THE FOLLIES OF THE KING
(*The eighth in the Plantagenet Saga*)

Edward the Second's first act on coming to the throne was to recall Piers Gaveston whom his father had banished because he thought he was having an evil influence on his son, and the new King's devotion to the shrewd and avaricious Gaveston soon became a scandal. It was thought, however, that when Edward married the Princess who was reckoned to be one of the most beautiful in Europe, his inclinations would change. But nothing could make him swerve from his attachment to Gaveston, and Gaveston was clearly the man to make the most of royal favour.

The new Queen Isabella, accustomed to adulation, was at first nonplussed by the King's attitude and then bitterly humiliated; and she was not a woman to forget or forgive. The country was in turmoil. The death of the first Edward had given the Scots the chance they had longed for and Robert the Bruce was the man to take advantage of it in such a way that he was finally able to defeat the English at Bannockburn. The influential barons rose in protest against the rule of Gaveston and led by the King's cousin, Lancaster, threatened civil war. Gaveston's arrogance and the King's folly in due course led to the murder on Blacklow Hill.

But when the handsome Hugh le Despenser was brought to the King's notice there was another to take Gaveston's place in his affections.

The King was making enemies throughout the country but he did not realize that the most deadly of these was the Queen. Cleverly biding her time Isabella waited until her schemes could mature, and when she met and fell in love with Roger de Mortimer, she knew the time had come; they worked together to overthrow the man who had humiliated her by showing his preference for handsome young men.

Alluring, powerful and ruthless Isabella emerges as the triumphant conqueror while Edward plunges along that road on which his follies have set him and which ends in history's most horrific murder within the thick dark walls of Berkeley Castle.

For a complete list of books by Jean Plaidy
see pages 333 and 334

THE FOLLIES OF
THE KING

JEAN PLAIDY

ROBERT HALE · LONDON

© Jean Plaidy 1980
First published in Great Britain 1980

ISBN 0 7091 6932 9

Robert Hale Limited
Clerkenwell House
Clerkenwell Green
London, EC1R oHT

Printed in Great Britain by
Richard Clay (The Chaucer Press) Ltd, Bungay, Suffolk

CONTENTS

BIBLIOGRAPHY

Aubrey, William Hickman Smith	*National and Domestic History of England*
Bain, Joseph	*The Edwards in Scotland*
Barron, E. M.	*The Scottish War of Independence*
Barlow, F.	*The Feudal Kingdom of England*
Bryant, Arthur	*The Medieval Foundation*
Costain, Thomas B.	*The Pageant of England 1272–1377*
	The Three Edwards
Davis, H. W. C.	*England Under the Angevins*
Green, Mary Anne Everett	*Lives of the Princesses of England from the Norman Conquest*
Guizot, M. (Translated by Robert Black)	*History of France*
Hume, David	*History of England from the Invasion of Julius Caesar to the Revolution*
Johnstone, Hilda	*Edward of Caernarvon*
Johnstone, Hilda	*The Eccentricities of Edward II*
MacKenzie, Agnes Mure	*Robert Bruce, King of Scots*
Norgate, Kate	*England Under the Angevin Kings*
Peers, Sir Charles R.	*Caernarvon Castle*
Stenton, D. M.	*English Society in the Middle Ages*
Stephen, Sir Leslie and Lee, Sir Sidney	*The Dictionary of National Biography*
Strickland, Agnes	*Lives of the Queens of England*
Tout, T. F.	*Place of Edward II in English History*
Wade, John	*British History*
Warburton, Rev. W.	*Edward III*

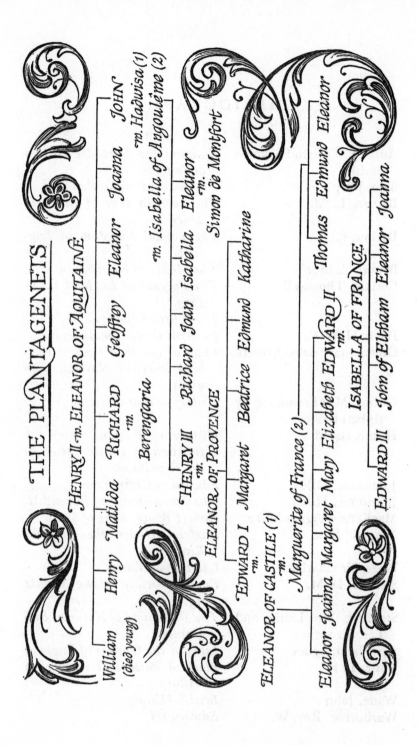

THE PLANTAGENETS

HENRY II *m.* ELEANOR OF AQUITAINE

William (died young) — Henry — Matilda — RICHARD *m.* Berengaria — Geoffrey — Eleanor — Joanna — JOHN *m.* Hadwisa (1) *m.* Isabella of Angoulême (2)

HENRY III *m.* ELEANOR OF PROVENCE — Richard — Joan — Isabella — Eleanor *m.* Simon de Montfort

EDWARD I *m.* ELEANOR OF CASTILE (1) *m.* Marguerite of France (2) — Margaret — Beatrice — Edmund — Katharine

Eleanor — Joanna — Margaret — Mary — Elizabeth — EDWARD II *m.* ISABELLA OF FRANCE — Thomas — Edmund — Eleanor

EDWARD III — John of Eltham — Eleanor — Joanna

GAVESTON

BELOVED PERROT

THE old King was dying. There, in the little village of Burgh-on-Sands where he was in sight of the Solway Firth beyond which lay the land he had planned to conquer, he had come to the end of a long life of endeavour and triumph. He had brought his country out of the pit of disaster into which the ill rule of a demoniacal grandfather and a weak father had led it and he had made England a proud country again. His ancestors, chief of them that great William who had become known as The Conqueror, would be proud of him.

But God had seen fit to take him before his work was completed. He had done much but not enough. He had known he had been inspired and he would become a legend. His enemies quailed before him and wherever Edward had ridden into battle that aura of invincibility had gone with him.

'When I am dead,' he said to his son, 'let my bones be placed in a hammock and carried before the army that the enemy may know that I am there in spirit.'

Young Edward was paying little attention. There was one subject which occupied his mind.

Perrot! he was thinking. My dearest, my beloved, my incomparable Perrot, when the old man is gone the first act of my reign shall be to bring you back to me.

He was vaguely aware that his father was babbling on about sending his heart to the Holy Land with a hundred knights who should serve there for a year and was wondering how soon he could despatch a messenger. Perrot would be waiting. For so long it had seemed that the King was near to death.

He had, in fact, lived for sixty-eight years, which was a long span. But Edward had always seemed different from other men. Some of his subjects believed that he was immortal and he had appeared to have that notion of himself ... until now.

The old man was uncanny. He had always had a gift for reading the thoughts of those about him. Even lying there, with death at his elbow, when he should be thinking of facing his Maker, he gave his son a shrewd look and said: 'Never recall Piers Gaveston without the consent of the nation.'

Uncanny! Yes, as though he knew that the tall, handsome young man at his bedside—so like the young man he himself had once been but only as far as his appearance was concerned—was not thinking of his dying father but of his dear friend Piers Gaveston, his Perrot.

'Yes, Father,' he said meekly, for he saw no point in arguing on a matter which he was determined was to be his first act on gaining authority. In any case the old King would be unable to prevent it when he was dead.

And as he stood by the death-bed he knew that his father despaired of him and the country's future, yet all the young Edward could think of was: 'Soon my dear Perrot, you shall come to me.'

Then the end was very close. The old King lay back whispering of his faith in God—and soon he was dead.

Now men were looking at the young King with that awed respect they showed to the crown. He was his father's son and therefore they must give him allegiance.

A great triumph came to Edward. A new reign had begun. His reign.

*   *   *

'My lord,' they said, and knelt before him. They kissed his hand, those barons who had, on more than one occasion, proved they could give less than absolute loyalty to their King. He must be wary of them. He must not show them just yet how different life was going to be. There must be no more of this obsession with Scotland for one thing. He hated the place. He longed for Westminster, Windsor and the south. He was already planning to leave an army up here and return to London ... but he would have to go carefully. He fully

realized that. Lincoln, Warwick and his uncle Lancaster ...
all of them had too high an opinion of themselves and on
account of his youth they wanted to guide him. He would
let them believe they were succeeding ... just at first.

Walter Reynolds was different. Reynolds was his friend,
and always had been, ever since he had come into his personal
household. Perrot had liked him and Reynolds had joined
them in their exploits and very often had given a spice to
them which even Perrot had admired. Reynolds secretly
laughed at authority—particularly had he mocked the tradi-
tions which the old King had been so eager to maintain. They
had found great excitement in flouting authority. Often, when
he was merely Prince Edward, he had wondered why his
father had allowed Reynolds into his household and, when he
had raised the matter with his intimate cronies, Reynolds had
explained rather slyly that even the most virtuous of men,
upright, just and honoured though they might be, at times
found it necessary to transact little matters which must be
performed in secret if the aura of honour, justice and nobility
was to be maintained. Then they turned to those who would
serve them in certain capacities ... and keep their mouths
shut. Reynolds' talk was always full of innuendoes. Even
Perrot had been fascinated by it.

Reynolds was a priest, which made it all so much more
amusing, but he was very good at theatricals; he knew where
to find the best musicians and liked to dress up and act himself. They had had good times together, and when the King
had reproved his son for his extravagances and cut off his
allowance, it was Walter Reynolds who had contrived to
have him supplied with what were called household neces-
sities and which turned out to be a new set of kettle drums or a
case full of fine materials for making costumes.

Walter Reynolds was his friend; they had mourned together
when Perrot had been sent away. It was Walter who had
slyly whispered that it might not be for long by the look
of things and had nodded and winked and pranced about as
though he were following a funeral bier.

Walter was a vulgar man. But young Edward liked vulgar
men. His sisters and his parents had never understood why he
preferred the company of his servants to that of noblemen.
There were exceptions of course. There was Perrot who was
full of court graces. None could dance as he could. None

looked so beautiful or loved fine garments more. But even he was not royal ... only the son of a Gascon knight whom the King had favoured because he had done him some service.

'Walter,' he said when the man appeared before him, 'it is time for action.'

'What are your wishes, O King?' replied Walter, smiling that sly secret smile of his.

'They will be leaving with my father's body ere long.'

'True, my lord. And you must needs remain here with your army and that grieves you, I'll swear.'

'It'll not be for long. I must make a show of carrying out my father's wishes.'

Walter nodded grimly.

'But I shall soon be in Westminster.'

'What mean you, lord King? To leave garrisons here as your father did?'

Edward nodded. 'It is all I will do, and it is enough. With all his fine battles what has my father won? Here we are facing the Scots as he was years ago. It's a lost battle, Walter, and I have had enough of it.'

'Yet, my lord, your uncle Lancaster ...'

'That man's a fool. I shall soon show him that. But I sent for you, Walter, and I think you guess why.'

Walter nodded laughing.

'I am to go south ... with all speed. I am to send a messenger to France ...'

'That is it. Tell my dear Gaveston that he must come back to me. Tell him the King commands him ... without delay.'

'Aye, my King. I'll tell him. I'll warrant he is all ready to leave. He'll be waiting the signal. Depend upon it. He'll be all eagerness to kneel to his King, mark my words.'

'And no more eager than his King to touch his dear face.'

'I'll tell him that, my lord. I'll tell him that. And now my lord King, with your permission, all speed to Perrot Gaveston.'

*   *   *

It was good to be riding south. He had done his duty. He had directed the army—his army now, he thought with a smirk—to Falkirk and Cumnock, though he had not exactly led it after his father's fashion. He had directed it from the rear—far safer, more comfortable and suited to a man who believed there was something rather ridiculous and pointless in going to war. He had it was true received the oaths of fealty from one or two of the Scottish lords, and then he had decreed that it was safe enough to leave Scotland well garrisoned and return to London.

There was his father's funeral to be attended to and that must be followed by his own coronation and his marriage ... oh yes, he would have to marry soon now. He was already betrothed to Isabella daughter of the King of France who was reported to be the most beautiful princess in Europe.

'Princesses are always beautiful,' Perrot had said. 'And is it not odd that their beauty grows in proportion to their royalty and their endowments?'

'Then it would seem that Isabella is richly endowed,' he had replied, 'for reports of her beauty come from all quarters.'

Perrot had shrugged his shoulders. He performed that gesture with more grace than any other man.

'She will take you from me,' he said quietly, almost petulantly.

'She never shall,' Edward had declared. 'No one on earth could do that.'

Perrot pretended not to be reassured but he was. He knew ... they both knew ... that the affection they gave to any would never rival that which they gave each other.

He was smiling, thinking of Perrot, and his cousin Thomas Earl of Lancaster who was riding beside him murmured that he trusted there would be no perfidy from the Scots.

'Ah the Scots,' replied Edward with a yawn, 'a tiresome race. Did you ever try their oatmeal porridge, Tom?'

Thomas said that he had tried and loathed it.

'Good Thomas, I agree with you. Let us thank God that we have turned our backs on the bleak inhospitable land.'

' 'Tis natural enough to be inhospitable to unwanted guests, my lord.'

Edward laughed. 'You speak truth there. Let us go where we are wanted. I wonder what sort of welcome the people of London will show me?'

'A grand one, I'll warrant. You are the son of your father and looking at you, my lord, none could doubt it.'

'Nay, my sainted mother was never one to stray from the marriage bed even though my father did desert her often enough for his wars.'

'She followed him in battle, my lord, and was never far behind.'

'Ah, battle ... battle. His life was one long battle.'

'A great King, my lord.'

'Don't say it in that way, Tom. I forbid it.'

'In what way, my lord?'

'In a we'll-never-see-the-like-of-him-again kind of way. I tell you this, his son has no intention of being his father's shadow and the sooner you and the rest realize that the better.'

'I doubt those close to you expect it,' retorted Thomas.

'Then that is well. Now we must give the old man a worthy send-off. I'll plan it myself. Gaveston will help me.'

'Gaveston, my lord?'

Edward looked slyly at his cousin. 'Piers Gaveston. You know him well.'

'But he ...'

'Will be awaiting me on my return to Westminster I believe.'

'It was the King's wish ...'

'That King is dead, cousin.'

'It was his wish ...' Thomas's face was serious. Thomas gave himself airs, believing himself to be as royal as Edward and so he was in a way although not in the line of succession. He was the eldest son of Edward's father's brother Edmund, first cousin to the King and because his father had died while Thomas was a minor in the King's care he had become the Earls of Lancaster, Leicester and Derby. Weighty titles which allied with royalty had given Thomas a high opinion of himself. No wonder he thought he could be on familiar terms with a king.

'I repeat, cousin,' said Edward firmly, '*that* King is dead. This one now riding beside you lives.'

'Aye, 'tis so,' replied Thomas non-committally.

They would learn, thought Edward smiling.

'You're glum, Thomas,' went on the King. 'Think you Richmond and Pembroke will not look after the affairs of the Border?'

'The late King had planned to do battle. Robert the Bruce has returned.'

'I have told you, Thomas, that we will not discuss the late King, except it be the matter of his obsequies. We will make our way to Waltham where he lies and then take him to

Westminster. He shall have a funeral worthy of him. Methinks he would wish to lie beside his father. He loved him dearly. I remember well the stories he told us of our grandfather.'

'The King was always a family man.'

'He was a paragon of virtues to those whom he favoured. There are some who would consider him less so. But ... I will not speak ill of the dead. Death sanctifies. Even those who failed to gain respect in life can do so often enough in death. So my father whose stature was great in life will become a giant in death. Therefore, good Thomas, we will bury him with such pomp as will satisfy the people of London.'

'You will remember his request that his bones should march with his army.'

'I remember it, cousin.'

The King rode forward ahead of Lancaester. He was in no mood for further conversation. He was thinking of reaching London, of his father's funeral, of his own coronation.

Gaveston would be there.

* * *

The journey to Waltham lasted two weeks and every day the King chafed against the delay. Now he must make the solemn entry into London and there his father must be laid to rest in the Abbey of Westminster. It must be a grand funeral. The people would expect it. He could imagine the old man's wrath if he were looking down on the scene. So much good money wasted, money which might have gone into armaments to wage war on the Scots and keep the rebellious Welsh in control.

Such a great King! Greater dead than he was alive. He had had enemies then. He always had to be watchful of the barons who had been given a high opinion of themselves since Magna Carta. Old Longshanks knew how to keep them in order, but even the mighty fell in due course. In the coffin lay the remains of a once great King, whose very bones—so he thought —would strike terror into an enemy. Nothing but bones!

And here he was in London, the capital. *His* capital now. He loved the city. It had been a custom of his to wander with Perrot through it incognito, to mingle with the crowds, to take on the roles of noblemen, merchants, strolling players ... just as the mood took them. *His* disguise had never been easy to achieve. He was so tall and flaxen-haired and so like his father that he could be easily recognized. It had been a special challenge and how he and Perrot would congratulate each other if they came through a nightly adventure identity intact! Edward sometimes wished he had not been born his father's son. To wander down the Chepe over the uneven stones where the kennels running down the middle were often choked with refuse, past the wooden houses, shops and stalls with their signs and lanterns swinging on straw ropes, that was adventure. To drink a flagon of ale in the Mermaid or Mitre Taverns, to mingle with merchants and beggars, milkmaids and moneychangers, honest traders and those bent on nefarious traffic—that was living and he and Perrot, with a few well chosen companions escaped to it when they felt in the mood to do so. They had been happy days of adventure and pleasure.

And afterwards ... to wash the grime of the streets from their hands and faces, to throw off their humble garments, to dress in silks and brocades and fine jewels and perhaps call the players to perform for them, that was pure pleasure. There was a great deal of fun to be had and Perrot knew how to make the most of it. Perrot could act and dance better than anyone else.

As ever his thoughts came back to Perrot.

And so to Westminster, there to make arrangements for his father's funeral. Lancaster had been right. The people were ready to give him a royal welcome. He was so like his father who was making rapid progress towards sainthood. People were talking of his just good rule which a few years before had been called harsh and cruel. 'Edward has not left us,' they said, 'but he lives on in his son.' A few very old men remembered when the old King had come from his crusade in the Holy Land to be crowned King of England. Towering above other men because of those long Norman legs which had given him the affectionate nickname of Longshanks, he came with a beautiful wife who had followed him romantically to the Holy Land that she might not be separated from him. So Edward I had come in as a romantic hero and had gone out as a saint, his glorious deeds remembered, his misdeeds forgotten.

So the people loved his son. They welcomed him. They wanted to see him crowned; they wanted him to have a beautiful bride.

Well, that must come.

He would have preferred not to marry but he had always known that it would be required of him. Perrot and he had discussed it often. Isabella—the most beautiful girl in Europe —royal, well endowed, daughter of the King of France. Everyone would approve of that.

He began to laugh suddenly. If he married, Perrot should have a bride too. Why not? He pictured Perrot's face when he put that proposition to him.

To the Palace of Westminster then which had been so beloved by his grandparents who had refurbished it, spent a fortune on it and had added exquisite murals and painted ceilings. Perrot liked it. It was here that he had talked of his ambitions.

'You are a prince,' he had said, 'the heir to the throne and I am but a humble knight. It bemeans you to be my friend.'

For the moment Edward had been stunned. Perrot who was always so sure of himself! Perrot who walked like a king and who could, by a show of displeasure, reduce Edward to humility. He could see nothing bemeaning to him. He could only be grateful to God for giving him such a friend.

Then it came out. Perrot had wanted honours. 'So that I can stand beside my friend ... not as an equal ... none in this realm can be that, but worthy of him,' he had explained.

He had wanted Ponthieu. 'Ask the King. Tell him you think some honour should be given me. Tell him what a good friend I have always been to you.'

Edward, who wanted above all things to please his friend, felt uneasy. He knew that their enemies looked askance at their friendship. Some of them had whispered to the King that it was not good for the Prince to be so often with Piers Gaveston.

He had seen the wistful look in Perrot's eyes. Perrot wanted to be an equal of those others about him. Lancaster and Lincoln treated him as though he were some higher servant.

Wanting to show Perrot what he would do for him he had actually asked his father for Ponthieu.

What a scene there had been! The old man had turned scarlet in the face. The Plantagenet temper which had haunted the family since the days of Henry II was ready to flare into being. They had all had it. In Edward I it had been largely held in check. In King John it had run so wild that he would have a man's eyes plucked out or his ears or nose cut off simply for having aroused it.

Well, he, Edward had seen it in his father's eyes when he had asked for Ponthieu for Perrot.

All his father's fears for the future, all his dissatisfaction with his son was there in that moment when he seized him by the hair and had even pulled out some by its roots.

Edward touched his head now remembering. It was still sore from the attack. In it had been all his father's resentments, his dislike of his son's way of life, his longing for a son who would follow him to battle and of whom he would have made a king to match himself.

It had been a mistake. It had resulted in Perrot's banishment. Perrot and he had slipped up there. Edward had been lenient with his daughter's misdemeanours. When his sister Joanna had been alive, she had twisted her father round her finger many times. But she had been a girl, and the King had doted on his daughters. But his son had failed to give him what he wanted. He cried out for a brave son who would go to war and bring Scotland to the crown; and fate had given him Edward, who was handsome but not in a manly way, who was clever enough but lazy, who had no taste for battle and liked better to frivol with his giddy companions, roistering in the streets, or playing music and dancing and lavishing time and attention on his players. Edward's little half-brothers, Thomas and Edmund, fruit of the King's second marriage, were as yet too young to show what they would be.

So ... his coronation, then his marriage ... but first there must be his father's burial.

The casket which would hold the dead King's body was being prepared. It was simple, as the King would have wished, and made of black Purbeck stone. It was not to be sealed for they would have to make a show of carrying out his orders which were that his bones be carried in a hammock before the army when it marched against the Scots. Every two years, according to his orders, the tomb was to be opened, and the wax of the cerecloth renewed. His tomb should not be sealed until complete victory over Scotland was achieved.

They would do it of course. They were afraid to do anything else. Dead Edward was as terrifying as living Edward had been.

There was a light tap on the door and one of Edward's attendants looked in. He seemed apprehensive. The King started up as the messenger bowed low.

'My lord, a man waits without. He says to tell you to be prepared for grave news.'

'Grave news! What news? Who is this man?'

'He will tell you himself, my lord. Those were his orders. Will you see him?'

'Send him to me without delay.'

He was frowning. Grave news! What now? He wanted nothing ... nothing but news of Perrot.

The door opened. The messenger was back. He bowed low. 'Come in, my lord,' he said. 'The King will see you.'

Into the room came a figure wrapped up in an all-concealing cloak. The messenger stepped backwards, bowed and shut the door on them.

'Who are you?' cried the King. 'Why do you come in this way...'

The cloak was flung off and, as it fell to the floor, Edward gave a cry of great joy and flung himself into the arms of his visitor.

'Perrot! Perrot?' he cried. 'Oh, you villain ... to hold yourself back from me even for those moments ... This joy has been delayed.'

'That my beloved King might find it all the more precious.'

'Oh Perrot, Perrot, if you but knew what it has been like without you.'

'I know that full well, my beloved lord. Have I not been without you? But it is all over now. We are together again and you are the King. You are the master now, sweet friend. The old man delayed his departure too long but at last he has gone.'

'Oh Perrot, what joy! What *joy!* You came with all speed then.'

'I was ready awaiting the signal. I had news that your father was nearing the end. As soon as I saw your messenger I knew. I was ready and waiting.'

'Let me look at you, sweet Perrot. You are a little different. What is it? Your long dark clever eyes. No. Your dark curling hair, your rather arrogant nose, your laughing mouth ... no it is not these.'

'It is this silk robe. Where have you seen silk like this? I must show you the cotehardies I have brought with me. You will be amazed. What a becoming garment. I promise you you will love it.'

'Talk not to me of clothes, Perrot. What care I for clothes? You rogue, you, to talk of grave news ... a messenger ... from afar. How could you keep me from this bliss even for a moment!'

'Pardon, sweet lord. It was a mischief in me. I had suffered so ...'

'Forget it. Forget it. You are back. How long it has seemed without you. You teased me then. You always did. How I missed your teasing. I am surrounded by these dreary lords. They depress me. They compare me with my father ...'

'You are incomparable.'

'Oh, Perrot, my love. I thought I should *die* when you went away.'

'Thank God you did not. For how could I have lived without you? It would have been a greater tragedy for Perrot to be robbed of his Edward than for England to lose her King.'

They were incoherent in the joy of their reunion.

'Let us savour just this,' said Edward. 'Tomorrow we will talk of many things.'

* * *

Lancaster burst into the apartment of the Earl of Warwick and seeing his expression Warwick immediately dismissed all those who were in attendance on him.

'By God, Warwick,' cried Lancaster, 'have you heard the news?'

'Nay, my lord, and if your looks express your feelings, I fear the worst.'

'He is back. That low-born traitor to the realm, the King's evil genius.'

'Gaveston?'

'Who else? By God, we should have had his head ere he left in banishment.'

'I think that the King's father would not have said nay to such an act. Had he thought his son would break his word to him Gaveston would not have lived to bring trouble back to our country. But 'tis no use brooding on what might have been. He is with the King, I'll swear.'

'Has been with him since the moment of his return. They'll

not be parted. It sickens me to see him there. The King will have him at his side, at his table, in his bed. He swears he'll never let him go again.'

'The King will have to learn that he rules by the will of barons. Even his great grandfather must have learned that lesson in the end.'

'I see trouble, Warwick.'

'Where Gaveston is there will be trouble. So it was when the King was but his father's heir. But Edward is King now. The people will support him ... for a time.'

'You mean we must do nothing to bring about Gaveston's banishment?'

'I think we should tread warily. Let us see what comes from his return. The King dotes on him and the people are with the King. They always are in a new reign. It seems likely that Gaveston will make such great demands and Edward doubtless grant them that the people will see for themselves what a menace this man is. They will not like the relationship between them. So what we must do at this time, my friend, is wait.'

Lancaster was disappointed. He wanted immediate action. He was noted for his impulsiveness and he was not an especially wise man. But for the fact that he was the grandson of a king he would have been insignificant, so reasoned Warwick.

So he was eager to impress on Lancaster that they must act with care. That the new King was self-willed was obvious, that he had perverted sexual tastes was another—well he was not the first king to have been afflicted in that way. He could be a good king for all that. Moreover Edward was young. He had much to learn. It was the task of his barons, who were eager to see peace and prosperity in the country to bring him to understanding of his responsibilities.

'So Gaveston is back,' he mused, 'though the late King banished him. We must accept that.'

'Aye,' cried Lancaster, 'and the late King advised us and his son never to have him back.'

'Young Edward is the ruler now, my lord. And he has commanded Gaveston to return.'

'That he may shower gifts on him ... lands, possessions, titles ... It is going to be Henry the Third with his extravagant friends soaking up the country's life blood all over again.'

'They were his wife's relations, and they were numerous.

This is the King's lover. Listen, Lancaster, Edward must be married without delay. He recognizes the necessity to do so, I'll swear. He has to give us an heir or two and they say young Isabella is something of a siren. Nay, my lord, let us do nothing rash. We will acquaint the leading barons of Gaveston's return. We will have them on the alert, shall we say? We have to crown the King and when he is married to this beautiful girl ... Oh come, Lancaster. He is young yet. His father was stern with him. He is now free. Let us give him a beautiful wife and a chance. It may well be that Gaveston will mean nothing to him within a few months.'

'I think you take too facile a view of this, Warwick.'

'That may well be. But there is little we can do as yet. He has sent for Gaveston and Gaveston has returned. Let us get the coronation over and the King married and then if ...'

'Yes,' said Lancaster. 'And then?'

'Then, my lord, if Gaveston is a danger to the King and the country we must find some means of disposing of him.'

Lancaster looked into the shrewd dark-skinned face of the Earl and nodded.

*   *   *

'Perrot, they say I must marry and soon.'

They were walking in the gardens arm in arm. They had not been out of each other's company since Gaveston's return.

'I know it. They seek to turn you away from me.'

'Fools! It would be easier to conquer Scotland than do that.'

'I had hoped that it would be an impossible task.'

'Absolutely impossible, dear Gaveston.'

'Well, you must perforce marry, get the wench with child and do your duty to your crown.'

'Well, I will do it for them.'

'They say she is a beautiful girl.'

'They say ... they say. As you once said before, she is the daughter of the King of France. My stepmother remembers her. Isabella was but a baby when Marguerite left France to marry my father. There is a tradition of beauty in that family. Her father is Philip le Bel and her aunt was so noted for her charms that my father dearly wanted to marry her and he got her sister, my stepmother, instead. Marguerite is not uncomely. Yes, I do think I shall have a beautiful wife.'

Gaveston pouted. 'You talk thus to plague me.'

'Never, Perrot. She will mean nothing to me. But I am the King and there are certain duties I must submit to.'

'Hateful duties.'

'Dear Perrot, I know your feelings well. Do not imagine that I shall not compensate you. I have news for you. You will not long be plain Piers Gaveston, you know. What would you say to an earldom?'

'I should say my gracious thanks, my lord; and my heart would rejoice ... not in the earldom ... others have those ... but in the love of my lord which is beyond price, beyond assessment and means more to me than any titles or lands.'

'It shall be an outward sign of my devotion, dearest brother.'

'My brother indeed.'

When they were young in the royal schoolroom—where Edward's father had put young Piers out of gratitude to the boy's father who had performed a service for him—they had taken an instant liking to each other. That attraction had never wavered and the first thing of consequence Edward had said to his young friend had been, 'You are my brother.' From then on they called eath other 'brother' and still did so in moments of nostalgic tenderness.

'Listen, Perrot. What earldom do you think? Nay, I'll tell you. You are to be the Earl of Cornwall.'

Even Gaveston, growing accustomed to lavish gifts, could not believe his ears.

'Cornwall! That is a royal title!'

'Well, Perrot, do you not like it?'

'My lord, what can I say?'

'You can say you believe now that your King loves you. Come, my lord earl, let us discover what manors, castles and lands are attached to your new title.'

Gaveston felt giddy with power. He was realizing that there need be no end to his good fortune. Edward was so besottedly in love with him that there was nothing he could not have. He could be King—for Edward would do anything to please him. The old barons would not like it. He would have to watch them. Old fools most of them; they would have to learn that Gaveston could outwit them—with the King beside him. Edward would be called the King, but it would be Gaveston who would rule.

They had always resented him in the royal household—

those scions of noble families. They had sneered at his low birth. He was the son of a Gascon knight whereas many of them considered themselves as royal as the King. Some of them had in fact been royal. He had always felt a certain rapport with Edward's sister Joanna—alas now dead. She had had an adventurous spirit and an eye for an attractive man. Not that Gaveston was her kind, but she appreciated his cleverness. She herself had married Ralph Monthermer—one of the handsomest men at court and of humble birth—in spite of the King's wrath which she had had to face afterwards. So she could not very well despise *his* low birth. Nor to do her justice had she shown that she was aware of it. She had been a good companion until her sudden death—by far the most friendly towards him of any member of the royal family.

Now he was to be Earl of Cornwall. He was equal with any of them.

'And, Perrot,' went on the King, 'as I am to have a bride, so shall you.'

'A bride, Edward. You are jesting.'

'Oh no, sweet friend. Indeed I am not. Only the most noble bride is good enough for my Perrot so whom do you think I have chosen for you?'

'Tell me.'

'Joanna's girl—Margaret de Clare.' Edward stood back a little to see the effect on his friend. Gaveston found it hard to hide the upsurge of delight. The girl was one of the richest in the country—and with strong royal connections too, since she was the King's niece. This was indeed favour. 'Well,' went on Edward, 'what say you, Perrot?'

'I would say that you are determined to honour me, sweet lord. I have no wish to take a wife but who could say no to being connected to his royal lord through marriage.'

'She is young and you need see little of her. But she will bring you much wealth. I said to myself: Hugh le Despenser has her sister Eleanor, so my Perrot shall have Margaret, I long to tell the child of her good fortune.'

'Let us hope she will consider it such.'

'How could she fail to admire you? And if she is a dutiful niece she will love one whom her lord uncle and King so cherishes.'

Gaveston was still stunned. He had expected favour but not quite as strong as this.

Edward was certainly impulsive. There was no doubt that the barons would soon be made aware of his intentions, and then there would be stern criticism.

'We must make immediate plans for your marriage,' went on the King. 'I want it performed without delay, before our enemies can raise their objections.'

'My clever friend thinks of everything.'

'Where your welfare is concerned, Perrot, indeed I do.'

It was such pleasure to be together. They laughed immoderately at the effect this announcement was going to have on the ponderous barons.

Perrot amused himself by giving them nicknames. Thomas Lancaster, for whom he had the utmost contempt, was the Fiddler.

'He should have been a fiddler,' commented Gaveston. 'Yes, he would have done very well fiddling his tunes. He could have played at country fairs. The rustics would have loved him.'

'Perrot you are talking of my cousin.'

'It was a joke of the Almighy mayhap. Or perhaps He was saving up all perfections for the King's son and so had none to spare for others. The one we have most to fear is the black hound of Arden. You know who I mean.'

'I'll guess Warwick.'

Gaveston nodded. 'And as for old Burst Belly he counts not at all.'

'You mean Lincoln. Oh, Perrot, you will kill me with laughing. Yes, if he gets much bigger he will certainly burst.'

It did him good to hear these mighty barons ridiculed. He could be afraid of the Earls of Lancaster and Lincoln—but not when he thought of them as Fiddler and Burst Belly.

'I will tell you this, Edward,' went on Gaveston, 'these gentlemen are not one twentieth as valiant or as significant as they believe themselves to be. And we shall prove this to them.'

'How?' asked Edward.

'We will begin by giving a tournament. I'll gather together the best knights of France and England. All young ... unknown. I can bring them here. Then we shall see these mighty barons brought low. How is that for a start?'

'A tournament. I shall enjoy that. And you will be the finest of them all.'

'Bless you, sweet friend. It is an honour I shall share with you.'

They laughed together, making plans. Everything, thought Edward, becomes interesting and amusing when Perrot is here.

*   *   *

On a cold October day the funeral of the King took place and his body was laid in the tomb prepared for him in Westminster Abbey. In the streets the people talked of his greatness but they were already thinking of the new reign. Young Edward's flaxen good looks so like his father's endeared him to them but they were hearing whispers of the favourite Gaveston against whom the barons were murmuring and the first breath of uneasiness was beginning to touch them. There had never been scandal about the dead King; he had been an example to all fathers and husbands and as such had had a good effect on the country.

'The new King is young,' said the women, 'and very good-looking. He is going to have a wife soon. Then he will settle down.'

The men said that the country's troubles always sprang from foreigners, and Gaveston was a Gascon. Let the King send that creature packing as his father had done and all would be well.

But it was early days yet and the King's popularity had waned very little because of the first touch of scandal.

A few days later when Piers Gaveston was married to the King's niece Margaret de Clare the uneasiness increased. The barons were very sullen, disapproving strongly of this marriage. The King, though, had said it should be, and one hopeful factor was that as Gaveston had a wife there might be a stop to the gossip about him and the King.

Young Margaret, who was only a child, thought her bridegroom the prettiest creature she had ever seen, so she was not at all displeased with her marriage and he spent so little time with her that she said it was scarcely like being married at all.

Perrot lay stretched out on the King's bed and Edward watched him with admiration. He was as graceful as a cat and as dignified as a king should be but was not always.

Gaveston was pleased with himself. He was fast becoming

the most important man in the kingdom, for whatever he wanted he must have—his wish was Edward's

They had been talking about Walter Langton whom they both referred to as 'that old enemy'.

'It seems to me an odd thing,' Gaveston was saying, 'that our old enemy should still hold his office of treasurer.'

'Not for long, Perrot, no, not for long.'

'Methinks he has held it long enough. 'Tis my belief, and one which I know my dearest liege lord shares, that those who have been good friends to us ... to you, dear boy ... should be rewarded and those who have been our enemies made to understand that their fortunes have taken a turn for the worse.'

'I have been considering Langton,' said Edward.

'Then let us consider him *now* and let us not stop considering him until he is no longer in a position to annoy us.'

'Turn him out,' said Edward.

'Precisely,' replied Gaveston.

They laughed, recalling their skirmishes with Langton who had, unfortunately at the time, been in favour with Edward I.

'Do you remember the time we broke into his wood?' prompted Gaveston.

Edward did remember. There had been a great deal of trouble about that and he recalled vividly his rage at the humiliation which had been heaped on him at the time, for his father had been on the side of Langton over the affair.

It was characteristic that this man Langton whom young Edward had so hated should be favoured by his father. The old King had had such a high opinion of Walter Langton, Bishop of Coventry and Lichfield, that he had made him his treasurer. He would listen to his advice and often took it for he had often declared that the Bishop's long experience was of great service to him.

Prompted by Gaveston, Edward had chosen Langton as a butt for his dislike. As treasurer Langton was always questioning young Edward's expenditure, nor was he averse to complaining to his father about it. It was galling that the old King took the treasurer's side rather than that of his son and, complained Gaveston, treated the Prince as an erring schoolboy in the presence of the Bishop which made that old hypocrite more determined than ever to spoil his pleasures.

It was Gaveston who pointed out that Reynolds could be of use to them. 'That other Walter,' as Gaveston called him. As treasurer of the wardrobe Walter Reynolds could contrive a little juggling over clothes which he was very willing to do. Indeed Reynolds was very happy to put his scheming head together with that of Edward and his minion and laugh over ways of deceiving the King and Langton.

It was only natural that when Edward and Gaveston were riding near Walter Langton's lands they should break into a wood of his and hunt the deer. They had not been without success and had just brought down a fine buck when Langton's gamekeepers had come upon them, surrounded them and in spite of Edward's protests that he was the Prince of Wales, had taken them, in a most humiliating fashion, to their master as though they were common poachers.

Moreover, even when he saw who the captives were, Langton had shown an equal lack of respect.

'How dare you trespass on my land and steal my deer?' he had demanded.

Edward had replied haughtily, 'These lands come to you through my father's grace. I am his heir and therefore claim the right to go where I will.'

Gaveston had nodded approvingly which gave Edward the courage he needed to stand up to the formidable old bishop.

'You have not stepped into your father's shoes yet,' cried the Bishop, 'and I pray God the time will be long before you do. Let us hope that when that time comes—and it could be a tragedy for the nation—you will have learned more sense.'

Now this had been more than Edward could endure and he began abusing Langton in somewhat coarse terms which seemed more amusing because they were addressed to a bishop and Gaveston had been looking on convulsed with laughter.

'I can tell you this,' the Bishop had replied, 'the King will not endure your frivolous behaviour, your extravagance, your dalliance with companions who are no good to you ...' Gaveston had smirked and mincing up to the Bishop had struck a mock pleading attitude which made Edward gasp with laughter. The Bishop had turned a shade paler as he had said: 'I shall report this matter to the King.'

'Pray do,' Edward had replied, 'and I shall report to him the insolence of a subject towards the King's son.'

Langton had arrived first before the King. He had been distraught and sorrowful and the King had been furious when he heard what had happened.

He had sent for his son and the lights of the dangerous Plantagenet temper had been visible in his eyes. Young Edward was the one person who aroused that more than any other. The King's voice could be heard through the palace and the things he had said were very uncomplimentary to his son. It was maddening that he should have been entirely on Langton's side. 'How dared you go into the Bishop's woods? How dared you hunt his deer? It's a punishable offence. You know that.'

'A King should hunt where he wishes,' Edward had replied.

'Remember this,' thundered his father, 'you are not yet a king. And I tell you there is considerable unease in this realm at the prospect of your becoming one. You will have to mend your ways or by God and all his angels I will mend them for you.'

'My lord it is demeaning to our state ...'

'*It* is demeaning. *You* are demeaning. You and your evil counsellors.'

Little darts of fear had entered Edward's heart then. He had always been afraid when the King's thoughts turned to Gaveston.

He had become quieter, more humble. He had listened to his father's tirade and when he was told that he was banished from court he had bowed his head and accepted the exile. It had been irritating but it would be simply dreadful if his father began blaming Perrot and decided to part them.

He guessed that when his father did banish Gaveston—a few months before his death—that this affair had first put the idea to do so into his head.

So now when Perrot reminded him of the time they had broken into Langton's wood he remembered not only the incident but the parting with Perrot which had followed and a great anger rose in him against Langton who had been one of their worst enemies.

'And he remains your treasurer,' pointed out Gaveston. 'Dear friend, you are too good to that old rogue.'

'Someone will have to replace him.'

'But indeed it is so and there is our old friend, that other Walter. He is just waiting for his chance and sweet Prince, why should he not have it?'

'Reynolds!' cried the King.

'Who else? Has he not served us ... you ... well?'

'You are right. It shall be. Who shall we send for first?'

'Let's have our sport with the Bishop.'

Edward slapped his thigh with excitement. How different from when they had been taken to his presence like humble foresters. Now it was his turn.

'Let's tell Reynolds,' said Gaveston. 'We'll hide him in the chamber and he can hear the great man receive his dismissal.'

'You always think of the most *amusing* things, Perrot.'

'It is my duty to amuse my lord. Sometimes I think my role is that of court jester.'

'There never was a more handsome, witty and charming one ... nor such a rich one.'

'There's truth in that, I'll swear. Now to the fun.'

*   *   *

The Bishop received his dismissal with dignity. It was clear though that he would soon join up with Lancaster and Lincoln, Warwick and such malcontents who were already raising their eyebrows at the King's preoccupation with Gaveston even though Gaveston had been recently married. He was rarely with his wife and that marriage had obviously been a means of bringing him a fortune.

'I will be magnanimous, my lord,' said the Bishop as he was departing, 'and ask God to help you.'

'But, my dear Bishop,' said Gaveston, 'it is you who will need His help and I am sure that, seeing the pious life you have led, He will not deny it now.'

The Bishop ignored Gaveston. Poor Perrot, that angered him more than anything. He could not bear to be treated as though he were of no importance.

Walter Reynolds came in rubbing his hands together.

'My lords, my lords, it was as good as one of our plays. You showed him the door, indeed you did. I'll warrant the old prelate is trembling in his shoes.'

'Methinks he was expecting it, Walter,' said Perrot. 'He could not hope to go on in office after all he has done to our gracious King.'

'Well, Walter,' said Edward, 'what would you say if I set you in the old rogue's shoes and made you my treasurer?'

Walter's answer was to go down on his knees and kiss the King's hand.

'Get up, Walter,' said Edward. 'You deserve your honour. Serve me well and there will be more. I remember my friends.'

'And must not forget your enemies, dear Prince,' said Gaveston.

'Nor shall I. It was good fun was it not seeing the old fellow brought low?'

'Now we shall cease to be plagued and must think of others who have offended you.'

'And of those who have been my friends. I intend they shall never regret it.'

'This is a great day for those who long to serve you well, my lord. I shall let it be known that good and loyal friends had cause for happiness this day. Even our little drummer Francekin shall have a pair of kettle drums.'

'That pleases me,' said Gaveston. 'Francekin is a good little nakerer and pretty withal.'

They were happy together making plans for the future.

*   *   *

The tournament had been planned to take place in the old town of Wallingford which was situated in the Thames valley between Reading and Oxford. Gaveston had arranged it and to it he invited all the knights renowned for their chivalry.

Gaveston was smarting a little from the treatment he had received at the hands of some of the leading barons of the country—men such as Lancaster, Lincoln, Warwick, Surrey, Arundel and Hereford. They had their followers too, and they all showed clearly how much they deplored his friendship with the King. Moreover they were constantly stressing the lowness of his birth—a very sore point with Gaveston who considered himself their superior in every other way. They were never going to let him forget that he was the son of a humble Gascon knight while they belonged to the greatest families in the country. Many of them were royal or connected with royalty and they believed that the King should take his friends and counsellors from their ranks instead of surrounding himself with minions of low birth.

Gaveston planned to teach them a lesson. He was going to show them that he could outshine them all in that display of chivalry which was considered to be at the very heart of good breeding. He was not only graceful on horseback but there

were few who could handle a horse better. Edward said that
when he watched Perrot on horseback he could believe he was
some mythical creature, half-horse half-man, so well did he
and the horse move together.

The days which preceded the tournament were full of excitement. Edward and Gaveston laughed together at the trick
they were going to play on the arrogant barons. They were
bringing into the country many young men from France who
had not yet made their names but whose skill and vitality
could, Gaveston was sure, outwit and overcome the proud
barons at every turn. Perrot would lead them and the King
would be seated under his canopy to watch the play and to
present the trophies.

It was going to be a most exciting occasion.

On the appointed day people came from miles to see the
contests. The roads were full of travellers with the usual company of beggars and pickpockets in their wake. Pennants
fluttered from those pavilions in which knights donned their
armour and waited to be called to the fight. They were beautiful, those pavilions, many made of double satin, the valences
embroidered with their owner's motto. The Royal Pavilioners
and Sergeants of the Tents were busy all through the day preceding the tournament, setting them up and making sure they
were not damaged. Merchants of London and the big cities
vied with each other to obtain contracts for making and main-
taining these pavilions. And a colourful sight they were.

When the King appeared there was a great shout of greeting
from the people, for there was nothing they loved more than
displays of this sort and the rumour had already been circulated that the King was at some variance with certain members
of his court who did not like his friend Gaveston. They knew
of course that the late King had banished the Gascon and that
the new King had recalled him and given him, as well as a
rich and royal bride, great honours.

The feeling had seeped out that the tournament was in
some way a contest between the King, who had his own idea
of what a King's duties should be, and those barons who
wanted to impose their will on him.

As yet the outcome of this struggle seemed of little importance to the people. What they wanted to see was an exciting
tournament and when the combatants emerged they would
pick their favourites.

The King had taken his seat beneath the royal canopy and among his party was Margaret de Clare, his niece, the newly married wife of Gaveston. As soon as the knights appeared in their splendid armour her eyes sought her husband among them and as she recognized him they shone with a pride which was matched by the King's own obvious love for his friend.

Gaveston was chafing against the fact that he had been designated as one of the challengers, believing that he should have been greeted as a champion. Well, he was here to show these arrogant knights what he thought of them. He and his group of challengers were determined to inflict such defeat on them as they would never forget.

His friends understood what was expected of them. They were young, vital and spoiling for the fight. Although the leading champions were here some of them were not in the first flush of youth; their limbs might well be stiffening a little and it was speed and agility which were needed in the fight ... not arrogance and strains of royal blood.

It was a brilliant show. Edward knew that his Perrot was going to succeed. There was an air of confidence about him and for days he had been complaining bitterly of the treatment he received from many scions of ancient houses.

They were going to be taught a lesson and Edward was longing to see it administered.

Edward had made it clear that the tournament had been devised by the Earl of Cornwall (he and Gaveston had decided that that was the title by which he must be referred to from now on) for their pleasure and that it was a Joust à Plaisance which meant that it was purely for sport and that each lance would be fitted with its coronel—an iron head roughly shaped and with several blunt points which would prevent harm coming to the combatants. This was different from a Joust à l'Outrance which meant that the contenders fought until one was forced to surrender and would surely be wounded—often severely—or even killed, for such jousts as these were fought with a sharp lance or spear.

Gaveston distinguished himself with great éclat. In a very short time he was tackling one of his greatest enemies the leader of the champions, John Warenne, Earl of Surrey and Sussex. With great panache and with a certain malicious delight he went into the fight. He had challenged Warenne because he knew that he was one of those who deplored the King's friendship with him and had not hesitated to make his feelings known.

Warenne was a handsome young man just about twenty years of age. His father had died when he was six months old and he had not long before succeeded to his titles on the death of his grandfather. During the preceding year he had been married to the King's niece, Joanna, the daughter of Edward's eldest sister Eleanor and the Count of Bar, so he considered himself a member of the royal family through marriage. He was a proud young man and pleased to be connected with the King and on more than one occasion he had done his best to humiliate Gaveston.

He was noted for his skill in the joust and had become an acknowledged champion of that art, and there could be no doubt that he was delighting in the opportunity offered him of humiliating the King's dear friend. Gaveston was, of course, determined that it should be the other way round.

There were many who were aware during those tense moments that this was something more than a Joust à Plaisance. The feeling that a great deal was at stake had permeated the atmosphere and the tension was growing.

As the two men rode into the field and came at each other with their blunted lances the King leaned forward in his seat.

'Go to it, Perrot,' he murmured to himself. 'Make Warenne grovel in the dust.'

They tilted, each highly skilled. Everyone knew that Warenne was a champion so it was Gaveston who surprised them most. All the skill of the champion was his. That much was clear. The thunder of hoofs as they galloped towards each other; the clash of steel as they met and then suddenly a cry went up. One of them was down.

The thundering of Edward's heart matched that of the horse's hoofs. A mist swam before his eyes so that he was not sure which was which.

'Oh God, yes it is ... it is ...' he murmured. 'Warenne is down.'

What a moment of humiliation! What a moment of glory!

Warenne would never forget nor forgive this moment.

Defeated, he a champion, beaten by an upstart Gascon knight who owed his title to the King's favour for questionable services performed.

Even Edward could not help feeling a little sorry for Warenne in that moment.

He had returned crestfallen to his pavilion, the roars of the
crowd in his ears, hatred for Gaveston in his heart.

And then Arundel.

Gaveston's friends were warning him. 'You cannot hope for
your luck to continue,' they said. 'Leave Arundel to one of
us.'

But Gaveston was drunk with success. He was supreme. He
was sure of it. He had staged this tournament that he might
show these people that he was superior to them in every way
and he was going to prove it. This was his triumph.

He knew that fortune was smiling on him that day. He was
aware of the King's burning gaze. He felt as though he had
been born for this day. From henceforth these men who had
set themselves against him should acknowledge their superior.
The tournament was a symbol and they knew it.

And so to Arundel—Edmund Fitzalan who had recently
married Warenne's sister Alice. They were a close community, these noble lords. Arundel had behaved arrogantly
to Gaveston. He was another one of those who resented the
friendship with the King.

Determination rode with Gaveston. Every bit of skill he
had taken such pains to acquire must do him good service.

The roar of the crowd was deafening. He looked towards
the canopy. Gaveston knew his dear friend was watching,
praying, hoping...

Arundel was down. A silence, then the uproar.

Gaveston—no, the Earl of Cornwall—had proved himself
to be a champion of champions.

Two of the greatest jousters of the times and both defeated!
This was triumph indeed.

'You have done it,' said Walter Reynolds. 'Rest on your
laurels, Perrot. You have brought these two down.'

But Gaveston shook his head. 'No, it shall be Hereford too.
I'll not rest until I have defeated the three of them.'

'My dear lord, you tempt the fates.'

'I have done that all my life, Walter. And today the fates
are with me.'

There was no dissuading him and soon he was riding out to
meet Hereford, proud Humphrey de Bohun, Constable of
England and another of those who considered himself part

royal because he was married to a sister of the King's. He was considered to be a great champion at the joust and his wife Elizabeth was seated under the royal canopy with her brother the King.

Elizabeth would be praying for her husband; but the King's thoughts, of course, would be all for his beloved Gaveston.

Gaveston felt like a legendary hero on that day. He knew he could not be beaten. Fortune was smiling on him. He, the son of a humble Gascon knight, was becoming the most important man in the realm.

Even as Hereford rode towards him, he knew.

And incredibly it happened. The mighty Earl, the champion jouster, was lying in the dust and the new champion Piers Gaveston, Earl of Cornwall, was riding round the field to come to rest before the King.

Edward could not hide his joy and pride. There were tears in his eyes.

'My champion of champions!' he murmured.

So the day ended in a resounding victory for Gaveston and a humiliating defeat for his enemies. The crowds were shouting Gaveston's name and vying with each other to wear his colours.

Gaveston asked the King if his lord was pleased with the little entertainment he had devised for his amusement.

'Dear Perrot,' replied the King, 'I am more than delighted. But I see some black looks around here. Do you?'

They laughed together—intimate laughter, implying shared secrets.

'My dear lord,' said Gaveston's young wife, 'you were wonderful. There can never have been such a noble knight.'

'Is that so?' said Gaveston. He glanced at her briefly and turned to the King.

'Magnificent Perrot,' cried Edward, 'I will come with you to your pavilion. I want to tell you of my special appreciation.'

Margaret was about to follow them when her husband turned to look at her. There was that in his eyes which commanded her to stay where she was. She stood, disconsolate, looking after the King and her husband as they made their way to the most brilliantly luxurious of all the pavilions.

'My lady,' whispered Walter Reynolds who was standing by and had seen what had happened, 'you cannot hope to come between such friends.'

Margaret looked as though she were about to burst into tears.

'My lady is but a child,' murmured Walter Reynolds.

The Earl of Warwick asked Margaret if he might escort her to the palace.

'It will be a pleasure to do so, dear lady, since your husband is engaged with the King.'

Gaveston looked round and saw Warwick with his wife. His voice always resonant and clear came to them as they stood there.

'Look Edward. The mad hound is taking charge of my wife.'

Their laughter floated back to the group.

The Earl of Warwick had flushed scarlet. He knew that people instigated by Gaveston called him the Mad Hound behind his back and it was true that he had an unfortunate habit of spitting as he spoke which Gaveston called foaming at the mouth.

'He may call me the mad Hound,' muttered Warwick. 'One day that mad hound will seize him and destroy him.'

* * *

How they rejoiced. How they laughed. Walter Reynolds said they must have a special play to celebrate the occasion. The arrogant nobility had been bitterly humiliated.

'They say,' commented Gaveston, 'that Hereford, Arundel and Surrey will never get over it.'

'I hope they will not try to take their revenge,' commented Edward uneasily.

'I would challenge them again tomorrow,' boasted Gaveston.

'Oh, but I did not mean at the joust. I fear they will put their heads together and talk against us.'

'Men will always slander those of whom they are envious.'

'Why should they be envious? They are rich men and have all they want.'

'They do not have your love, my lord, as I have it.'

'They should know that is for one alone.'

'We should be watchful, my lords,' said Reynolds. 'They are in conference with your cousin Lancaster and Warwick.'

'I'll warrant the mad hound is foaming at the mouth,' cried Gaveston.

'And that Lincoln strokes his fat belly and is taking a little more food and wine to comfort him.'

'And Lancaster fiddles away to get them dancing to his tune.'

'While our one-time champions lick their wounds.'

There was much laughter in the royal chamber and when the players came in they made little Francekin perform for them on his new kettle drums. Francekin was such a pretty boy.

Then they gave themselves up to the pleasure of planning Christmas. How wonderful it would be to spend it together. Edward had a special cotehardie for his friend. It was set with the most valuable jewels he could find. How delighted Perrot would be with that. He could scarcely wait to give it to him.

He lay dreaming of the joy in store for his dear friend.

But Gaveston's thoughts were on another prize.

'You know, dearest boy,' he said, 'that you will soon have to go to France.'

Edward pouted. 'Oh pray, Perrot, do not remind me of it.'

'You will not stay long, just long enough to pay your respects to the King of France and marry his daughter. Then you will return to your Perrot. But while you are away there must be a Regent. You will have to appoint him before you go.'

'You know who that will be, Perrot—my cousin Lancaster.'

'Old Fiddler! Oh no, that must not be.'

'It will be only for a short time. I know he is stupid but there will be plenty around him to keep him in order.'

'Dear lord, you know that I have beaten three so-called champions in combat. I have shown myself to be superior to them, have I not?'

'Indeed you have, Perrot.'

Gaveston seized the King's arm. 'Then give *me* this chance. Show your trust in me. Let me hold the power for you while you are away from these shores. Only that can give me a crumb of comfort.'

'Perrot! They would never agree ...'

'Why, my lord? Who would dare to disagree with the King?'

'They will say that it should naturally go to Lancaster.'

'Let them say what they will. It is for you to bestow the Regency on whomsoever you wish. And I venture to believe that you have more trust in me than in the Fiddler or Burst Belly or even the Mad Hound.'

'By God's ears, Perrot, I'll do it.'

'Oh, my lord, my sweet lord.'

'So you are content then, Perrot?'

'Content when my lord plans to leave me ... even though the parting will be brief? It must be brief. How can I live without you? But I will take the Regency and I will say this is a symbol of his trust in me and believe me, dearest lord, it will not be the power which comes to me in which I shall delight but the knowledge of the trust my dear lord has in me.'

'Oh, Perrot, Perrot, I shall soon be back with you.'

Gaveston grimaced. 'A husband. Fancy that, lord. You will come back with a wife.'

'What you have, I shall have. Nothing more.'

'Let us hope,' said Gaveston gaily, 'that our wives will be good friends and that their friendship will compensate them for their husbands' neglect.'

Gaveston was feeling intoxicated with power. He had not really believed it. Surely Edward would have stopped at the Regency. It was clear though that there was no end to his infatuation.

This, said Gaveston to himself, is but a beginning.

*   *   *

The lords had met. Among them were Warwick and Lancaster and, still licking their wounds, Hereford, Sussex and Arundel.

They were incredulous.

'It cannot be true,' cried Arundel. 'The Regency. This upstart. My God, Thomas, it should be you.'

'I cannot think what madness has beset my cousin,' said Lancaster. 'I had naturally assumed that I should be the one.'

'Gaveston,' cried Hereford, 'to be put above us all. This nobody. It's a madness.'

It was Warwick who begged them to be calm.

'He can do little harm. We shall see to that and it will not be long before the King returns.'

'And if he attempts to rule the country ... and us?' asked Hereford.

'We shall know how to deal with him,' answered Warwick.

'Nay, the King will return a husband. His bride is noted for her beauty. Philip will have them married with great pomp and when the King has a beautiful wife he will grow away from Gaveston.'

'Do you think he will ever grow away from Gaveston?' asked Arundel.

Warwick's dark eyes glowed suddenly.

'If he does not, my lord, it will be our duty to see that Gaveston is removed.'

Removed. A good word. It covered so many meanings. That was what they were all thinking as they looked at Warwick.

Little flecks of foam were visible on his chin. The Mad Hound, Gaveston had called him. They remembered Warwick's words. 'He will find that the Mad Hound can destroy him.'

Perhaps it would not come to that. Who could say? Warwick was smiling almost blandly. 'Give the King a beautiful wife. If anyone can change him, can take him away from this passion for Gaveston, Isabella can.'

There was a sense of relief in the room. Warwick was right. Edward was young yet. He was weak; easily influenced, and Gaveston they all had to admit was clever.

Marriage was the answer. Beautiful Isabella would save the King.

'We must impress on the King that he should leave without delay,' said Arundel.

'So that,' went on Lancaster, 'on his return we can go ahead with plans for the coronation.'

They nodded.

They were convinced—most of them—that Isabella might well make a good husband and father of Edward, and so weaken and, hopefully, destroy the evil influence of Piers Gaveston.

THE QUEEN'S DISCOVERY

THESE were exciting days for the Princess Isabella and she was gratified to be the centre of attention. They were all so pleased about the proposed match; and so was she for she had heard that her bridegroom-to-be was one of the most handsome men in the world. She had never seen him but those who had, assured her that there had been no exaggeration of his good looks.

'He is tall,' they said, 'with flaxen hair. He is just like his father and he was known in his youth to be a fine-looking man.'

'You will be a Queen,' they went on. 'Queen of England—think of that.'

She had thought about it and it pleased her. She patted her luxuriant fair curls and assured herself that she would be a good match for this handsome man, for she was an acknowledged beauty herself. She had seen even her father's eyes soften at the sight of her and everyone knew what a ruthless man he was. He was the most powerful King in Europe and her mother had been a Queen in her own right before she had married, so none could be more highly born than the Princess Isabella.

Therefore it was only to be expected that because of her high rank and outstanding beauty she would make a grand match.

Her brothers—Louis, who was always quarrelling, Philip who was tall and aloof and Charles who was so good-looking that they were already calling him Le Bel, a title which in her father's heyday had been given to him—were pleased with the match. So were her uncles Charles de Valois and Louis d'Evreux. In fact the uncles were to go to England when she and her bridegroom left for his country.

She was glad of that. It would make the parting less acute, although of course she had always known that, as a Princess, she would have to leave her home one day. It was the fate of all princesses. It had not worried her unduly, and even though at this time she was barely sixteen years old she was prepared for what life would offer. Her strong-minded mother, who never forgot that she was the Queen of Navarre as well as France, and her ruthless father had endowed her with something of their own natures, and she was quite ready to hold her own position in whatever society she found herself.

She only had to see her reflection to receive assurance and, if she could not have seen for herself in her mirror, the eyes of the men at her father's court told her that without doubt she was possessed of a rare attraction.

Five years previously she had been solemnly betrothed to Edward, Prince of Wales. This had taken place in Paris and she remembered it well. The Count of Savoy and the Earl of Lincoln had represented the Prince of Wales and her father had given his blessing and her hand to the heir of England. It had been a very impressive moment when she had placed her hand in that of Père Gill, the Archbishop of Narbonne, who had stood proxy for Edward. From that moment she had known that as soon as she was old enough she would become Edward's wife. Since then she had tried to learn all she could about Edward. She had discovered that he often disobeyed his father and she was amused. Her father had talked of the King of England as that wily old lion and gave the impression that he did not by any means love him, although he respected him. 'We must always be watchful of the old lion,' he had said, and he was always delighted when the Welsh and the Scots gave his rival trouble. But he was eager for this marriage and so it seemed was the old King of England.

Her mother had explained it to her. 'Alliances such as you will make with the Prince of Wales are a safeguard of peace. And when you are Queen of England never forget France.'

She had sworn she never would.

It was comforting too that her aunt Marguerite was now the Dowager Queen of England. She was coming to France for the wedding. Queen Jeanne, Isabella's mother, often talked of Marguerite.

'Your aunt is a good woman, Isabella. She was happy with the old King. But Marguerite is such a meek and docile woman that she would believe she was happy as long as her husband did not ill-treat her or too blatantly consort with other women. The King of England was a faithful husband and that is considered rare. Therefore your aunt was a very happy wife. She has said so often.'

Isabella was well aware of the story of her aunts. She could just remember beautiful Aunt Blanche who had married into Germany and died soon after. They had thought that Blanche would marry the King of England at one time—at least the King of England had thought it, but Philip le Bel had had other ideas for his sister and had tricked Edward into taking Marguerite instead. Isabella reflected that her father could be very wily. She admired him for it although she supposed some would call it dishonourable.

Isabella had always been a girl to keep her eyes and ears open. She liked to sit at her father's table—and he liked her to be there because he was proud of her beauty—and she would be alert listening to talk. It was gratifying to learn that she was the daughter of the most feared man in Europe.

Philip le Bel! They still called him that although it scarcely fitted now. She had heard that when he had come to the throne at the age of seventeen he had been so handsome that men as well as women found it difficult to take their eyes from him. He had a cold nature though and rarely any warmth showed. Sometimes she thought he admired her because she had inherited many of his characteristics—the most obvious being beauty. He no longer possessed his—he had grown too fat and florid—but if he had lost his looks he had gained in power. Some said he was the most ruthless man in Europe. He was cold, harsh and caluculating and the more power he achieved the more he wanted; and he had few scruples when it came to attaining it. That he was vindictive and completely without mercy was well known. It was one of the reasons why he was so feared. He sought not only to rule France but the whole world and even that did not seem to him an impossible dream.

Isabella knew how pleased he was that Edward of England was kept busy with his border rebels. Of all men the King of

France feared the King of England and Edward's obsession to bring Wales and Scotland under the English crown was as great as Philip's dream of complete domination. Edward had died without achieving this success and there was no doubt that her father had looked upon Edward's death as a happy augury for France.

She had heard him say. 'This young cub, my son-in-law, will give me no trouble. Or if he does I shall know how to deal with him.' Then seeing the look in his daughter's eyes he had become alert. He added: 'My daughter will help me, I know, and she is going to be a power in that troublesome kingdom.'

It was flattery of course and a reminder. Never forget that you are French, daughter. Always remember where your allegiance lies.

When a Princess married a King and became a Queen his country was hers and it was to that, she would have thought, to which she owed allegience. But Isabella wondered whether she would ever owe allegiance to any but herself.

If this were so she was following the teachings of her father. She had learned not so much through what he had said to her as by watching his actions.

She had lived through stirring years in the history of her country. She knew that her father had always tried to curb the power of Rome and how it infuriated him to realize that to many of his subjects the Pope stood above him and that they believed they owed first allegiance to the Church rather than to the State. There had been a bitter quarrel with Pope Boniface who had dared say that if the King of France did not mend his ways he would be chastised and treated as a little boy. With this admonition had come the threat of excommunication and this was something all dreaded. A weaker man might have sought to placate, but Philip looked for revenge. He demanded that his subjects support him against the Church and so did they fear his ruthless revenge if they did not that most were ready to obey him. The rich Templars were one community which refused to do so.

Vindictive as he was Philip vowed he would not forget this and although he never scrupled to break a promise if he saw an advantage in doing so, a vow such as this was one he was determined to carry out.

He was a strong man, her father. Only fools would go against him. Even the Church should have considered before acting rashly. She admired him so much. She was proud to be his daughter.

Philip had sent Guillaume de Nogaret, his trusted minister, to Rome to conspire with the Pope's enemies against him. This he did so successfully that they captured Boniface in the town of Anagni and held him prisoner. He was rescued but that incident had impaired his health and his reason and he had died soon after. A new pope was elected who was sponsored by the King of France. This was Benedict.

Isabella had glowed with pride at her father's success. Men were right when they said that he was the most powerful man in the world. Even the Popes must obey him. But the Pope was far away and Benedict must have forgotten his promises to the King of France which he had given in exchange for his support at the time of his election, for very soon he was talking of excommunicating any who had brought harm to his predecessor Boniface and wanted the matter of his imprisonment and death enquired into.

When the shadow of excommunication hung over her powerful father Isabella had shivered with fear and even he was downcast, dreading that the sentence might be carried out. It was not so much that he would fear to dwell in that unsanctified state as that his soldiers would believe themselves beaten before they went into battle and his ministers would have the idea that working with the King was working against God.

The King did not fly into tempers; his rages were cold and calculating and his revenge on those who displeased him could be terrible.

She had been working at her embroidery one day when her mother had come to her and sat beside her.

'The King is in high spirits this day,' she had commented. 'The Pope is dead.'

'Oh,' cried Isabella, 'that is good news for France.'

'A foolish man,' commented this Queen. 'He thought to break his promises to your father.'

'Then he deserves to die,' said Isabella. 'He did not reign long as Pope. Was he an old man that he should die so soon?'

The Queen smiled slowly. 'Let us say that he was a greedy man. A basket of fresh figs was sent to him. He ate too many of them.'

'Could he die through eating figs?'

'This Pope did,' said the Queen still smiling.

What rumours there were about that basket of figs. It was said that the Roman enemies of the Pope had had poison inserted into the luscious fruit before they had been sent to Benedict. It was even whispered that Guillaume de Nogaret had done it. But the chief suspect was one few dared name. The King of France.

Philip was certainly ready to seize the advantage and was determined that the next Pope should be his man. His choice fell on Bertrand de Goth, a man of great ambitions, and one who would be ready to do anything to gain his ends. The very man for Pope. But what chance had the Archbishop of Bordeaux of reaching that mighty pinnacle? None without the help of the most powerful man in Europe. And if he had that help?

'Why should we not make a bargain,' demanded the shrewd King of France.

A hard bargain it was but the Archbishop knew very well that it was his one hope of becoming Pope, and being the man he was he seized it. In a short time he had become Pope Clement V.

The papal resident had been moved from Rome to Avignon. This Pope was undoubtedly the King's man.

Isabella knew that one of a ruler's most urgent needs was for money. It was often the topic of conversation in intimate family circles. Subjects thought their rulers were possessed of inexhaustible coffers into which they had but to delve. How different was the truth. Those coffers had to be filled and one of the main preoccupations was how to replenish them. Philip was like the rest in this. He had no alchemist's secret of turning base metal into gold. So he must look about for other means.

He had hated the Templars since they had opposed him and the desire for revenge on them had been festering in his mind for some time. He would have taken that revenge before had he not been so immersed in papal affairs. Now he saw a means of satisfying two cravings at the same time. He could gain a great deal of money while taking revenge.

About two years before when there had been riots in Paris he had been in danger and it had been necessary for him to seek a refuge. This had been offered to him by the Templars in the Temple Palace and during his stay there he had become aware of the enormous amount of treasure which was stored in their vaults.

Isabella had heard a great deal about the Knights Templars —the Order of the Knights of the Temple of Jerusalem. They were a military religious order of knighthood which had been formed to protect the pilgrims to the Holy Land. They had done good service during the Crusades and they had been maintained and rewarded in many countries and this had been the foundation of their great wealth.

Lately stories had been circulated about the order. Being a rich and successful one it had generated a great deal of envy. Isabella listened wide-eyed to the gossip. Her women talked of the Templars in hushed whispers while they assisted at her toilette.

The stories grew more and more outrageous.

'They have strange ceremonies. They have a Grand Master who is all powerful. They say that what goes on at the initiation is too evil to be spoken of.'

'But I wish to know,' Isabella had said.

Glances were exchanged, reproving ones. 'These things should not be spoken of before the Princess. They are not for my lady's ears,' said one.

Nothing could anger Isabella more. She wanted to hear everything and the more shocking the more necessary was it for her to hear about it. When her temper was aroused she had been known to administer many a painful slap or nip.

'You will tell me,' she said.

There was a moment's hesitation but only a moment's, for her attendants had learned it was unwise to offend their imperious mistress. One of them whispered: 'They spit on the crucifix and deny God.'

'What else?' demanded Isabella.

'They have to behave ... indecently on the altar ... with each other.'

Isabella wrinkled her brows trying to imagine what acts were performed and as she saw that some of her women had a notion of this she was loth to show her ignorance, so she repeated: 'What else?'

'They make obscene images and they worship goats and cats. And there are indecent acts with animals. They kiss them ... in all manner of places ...'

This was easier to understand and Isabella stared round-eyed with wonder.

'They have children,' whispered one woman, 'when they should not according to law have them. Then they seek to destroy them.'

'How?'

'They roast them alive over a pan into which the fat drips and this fat they smear over their idols. It is a sort of sacrifice . . . an offering.'

'It makes me feel sick,' said Isabella.

'I know we should not have told you, my lady.'

'When I command you to tell me you will tell but I do not believe knights would behave so.'

The women fell silent and then Isabella said: 'But perhaps they do. My father hates them. He is going to make them sorry for these evil deeds.'

Then the women shivered for they knew some evil fate would befall the Knights Templars.

And they were right.

They were filling the prisons now; they were confessing their sins. There was only one way of dealing with such wickedness, declared the King. From the squares in Ile de la Cité the smoke could be seen rising and in the air was the acrid smell of burning flesh. The persecution of the Templars was providing a rich haul, for when a Knight was condemned to die for his sins his treasures fell naturally into the hands of the King.

'We must impress the English,' he told Isabella, 'and as my daughter you must have a dowry worthy of you. We must make much of your bridegroom when he comes to marry you because he is the King of England.'

She liked to gloat over her treasures with her attendants round her. Her father was true to his word. She was to be magnificently equipped and for this she must thank the Knights Templars for she knew she owed her rich possessions to them.

'It was God's will that I discovered their villainies at this time,' commented the King with a wry smile. 'And there is more to come.' He rubbed his hands together in glee and the Princess smiled at him. Her brothers thought their father very clever and so did she, but she hated the smell of burning flesh, which seemed to permeate the air. She would not think of it. After all it was very wicked of them to burn their babies —even though they should never have had them in the first place—and rub their fat over their idols. That image haunted her, sickened her, so that she turned to her treasures and thought how much better it was for a beautiful young girl to have them than that they should be buried away in chests in some gloomy vault.

She had two golden crowns decorated with magnificent jewels and she knew that the jewels had been taken from the Templars' store and her father had had them set into the golden crowns for her.

'Remember always, daughter, that you *are* my daughter. You will have a young husband who is not very serious-minded. You must always remember to make him the friend of France.'

'Oh, I will, my lord, I will.'

'Then you may have these, my child. See how pretty they are. Golden drinking vessels. Shall we wager that they came from the East? Those wicked men picked up many of their treasures there. And see here are silver cups to match. Remember me, dear child, when you drink from them and that you owe your good fortune to your father. Here are golden spoons and look at these porringers, all solid silver.'

'They are beautiful, my lord.'

'They are yours, child. Part of your dowry. I would not have your bridegroom think you go to him as a pauper. It is well that he should know the King of France is in a position to send his daughter to her husband in fitting manner. He must know that whether it be a daughter or an army there is no lack of treasure to fit out what should be done in a costly manner.'

So many beautiful garments she had. There were eighteen dresses—all splendid colours and most becoming to her dark beauty—greens, blues and scarlets, all of the finest materials that man could devise. There were surcoats of satin and velvet. There were wimples and fillets for her head and gorgets for her throat. There were many costly furs to keep her warm in winter, some made into cloaks, some edging her gowns and others to use as coverlets for her bed at night. There was everything she would need, even tapestries to hang on her walls, for these had become fashionable in England since they had been brought in by the late King's wife, Eleanor of Castile.

The time had come for her to leave for Boulogne whither she was to travel with her parents and other members of the the family. It was a brilliant cavalcade and she was at the heart of it, riding beside her father and her mother who were clearly proud of their beautiful daughter.

The princes and members of the nobility were led by her brother Louis, who was the King of Navarre, a title his mother had assigned to him, and like her father he impressed on her the need to remember that she was a daughter of France and that in her new life she must never forget it. She listened intently and assured them fervently that she would remember.

And in Boulogne Edward was waiting for her. He was every bit as handsome as they had said. Her heart leaped with delight when she saw the flaxen hair stirred slightly by the breeze and the bluest eyes she had ever beheld. Moreover he was tall and held his head like the King he was.

Isabella had fallen in love at first sight with the King of England.

*   *   *

He was charming and courteous to her and her parents looked on at the young couple with unfeigned delight. Dear Aunt Marguerite, who herself had gone to England as a young girl to be the bride of the King, the present one's father, was clearly moved. Aunt Marguerite was gentle and kind and she whispered that she hoped Isabella would be as happy in England as she had been. If there was a faintly apprehensive look in her eyes as she spoke, Isabella did not notice it.

She noticed nothing but Edward.

He took her hand and told her how enchanted he was by her beauty. He had heard word of it of course but it exceeded all expectations, and he eagerly awaited their marriage.

The preparations had been made with the utmost care, and the ceremony in the church of Notre Dame was most impressive. The handsome distinguished looks of the bridegroom, the fresh and startling beauty of the bride, were marvelled at and to those who knew nothing of the King's infatuation for Piers Gaveston it seemed the perfect match.

Isabella was one of those and she often thought afterwards that had she received some intimation of what she would have to expect she might have been able to handle the situation more wisely. For one thing she would never have allowed her-self to fall in love.

Those were happy days—perhaps the happiest of her life. She loved the pomp and ceremony; she loved the homage to her beauty and her rank. In the church of Notre Dame she had become a Queen as well as a wife and Edward appeared to have fallen as deeply in love with her as she with him.

Edward was in fact chafing against his separation from Gaveston. He knew he must accept this because this marriage was necessary. Isabella was a beautiful girl and she was most flatteringly enamoured of him so he was lucky for he might have had someone he could not take to at all. This beautiful daughter of the King of France must bear him a child and quickly. Both he and Perrot had agreed on that. He was glad therefore that she was not repulsive to him, and that he could, with some conviction, play the part of the devoted husband.

This he did and with such success that Isabella believed herself to be the happiest woman in France. Marriage suited her. She had always known it would. She had always liked to hear about her women's love affairs. Now she understood so much that she never had before and she was going to have few regrets at leaving France because she was going to Edward's country which she would rule with him.

She realized quickly that Edward was pliant as well as ami-able and that delighted her. She believed he was the kind of man whom she could govern. He clearly wanted to please her. It was a good sign. She must keep him thus.

She soon began to suspect that he was a little lazy. So much the better. She had energy enough for them both. He would discuss everything with her. They would work together but it would be her will which would be done.

Oh, she was deeply content in her marriage.

*　　*　　*

The King of France walked arm-in-arm with his son-in-law in the gardens of the palace.

'It gives me the greatest pleasure,' said Philip, 'to see your happiness with my daughter.'

'Your daughter is the most beautiful girl in France,' re-plied Edward.

'I see we were meant to agree.' Philip gave his sly quick smile. 'It is a good augury for the future, my son, when France and England walk together in amity.'

'There will be many in France and England who will rejoice at this time.'

'My dear son, let us keep it so. Let us make a vow of friendship.'

They were both ready to swear to that for neither would be entirely scrupulous if the need arose to break a vow or two.

'You have heard of the wicked doings of the Templars, I doubt not,' went on Philip.

Edward replied that he had. It was difficult to be in France and not know that they were being arrested all over the country and put to the torture in castle dungeons where they admitted that they were guilty of the most horrifying crimes.

'There can be no peace in countries where such wickedness is allowed to flourish.'

'That must be so,' agreed Edward.

'What of those who have sought refuge in England? There are many of them.'

'Oh, many of them.'

'You must hunt them out. You must not allow them to pollute your country.'

'Oh no, they shall not,' replied Edward; he was not thinking of the Templars. He was wondering how Perrot was faring and whether he was having trouble with the barons who had been so jealous about the Regency.

'Arrest them. Bring them to trial. Make them confess their abominations. It is the only way.'

'Oh yes, the only way.'

'Put them to the torture. Nothing is too fierce for them. You will wring the confessions from them. Then you confiscate their goods. They have managed to build up treasures I can tell you.'

'I am sure of it.'

'Why should that wealth not be used in the service of the country?'

'Why not indeed.'

'I shall be interested to hear what comes of this.'

'You shall be kept informed.'

The King of France looked satisfied. They went into the palace together.

'I am glad you are of my opinion and that we are in agreement on this matter,' said Philip.

What matter? wondered Edward lightly. What had the old man been talking about?

Isabella joined them.

'She is upbraiding me for keeping her husband from her,' said Philip with a roguishness which did not match his shrewd face.

Isabella took Edward's arm. 'Well, I have found you now.'

'We have had an interesting talk,' said her father, 'and we see many things from the same angle. This is a happy time for our two countries.'

Philip led them into his private chamber and there he took a key from his chain and opened a wooden box with a strong iron lock. From it he lifted a heavy chain of gold studded with rubies and diamonds of an unusual size and of great beauty.

This he placed about Edward's neck.

'A gift to you, my son. An outward sign of our promise to work together.'

'But it is magnificent!' cried Edward.

The King took a ring from the box. It was set with rubies and diamonds and matched the chain. Philip put the ring on Edward's finger.

'A token of our friendship,' said Philip. 'You are my son now.'

Edward was astounded at the magnificence of the gift and he immediately wondered what Perrot would think of them. Perrot loved rubies almost as much as he loved diamonds!

Philip was in a generous mood, which was unusual with him, and added a special significance to the gifts. There were more of these to come for he had acquired so much booty from the Templars that he could well afford to part with some of it. He produced a belt and two fine brooches all set with glittering jewels and some bales of linen and velvet.

It was a token of friendship and the knowledgeable agreed that Philip's generosity meant that he intended to rule England through his son-in-law.

*   *   *

'My father loves you,' said Isabella.

They lay on their bed together, his arm about her, her lovely hair loose about her shoulders. Now and then she paused in her conversation to kiss him lightly on the cheek, lips or brow. He smiled benignly at these caresses. She was a beautiful and passionate girl and it had not been as difficult as he had thought it might be to do his duty by her.

'How shall I like England?' she asked.

'You will love it.'

'Because it is beautiful or because you will be there?'

'For both reasons,' said Edward.

'Will the people love me?'

'How could they help it?'

'The French can be difficult. They are quickly angered. There are riots now and then and people speak against the royal family.'

'This happens now and then. But when the people see you they will love you.'

'Do they love you.'

'So far, yes.'

'You think they will change?'

'They are fickle. They will tell you my father was the greatest of kings now that he is dead, but they did not always think so while he lived.'

'But they love you in spite of the fact that you are alive.'

'I am a new King and they have not yet learned to hate me. At this stage they blame others for my shortcomings. Perrot ... for instance. They blame him.'

'Perrot?'

'Oh ... he is just one of the knights. The Earl of Cornwall in truth.'

'Why do they blame him?'

'They must blame someone. Now let me tell you what I have done for you. We shall go to Westminster Palace. You will see what I have ordered to be done and it is all to please you. I have had the gardens returfed and trellisses built and flowers planted just for you. And I have had a new pier built which shall be called the Queen's Bridge.'

'All for me.'

'Yes, for you. You will find I am ready to do a great deal for you.'

She kissed him again and again – light butterfly kisses at first.

His arms tightened about her.

Oh yes, it was certainly a great deal easier than he had believed possible. He wondered if Perrot had found it equally so with his bride.

*　　*　　*

The Dowager Queen of England came into her niece's chamber and, as she indicated that she wished to speak to her alone, Isabella's attendants disappeared.

'It is nothing much,' said Queen Marguerite. 'I merely thought that as what is happening to you is so like what happened to me we might have a little chat.'

'My dearest aunt, you were very happy in England were you not?'

'I was completely happy. Your husband's father was good to me. I was afraid when I left France. You are not afraid, Isabella?'

Isabella shook her head.

'That is well, dear niece. You are young and beautiful and strong-willed. I was young but that is where the comparison ends.'

'Oh, but Aunt Marguerite, you were always very pretty and still are.'

'There are some in our family who have outstanding beauty. You are one. Your father was another and so was my sister Blanche. Edward had heard of her charms and wanted to marry her. Then your father changed his mind and I was sent in Blanche's place. It was not a good beginning. But Edward never showed his disappointment. He said afterwards how glad he was that I came instead of Blanche. It was a very happy marriage. But then Edward was a good husband ... a good father. He loved his family dearly. I wonder if ...'

'If my Edward will be the same. Dear lady, do not worry. I intend that he shall be.'

'Yes, you will see to that. Of course Kings have such power and so many seek to please them. Often they are tempted ...'

'Tempted?'

'To take ... lovers.'

Isabella laughed. 'There shall be none of that. Why, my lady, Edward is a meek man. He is a man who would not seek trouble. Never fear, I shall know how to deal with him.'

'Of course you will, my dear.'

'You are looking uneasy. Tell me, is there some scandal in Edward's life of which I have not heard? I shall ask him. I shall demand a full confession.'

'Oh no, no ... You must not do that. All will be well. I was just over anxious ... nothing more. Pray forget what I have said.'

Dear Aunt Marguerite! She was rather a simpleton, but she had the kindest heart in the world. She was merely trying to warn her young niece of the ways of men.

Isabella kissed her warmly.

'There is one thing you must know,' she said. 'I am able to take care of myself ... and Edward.'

The Dowager Queen nodded eagerly. Of course it would be all right, she assured herself. Now that he had a beautiful young wife, this regrettable liaison with Piers Gaveston would cease.

*   *   *

It was time to leave for England. The young bride had said farewell to her parents who had solemnly placed her in the care of her two uncles, Charles de Valois and Louis d'Evreux.

'If you need advice on any matter, my child,' said her father, 'go to your uncles. They will tell you how to act.'

She promised that she would do this and Philip seemed satisfied.

The journey across the Channel in spite of the bleakness of the February day was a calm one. Isabella stood on deck beside her new husband and watched with some emotion the approaching white cliffs. She glimpsed the castle high on the hill, that almost impregnable fortress which she had heard called the key to England.

Her eyes shining with happiness she grasped Edward's arm and told him that she knew that the happiest time of her life lay ahead of her.

He kissed her hand and murmured that it was going to be his joy to make her so. She did not know how lightly he spoke and that the excitement in his eyes was not there because he was bringing home his bride but because soon he would see Gaveston.

There were crowds waiting to greet them. Isabella could see the banners as they came in; she heard the shouts of the people. This was indeed a royal welcome.

Edward took her hand as they went ashore. She heard someone say, 'She is indeed a beauty.' Then the crowds took up the cry. 'Long live Isabella the Fair. God bless our Queen.'

She felt intoxicated with joy. She was a Queen; she had a handsome husband whom she could love; her new people admired her and welcomed her warmly to her new land. It was beyond anything she had imagined.

This was happiness.

There was a sudden silence in the crowd. A man had stepped forward. He was clearly of great importance for he was surrounded by extravagantly clad men who were in attendance on him. He was like a king himself—even more magnificent. He must be an Emperor, she thought, or some ruler of even greater rank than the King himself.

His cotehardie glittered with jewels and the purple velvet cloak—surely a royal colour—was trimmed with miniver. He was dark-haired, dark-eyed, very handsome, lithe and graceful.

'My lord,' he cried and then he and the King were embracing as though their reunion was the sweetest thing in the world to them both.

Edward was murmuring, 'Brother ... my brother ... It has seemed so long.'

'Forsooth, Edward, you are back now. God's ears, I thought the time would never come. It has seemed an age.'

'Perrot ... how has it been? What of the lords ... ?'

'Fiddler has been fiddling, and the Mad Hound foaming. What did you expect, dear lord?'

'Oh it is good to be back.'

Isabella said: 'My lord, I pray you present your friend to me.'

'My dear Isabella, of course ... of course ... This is the Earl of Cornwall, my brother.'

'I did not know of this brother. I thought your brothers were but children.'

Edward laid his hand caressingly on Gaveston's arm.

'This is *my* beloved brother. We were together in the nursery and there he became my best-loved brother. He has remained so ever since. You will love him, Isabella. He is the most amusing, interesting, charming, delightful of all our lords.'

She thought she detected an air of insolence in the manner in which Gaveston regarded her. She thought: The Earl of Cornwall, indeed! I shall soon put this fellow in his place. What possesses Edward to make so much of him?

She inclined her head slightly. She was then aware of a certain tension which had fallen on the watchers.

'Let us go into the castle,' said Edward.

They walked up the steep incline, the crowds parting to let them through. The shouting for the King and Queen persisted, but the Queen detected that there was a certain difference in these and those which had at first greeted her.

It was irritating that the Earl of Cornwall should walk beside them as they made their way into the castle.

*   *   *

There was a banquet to celebrate their arrival and as her women prepared her for it and kept exclaiming at her beauty, reminding her how the people who had gathered to see her and the King had been completely charmed by it, her spirits rose.

She had allowed herself to be irritated by that arrogant man who really had been ridiculously overdressed and tried to take up the King's attention. That was something she would not endure. She would speak to Edward about him at the first opportunity.

She asked her women: 'Why does the Earl of Cornwall give himself such airs?'

There was a brief silence and she went on sharply: 'Answer me. Are you all struck dumb?'

'My lady, he is a great friend of the King.'

'A great friend indeed! Methinks he had the appearance of an eastern ruler. He was more richly dressed than the King or I were, and his jewels ... If they are real they must be worth a fortune.'

'The Earl is a rich man, my lady. Since the King bestowed such titles on him, they say he is the richest man in the kingdom. He is connected with the royal house, too, for his wife is the King's niece.'

The young Queen seemed slightly mollified. She thought

she understood. He had recently married Edward's niece and because of this had had titles bestowed on him. His newly acquired honours had gone to his head. This was often so. But he would have to be taught to mend his manners.

The women having started to gossip seemed to find it difficult to stop.

'He was Regent during the King's absence. Some of the barons were not very pleased.'

'Regent! That popinjay.'

'The King thinks him very clever. The King is his great friend.'

Isabella could not quite understand the meaning of one woman's expression. She was on the point of demanding an explanation but thought better of it. She would speak to Edward.

What a fanfare of trumpets burst forth as she and Edward entered the hall. There had been no time to speak to him as yet for he had only arrived in time to conduct her to the banquet.

She heard the exclamation of amazement and she knew it was because of her beauty. She saw her uncles exchange gratified glances. Edward pressed her hand.

All was well.

She sat beside the King and to her dismay on the other side of him was the Earl of Cornwall. He had changed his elaborate garments for even more splendid ones. Indeed, who did he think he was? The King? Oh yes, she would certainly speak to Edward.

The Earl of Lancaster was beside her. He was the most important of the barons because he was the son of Edward the First's brother Edmund and therefore her husband's cousin.

She found him excessively dull and it was irritating that Edward should have bestowed so much attention on his neighbour. They were laughing together and clearly had a great deal to say to each other. Of course he had held an important post during Edward's absence. Perhaps that explained it.

After the meal there was music and she played her lute to them for she wanted them to realize how accomplished their new Queen was. She knew that she looked very beautiful with her hair falling over her shoulders. She had refused to have it confined by wimple or any such head-dress. It was really

very beautiful hair and should be displayed to her new subjects, she believed. So she sat with her lute and sang the songs
she had learned at her father's court and afterwards she and
Edward led the dance.

She whispered to him: 'You talk a great deal to the Earl
of Cornwall.'

'Oh, Perrot! He has always been a close friend.'

'Some were not very pleased.'

'Some will always be displeased no matter what one does.'

'*I* was one of those who felt displeasure.'

'*You*, Isabella? Oh you will soon be used to Perrot. I want
you to appreciate him. I am most anxious for you two to be
friends.'

'I like not his arrogant manner and his style of dressing to
outdo us all.'

'Oh . . . that is just Perrot. You will understand.'

It was difficult to talk seriously while dancing so she did
not tell him that she had taken an instant dislike to his Perrot
and she thought it very unlikely that she would become his
friend.

Edward was with her for the rest of the evening and she
was longing for that time when they should be alone together.
Dear Edward, he was so handsome and he hated conflict. He
would be ready to do exactly as she told him. It was a very
pleasant prospect. One of her first tasks would be to put a
stop to the friendship between him and the Earl of Cornwall.
She would do it gradually so that Edward would not realize
it was happening.

Now she longed for him to come. She had scented her hair
with special perfumes which she had brought from France.
She would lavish her caresses on him; she would make him
weak with love for her and after that when they lay languorous
together she would hint to him that she wanted Gaveston to
be less prominent at Court.

Her women had left her and she lay in anticipation of his
coming. 'Tomorrow, my lord of Cornwall,' she murmured to
herself, 'you are going to find yourself decidedly out of favour.'

She smiled to herself. Dear Edward. He was always so
tender, so eager to please.

He was long in putting in an appearance. He might be
delayed of course. It was his first night in his country. Surely
none of those dreary barons would detain him tonight? This

was not the hour for talking State business.

But how long he was!

An hour had passed. And still he had not come. What could it mean?

She rose from her bed and went to the door of her chamber. One of her women came to her at once.

'Is aught wrong, my lady?'

'The King has been delayed. He has not yet come to his bed.'

The woman had averted her eyes and Isabella caught her by the wrist.

'Do you know where he is?'

'No, my lady.'

'Find out.'

The woman escaped. Isabella went back to her bed. She sat on it, her eyes on the door. At any moment he would come. She would scold him, pout a little, insist that he placate her.

But he did not come.

In due course the woman came in, nervous, eyes downcast.

'The King was seen in conversation with one of his ministers.'

Isabella curbed her rising anger. She did not want to betray her feelings. People gossiped. She would not let Edward know how much he meant to her. That would be unwise.

'State matters,' she murmured yawning.

'It is so, my lady.'

She was angry. Her mother would have said: 'A King is first a King. You must remember that.'

Her father was a man who would always consider his kingship before anything else.

But Edward ... who would have believed it! She was going to be very angry with him.

*   *   *

It was late next day when she saw him. He was in the company of Piers Gaveston. They were seated together in a window-seat the light falling on Edward's flaxen head which was very close to Gaveston's dark one. They were laughing and whispering together. Of State matters! she thought angrily.

She advanced into the room.

'Edward.' Her voice was cold with its suppressed anger.

'Ah!' Gaveston had risen. He gave a bow which might be called ironic. 'The Queen.'

'Isabella!' Edward sounded suitably contrite.

'So you are here,' she said advancing. 'Are your State matters so pressing then?'

There was a short silence then. She stared for she could not believe what she saw—Piers Gaveston was wearing the diamond and ruby chain—Templars' spoil—which her father had given to Edward.

Gaveston knew that she was startled. He lifted the chain with a delicate hand on which she immediately recognized the ruby and diamond ring, another of her father's gifts. She was too bewildered for speech.

'Very pressing,' Gaveston was saying. 'It is long since the King and I were together. We had much time to make up for. Is that not so, dear lord?'

'Oh yes, yes,' said Edward.

Isabella turned to the King. 'The chain,' she said, 'the ring. He must have stolen them. Have you not seen ... ?'

Gaveston laughed. 'Are they not beautiful? I could have swooned with delight when my dear lord set the chain about my neck and put the ring on my finger.'

Edward spoke then haltingly, his eyes still on her, a little fearful and yet faintly defiant. 'Perrot loves rubies almost as much as diamonds ...' he said.

'And the two combined are quite irresistible,' added Gaveston.

'These are priceless ornaments,' cried Isabella. 'They are my father's gifts to us. They are for our children. You cannot let this man wear them.'

'Ha!' retorted Gaveston with a smirk. 'My lord the King would never attempt to stop me wearing what is mine. Very precious they are to me but more because of the giver than for their value.'

It was like a dream, a nightmare. Why should Edward give costly gifts to this young man? Why should he desert her for him?

She felt dizzy with apprehension. She remembered sly looks which she had failed to interpret.

She said: 'I do not understand what this means. Edward

pray dismiss this man. I have much to say to you.'

Edward looked at Gaveston who slowly shook his head.

'Edward,' cried Isabella, arrogant and appealing all at once.

Edward said: 'I will see you later, Isabella. You see, my dear, having been away there is so much to say to Perrot. Later I will explain.'

She felt weak and inadequate to deal with this situation and that was not due to Edward but to Gaveston.

She turned and went back to her chamber. She turned her attendants away. She lay on her bed and stared at the ceiling. Understanding was beginning to dawn on her. How many Princesses had married, gone to a new country and found themselves confronted by a husband's favoured mistress.

She did not have to face a mistress. She had to face Gaveston.

*   *   *

Perhaps her Aunt Marguerite was the best choice of confidante for she understood now that her aunt had made an attempt to prepare her.

What sort of man had she married? This was monstrous. How could he have deceived her so? She wished she had been told from the beginning. She had heard of these matters. Richard Coeur de Lion had loved his own sex and had neglected his wife; consequently he had left no heirs and the kingdom had passed to his brother King John. Was that what was going to happen again? She would be no barren Queen. She would be the mother of kings. She had determined on that.

She took her aunt's hand and said to her: 'I want you to tell me the truth. What sort of man is this I have married?'

The Dowager Queen flushed to the roots of her hair. 'So,' she said, 'you know about Gaveston.'

'I know that I saw the King not all through the night. Do you mean he shared that man's couch?'

'It has been an unfortunate friendship,' said the Dowager Queen. 'His father feared it and sought to break it. He banished Gaveston but as soon as Edward became King he recalled him.'

'He must be banished again. He is a loathsome creature.'

'I agree, my dear, but will Edward?'

'He must be made to.'

'The barons would be with you.'

'Ah the barons. Then there is hope. Oh, my dear aunt,
I was so happy. Edward seemed ... perfect. I cannot believe
this. I saw that man wearing the jewels my father had given
to my husband. How could he give them to that man!'

'He will give anything to Gaveston.'

Isabella stamped her foot in fury. 'I'll not endure it. I'll
not. He has deceived me. If my father had known this he
would never have allowed me to marry him.'

The Dowager Queen looked sad. Of course her brother had
known of it. Everyone knew of it. But Edward was a king
and his friendship for another man need not prevent his
having children. Philip wanted a bond between England and
France. He wanted peace for a while so he had agreed to the
marriage. He would reason that Isabella was a beautiful and
virtuous young woman. It was for her to wean Edward from
Piers Gaveston.

'My dear aunt, you must help me.'

'It is what I want to do, my child.'

'How can I be rid of that man?'

'The barons are in revolt against him. It is said in some
quarters that they will not endure him for much longer.'

Isabella narrowed her eyes. 'It shall be so. I shall do all I
can to help them. When I saw him wearing the chain and the
ring, I could not believe my eyes. I thought of my sisters-in-
law. Do you remember when you visited us once you gave
them costly gifts of jewels. They gave them to their lovers who
foolishly wore them at Court ... flaunted them that all might
know of their relationship with these foolish women. My
father saw them. He was furious. You know how angry my
father can get.'

'I never knew any who could be so coldly ruthless.'

'My dear aunt, he arrested those two brash young men.
Do you know what happened to them?'

Marguerite shook her head. She did not want to hear but
Isabella was determined to tell. 'They were flayed alive and
my sisters-in-law were sent to prison. They are still there.'

Marguerite covered her face with her hands. She has grown
very soft here, thought Isabella. But then she always was. It
was good that she married an old man who, wicked though
he no doubt was, was ready to be a good and faithful husband
to a docile wife.

Isabella knew what her aunt's advice would be. She would

tell her *she* must be a docile wife, that she must accept her husband's peculiarities; she must hope that he would not ignore her altogether and that she would in due course bear the heir to the throne.

But there was nothing docile in Isabella's nature. She was not like her predecessor Berengaria who had meekly waited for her husband's attention. She wondered what had happened to that gentle Queen. She had died neglected and there had never been any children to comfort her.

It was unfortunate that Edward was the man he was. She hated to think how he had deceived her and how she had allowed herself to become enamoured of him. She would not sit by quietly and wring her hands.

Gaveston ... and Edward ... had better beware.

*　　*　　*

She had seen very little of Edward since that meeting with him and Gaveston. Edward was evading her, which was typical of him. He hated conflict and he knew that she was deeply offended. She had time to overcome her shock and rage in some degree and could plan more calmly what action she should take. Her first impulse had been to go to her uncles and demand to return to France, but she knew that would not be permitted. She was Queen of England and that was what her father wanted her to be, so here she must remain.

When she next saw Edward alone she was aloof and cool. He pretended not to notice this and behaved as though he had not neglected her and everything was as it had been before her discovery.

'My dear,' he said, 'the coronation is approaching.'

'So I am to be crowned your Queen?'

'But of course.'

'I thought you might have reserved that honour for Gaveston.'

He looked at her uneasily and laughed as though they shared a joke.

'He is making the arrangements,' he said quickly. 'There is no one who can manage these matters better. You will have the most splendid coronation, I promise you.'

'This Gaveston ... has he estates outside England?'

'He is rich. He has estates in Gascony.'

'Of course, he is a Gascon. He must sigh for his native land.'

'Oh, he is happy enough here.'

'I doubt it not but the happiness of others must sometimes be considered besides his, I daresay.'

'The people are very happy. They are looking forward to the coronation. Lancaster says they took to you at once. They do not always, you know. The people can be very unkind. Do you know the Londoners nearly killed my grandmother once because they were displeased with her.'

'It is only when kings and queens have complete power that they can afford to offend the people. I suppose that is something we should always remember.'

'It was what my father always said.'

'He was a wise man and it is never easy to follow such. People make comparisons. To follow a strong man one must be seen to be as strong.'

'My father's shadow has always haunted me.'

'I doubt not that it will be more than his shadow that haunts you if you do not mend your ways.'

'Isabella!'

'Yes,' she cried suddenly her anger rising. 'I have no intention of being set aside for your paramour.'

'I ... I don't understand.'

'You understand very well. Everyone knows of your relationship with this man. It is unnatural. It must stop. You have a queen now. It is our duty to produce an heir.'

'I know ... it is what I want.'

'Then dismiss this man and behave as your people expect.'

Edward realized for the first time that his wife was by no means the meek girl he had been telling Perrot she was. She was a virago facing him now. She clenched her fists, her eyes blazed and she trembled with rage.

'I will not have people talk. I will not be your neglected wife awaiting your pleasure. I will not endure this insolent fellow. Do you hear that? I shall see my uncles. I hear there are many in the country who do not care for this man Gaveston. You will banish him as your father did ... or it will go ill with him, I promise you.'

Edward was dumbfounded. He had come to discuss the coronation and the beautiful clothes she would wear and to tell her how she had enchanted his people with her grace and beauty. And this had happened.

He hated trouble. He turned abruptly and left her.

* * *

The barons had arrived at the palace for an audience with the King. Lancaster, Pembroke, Lincoln and Warwick were among them.

They had come, they said, to speak of the approaching coronation with the King as they had heard disturbing reports of it.

Edward, fresh from his interview with Isabella, received them cautiously.

Lancaster was the spokesman. 'My lord,' he said, 'we are made uneasy by rumour.'

'You should not allow yourself to be made uneasy by rumour, cousin. If you do you will never have a moment's peace.'

'We have had little since we have heard of the Queen's displeasure, my lord.'

'The Queen's displeasure! What means this?'

'It has been brought to our notice that her royal uncles are not pleased with her treatment here and it is certain that they will carry ill reports to her father, the King of France.'

'The King of France has enough to concern him in his own kingdom.'

'His daughter's welfare must be one of his main concerns.'

'Do not believe it, cousin. The King of France concerns himself only with his own advantage.'

'His daughter is part of that, my lord. We have come to ask you that the Earl of Cornwall be sent out of the country.'

Edward was scarlet with rage.

'You must be mad. Why should I banish the Earl of Cornwall?'

'Because he is a disruptive presence and he has displeased the Queen and her uncles.'

'The Queen must conform to our ways,' mumbled Edward.

'This is a matter to which she will not become reconciled. My lord, we have come here to tell you that we will not have Gaveston at the coronation.'

'Not have him at the coronation ... *my* coronation! It is he who has made all the arrangements. They are almost complete. The coronation is to take place in a few days. What do you mean you will not attend?'

Warwick, foaming at the mouth with suppressed anger, said: 'We are not alone, my lord. We represent a large company. We were with your father when he banished Gaveston. We want you to do as your father did.'

'I am heartily sick of being compared with my father.'

'It is understandable,' said Warwick wryly.

'I will rule in my own way. I will brook no interference.'

'In that case, my lord, more barons will absent themselves from your coronation than will attend.'

Lancaster bowed and stepped backwards towards the door. The others followed him.

Edward stared after them.

'The insolent dogs!' he cried. But he was afraid.

*   *   *

It was necessary to postpone the coronation. Obviously it could not take place with so many barons absenting themselves. They must be there to acclaim him as King and show their allegiance.

How difficult they were! After Perrot had made such grand arrangements! Perrot was going to carry the crown and sword before him and he was so looking forward to doing it. The people of London were anticipating it with pleasure, too. They loved such celebrations and the King so newly married to a very beautiful wife would make it a doubly joyous occasion. Moreover the Queen was the daughter of the King of France and that could mean peace on the Continent. Such linking of families always benefited those who might be called on to fight. It could be a happy occasion and the barons were going to spoil it because of Gaveston.

As it was impossible to let the coronation take place on the appointed day and the King was most anxious that the people should not know that it was postponed because of his disagreement with the barons; he had a ready excuse. Robert de Winchelsea, Archbishop of Canterbury, was absent on the Continent. He had been banished by Edward the First with whom he had been in continual disagreement, but on his

accession Edward the Second had sent for him to return to
England. Alas, the Archbishop's ill health made the journey
back to England very arduous, and it was therefore plausible
enough to hint that the coronation should not take place
because of the absence of the Archbishop.

The Queen was aloof; her uncles were suspicious; and the
people did not want the coronation delayed. If the Archbishop of Canterbury was absent what was wrong with the
Bishop of Winchester? They wanted their coronation.

In desperation the King sent for those barons who had confronted him before. They must change their minds, he told
them.

'There is only one thing which will make us change our
minds,' Warwick told him. 'Your promise to banish Piers
Gaveston.'

The King was dismayed, but he saw the purpose in their
eyes. This could be disastrous. It could even be the beginning
of civil war. Oh, it was cruel. Piers had only just been returned
to him and now they wanted to send him away again.

But there was purpose in their eyes.

'The coronation must take place ... soon,' said the King.

They agreed. If not the people would know that something was very wrong.

'What can I do?' cried Edward.

'Please the Queen and the people,' he was told, 'by banish-
ing Gaveston.'

'You don't know what you ask?' cried the King in anguish.

'What we do know,' said the implacable Warwick, 'is what
will happen if you do not.'

These barons! They had too much power. Ever since
Magna Carta a king was not in truth a king. He had to bow
to their will or face ... disaster.

The King knew he had to promise. After all promises did
not necessarily have to be kept.

*   *   *

The coronation was a disaster. The fact that it was postponed had tarnished the whole affair in some way, and the
people were aware of certain tensions. Nevertheless they
turned out in their thousands and the press in the streets and
about the abbey was so great that when one of the knights,

Sir John Bakewell, fell from his horse he was trodden to death before he could be rescued.

Gaveston had insisted on making the arrangements. He had intended that this coronation should be more splendid than any which had gone before—and he the most splendid figure in it. But his numerous enemies had decided on quite the opposite and on this occasion they proved more effective than he was.

The service was delayed and darkness had descended just after the consecration of the King and Queen. When they arrived at the banqueting hall by torchlight it was discovered that the meal was not ready in spite of the delay. The barons were very hungry and they complained bitterly and there were audible whispers that Gaveston's departure must not be delayed. When the food did arrive it was proclaimed to be cold and ill-cooked and disgruntled looks could be seen everywhere.

The Queen's uncle Charles who was close to her said: 'This is an affront to you and therefore to France. It shall not be forgotten.'

'You must write your account of this matter ... and others ... to your father and we will see what he has to say,' added Louis.

Isabella had every intention of doing that.

Her coronation had been a disaster and she had not been the centre of attraction, for all eyes had been on that impossible outrageous creature, Gaveston. True the looks cast in his direction had been far from friendly but still it had been as he had intended it should from the first: His day.

The Queen was ready to upbraid the King and tell him that she would complain to her father, but he did not come near her. He must spend as many hours as he could with his beloved Gaveston, particularly now the threat of separation hung over him.

Isabella wrote home to her father: 'What sort of man have I been married to? I see little of him. He prefers the couch of his favourite Gaveston to mine.'

Her uncles informed the barons that they were displeased by the treatment given to the Queen and that they would consider it their duty to explain the situation to her father.

Lancaster replied that the Queen's uncles could be no more displeased with the state of affairs than the barons were and that before long they intended Gaveston to be banished from the country.

Charles de Valois discussed the matter with his brother Louis and they wondered whether it was wise to advise the King to send his favourite away.

'If he does not,' said Charles, 'the barons will rise in revolt.' He smiled slowly. 'Our brother will not be displeased at that I am sure.'

'And Isabella?' asked Louis.

'Never fear, we shall take care of our niece.'

Charles was right. When the brothers returned to France the King was most interested to hear of the English barons' dissatisfaction with their King.

'Good,' he said. 'We must let them know that if they should decide to rise against him we should not come to *his* aid.'

'As your son-in-law would he not expect it?' asked Louis.

'There is no harm in his expecting it. But Edward is not entirely a fool, my son. Every King of England knows that every King of France cannot help but watch with interest any disaffection in his realm; and since we can never be sure when he will seek to take advantage of us, we must be somewhat relieved to know that he has his troubles elsewhere.'

'Do you propose to take action, my lord?' asked Louis.

The King smiled slowly. 'Secret action. It shall be known that if the barons needed help we might be prepared to give them ... a little.'

*　　*　　*

Lancaster had received word from the King of France that Philip was displeased with Edward's treatment of his daughter and, if Lancaster were to make himself head of that party which demanded action against the King's favourite, he would have the support of the King of France.

This decided Lancaster. The party was more powerful than many of them would have believed possible. The King had vowed to banish Gaveston. He and they must make him realize that it was within their power to force him do so.

Lancaster called together a meeting of the barons.

'It is clear,' he announced, 'that we cannot continue in this way. Gaveston must go. The King of France desires it and no wonder. Gaveston's presence at court is an insult to the Queen.'

The barons agreed with one exception. This was Hugh le Despenser, Earl of Winchester, an ambitious man—more than that, an avaricious one. He had served in Scotland with the King's father and, eager to curry favour with the younger Edward, he saw an opportunity here. He had asked for an audience with the King and being admitted found him with Gaveston, both of them rather gloomy for they knew that the barons were standing together against the favourite.

Winchester told them that the barons had called a meeting and intended to confront the King and command Gaveston's banishment.

'I will not let him go,' cried Edward petulantly.

Gaveston said: 'They may force you to do so, sweet lord.'

'I will not be forced. Am I the King or am I not? God's teeth, I have not reigned a year yet and they would seek to rule me.'

Winchester said: 'I fear my lord that they are going to insist and it may be necessary for a while to do as they wish. But need it be for long, and why should you not decide where the Earl of Cornwall should go?'

'They want to send him to Gascony.'

'He could go to Ireland, my lord. There he could act as your lieutenant. He could be given a grant of money and live in comfort until you could see fit to recall him. You see if there were trouble in Ireland it would be necessary for you to consult with him. And then you could meet somewhere half way. You could accompany him on his journey until he takes ship. Perhaps this could break the melancholy a little.'

Gaveston's face had brightened but Edward was still downcast.

'I do not wish him to go at all,' he cried peevishly.

'My heart is torn in pieces,' added Gaveston, 'but my lord Winchester is right. We can soften the blow. We can rest assured that they are determined to part us, and I fear they may succeed. But let us make our parting as brief as is possible. Let us see if we cannot outwit them in the end.'

Edward could not be comforted. He said he could not bear to be parted from Gaveston even for a night.

Hugh le Despenser watched them together and thought how weak the King was and how completely Gaveston controlled him, but with Gaveston out of the way would the King be looking for new favourites? It was not that Despenser wished to take Gaveston's place. None could do that. But a weak King could be flattered and worked upon and Hugh le Despenser might be the man to do it. Gaveston was going. That was clear. The barons had decided on it and they had even hinted at civil war if Edward did not obey them. He had to make a choice. If Hugh le Despenser threw in his lot with the barons he would have many rivals. Lancaster—though not the most astute of men—would lead them. There was Warwick, Lincoln, Pembroke ... too many strong men. But if he supported the King he might become more powerful than any of them. Even if Gaveston returned he would be grateful to him for he was going to speak for him at the council meeting which would be held.

He had made up his mind. Hugh le Despenser, Earl of Winchester, had thrown in his lot with the King and Gaveston.

Edward was still King and would remain King. It was far-sighted to curry favour with kings if one could keep that favour.

The next day at the meeting of the council, Hugh le Despenser was the only one who spoke against the banishment of Gaveston. The barons rounded on him, hinted that he was a traitor, but he merely laughed.

He was sure that he had taken the right action and that he would lose nothing in the long run.

He was present when the ultimatum was put to the King. The barons were threatening civil war if Gaveston did not leave the country.

Edward had no alternative but to submit, but he had expressed his gratitude to Hugh le Despenser for his support.

'I shall not forget my friends,' he said, and when shortly afterwards Hugh le Despenser was dismissed from the council he remembered those words.

*   *   *

The King rode with Gaveston to Bristol, seeking to make the journey as long as possible.

He was sick at heart. There was no joy in life for him without his beloved Perrot. Gaveston declared that his own sorrow at the parting was as great if not greater than the King's.

This was not true of course. In fact Gaveston was some-what excited at the prospect of governing Ireland. There he would be treated like a king. He had come with all the trap-pings of royalty and he intended to be treated as such. It had been a stroke of brilliance to have thought of Ireland. He was determined to succeed there. That would be a blow for his enemies. They thought he was frivolous but he was by no means so. He frivolled to amuse the King, that was all. The King's favour was necessary to him. Because of it he was the richest man in England; and he had been careful to get his treasures out of the country because he could never be sure when those barons were going to trump up some charges against him, and who knew they might take it into their heads to confiscate his goods. So he had made sure that his wealth was taken into Gascony where he had some estates and there it awaited him if at any time he had to leave the country in a hurry. Edward was the most generous of men and he had bestowed on him the funds which the late King had gathered together for a crusade. Gaveston grimaced. He could make much good use of such treasure. Better for him to possess it than that it should be frittered away on some useless cam-paign for killing Saracans and getting nowhere. When he thought of all that had been wasted in that hopeless endeav-our in the past he could feel really angry.

Well now he must say farewell to his sorrowing King and assure him that very soon he would be back with him.

'I intend to make such a success of this Irish campaign, sweet lord, that your barons will tear their hair and smite their breasts and like as not grovel on the floor and eat the rushes.'

'That was what my great grandfather used to do.'

'They shall do the same, I promise you.'

'Promise me one thing more important, my dear one. That you will never forget me and come back as loving as you left.'

'I give you my word, dear lord.'

Edward stood on the shore and watched the ship sail away.

Then he turned sorrowfully away. 'I can know no hap-piness,' he said, 'until Perrot comes back to me.'

MURDER ON BLACKLOW HILL

EDWARD was desolate but Isabella was triumphant. She was furious, of course, to have been set aside for Gaveston and her inclination was to scorn her husband, but she had grown up since her marriage and was not going to act in a manner which might bring no good to herself. Strangely enough she was still physically in love with her husband. When she looked round the Court she could not find one man who was as handsome in her eyes. As for Edward, he was pliant, amiable and anxious to placate her and she found his melancholy attractive. She thought how gratifying it would be to win him away from Gaveston and when that fellow returned, as he undoubtedly would, it would give her immense satisfaction to see Edward turn away from him because of his love for his wife. It would be a difficult task to achieve with one of Edward's proclivities but the very immensity of it intrigued and inspired her. There was one other consideration—and this was the chief of all: she wanted children. She must have a son who would inherit the throne. If she did, then she could guide and rule him; and if Edward so displeased the barons and they deposed him—which, it had already occurred to her, was not an impossibility—she would be there with her son who would be ready to take the crown. That was looking forward a good many years but she was becoming shrewd and wise. Edward had humiliated her beyond normal endurance. Very well, why should she not use him to get what she wanted from life? Determination had taken the place of humiliation and life had become quite amusing and exciting.

It was by no means so for Edward. He missed Gaveston desperately. Sometimes he thought of giving up everything and joining him in Ireland. He could not do that of course and secretly he wondered whether Perrot would find him so attractive if he were not King. He must keep his royalty—Perrot set such store by it. He loved to see Perrot's face light up when some gift was bestowed on him and only kings could provide the sort of gifts which Perrot wanted.

There was trouble in Scotland. Robert the Bruce, who had been crowned King there, was endeavouring to regain the whole of his kingdom and drive out the English. The best thing that had happened to Scotland from Bruce's point of view was the death of Edward the First, he whom they called the Hammer of the Scots, that Edward who had commanded that his bones be placed in a hammock and carried before his army. Bruce said cynically that he feared the bones of Edward the First more than he feared his son and any army led by him. Insulting words, but let be, thought Edward. How can I be in Scotland when there is so much to be done here and I am unsure of the fidelity of those about me?

His father-in-law was offering advice. In fact since the marriage Philip had made it clear that he took a great interest in Edward's affairs. Philip had the Pope dancing to his tune; he wanted his son-in-law to do the same.

A messenger from the Pope had arrived in England and he told the King that his master was much disturbed by the practices carried out by the Knights Templars and that he wished the Order to be suppressed in England as it was being in France.

Edward was alarmed. He had always believed there was something holy about the Templars. He knew that over the centuries they had amassed great wealth but he remembered his father's saying how magnificent they had been during his crusade and how their presence there had been such a help to the soldiers.

He sent for Walter Reynolds who had been a great comfort to him since the departure of Gaveston.

Walter was thoughtful when he heard of the Pope's instruction. 'You can depend upon it this does not come so much from His Holiness as from the King of France,' was his comment.

'Philip has started to suppress the Templars. Walter, I

fear it will bring me ill luck. I fear if I do this something awful will happen. I might never see Perrot again.'

'The King of France has amassed great wealth through the suppression of this Order, my lord.'

'I know it well.'

'And a king never needed money more than you do.'

'It seems the wrong way to get it.'

'If it is true that they practise these obscene acts . . .' Walter licked his lips and Edward knew that Walter was thinking how he would like to witness some of them.

'Do you believe it, Walter?'

Walter shrugged his shoulders. 'It would be a way of replenishing the royal coffers,' was his comment.

Edward shuddered. 'I will not do it,' he said. 'Frankly, Walter, I do not believe it. My father-in-law is a ruthless man. He needs money so he looks round to see who has some. He has alighted on the Templars. I think this will bring him ill luck. The Templars are . . . or were . . . men of God.'

'You will doubtless put it before the council.'

'This I must do, but somehow, Walter, I fancy they will not wish to do it either. The Templars have lived peaceably here for many years. I had rather they continued to do so.'

'The King of France is the most powerful man in Europe, my lord. It is a blessing that you married his daughter.' Walter smirked. 'The lady seems a little more pleased with life of late. I doubt not this state of affairs has reached the French King's ears.'

'If he thinks to rule me,' said Edward somewhat petulantly, 'I shall defy him.'

'Who is the King of France to govern the King of England! He is determined though that the Templars be suppressed and not only in his own country. It may be that he wishes to ease his conscience by letting others share his guilt . . . if guilt it is.'

'If these men are innocent, Walter . . .'

'I doubt they are that. It is not the nature of men to be innocent and when an Order amasses great wealth it can become obsessed by that wealth and eager to see it multiply. They say that there was much indulgence among these men. They lived in luxury, they belied their holy laws. Oh yes, that seems very likely, my lord.'

'But does this deserve torture and death?'

'The King of France thinks so.'

'Do you think he has lived such a virtuous life?'

'That is beside the point if I may say so, lord. Philip is a
king; these men proclaim to be holy knights. They have been
foolish. They should not have become so wealthy for where
there is wealth there will always be those who covet it and
scheme to take possession of it. There is no doubt that Philip
is determined on their destruction. He sent for the Grand-
master, Jacques de Molai, on pretext of wishing to talk to him.
Molai came to Paris from Cyprus and was treated well at first
to allay his suspicions. Then suddenly Philip swooped on
Molai and sixty of his knights of high order. They were taken
to noisome dungeons and there daily these Knights Templars
are submitted to hideous torture.'

Edward covered his face with his hands. 'I hate to hear
of it, Walter. I will not allow it here.'

'Under this torture many of the knights have confessed to
obscene practices.'

'What they say under torture does not count.'

'Indeed it does. The purpose of the torture is to reduce
them to such agony that they will do anything to stop it.'

'I do not want it here, Walter. I do *not* want it. Why cannot
people be merry and gay and laugh and sing together? Why
does there have to be this vileness?'

'Ah, my lord, you are gentle and kind. All kings are not so.
Least of all your father-in-law. He acts with demoniacal fury
against the Templars. He wants their money and treasure and
he wants an excuse for taking it. Doubtless they would be
willing to give it to him but that will not suit him. He must
ease his conscience. Therefore he must prove to the world
and himself that these men deserve to be dispossessed. This
he does through torture when they confess to the sins he and
his friends like Philip de Martigny, Archbishop of Sens, and
his minister, Guillaume de Nogaret, have thought up for
them.'

'Perhaps they will refuse to confess,' said Edward. 'What
then?'

'Then there will be further torture and that such as few can
withstand. I have heard that many have lost the use of their
feet after being submitted to a certain form of treatment in
which the soles of the feet are greased and set in a screen
which is placed before a fire. I have heard that the slow

burning of the feet is one of the most agonizing tortures devised by man. There are many others ...'

'I do not wish to hear of them,' cried Edward. 'Walter, I do not wish that the Templars in England shall be arrested. Perhaps they could be warned. Perhaps they could give up some of their wealth ... but I do not wish them to be tortured or burned at the stake. I am sure Perrot would agree with me if he were here.'

'Ah, Perrot,' sighed Walter. 'But what good news of him in Ireland!'

Edward brightened. 'I am so proud of him. Even Mad Dog Warwick had to admit that the news was good. The way in which he dealt with the rebellion in Munster was magnificent.'

Walter nodded. 'If he goes on like this, my lord, you might suggest he comes back.'

'Do you think they would listen?'

'Who knows? They might be ready to. Let him go on for a while as he has begun and even his worst enemies won't be able to deny that he has made a good job of Ireland.'

Edward forgot the distress he felt at the treatment of the Templars, in contemplation of that glorious possibility.

But when he sat with his council and expressed his views regarding the Templars, he was pleased to find that the majority of his ministers agreed with him.

* * *

Each day there was news of the terrible fate that was befalling the Templars in France and of how many were arrested and taken before the council set up by the Archbishop of Sens. Some would not confess to their alleged sins even under the most violent torture and were taken to the stakes which were set up all over Paris and burned to death.

Nothing was too revolting to be laid at their door, and their enemies were hard put to it to think up new crimes they could have committed. Many of them were escaping from France and that did not suit Philip. He wanted the entire Order wiped out. He demanded that other countries follow his lead; he was most displeased at the attitude of his son-in-law. His greatest advantage came from his puppet the Pope. The Templars must be destroyed, thundered Clement.

Excommunication could well be the wages of those who ignored the command.

The threat of excommunication could always arouse alarm. Edward was persuaded by his ministers that although he might defy his father-in-law he could not defy the Pope. That the Pope was acting on the instructions of the King of France was true, but behind the Pope was the image of the Holy See and the people feared it.

There was a half-hearted attempt in England to suppress the Templars, but this could not be allowed to proceed and in a short time the Pope had sent his inquisitors to deal with the matter. It was the first time that the Inquisition had been set up in England; many determined at that time that it should never come to their shores again and by great good fortune it never did. It brought with it a change in the attitude of people. Fear had come into the land. There had been persecution before of course; there was cruelty; but the sinister body of inquisitors shrouded in religious fervour with their instruments of torture and their secret administrations had brought something to the country which had never been there before.

The Inquisition did not lack victims. Countless arrests were made. The tales of what happened in those sombre chambers of pain were whispered in dark corners. Insecurity was in the air.

Edward had said that he would have no burnings at the stake and it was ordained that the Templars should be disbanded, their property confiscated and they could find places where they could settle into civil life.

The Templars could not believe their good fortune for they were well aware of what was happening in France. True, they must find news ways of existence but at least they had been left with their lives.

The Inquisition finally departed from England to the great relief of the people.

Never, never they vowed, should it come to these shores again.

Meanwhile the horrible tortures persisted in France and the Grand Master himself suffered. He was in his seventies and to the delight of the King of France could not stand up to torture and was ready to confess anything of which he might be accused, but it was not possible for Philip to consign him to the flames. He must receive his sentence of death from the Pope. That would come in due course.

Meanwhile Philip contented himself with lesser men and revelled in their property which was more than even he had dared hope.

Edward had replenished his exchequer also, which gave him much relief, but was glad he had not the sin of murder on his conscience.

His behaviour over the matter of the Templars had brought him a certain popularity with the people. In fact they had always been fond of him and had blamed Gaveston for the troubles in the kingdom. When he rode out with the Queen he was cheered and seeing them together the people thought that the scandalous affair of the King and Gaveston was over now.

If the Queen could give birth to a son they would be popular indeed.

* * *

In his heart Edward did not greatly care. All he wanted was the return of Gaveston and he began to plan for his return.

Perrot was clever. He was doing so well in Ireland that even his greatest enemy—Warwick perhaps—had to admit that this was so.

As for Edward he sought to placate those very men who had dismissed Perrot, and they were not unwilling to be placated. He was after all the King and the King's friendship must mean a good deal to them all. Edward was realizing more and more that there was only one thing he desired—that was the return of Gaveston, and he was ready to do anything to bring it about.

His friendship with Walter Reynolds had always been a source of irritation to the nobility who deplored the King's partiality for those of humble birth. He had recently made Walter Bishop of Worcester and had actually attended the consecration by Archbishop Winchelsey at Canterbury. That was a great mark of favour. Walter was well known as a crony of the King and Gaveston; he was standing with Edward now against the barons and was believed to be working for the return of Gaveston. So it was clever of Edward to send him off on a papal mission to the Court of Avignon where he would have to remain for some time. That was not all. There was one man whom Gaveston's enemies were very eager to see removed from his position near the King. This was Hugh le Despenser. He had been dismissed from the council at the time of Gaveston's banishment but he still remained near the King.

The departure of Walter Reynolds had so pleased the barons that Edward had another idea which he confided to Hugh.

'My dear friend,' he said, 'you know my regard for you. You must never think that it has faltered. I am a faithful friend, I trust, to those who serve me well.'

'Your fidelity to the Earl of Cornwall can never have been surpassed,' said Hugh.

'Ah Perrot! How I miss him. But he will come back to us, Hugh. I am determined on it.'

'I pray so night and day, my lord.'

'I know you are our good friend, Hugh. That is why you will understand what I am going to do. I must have Perrot back. I shall die if he does not come to me soon. I have sent Walter to France. Did you see the effect of that? They could not believe it and they took it as a sign that I have reformed my ways and am going to be the sort of King they want me to be.'

'I have noticed it, my lord. Walter was desolate to go and you to lose him.'

'He understands, as you must, Hugh. I am going to dismiss you.'

Hugh's face was blank. He was so eager not to show his emotions.

'It will seem that you no longer please me as a close friend but that is untrue. You must understand that. I shall be seen everywhere with Isabella. Please understand what this means to me. I must have Perrot back.'

'I understand well, my lord. You will win the barons and the Queen to your side and then you will say that there is no reason why the Earl of Cornwall should not come back. He has proved himself an able lieutenant and good servant of the country; and you must have grown out of your infatuation with him for you are dismissing your old friends and becoming a good husband to the Queen.'

'You have it, Hugh. Do you think it will work?'

Hugh was thoughtful for a while. Then he said: 'It may well. As for myself, although I shall be desolate to be dismissed, I am ready to do anything in your service.'

The King embraced Hugh.

'My dear good friend, I shall not forget this.'

* * *

The barons were, as Edward had foreseen, duly impressed by these signs of reformation but they were not to be entirely deceived.

The King was too extravagant. There were too many Court officials who had too much power. The laws of justice needed revising and there should be more drastic action against those who debased the coin. In fact the barons drew up a long list of necessary changes.

When these were presented to him Edward said: 'I would be ready to agree to these on one condition.'

'And what condition is this, my lord?' asked Warwick.

'That the Earl of Cornwall return to England and his estates be restored to him.'

There were grave faces round the table but he could see that some of them wavered. They agreed that they would like to discuss the matter if the King would give his permission.

All gracious charm and tolerance, the King agreed. They came back to him. He could see that Lincoln was half apologetic but Warwick was adamant. He would be. He had never forgiven Perrot for his success at the tournament and most of all for giving him the nickname of the Mad Hound.

Warwick was the strong man and Warwick was firm in his denunciation of Gaveston and stressed his determination not to allow him back in the country.

Edward could have wept with rage. He wanted to arrest Warwick and have him sent to the Tower. But he had grown wily in his great desire to bring Gaveston back.

He bowed his head and accepted the judgment of the barons. So the time had not yet come.

But the next day three of the barons asked for an audience with him. They were Lincoln, Pembroke and Surrey.

Lincoln was growing more and more unwieldy. Poor old Burst Belly! Edward could hear Perrot's derisive voice and

the longing for him was almost unbearable. Then there was
Aymer de Valence, Earl of Pembroke, who thought himself
royal because his father was the half-brother of Henry III.
Perrot had had a nickname for him too: Joseph the Jew,
because he was dark, of pallid complexion and had a hooked
nose. Then there was John de Warenne, Earl of Surrey, one
of those whom Perrot had defeated at the tournament.

Lincoln was their spokesman. He had come, he said, to
tell Edward that he and his friends deplored the state of
enmity which appeared to exist between the King and the
barons and since the King had shown himself willing to accept
their reforms they would show their appreciation by agree-
ing to his side of the bargain.

Edward felt dizzy with joy. He had succeeded. Oh, how
clever he had been. Soon Perrot would be in his arms. How
they would laugh together when he heard of Edward's cunning diplomacy. To think that he could win over old Burst
Belly to their side. The Mad Dog was still foaming venom
at the mouth, but a plague on the Mad Dog. They would
get along very well without him.

'Piers Gaveston has it seems done well in Ireland,' said
Pembroke. 'It may well be that he has grown serious-minded
and changed his ways.'

'Oh God forbid that he should do that,' prayed Edward.
'Let my Perrot return to me exactly as he was when he went
away.'

'His titles must be restored to him,' said Edward, a trill
of happiness in his voice.

'It would be well,' advised the ponderous Lincoln, 'for him
to behave with greater decorum than he did before he went
away.'

'He has learned his lesson,' said Edward; and he thought:
And so have I. Once you are back, sweet Perrot, there shall
be no more wanderings.

'I can promise you he will,' said the King.

Surrey held up a hand. Edward guessed that he had come
scarcely of his own free will. He reckoned they had had to
argue with him, placate him. He would never forgive Perrot
for defeating him at Wallingford and snatching his champion-
ship from him for ever.

Surrey said: 'Gaveston will have to tread with the utmost
caution.'

'I promise you he shall,' cried Edward.

It was clear that they had agreed reluctantly to the return of Gaveston.

* * *

Edward lost no time. He sent the messenger without delay. 'Come back, brother Perrot. I am waiting for you.'

Edward went to Chester. That beautiful city which was to be their meeting place. Gaveston meanwhile had left Ireland immediately. He came like a great warrior, for he retained his love of pomp and ceremony—with himself at the centre of it. He landed at Milford Haven with a retinue of followers—Irish, English and Gascons.

Impatiently the King waited for him. He stood on the top of that wall which had been built by Marcius, King of the British, and looked out for the coming of his friend. He walked the two red-stoned miles of the walls and had climbed to the top of the old square tower of Julius Caesar when finally he saw Gaveston coming.

He called for a horse and galloped out to meet him.

There they embraced.

'Perrot, Perrot, my beloved. At last you are home.'

Gaveston looked eagerly into the King's face. 'Nothing has changed,' he said. 'Tell me nothing has changed.'

'It is as it always was, dear friend,' the King assured him.

* * *

The Queen was incensed. So they had brought back Gaveston! Edward was completely infatuated with him. It sickened her. So far she was not pregnant. If she had been she could have been more reconciled. It was maddening that she, one of the most beautiful of queens, should be so neglected. One day she would have her revenge.

If she had not been a queen she would have taken a lover. There were plenty who would be ready to risk a great deal for her. But no, even she dared not. There must be no doubts as to the royalty of her children. It was to be the old battle with Gaveston again.

She realized with a certain exultation that Gaveston was a fool. He had suffered banishment more than once and he should have been warned; but it seemed the man's overweening vanity would be his downfall as it had on previous occasions. One would have thought that having felt the power of the barons he would have done his best to keep in their good graces. Heaven knew they had been given grudgingly enough. But no! Edward's Perrot could not forget that he was the King's favourite; he wanted to rule the country through the King and this was what he was attempting to do. As for poor besotted Edward he could deny his minion nothing. It was nauseating.

But she could watch with amusement because she knew that Gaveston's downfall could not be far off. It was her duty to lure Edward to her bed when she could. She had impressed on him the need to get children and he did realize this. By God, she thought, if this were not the case I would scorn you, Edward Plantagenet. Do you think I have no pride? I, a Princess of France, to be set aside for a low born adventurer!

In her heart, though, she knew that one day she would be revenged.

Meanwhile she watched foolish Gaveston prance about the Court. She saw the offence he gave to high and low. He was becoming more and more insolent every day and would talk audibly of Monsieur *Boele Crevée* in the presence of the Earl of Lincoln, calling attention to the Earl's enormous paunch, and although humbler men might take up the soubriquet of Burst Belly, they did not admire Gaveston for using it.

Gaveston's brother-in-law, the Earl of Gloucester, who had been a good friend to him once, irritated him and he had the impudence to dub him a whore's son, which was a slight on his mother—Joanna, the King's aunt.

Gaveston believed that the great esteem which the King had for him entitled him to behave exactly as he felt inclined by the mood of the moment.

Let him, thought Isabella. He is sharpening the axe which will one day sever that insolent head from his shoulders.

*　　　*　　　*

Gaveston had been back but three months when Edward called a council to appear in York. It was disconcerting when a number of the barons, led by Lancaster, refused to appear, and when the King demanded to know the reason why he was told quite bluntly that it was because of Gaveston's presence.

'They are all jealous of me,' said Gaveston blithely. 'They envy me your lordship's love.'

But he did not really think that was the reason. They envied him because he was richer, more handsome and so much more clever than they were.

'A plague on their council,' he added. 'Come sit, my lord, and let us talk of other matters than this dreary community of slow-witted oafs.'

Edward said: 'You must not talk so of my relations, wicked one.'

'As I have told you many times, my lord, the perfections allotted to your family were all saved for you.'

So they laughed and snapped their fingers at the barons, but those about them knew that they were moving towards a repetition of what had happened before.

'Let us do a play for Christmas,' suggested Gaveston. 'What say you, lord?'

'You always know how to divert me.'

'Then we will go to Langley and have Christmas there together. Oh how the thought of that pleases me!'

'It fills me with joy to have you back with me,' said Edward fondly.

So they spent Christmas at Langley, in Hertfordshire, and they were very merry and for days they were happy together. Edward showered gifts on Gaveston and calculating their worth Gaveston felt it was indeed a pleasant Christmas that they spent at Langley.

February came and it was time to attend the Parliament at Westminster. Edward and Gaveston came south together lamenting that the happy days of Christmas were over.

They knew there would be trouble. What had happened at York had been a pointer to that. This would be more serious. This was Westminster. If any of the barons refused to attend the Parliament and gave as their reason the presence of Gaveston that would have to be taken seriously.

Edward was downcast, terrified that it would mean separation again. Gaveston was more optimistic.

'We will find a way, sweet lord,' he said. 'Leave it to me.'

'You are clever, Perrot, I know,' replied Edward. 'But how I hate these men! I think most of all I hate Warwick. Your name for him is apt. He is like a mad dog and I fear mad dogs. Their bite can mean death.'

'We will draw the fangs of this one, Edward, before he has time to infect us with his venom.'

But it was as Edward feared. Warwick, Oxford, Arundel and Hereford, led by Lancaster, refused to attend. Their reason for their absence was as before. Because of the presence of Piers Gaveston.

Edward was in a quandary. There must be a session of Parliament for he needed money and only the Parliament could grant it. Also there was animosity in the air and he knew towards whom it was directed.

He was afraid for Perrot.

They discussed the matter together and even Gaveston dropped his easy optimism. They were out to destroy him and he knew it.

'You must get away from here,' said the King. 'It breaks my heart but you must go. I cannot be at peace while you are here for I fear for you. Leave at once for the North. I will join you as soon as I can. Then I will call the Parliament and they will assemble because you are no longer with me.'

It was drastic. It was infuriating. But they both saw that a separation arranged by themselves was better than one which would be forced on them.

So they parted and Gaveston rode north.

*   *   *

It was unfortunate that about this time the Earl of Lincoln died. It was true that he had become alienated from the King because of Gaveston and had deeply resented the insolent name of Burst Belly being applied to him; but although he was somewhat ponderous he had been a steady influence and had won the respect of Edward the First. It was because the second Edward was so unlike his father that Lincoln had swerved in his allegiance, but what he had done had been that which he thought right for the country.

The reason why his death was such a blow to the King was that Thomas Earl of Lancaster, who had married Lincoln's daughter, on Lincoln's death inherited the earldoms of Lincoln and Salisbury through his wife. As Lancaster already had, besides his royal birth, the earldoms of Lancaster, Leicester and Derby he was without doubt one of the richest and most influential men in the country.

Being seven years older than the King and considerably more mature, he had overnight become an even greater power in the land than he had been before. He had shown himself to be one of the fiercest enemies of Piers Gaveston, and with Lincoln dead, discontented barons looked to him to lead the faction which was going to demand the final banishment of Gaveston.

The King was very worried.

Edward had lost no time in joining Gaveston under the pretext of making war on Scotland and he was at Berwick when news came to him of Lincoln's death and Lancaster's accession to the earldoms.

It was pleasant to be far away from the conflict, and Gaveston said: 'You know, lord, we should be grateful to your enemies the Scots.'

Then they laughed together and talked in that intimate fashion which was such a delight to the King and they wondered how long they would be left in peace to enjoy each other's company.

Their pleasure was interrupted by an announcement that Lancaster was on his way north to pay homage to the King for the earldoms of Lincoln and Salisbury which he had just acquired. That, he said, must be his first duty.

'A plague on him,' cried Edward. 'I never trusted that man.'

'He'll be insupportable now,' agreed Gaveston, and added enviously: 'He will be the richest man in the kingdom ... with no exception.'

'My Perrot must run him pretty close,' said the King fondly.

'But five earldoms! He will think himself more important than the King.'

'He did that with three.'

'We must find a way of cutting that arrogant fellow down a little, my lord.'

Edward agreed, but it was Lancaster who was to cut Gaveston down.

One of Lancaster's men arrived at Berwick with a message from his master.

The King heard what the man had to say and his brow darkened with anger.

Gaveston was with him and his indignation was as great as the King's because Lancaster's message was that he refused to come to Berwick. He owed allegiance to the King for his lands in England and as Berwick was over the Border into Scotland it would not be proper for him to come to the King. The King must come to him.

'I never heard such insolence!' cried Gaveston.

Edward was uneasy. 'Some would say he was right. Berwick *is* across the Border and we are just inside Scotland.'

'So you will give way to this man.'

The messenger said: 'My lord has said that if you will not accept his allegiance he must return south without it.'

Edward realized what that meant. At any time Lancaster could raise an army against him—and he was capable and rich enough to do that—and not put himself wrong with the law because he had sworn no allegiance.

'There is nothing to be done but cross the Border and meet him,' said Edward. 'He *must* take his oath of allegiance.'

Gaveston had to agree and the King sent the messenger back to say that he would see Lancaster at Haggerston, a small place close to Berwick and just within the English border.

There they met—a very arrogant enriched Lancaster, and a somewhat humiliated Edward with Gaveston who felt mischievous and at the same time excessively envious of this man whose birth and marriage had brought him five earldoms and all that went with them.

The King received the Earl's homage with Gaveston beside him. Lancaster's behaviour was very correct as far as the King was concerned but the contemptuous manner in which he ignored Gaveston was obvious. Edward felt furious but could do nothing about it in public although he raved against Lancaster in private.

As for Gaveston he was furious and with his fury was mingled a deep apprehension. He had realized that the powerful Lancaster was the bitterest of his enemies next to Warwick and with these two men—and many others—against him his position was very precarious indeed.

Lancaster left and Edward with Gaveston returned to Berwick, but they both knew they could not remain together much longer. The King must go to London for another session of Parliament.

Fearfully they left Berwick together but the parting was near.

'Let it be Bamborough Castle,' said Edward. 'It is a strong fortress and I shall feel that you are far enough from Westminster there to be safe until we can be together.'

So to Bamborough they rode and in the formidable castle there, set high upon a perpendicular rock looking out to sea, they took a painful leave of each other.

The King rode south determined to defy his barons while Gaveston within the stone walls of Bamborough assessed his case. He had held the King's favour for a long time, far longer than he had dared hope. He was a rich man. He had been wise in getting a great deal of his wealth out of England because he had always been aware that one day he could lose everything that remained there. His estates and possessions in Gascony were vast. At any time he could slip away to them. But he loved possessions so much that he could never resist the desire to gain more. He was fond of the King. He was greatly flattered to be so beloved by him. Edward had been faithful since the days of their childhood, and Gaveston was wise enough to know that his fame and fortune rested entirely on the King's favour. But the day would come when he must leave that rich field even though there was still much to be gleaned. He would have to choose that moment and not allow his avarice to overcome his common sense.

There in Bamborough, this castle which had stood on its cliff of rock since the days when the Romans had built it, he could look out on a stormy sea and contemplate his fate as so many others had before him. Bamborough, named after Queen Bebba the wife of King Ida of the Angles who had turned the Roman fortress into a castle, could provide only a temporary refuge. He paced the walls and thought of Edward and wondered what the outcome of this visit to Westminster would be.

*　　　*　　　*

'Banish Gaveston!' That was what they wanted.

They were too strong for him. It was: Gaveston must go or civil war.

Was ever a king so plagued? They would rob him of the most important thing on earth to him and he the King who could have commanded them all! The barons should never have been allowed to become so powerful. They had forced his great grandfather King John to sign Magna Carta and ever since then it was not so much the King who ruled the country as the barons.

Civil war. He contemplated it. It would be insupportable. He pictured himself and Perrot flying before them, being captured by them and then what would they do to Perrot? They would kill him as a traitor. That was what they wanted to do. Banishment was the better alternative. At least he would know that Perrot was alive and awaiting that moment when he could return.

He tried to resist but it was useless. They were bent on Perrot's leaving the country. How he argued; he even pleaded. They were adamant. Gaveston must go.

It was Gaveston who tried to comfort him.

'My friend,' he wrote, 'if they banish me, I shall be back. Do you think they can keep us apart for ever? No, we will overcome this as we have those other occasions. Be of good cheer, my dear lord.'

It was no use. He was desolate.

The barons had given their ultimatum. Gaveston must leave the country by the first of November or face arrest.

*   *   *

Isabella was with the King again. She was cool with him but did not reproach him. She was so eager to have a child that she was prepared to set aside her anger at his treatment of her. One day she would be revenged on him, but it was clear that that time was not yet. It was no use writing to her father and complaining. He had no time to listen to her. He was too busy with his own concerns; he was continuing with his persecution of the Templars and Jacques de Molai was still his prisoner awaiting the sentence of death from the Pope.

Isabella was sorry that the barons had not killed Gaveston. They were still perhaps a little afraid of Edward otherwise they might have done so. Perpetual exile they insisted on for Gaveston. Death would have been better, for while he lived Edward would continue to yearn for him.

Still she must make herself sufficiently pleasant to her

husband to assure his visiting her bedchamber now and then. It was irksome, humiliating in the extreme but of course necessary.

Edward himself was constantly looking for messengers who would bring him news of his dear Perrot. What was he doing now? Who was benefiting from his sparkling wit and the sheer joy of looking at his handsome graceful form? Was there anything he could do to help his beloved friend? He had been forbidden to go to Gascony by those harsh barons so he would be wandering about in France not knowing where he was going to find refuge. The King of France would not help him. He must have heard evil reports of him from Isabella. He could hardly blame Isabella for her attitude towards Gaveston. He must be fair to her. She had been as good a wife as he could expect. He was ready to admit that his passion for Perrot must be a trial to her. That was why whenever he could bring himself to do so he would spend time with her. He would be as delighted as she was to hear that she was with child. That would salve his conscience considerably.

What could he do to ease his sorrow? He thought continually of Perrot and those places where they had been together and he made a habit of visiting them and trying to recapture those happy times.

Wallingford! How often they had been together there in that ancient castle on the west bank of the Thames. He had always been fond of it since he had heard as a child that his great ancestor William the Conqueror had been invited there by the Saxon, Wigod, who owned it, to receive the homage of the principal nobles before marching to London.

Perrot had loved the place. It was here that he had excelled at that never-to-be-forgotten tournament when he had so humiliated the champions that they had never forgiven him.

Christmas would soon be upon him. How dreary it would be without Perrot!

There was a gentle tap at the door. He called permission to enter. He stared. He could not believe his eyes. Then the wild joy took possession of him.

'Perrot.'

'None less,' exclaimed Gaveston. 'Once again I faced perils to be with my lord.'

They were in each other's arms and Edward was trembling

with the wild joy which possessed him.

'So you came home to me. Oh Perrot, Perrot, my beloved friend!'

'I am no wanderer, Edward. I want to be with my dear King. I care for nothing, as long as we are together.'

'Perrot, what will they say? What will they *do*?'

'That is for tomorrow,' said Perrot blithely.

*   *   *

He kept him with him. They could not bear to be separated. Perrot could stay away no longer. Where would he go even if it were possible to be happy away from his King? Holland? France? The first bored him and he was hardly likely to be welcomed by the Queen's father. Gascony, his native land, was denied him. He ground his teeth to remember all the treasure he had stored safely away in Gascony. But this was not the true answer. It was the need to be with his beloved King which had made him face the anger of those dreary barons in order to be with him.

What could they do? There would be trouble when it was known that he was back. He had been ordered to leave and had given his word that he would.

'For you, my King, I would break a thousand oaths,' said Gaveston.

'And I for you, dear friend.'

The Queen was incensed when she heard that Gaveston had returned. She came to Wallingford and burst in upon the King. Fortunately it was one of those moments when Gaveston was not with him.

'Gaveston is mad,' she cried. 'The barons have ordered him out of the country.'

'The barons will have to accept the fact that he has returned.'

'Edward, do you want to plunge this country into civil war?'

'You are too dramatic, Isabella. There cannot be war because one man returns to this country when they want him out of it.'

'There can be,' said Isabella, 'and there will be.'

She thought of her recent ride through London and how the people had cheered her. Isabella the Fair, they called her. They loved to see her bright beauty and they were indignant because the King ignored her. They could not understand how he could prefer that mincing friend of his to his beautiful Queen. They loved Isabella the more as their hatred for Gaveston grew. Oddly enough they did not blame the King so much as Gaveston. Perhaps if he had been less handsome, less tall, less like his father, they might have done. But Edward was their annointed King, his father's legacy to them and they wanted him to remain their King but to behave as his father had.

Isabella knew that she had the people with her. What she wanted was a son—a son who should look like his grandfather and be like his grandfather and then the people would be very pleased to rally to him, and in charge of him would naturally be his mother. Perhaps then Isabella could pay back some of the insults she had had to accept from Edward and Gaveston.

But it was not to be yet. How could she become pregnant when her husband's attentions were so sporadic? They slept together only for duty on his part, ambition on hers. One day, she promised herself, she would have a lover who would match his passionate nature with hers. But first she must get her child. She longed for it; she prayed for it; and it was the only reason why she suppressed her contempt and hatred for her husband.

In a measure she exulted in Gaveston's return, for in coming back he had defied the barons and the Archbishop of Canterbury. She knew that none of them would meekly accept such blatant contempt for his word. Trouble was brewing for Gaveston and if he and the King were too infatuated with each other to see it, let them frivol away the hours for a while before their fate overtook them.

She was right. News came from London. It was known that the favourite had broken his vows and returned. It was known that he was with the King and that Edward was with him throughout the days and nights.

Bands of men trained as soldiers marched through the streets of London. They wanted the favourite to lose his head in England since he would not lose himself abroad. Isabella was a saint. London loved her as much as they hated Gaveston. She was the wronged wife, the beautiful Princess who had charmed them, whom they had believed would make a man

of their King. And what had happened? He neglected her.
He treated her with contempt; he spent his nights in the
licentious company of Piers Gaveston whose mother, rumour
had it, had been burned as a witch. Gaveston had clearly inherited some of her powers for he had completely bewitched
the King. They wanted Gaveston's blood. They wanted him
brought to London and his head cut off and stuck up on
London Bridge.

Worse still the barons were gathering together. It was unthinkable that they should allow Gaveston to flout them. The
Archbishop of Canterbury, old Robert de Winchelsey, excommunicated Gaveston for breaking the oath he had made
to the barons. That frightened Edward but Gaveston shrugged it aside.

'The old fool,' he said. 'It is time he was dead. You should
make Walter Reynolds your Archbishop of Canterbury. Why,
there is a man who would work for you.'

'I will,' cried Edward, 'as soon as Winchelsey is dead—and
he cannot last much longer.'

'If only he were in that position now.' Even Gaveston was
a little afraid of excommunication. Edward noticed that his
friend's appetite waned and that he had lost a little of his
glowing health.

Isabella knew that the barons were getting together and
would march against Edward. Oh God, she thought, if I but
had a child, a boy who was heir to the throne! Then I do
believe they would be ready to depose Edward and make my
son the King and I his mother would be Regent, for the people
love me and want to recompense me for the wrongs I have
suffered through Edward. It was true. They were ashamed
of their King. That he should marry a beautiful French
Princess and neglect her for a foppish minion was disgraceful. They were ashamed of their English King. Yes, they
would be with her and against her husband while he kept
Gaveston at his side.

Oh, for a child! How she yearned for one, prayed for one,
and exerted every wile she knew to lure Edward to her bed.
There was one thing which could bring him there and that
was duty and the thought that if she were once impregnated
with his seed he could be left in peace.

Meanwhile Gaveston languished, and the King was distraught. If they had been in London he would have had his

physician at his friend's bedside. He did the next best thing and sent for the finest doctor in the North, William de Bromtoft. Gaveston would recover, Edward was told. He needed rest. 'I will give him a potion to make him sleep. It is rest he needs more than anything.'

And while Gaveston slept Edward sat by his bedside until the Queen glided quietly into the bedchamber.

'How fares he?' she whispered.

'He murmurs in his sleep.'

'He is aware of you here. The doctor said he needs peace and rest. Leave him, Edward. Let him sleep alone. He will best recover then.'

'What if he should wake and want me?'

'Then he will call for you. At this moment he is aware of you and it worries him that he cannot speak with you.'

At length Edward allowed himself to be led away. In his bedchamber the Queen soothed him with a special posset women made in France to rouse their lovers' ardour. She took him to her bed and with the help of her ministrations, her prayers, and perhaps the posset, that night she became pregnant.

*   *   *

Gaveston slowly recovered. The spring had come and it could hardly be expected that the barons would allow him to continue to flout them. The Lords Ordainers, those earls, barons and bishops who had drawn up the Ordinances for the reform of the realm had met and sworn to defend them and for this reason they were ready to march against the King, for by receiving Gaveston and restoring his possessions Edward had openly defied them. It was clear that he had to learn his lesson.

Lancaster, with his newly acquired power, was the most important of the earls. He had his own private army. It was arranged that the earls and barons should organize tournaments in their castles where men prepared for war should muster. When they were ready they would band together and march north to where the King and Gaveston were living together. They would take Gaveston prisoner and if the King objected, there would be nothing left but to take arms against Edward.

It was a dangerous situation and it was hoped that the King realized how serious.

Edward did. To his great joy Gaveston had completely recovered and there was another reason for rejoicing. Isabella was with child.

Edward was delighted. None could say he had not done his duty. Fervently he prayed that the child would be a boy.

It was May. Isabella had conceived in February and her condition was beginning to be noticeable. The King with his entourage had come to Newcastle and there it was they heard the news that the hostile barons were approaching.

'We must leave without delay,' cried the King. 'Where can we go? Oh, Perrot, what will happen to you if you fall into their hands?'

'They will trump up some charge against me doubtless and have my head to grace the Bridge.'

'I beg of you, do not talk so. They shall all be hanged before I'd allow it.'

Gaveston said sadly: 'Little King, would you be able to stop it?'

The Queen burst in upon them. She was afraid for the child. She said: 'Come, let us not wait here. Let us get away without delay. If we go to Tynemouth we could take ship for Scarborough and that will give us time to think.'

'Isabella is right,' said Edward. 'Let us go, Perrot.'

In due course they arrived at Tynemouth and there Edward at once ordered that a boat be made ready for them.

'We will rest one night and be gone tomorrow. The tide will be right and carry us to safety.'

Isabella returned to her bedchamber, leaving the friends together.

She wondered what the barons would do to Gaveston when they captured him, for capture him they would in time.

She thought of his enemies and chiefly of Lancaster. She had quite a fancy for Lancaster, and he for her. She had heard that his marriage was not a happy one. Alice de Lacy had brought him his earldoms of Lincoln and Salisbury but little happiness. She did not like her husband and made no secret of her feelings. He shrugged her dislike aside and it was said took many mistresses. He was the most powerful baron in the country and Isabella was attracted by power. *She* could never love *her* husband. He was too weak and that streak in his nature which made him the doting slave of Gaveston nauseated her.

Lancaster would lead the barons against Gaveston and because Edward had allied himself with his friend that meant against Edward. What a fool he was, this man to whom they had married her! Could he not see that he was placing his throne in jeopardy? They were fools both he and Gaveston. They seemed to be blind to where their folly was leading them. Why could not Gaveston have behaved with decorum? Why did they have to flout their relationship so that it was obvious to all? Why did Gaveston have to display his questionable wit and poke fun at men who were far more powerful than himself? How had Edward become so utterly his slave?

Never mind. One day it would be different. If this child she carried was a boy ...

She slept fitfully that night, for her sleep was troubled by dreams and vague stirrings throughout the castle; and in the morning she understood the reason for these disturbances.

When her women came to her for her toilette she knew at once that something was wrong.

'You had better tell me without delay,' she commanded grimly.

'My lady, the King has left. He and the Earl of Cornwall were off before dawn.'

She did not answer. She did not want the women to know how angry and humiliated she felt.

She waited.

'My lady, they say that the Earl of Lancaster is but a few miles from the castle and marching this way ... come, they say to take the Earl of Cornwall. The King was beset with anxiety and he and the Earl left without delay.'

So they had gone and left her to face his enemies. How she hated them, Edward as much as Gaveston! What did Edward care for her, the wife who was about to bear his son? Nothing mattered to him as long as Gaveston was safe.

'So,' she said, 'the Earl of Lancaster is close to the castle.'

'Surrounding it with his men some say, my lady.'

'It is all "they say" and "some say". You had better help me to dress. I must be ready for the King's enemies when they call on me.'

How well she hid her seething anger! How dared he! What were they thinking, these servants? So this is how he treats his wife. He has no thought for her at all. All that matters to him is his lover Gaveston. He should pay for this one day. Oh yes, one day the humiliation he had piled on her should be paid for with interest. Once this child was born ... and if it were a boy ... Oh God, let it be a boy. Then, Edward her faithless husband should beware.

She was dressed. The cold glitter behind her eyes if anything added to her beauty. She was maddened when she saw that glowing reflection, that outstanding beauty which had set the minstrels singing at her father's Court, because it had no effect on her husband. Why had they not married her to a man!

'Now,' she said, 'I would hear what is happening.'

It was Lancaster who made her aware of that. The castle could offer no resistance. Moreover the Queen was not sure that she wished it to.

Lancaster walked straight into the castle and when he learned that the King had flown with Gaveston during the night he asked for an audience with the Queen.

He bowed low and kissed her hand. His eyes told her that he thought she was a remarkably beautiful woman and as such he did homage to her.

'My lady,' he said, 'I beg you to forgive me for this intrusion.'

She smiled and she thought: Why was Lancaster not the King? I should not have complained if he had been my husband. It could so easily have been so. His father had been a brother of Edward the First and he was therefore first cousin to Edward her husband. He was royal; he was powerful and rich; and he was fully a man.

'Intrusion?' She lifted her brows and turned her head towards the window where she could see Lancaster's private army was encamped about its walls. 'It is a mild way of expressing it. Have you and your men taken the castle?'

'My lady, while you are here I would never allow that. We came for the traitor Gaveston who has broken his word and returned to England and who is under excommunication.'

'I would I could deliver him to you. He and the King left shortly before your arrival.'

'So he has slipped through our fingers. Never fear. We shall catch up with him.'

'The King is with him, my lord.'

Lancaster nodded gravely. 'That is a pity, but if it is so, then must he take the consequences.'

'What do you mean? Have you come against the King?'

'My lady, I have come to take Gaveston.'

'And if the King will not give him up?'

'We must perforce take him even so.'

'This could mean ... war?'

'War for a worthless adventurer! Nay, let us hope it will not come to that. But we are determined to have Gaveston. So you did not leave with them.'

'No.' She could not hide the venom in her voice. 'They did not think to save me from their pursuers. They thought only of themselves.'

'There is no need for you to fear.' He had taken a step towards her. '*I* would protect you against all who would harm you.'

'You are a good friend to me, cousin.'

'My lady, I would serve you with my liife. Depend upon this: no harm shall come to you while I am near to protect you.'

'Thank you, my lord Lancaster. In protecting me it may well be that you protect your future King.'

He smiled slowly. 'Is that so, my lady. Then we should rejoice.'

'Thank you, cousin.'

He took her hand and kissed it. 'I will rid you of Gaveston,' he said. 'I promise you that he shall not live much longer to torment you.'

'He has bewitched the King as you know.'

'It is sorcery. His mother was a witch. It is time that he was removed and if he will not leave the country then we must take measures to see that he leaves this world.'

'What shall you do now?'

'Pursue them, my lady. There is nothing for it but that. Pembroke and Warenne are on the march with troops. The King has not a chance of saving Gaveston. Rest here, my lady. I promise you no harm shall come to you.'

She gave him her hand. 'I will remember that, cousin,' she said.

He bowed and left her, his eyes lingering on her as though he found it difficult to take them from her.

When he had gone she listened to the sounds in the castle.

They were searching for evidence of where the pair had gone. They would soon discover that they had left by sea. They must be calling at Scarborough. So Pembroke and Warenne were marching north and Lancaster would march south.

Edward would have to deliver Gaveston to them or there would be civil war.

Thank God for the child. If it were only a boy she could look forward to the future with excitement. She was heartily tired of Edward and it was more humiliating because if he had cared for her she might have loved him. It would be hard to find a more handsome man. It was maddening and humiliating that he had left her to her fate in order to escape with Gaveston. How was he to know that his enemies would not regard themselves as hers too? Yet he had left her, pregnant as she was, to face them. What man worthy of the name would do that? If she had had a spark of affection for Edward it was over now.

She thought of Lancaster ... if she had not been a queen, if she had not to bear the King's son ... She had seen in his expression when he looked at her that he found her infinitely desirable.

He had a reputation for his affairs with women. It was understandable. He disliked Alice his wife and she him. That had been a marriage of convenience if ever there had been one. He had little to complain of though. No doubt Alice had. It had brought him the earldoms of Lincoln and Salisbury. What had it brought Alice? The Queen wondered about her and whether she had taken a lover.

If only ... thought the Queen. How easy it would have been with a man like Lancaster. He had shown her clearly that he would count himself fortunate if she beckoned to him. They would be discreet ... but there was no discretion that could save her from scandal. And she had the heirs to the throne to produce.

Isabella was a voluptuous woman but she was an even more ambitious one.

She wanted power through her children. She wanted to humiliate the man who had humiliated her. Perhaps more than anything she wanted revenge.

*　　*　　*

She was safe at Tyneside. Lancaster had promised her that no harm should befall her. He would rid her of Gaveston, he had said. It was a promise which she knew he would do his best to keep. She felt at ease. Her women said that the child was certain to be a boy. The wise old goodies could tell by the way she carried it. She was careful of herself. Nothing must go wrong. She must produce a healthy child. And if by the time of its birth Lancaster had kept his word and rid her of Gaveston who knew what would result?

She must have more children. They would not be born in love, of course. Never, never would she forgive Edward for his last insult. That he should leave her and their unborn child to his enemies was too much to be borne. How was he to know that his enemies might be her friends?

It was necessary, her women said, to take exercise. She should not ride. It could be bad for the child, so she took to walking in the fields and woods about the castle and it was here one day that she met the boy Thomeline. Poor wretched little orphan. He was half-naked and dirty and frightened and yet so desperate that he dared approach the Queen and beg for alms.

Her companions would have driven him away and she would have shrunk from him but she hesitated. It might have been because of the child she carried that she was interested in children. She was not sure but there was something in the boy's eyes which touched her unaccountably, for she was not a sentimental woman who brooded on the wrongs of others.

'Nay,' she said, 'let the child speak. What would you have, boy?'

He answered, 'I am hungry, Queen.'

'Where is your father?'

'Dead.'

'And your mother?'

'Dead too. The soldiers killed them. The Scots who came over the border. They burned our cottage and took all we had.'

'And they let you live?'

'They didn't find me. I was hiding in the bushes. They didn't see me.'

'Give this boy clothes and money to the value of six shillings and sixpence,' she commanded.

'My lady!' cried her women. 'He is a beggar with a beggar's tales.'

'He is a child,' she answered, 'and I believe him. Let it be done.'

The boy fell on his knees and kissed the hem of her gown.

She walked on, wondering at herself. There were many orphans in the world. Why be upset by one?

But she was glad that the boy had stopped her. Then she was pleased that she had acted as she had, for she heard the women talking together of her piety and good deeds. She must have the good opinion of her husband's subjects. When they turned from him they must look to her.

She thought a good deal about the boy and a few days later she wished to know if her orders had been carried out regarding him and asked that he be brought to her.

He came in his new clothes and he stood before her staring at her in wonderment.

'Well, boy,' she said, 'so you have eaten now and you have good clothes.'

His eyes filled with tears and he knelt and would have kissed her gown but she said: 'Get up. Come and stand near me. Where do you sleep at nights?'

His eyes shone with pleasure. 'There is an old hut. The Scots did not take the trouble to burn it. I found it. It offers shelter from the cold.'

She noticed how thin he was. He needed care. That much was obvious.

'When I am gone from here,' she said, 'you could go hungry again.'

He nodded. Then he smiled: 'But I shall always remember you. I shall never forget that I saw the Queen.'

'When you are cold and hungry and bigger, stronger people turn you out of the hut you will forget me.'

'I never will,' he said fiercely.

'You will always be my loyal subject then?'

'I'd die for you, Queen.'

'It was little I did,' she said. 'I would spend what I gave to you for ribbons for my waist.'

'So should it be,' said the boy, 'for you are beautiful as no one ever was before you. You are a queen and an angel from heaven.'

She said: 'I am a queen to all but only an angel to you. I

am going to make you love me more, little Thomeline. You shall not again be hungry, nor sleep in the hut. How would you like to go to London? But how can you know? You have no idea of what London is like, have you? I have an organist there. He is French and his name is Jean. He has a wife named Agnes. She longs for children and could never have them. So I am going to give her a little boy and you a mother and father. How would you like that?'

'Should I see you, Queen?'

'It might well be that you would.'

'Please may I go?'

'You shall go. You shall be well clothed and fed and taught many things. You need good food for you are not very strong. They will make you into a healthy boy.'

'Will they want me as their boy?'

'They will if I say they shall.'

'You can do anything, Queen,' he said.

She had him bathed and dressed and she kept him with her awhile. She enjoyed his adoration. It soothed the wound left by Edward's desertion. The boy's belief in her goodness and Lancaster's obvious desire for her comforted her a good deal.

She had sent a messenger to her French organist, Jean, and his wife, Agnes, to tell them of the child's coming and that she expected them to treat him as their own.

Then she sent him to London. He was reluctant to go, not because he did not want to but because it meant leaving her. His life had taken on a bewildering turn—the orphan who had been obliged to fend for himself was now regularly fed; he was taking lessons. Now and then he sat with the Queen.

So when he must leave her he was filled with sadness and although she too was sorry to see him go, she liked his feelings for her.

She marvelled at herself. She was not a soft and gentle woman. Perhaps it was because she was going to have a child that she had concerned herself with Thomeline. And then his rapt adoration had been irresistible to her.

However, there was a bond between them.

She thought: If the time came when I stood against Edward there would be one of my loyal subjects.

'Queen,' he said, for she had liked him to address her thus and had never stopped his doing so, 'you have done everything for me. What can I do for you?'

She smiled at him gently. 'Pray that I may have a healthy child ... a boy who will love me even as you do.'

'I shall pray for that, Queen. But it cannot be. No one can love you as I do ... even your own son.'

After he had gone, she thought what a pleasant interlude that had been.

*   *   *

Edward and Gaveston had reached Scarborough.

'We could do no better than stop here,' said Edward, and Gaveston agreed with him.

Scarborough indeed provided an ideal refuge. As its name implied it was a fortified rock. Above the bay rose a high and steep promontory on the highest point of which stood the castle. It had been built during the reign of King Stephen, and Edward the First had often held splendid court there, for it was easily accessible being a port, and from its harbour ships were constantly coming and going in various directions. It was a castle in which to shelter and from which it might be possible to escape should that be necessary.

Gaveston was less exuberant than Edward had ever known him and the King feared for his friend's safety. He had, after all, broken his word in coming back to England and had aroused the enmity of almost every baron in the country.

'We shall be safe here, dear friend,' said Edward, but he knew that their refuge would be temporary and after they had rested from their journey and lay talking together they agreed that they could not hope to rest peacefully for very long.

In fact the day after their arrival they discovered that the garrison manning the castle, although not openly disloyal to the King, were talking together of what they must do if the barons attempted to take the castle.

Rumours persisted that Lancaster's men were on the way.

'What *can* we do?' cried Edward. 'Do you think we can hold the castle?'

'For a time mayhap,' replied Gaveston.

'If I could gather together a force ...'

'You cannot do that here, my lord.'

'Nay. But I am the King. I could rally men to my banner. They would support the King. They do not like Lancaster.

Do you think they would follow Pembroke, or Warenne? Do you think the mad dog could raise an army against us?'

'They could,' replied Gaveston. 'But they might not if you had an army ... loyal men who supported the crown.'

'Then I shall leave here. I shall go to York first. I shall gather together my army and then I shall come to Scarborough and rescue you, Perrot. You must hold out until I come.'

For a rare unselfish moment Gaveston thought of what the King was proposing to do. He would gather an army in order to oppose Lancaster and those who came to take him, Gaveston. For his friend the King was proposing to plunge into civil war.

He should stop him. This could lose Edward his crown. But where should they go? Fly together? It was impossible. No, the only way was for Edward to defy the barons, to stand with his friend, to say to them: You have banished Gaveston, but I have taken him back. I have reinstated him and I am the King.

Yes, it was the only way.

'I will do everything I can to hold out until you return with your army,' said Gaveston.

'Then, my beloved friend, I must needs say good-bye at once.'

'We shall meet again, dear lord. One day we will show these dreary barons who is King. You and I will show them, Edward ... together.'

'Together,' said Edward, 'always together until the end of our days.'

*   *   *

Gaveston's enemies were at the castle gates. The garrison were offering but a weak resistance and it was becoming clear with every passing hour that they had no heart for the fight.

Gaveson tried to bestir himself but he felt defeated. How could the King rally an army and reach him in time? His servants disliked him. He had never bothered to cultivate their friendship. In fact he had never given a thought to anyone but himself. The King had adored him as much as he adored himself, and there had seemed no need to placate anyone in the old days. Everything he wanted was his, given to him by his doting King.

And now that the King was absent, there was no one whom he could really trust.

He noticed a marked change in the attitude of his servants. There was a certain veiled insolence and he judged their opinion of his chances by their manner towards him. Of course there was always the possibility that the King might rally his army and return to save him, so they dared not go too far. It was for this reason that they did as much as they were doing.

How long could he hold out? What stores were in the castle? Out there Pembroke and Warenne appeared to have settled down to wait. Doubtless before long they would be joined by Lancaster. His bitter enemies, all of them.

One of his servants asked leave to enter the room where he was disconsolately sitting.

'It is a messenger from the armies outside, my lord. He is asking if you will receive the Earl of Pembroke who would speak with you.'

'What! Let him into the castle. Pembroke!'

'He would come alone and unarmed, my lord. It is to speak with you ... to make terms.'

'I will see him,' said Gaveston. 'He is a man who prides himself on his honour. That is why they send him, I'll swear.'

Aymer de Valence, Earl of Pembroke, confronted Gaveston.

Pembroke was a proud man. He was the son of Henry the Third's half-brother—a third son but his brothers had died during his father's lifetime and he had succeeded to the title. His royal connections, his great title, his wealth and power had made him a force in the country; but he was a man who prided himself on keeping his word. It was a favourite maxim of his that honour and Pembroke were synonymous.

He looked at Gaveston with dislike. He had not forgiven him for the defeat at the Wallingford joust and he knew that because he was dark-haired, pallid, and his nose was inclined to be hooked Gaveston had delighted in referring to him as Joseph the Jew. Since the banishment of the Jews by Edward the First the epithet was even less complimentary than it had been before. Gaveston guessed Pembroke bore grudges.

Pembroke came straight to the point. 'The castle is surrounded. We can take it with ease. It may be that you prefer to surrender quietly.'

'Why should I? The King is on his way with an army to rescue me.'

'You cannot think that men would rally to the King to save *you*. There is not a man in England more loathed. I can tell you that.'

'The King is confident of raising an army.'

'Then the King lives in a dream. He will never raise an army to save you, Gaveston.'

'There are loyal men in England.'

'Loyal to England but not to a Gascon adventurer.'

'Do you forget you speak to the Earl of Cornwall?'

'I know full well to whom I speak. Come, man, be sensible. Do you want to surrender with dignity or be taken by force?'

Gaveston was silent for a few moments. It was true what Pembroke was saying. It would be a simple matter to take the castle. They would seize him ignobly, perhaps put him in chains. Pembroke was an honourable man. He knew that such an act might bring about civil war and he did not want to fight against the King. His quarrel was not with Edward but with Gaveston. But he would act if need be. Warenne would not hesitate to treat him with indignity for Warenne more than any had never forgiven him for the Wallingford joust.

Gaveston knew that this might be his only chance to make terms. He came to a quick decision. 'If I surrender to you,' he said, 'it will be on condition that I am allowed to see the King and be given a fair trial.'

Pembroke hesitated. He thought it would be unwise for Gaveston and the King to meet again. But Gaveston should have a free trial. He had no doubt that there was enough evidence against him to condemn him to death. He had run from Tynemouth so hastily that he had left numerous possessions behind and among them were some of the crown jewels. He would declare that the King had given them to him but that would not save him. He had no right to have them in his possession. Moreover he had been a traitor to England again and again. He had returned when he had been banished.

To take him now ... easily ... to bring him to trial, that would be a triumph. Warenne had agreed with him that they wanted no bloodshed.

'It shall be so,' said Pembroke.

'I have your word as a man of honour.'

'You have it,' was the answer.'

Pembroke left the castle to report to Warenne what terms
he had made.

*   *   *

The journey south was slow. Gaveston was a prisoner and he
knew it. He rode between Pembroke and Warenne and he was
never allowed to be out of the sight of one of them. At
night guards slept outside his door.

Each day he waited for a sign from the King. He looked
for evidence that his army was approaching. None came.
Then he told himself to be sensible. Who would fight
for the sake of Gaveston? Englishmen wanted the King
to give up his friend and live normally with his beautiful
Queen.

At length they came to Northampton and on a June evening they arrived at the town of Deddington, close to the
Thames, and here they decided they would rest.

Pembroke with Warenne selected a house in the town and
there Gaveston should spend the night well guarded.

They themselves rode on to a castle which was a few miles
away where they knew a welcome would be awaiting them.

A terrible sense of foreboding had come over Gaveston.
It was more than a month since he had become their prisoner
and very soon his trial would be taking place. He had not
seen the King and he wondered what Edward was doing now.
That he had failed to raise an army was clear. Did he know
what these men were doing to his beloved friend?

Sleep did not come easily, and he longed for it. The only
time he was at peace was when he could slip into dreams.
Then he would be back in the past with Edward beside him,
feeding him the sweetmeats of power, showing him in a
hundred ways that none other than his Perrot meant anything
to him. Sometimes his dreams would take the form of nightmare. His enemies would be surrounding him and at the head
of them would be one with a face like a dog ... a mad dog
foaming at the mouth, jaws slavering, trying to leap at his
throat. Of them all he feared Warwick. Pembroke was indeed
a man of honour, proud of his royalty, his good name. Not
so Warwick. He was the most ruthless of the barons. Then

there was Lancaster who hated him and who had, so he heard, promised the Queen that he would destroy the man she hated more than any in the kingdom—himself.

Perhaps he and Edward had not considered the Queen as they should. She had seemed so unimportant. Edward had admitted that he found times spent with her irksome because they took him from his beloved, and he had not hidden this from her. She had displayed an unnatural quiet which might be perhaps a smouldering resentment. She had inspired Lancaster with a determination to destroy him, for Lancaster it was said was half in love with her.

The Queen was in his dreams, her beautiful face a mask of resignation concealing her true emotions. Odd that he should think of that now. We should have paid more attention to the Queen. That thought kept going round and round in his head. It was absurd. What could a woman do? Women perhaps were more dangerous than some men because they acted in a more mysterious manner. Hatred was obvious in the dark eyes of Joseph the Jew and Lancaster's scheming face and the foaming lips of Mad Dog Warwick. But how could he know what schemes were planned behind the beautiful face of Isabella the Fair?

He was awakened from an uneasy dream. There were noises below. He heard the shouts of the guards and then silence. He started up but before he could rise the door was opened and figures from his dream were at his bedside.

Warwick, the Mad Dog, was looking down at him.

'So, my fine fellow, we have you, eh?' he said.

Gaveston looked up at that cruel dark face, noticed the spittle about the thin lips and said with an attempt at his usual cynicism: 'So the Mad Hound of Arden has come to Deddington Rectory.'

'Aye,' cried Warwick. 'He is here. He is taking you where you belong. Beware lest he take you by the throat and kill you.'

'You cannot touch me. I have the word of the Earl of Pembroke. I am to have a free trial and I am to see the King.'

'Since when has the Earl of Pembroke given orders to Warwick? Get up. Or we will take you as you are ... naked. The dungeons at Warwick are not made for comfort. Be wise and dress warmly. If you can do it quickly you may still have time.'

'I protest...'

'Take him as he is then,' cried Warwick. 'The pretty boy likes us to see himself as nature made him. He fancies he is prettier that way than in the finest garments. It may be, Gaveston, but we are not of a nature to admire. Get up. Or I will call my guards.'

Gaveston reached for his clothes and under the eyes of Warwick hastily dressed.

About his neck he wore a chain set with jewels and there were several rings on his fingers. They were all he had brought with him from Scarborough.

Warwick noticed them. 'The chain was a gift from the French King to our King,' he said. 'The rings are royal too, are they not? How you love jewels, pretty boy. Crown jewels preferred. You stole them from the Treasury.'

'I did not. I did not. The King gave me ... everything ...'

'Ah, he did so. His honour, his people's regard and mayhap his kingdom. Guards. Take him.'

'You will have to answer to the Earl of Pembroke. He had given me his word.'

'Leave the Earl of Pembroke to me. You should be concerned with yourself.'

As he stepped out into the night air, he knew where they were going and a terrible despair filled his heart.

*   *   *

When Pembroke arrived at the rectory to prepare to continue his journey he was horrified to hear that Warwick had taken his prisoner away.

'This is unpardonable,' he cried. 'I have given my word for Gaveston's safe conduct. This is a slight on my honour.'

He was in a quandary, for he had sworn to the King that no harm should befall Gaveston and he had pledged his lands on this.

Little could have been more dangerous for Gaveston than to fall into the hands of Warwick; and Pembroke knew that if anything happened to the favourite the King would be so mad with grief and that he would insist on Pembroke's being stripped of his lands.

He appealed to Warwick who laughed at him and declared that Gaveston was his prisoner and was remaining so. Lancaster, Hereford and Arundel were on their way to Warwick where they would decide Gaveston's fate.

Frantically Pembroke sought out the young Earl of Gloucester, Edward's cousin, for the King's sister, Joanna, was his mother. Gloucester had been neutral in the affair of Gaveston because his sister Margaret was Gaveston's wife. Poor Margaret, wife to such a man was an empty title and she had long ceased to admire him, which at the time of her marriage, when she was very young, she had done because he was so pretty. But when she learned of his true nature her feelings had changed. Yet at the same time Gaveston had become a member of the family and families usually clung together, though Gloucester had not come out in Gaveston's favour because the favourite had offended him on one occasion by calling him Whoreson—a derogatory reference to his mother, the Princess Joanna, who had married old Gloucester and almost immediately after his death had turned to Ralph de Monthermer and secretly married him.

Gaveston had been very sure of himself in those days. He was a reckless fool, like a gorgeous dragonfly revelling in the sun of royal favour, never pausing to consider that the baronial clouds could rise and cover it.

Gloucester shrugged aside Pembroke's suggestion that they should band together and storm Warwick Castle to rescue the favourite.

'You cannot expect me to go to war for Gaveston!' he cried aghast.

'The King would be on our side.'

'The King ... against Warwick, Lancaster, Arundel and God nows how many more! Do you want to plunge this country into civil war for the sake of that man?'

'I gave my word.'

'Then you should have taken more pains to make sure you kept it.'

'It seemed safe enough. He was well guarded. Warwick came by night with an overpowering force.'

'You should never have left him. You should have taken him to the castle with you.'

'I know that now. But at the time it seemed safe.'

Gloucester shrugged his shoulders.

'I have pledged my lands to the King for his safety,' pleaded Pembroke. 'I shall lose everything.'

'Then mayhap this will teach you to be a better trader next time.'

'But he was *promised* safe conduct.'

Gloucester turned away. He could not shut out the sight of Gaveston's face, the eyes glittering, the mouth slightly lifted at one corner. 'That Whoreson Gloucester ...'

Gaveston would now pay for the fury he had aroused in the hearts of powerful men.

It was their turn now.

* * *

Lancaster, Hereford and Arundel had arrived at Warwick Castle.

'So you have him here,' said Lancaster.

'He is in one of the dungeons. He has lost his bombast. He is now full of fear as to what we have planned for him.'

'So should he be,' replied Lancaster grimly.

'What shall we do with him?' asked Warwick.

'He must not be allowed to live,' Lancaster pointed out. 'Every day he is alive could mean danger. What if the King mustered an army and came to take him? What would our position be then?'

'We should be fighting against the crown,' put in Warwick. 'Civil war. There was enough of that under John and Henry.'

'There is one thing to be done,' said Lancaster tersely. 'We must pronounce sentence and carry it out. The man is a traitor. He has stolen the crown jewels. A fortune in treasure was left behind at Scarborough. He is under excommunication. He deserves death and at a trial he would be found guilty. My lord, there is one thing we must do. We must carry out the sentence before there is more trouble.'

'He deserves the traitor's death.'

'Hanged, drawn and quartered. Yes, but how? Moreover he is connected by marriage with Gloucester's sister which gives him a link with royalty. It is enough that he loses his head.'

'Who will strike the blow?' asked Hereford looking from Warwick to Lancaster.

Arundel said: 'The man who does that places himself in danger.'

'It is no time to think of that,' retorted Lancaster sharply.

'The blow must be struck. He must lose his head.'

'When?' asked Arundel.

'This night.'

'So soon?'

'Why, man, who knows what tomorrow could bring?' cried Lancaster. 'What if the King arrived to take him from us?'

'There will be no peace in this land while he lives,' said Warwick. 'The people will rise against the King if Gaveston goes back to him. They like not this relationship between them. They want him to be with his Queen. They want another man such as his father was ... a family man who will give the country heirs.'

'Great Edward the First gave us our present King. He was great in all things save one—the giving of an heir.'

'Hush, my lord. That's treason.'

'Treason ... among friends. We know it is all true.'

'That may be. But let us rid the country of Gaveston and see what comes then.'

'He must go.'

They all agreed to that. And who should actually strike the blow? That man would be the enemy of the King for ever.'

They came to a decision. It should be an unknown hand that killed Gaveston. The noble earls would merely be spectators, and the men who struck the blows should be humble soldiers whose identity would be lost when they mingled with their fellows.

It was the only way.

*　　*　　*

'Come, Gaveston.'

It was Warwick who spoke to him.

'It is time to go.'

'To go where?'

'Whither the Mad Hound leads.'

'You never forget that, do you?'

'There are some things which are never forgotten.'

'You harbour more resentment against me for calling you that than for snatching the championships at Wallingford.'

'Have done. There is little time for such badinage. You should be saying your prayers.'

'So you are going to kill me?'

'You are going to meet your deserts.'

'And my fair trial? And my meeting with the King?'

'*I* promised none of these things.'

'You will have to answer to Pembroke.'

'That will be no affair of yours, Gaveston. You should be praying for your black soul.'

'There is little time for that now.'

' 'Tis so. Then use it.'

They took him out of the castle. He saw the noble earls on horseback waiting. They were as still as statues cut out of stone.

They sat him on a horse. He savoured the smells and signs of the night. The good earth; the scent of grass; the dark star-speckled sky. He had never noticed their beauty before. He had loved the blue of the sapphire, the rich red of the ruby, the glitter of the diamond, because they had been the symbols of riches and power. Now he wanted to savour other beauties, but it was too late.

Where were they taking him? Away from Warwick? Why, he wondered. The Mad Hound had been eager to take him but perhaps he was not so eager to have a hand in his death.

He noticed then that Warwick was not among them.

It was Lancaster who rode ahead with Hereford and Arundel. They were going into Lancaster's estates, which bordered on those of Warwick and could not have come more than a few miles.

Were they on the way to Kenilworth?

But no. They had stopped.

He was ordered to dismount. He did so and a troop of soldiers surrounded him.

They walked forward; he with them then. They had come to a hill which he knew from the past. Blacklow Hill. He remembered passing it when he was in Edward's company. How strange that then he should have had no premonition of this.

The three earls did not follow him. He knew what that meant. They were afraid. They wanted him dead but they did not want to kill him themselves. That was a task for some-one else.

This was the moment then.

The soldiers were all around him. He stood at the foot of the hill. He looked back. His last look at the earth: the dark hill before him; the silence of the night broken only by the ripple of a nearby stream. The smells of earth, the beauty of the earth ... so much that he had never had time to notice before.

He glanced back at the figures of the three earls seated on their horses. The sentinels at the gates of the Earth, crying out to him: No admittance for you, Gaveston. You are banished ... banished from life.

Someone had come close to him. He was just in time to see the flash of steel. Then darkness and he was falling ... His life had been ended by an unknown hand but those men sitting on their horses, silent, still as stone, were the men who had murdered him.

He could hear a rushing in his ears. Vengeance, Vengeance, it seemed to say and then something else ... perhaps it was his own voice.

Edward ... Edward ... this is the end.

* * *

Warwick waiting in the castle was afraid of what they had done. They should have waited, given him his trial, for he must surely have been found guilty. But they had taken justice into their hands.

He had captured him, brought him to Warwick Castle, and sent word to Lancaster. But he had not gone out with them to Blacklow Hill.

There was a banging on the castle door. It echoed uncannily through the vaulted roofs.

Warwick opened the door. Two men stood there. They were carrying a headless corpse.

'He is no more, my lord. The Earl of Lancaster has his head. We have brought his body to you.'

Warwick stepped forward and looked at the grisly remains of that once graceful body which had charmed the King.

'Take it away,' he cried. 'Take it from here. I will have nought to do with it.'

'My lord, where would you have us take it?'

'Take it ...' He tried to think. 'Anywhere,' he cried, 'but away from here. Take it to the Dominicans of Oxford. They will give it temporary refuge.'

So wild did he look with the foam at his mouth—Gaveston's mad dog indeed.

The men hurried off. They knew that Gaveston could not be buried in consecrated ground. He had died excommunicated and with all his sins upon him.

* * *

Lancaster alone took responsibility for the death of Gaveston. He despised the others for their fear. They had hated the man even as he had and had agreed that he must die.

Nothing could have saved Gaveston before a court. He had disobeyed the laws. He had filched a fortune from the King. No, nothing could have saved him.

'I have no fear,' said Lancaster. 'The King will hate me for this but the people will be with me. The Queen will applaud me. I promised her to rid her of this man and I have done so. Why should I fear the King? I have my private army. I am as royal as he is. If the King cannot rule this land, then must others do it for him.'

Thomas Lancaster believed he could boldly admit to the judicial killing of an outlaw and a thief and a man who threatened the peace of the country.

'Gaveston is dead,' said Lancaster. 'We will go on from there.'

THE DESPENSERS

YOUNG EDWARD

WHEN the King heard of Gaveston's murder those about him thought his grief would drive him mad. For days he shut himself into his chamber and would see no one. His attendants heard him wailing in his misery. He found some relief in calling vengeance on Lancaster, Warwick, Hereford and Arundel who had been responsible for the death of the finest man on Earth.

No one could soothe him in those first days but later the Queen insisted on going to him.

She was large with child now and the sight of her seemed to give him some comfort.

She feigned compassion but she felt none, only exultancy because Gaveston was dead. She had thought often of Lancaster and the ardent look in his eyes when he had said: 'I will rid you of this man.'

He had meant it. He had taken great risks, and had removed Gaveston from their lives for ever.

Edward was babbling of his talents. She pretended to listen and she let her hand rest on the child and to herself she said: We will show this man for the fool he is, when you are born, my child. You will grow up and you will be a great King and your mother will always be beside you. The people despise your father but I will give England another King such as the first Edward and the people will welcome you in place of your ignoble father. How she despised him—his eyes red with weeping, his stupid babbling about the virtues of Gaveston. Gaveston had no virtue. All he had was a talent for self-aggrandisement and he was not even clever enough for that, for all that he had had a few years run he had ended without his head on Blacklow Hill.

Now she was going to be watchful. She was going to play her own clever game. She would be secretive and none should really know what was in her mind. She would use Edward to get her way. But as soon as the moment was ripe she would show him that he had never been forgiven for the humiliation he had poured on her. She would always remember that when she had come to him, a fresh young bride ready to love him, he had turned from her to Gaveston.

Edward said to her: 'To kill him so. To treat him thus. Oh Isabella, I cannot bear my life without him.'

She stroked his hair. What a fool he was! Like a girl. But he was indeed handsome. Who would have believed that those strong golden looks—inherited from his father—should disguise a girlish nature. A poor weak creature masquerading as a king.

He should be her puppet now. She had powerful friends. Lancaster was undoubtedly one and when the child was born if it were a boy . . .

If! It must be a boy. She willed it to be a boy. And if not . . . Then she must get more and more until she had her boy.

'What can I do without him, Isabella? You know what he meant to me.'

She said: 'He should be given decent burial. Why do you not have his body taken to Kings Langley? You have constantly spoken of the happy days you shared there with him in your boyhood.'

He seized her hands. 'Oh Isabella, you are good to me. You give me courage. You give me hope.'

Inwardly she laughed. You fool. Don't you know that I hate him more than any of them? He had earned Warwick's enmity by sneering at him and calling him the Mad Hound of Arden. He maddened others with his serpent's tongue. But none was humiliated as much as you have humiliated me, and I shall remember even as those barons did.

'Well, then,' she said, 'let us consider his tomb, and should not prayers be said for his soul? Remember,' she added maliciously, 'he died with all his sins upon him.'

'Gaveston will charm the angels. He need have no fear.'

'They may not share your tendencies, Edward,' she said

sharply. Then she added quickly: 'It would be well to have masses said for his soul. I am sure you see what I mean.'

'It shall be done. Oh Isabella, it must be done quickly. Nothing ... simply nothing must be forgotten.'

'We will arrange it together,' she said.

'I will have Lancaster's head for this.'

'You must be watchful of Lancaster, Edward. He is the most powerful man in the country.'

'But I am the King, Isabella. Have you forgotten that?'

'Not I. But others might. Much as you loved Gaveston, the people did not.'

'They were fed lies.'

'Oh, they liked not his influence with you. Barons like Warwick and Lancaster were determined he should die. He should never have come back.'

'Oh, no, no. If he had not he would still be alive.'

'Now he shall rest peacefully in Kings Langley. Edward, the barons are ready to rise against you. You will have to be careful with Lancaster.'

'Lancaster! I'll have his head.'

'Your own cousin. He is popular with the people.'

'I must remind you again, Isabella, that I am the King.'

'Kings fall. Remember your grandfather Henry. There was a time when Simon de Montfort made him a prisoner. Your great-grandfather John was in even worse plight.'

'I wish people would not always talk of those two. Look at my father. Men trembled at the sight of him and the sound of his voice.'

'Edward, you are not your father.'

He was silent. Even the mention of the old man could subdue him still.

'Listen,' she said. 'Pembroke and Warenne are disgusted with Lancaster, Warwick, Hereford and Arundel. Pembroke moans that he was forced to break his word and he fears he will lose his estates to you.'

'He should have taken more care.'

'He should indeed. Bind Pembroke to you, Edward. Don't you see that this split between the barons can be your salvation? Pembroke and Lancaster are engaged in a feud which is greater than that between you and Lancaster.'

'Nothing could be greater than that. I regard Lancaster as Perrot's murderer.'

'Yes, yes. But Pembroke is a powerful man. The people admire him. And because of what has happened he will be with you ... not against you. Don't you see, this has not turned out so badly. Oh, I beg of you do not start again on the virtues of Gaveston. We must put that behind us. Give him the best burial we can and a good chance in heaven by exhortations to the saints. Let us set up our candles and let prayers be said for his soul, but Gaveston is gone and we are here.'

Even as they were talking messengers came hurrying to the King from Pembroke. Lancaster, Hereford and Warwick were marching on London. They knew full well that the King would want to take action against them and they were taking action first.

Isabella smiled secretly. Lancaster was a bold man. This was not the time however to depose Edward. Her child must be born first. She must have a son, a symbol, a new King before the old one was set aside.

Gloucester was without. An earnest young man and loyal to the King. He knelt and kissed Edward's hand.

'Well, cousin?' said Edward.

'My lord, Lancaster marches on London. He has strong support. He must not be allowed into the city.'

'Let him come,' retorted Edward. 'I would have his head. I would show him what I feel for him now that he has robbed me of my best friend.'

Gloucester said: 'If he came to London there could be civil war. Let the gates be closed my lord and warn the Londoners to be on guard.'

Isabella interrupted: 'Our cousin is right, Edward. This is no time for conflict.'

So it was done and Lancaster himself was somewhat relieved that there should not be open conflict . Now there would be conferences between the barons which could last for weeks and meanwhile the King could subdue his grief and perhaps forget his ire; and it might well be that the difficult situation could be eased somewhat. It was hardly likely that the King would ever forgive the murderers of his beloved Gaveston. But it was always better to let matters settle down before rash action was taken.

*   *   *

The Queen had gone to Windsor for her lying in. At last the waiting was over and her desire to hold her child in her arms obsessed her.

She had chosen Windsor for the birth. It was one of her favourite palaces as it had been for Queen Eleanor who had brought the children there because she had thought the draughtiness of the Tower of London was bad for their health.

Isabella now lay in her bed and thought of how her life would be changed when this child was born. If it were a boy everything would have been worth while.

Her pains were beginning. She welcomed them. She was praying to the Virgin, who should intercede for women.

'O Holy Mary, give me a son. I have waited long. I have suffered humiliation which has been hard to bear for a woman of my proud nature. *Please* give me my son.'

Pain engulfed her. She did not shrink from it. Anything … anything but give me my son.

She lost consciousness and was aroused to the sound of the voices about her. Then … the cry of a child.

She heard someone say: 'Look the Queen opens her eyes.'

'My lady …'

How long they were! It seemed as though time had slowed down.

'My … child …'

Then the blessed words: 'A boy, my lady. A healthy boy … sound in limb and in good voice. A fine boy.'

A smile of triumph was on her lips as she held out her arms.

* * *

She caressed him. She examined him. He was perfect.

'His legs are long,' she said. 'He will be like his grandfather.'

They noticed that she did not mention his father.

'He is beautiful. Look … his hair is already so fair. Like a golden down. He's a Plantagenet. It is obvious already.'

They agreed with her. The nurses clucked over him. They had never seen such a child, they assured her. He surpassed all other children.

Of course he did. He was to be a king.

She said: 'I have decided he shall be called Edward.'

'The King will be pleased.'

She thought: Not after him. After his grandfather. I pray he may not be like his father. No, he should not be. Tall, fine, manly. A great king. But one who would listen to his mother.

Edward came. He stared at the child and none had seen him so delighted since Gaveston had died. He was smiling. Just for a few moments he forgot his beloved friend.

'He is ... perfect,' he cried incredulously.

'In every way,' the child's mother assured him. 'Give him to me. I cannot bear not to have my eyes on him all the time.'

'*My* son,' said Edward as though bewildered. 'My own son.'

'Your son,' she answered, 'and mine.'

'There is rejoicing throughout the land,' he went on. 'They are talking of it at Court. They want him to be named Louis.'

'I will not have it,' said the Queen. 'His name is Edward. Louis is not the name of a king of England but a king of France. He is Edward. I will have no other name.'

Edward knelt by the bed and kissed her hand.

'I am so proud of him,' he said. 'My son.'

'Yes, Edward,' she answered, 'and mine also.'

He took the child in his arms and walked about the room with it.

He has forgotten Gaveston ... momentarily, she thought.

She was glad to see his delight in the child but her intentions towards him had not changed at all. He had fathered the child, and they must have more. But little Edward was hers, entirely hers.

As she lay in bed with her baby beside her she thought of the future. The people would be with her. They liked her youthful beauty as soon as they set eyes on it and the King's treatment of her had incensed them so that they had immediately taken her part. That she had apparently forgiven him for his disgraceful behaviour with Gaveston and now had actually given them the heir they wanted, made her seem something like a saint in their eyes.

She must never lose the respect of the people and in particular those of the City of London.

She therefore decided to acquaint them with the arrival of her son, to send them a personal message and to order that there be rejoicing throughout the capital.

She wrote to the citizens of London.

> Isabella, by the grace of God Queen of England, Lady of Ireland and Duchess of Acquitaine, to our well-beloved Mayor and Alderman and the Commonality of London, greetings. Forasmuch as we believe you would willingly hear good tiding of us, we do make it known to you that our Lord in his Grace has delivered us of a son, on the 13th day of November with safety to ourselves and to the child. May our Lord preserve you. Given at Windsor on the day above named.

She sent messages to say that she wished the City to have three days of rejoicing in which to welcome the baby. Wine would be in the streets and she hoped that there would be none in the City who did not drink her child's health. She believed they would know how to make a merry time of it and she would be glad to hear of their rejoicing.

'God bless the Queen,' cried the people of London. 'God bless the little Prince.'

There were few cheers for the King. But it was said that the timely arrival of the baby had averted trouble with the barons, for everyone was so delighted that there should be a male heir that it seemed hardly likely that those critics of the King would stand a chance against him now. As for the King, he should forget his grievances against those who despatched Gaveston.

Gaveston was dead and a good riddance.

There was now a baby heir. Let the King settle down with his beautiful wife who was so popular with the people. Let him live a normal married life and beget more children.

THE CURSE OF THE TEMPLARS

AT this time the Archbishop of Canterbury, Robert de Winchelsey, died. He had been ailing for some time and was an old man so his death was not unexpected .

Walter Reynolds, Bishop of Worcester, who had been an intimate friend of Gaveston, asked for an audience with the King, which was immediately granted. Reynolds was a crafty man. He did not come straight to the point which he felt even Edward might consider a little audacious but it had always been Walter Reynolds' opinion that no delicacy of feeling should come between a man and his ambitions. The See of Canterbury was vacant. A new Archbishop would have to be appointed and in view of the closeness of his friendship with the King it could possibly be that Walter Reynolds might step into those shoes so recently vacated by Robert of Winchelsey.

Reynolds fell onto his knees and kissed the King's hand.

'My lord, my lord, I see how you still suffer from our terrible loss.'

'I think of him continuously,' replied the King.

'As I do also.'

'And the manner of his death, Walter, I shall never forget it or forgive it.'

'You could not, my lord. The happy times we had together ...'

They talked of them for a while, Reynolds deliberately arousing the King's despair. He was more likely to agree when he was in a maudlin mood. After all the three of them had been so much together. Reynolds had made it his duty to provide for their comfort. It had been Gaveston who had considered Walter should be rewarded in the first place.

At length Reynolds said: 'There is Canterbury.'

'Ah, yes. Poor Robert. I never liked him. An uncomfortable man but a good one by all accounts.'

'My lord will not be sorry to see him go. You must put someone in his place who will be your man.'

'The monks have already elected Cobham.'

'Cobham. That will never do.'

'You know they claim their right.'

'But, my Lord, the monks of Canterbury have no rights over their King.'

'They were always a tiresome company. They have made trouble for my ancestors through the centuries.'

'That is no reason why they should make trouble for you, gracious lord. Insolent fellows.'

Edward sighed. 'If *he* were here he would jibe at them.'

'He would be angry at the manner in which they treat you.'

'He was always eager to uphold me,' said Edward fondly. 'You know Clement issued a bull only a month or so ago reserving to himself the appointment of the archbishop.'

'Clement! He sways with the wind. The French King whistles and he comes. There is one thing I know of which could make him change his mind.'

Edward raised his eyebrows and Walter went on: 'Money. Poor Clement, what is he but Philip's puppet? Philip has him there at Avignon under his nose. Philip says, "Come here. Go there." "Do this. Do that." And what does Clement do? He obeys. He has persecuted the Templars. Why? Because Philip says so. There is one thing he can do without the help of the King of France and that is amass money. I have heard he will do a great deal for it.'

Edward was thoughtful.

'Why, Walter, how comforting it would be if you were Archbishop of Canterbury.'

Walter folded the palms of his hands together and turned his eyes up to the ceiling.

'I would serve you with my life, dear lord.' Then he fell on his knees. 'If only this could but come to pass! Can you not see our dear friend looking down on us from Heaven.

Sometimes I think, lord, that he is working for us. He could never forget us could he, any more than we could forget him? I wonder whether Clement would go so far.'

'Let us find out,' said Edward.

They did, and discovered that the Pope was ready to go a very long way for the sake of thirty-two thousand marks.

It was a great deal of money, but worth it to have in the important post of Archbishop of Canterbury a man who would serve the King rather than the Church, and if his reputation was hardly that to be expected of a good churchman the King did not care. It was comforting to have Walter in such a position. They could meet often and talk over old times. Together they could mourn for the incomparable Gaveston.

'The King is mad,' said Lancaster.

Pembroke agreed with him but there was a feud between them because Lancaster, Warwick and the rest had made him break his word. Pembroke was wooing the King, for he feared to be deprived of his lands.

If there had not been this rift between the barons they would have stood out against this appointment of Walter Reynolds to the important See of Canterbury but, as there was, it came to pass.

*　　*　　*

There was news from France of Philip's final acts against the Templars and when the story was told, Edward was glad that he had acted differently towards that company of Knights. In England they became absorbed into the rest of the community, and when they considered what had happened to their brethren in France they must be grateful to the King and the English for evermore.

Philip the Fair had pursued them with a ferocity which was hard to understand. True, he wanted their wealth but he could have taken that without inflicting such tortures on them. The rumours which came in from France were horrifying. The Queen listened to them and told herself that at least her father was a strong man. Frenchmen trembled at the mention of his name. It would never be like that with Edward. Even now many of the barons were against him and she guessed that Lancaster was waiting for the moment when he could seize power. Edward was weak. He was a fool and when the young Edward was older something would happen, she was sure of that.

In the meantime she must show a certain affection for her husband, even if she did not feel it. It was necessary to get more children and she was determined to. Her bonny Edward was the delight of her life. But she wanted him to have a brother ... several if possible.

Although many of the Templars had suffered the most cruel tortures and been burned at the stake, their Grand Master, Jacques de Molai, still lived. De Molai was a Burgundian nobleman who had joined the crusades and fought valiantly against the Infidel. When he had been invited to Paris some years before he came unsuspecting and almost immediately was seized on, fettered, and submitted to such excruciating torture that he had collapsed under it and confessed to the evil deeds of which it was suggested he was guilty.

That men of logic did not believe he was meant nothing. So rigorous had been the torture that few could have stood out against it, certainly not a man of de Molai's age.

At this time the Order had been suppressed and its riches were in the hands of the King of France, but the Grand Master and the Master of Normandy still lived because it had been discovered that, on account of their rank in the Order, their death sentence must be sanctioned by the Pope.

Realizing that death was at hand, and as he had suffered so much that his poor pain-racked body was indifferent to more suffering, the Grand Master made a declaration that he deeply regretted his previous statements. He had spoken as he did under duress. He wanted now to tell the King of France and his accusers that his confession had been wrung from his weak body. His soul was in protest and he now wished to state the truth. He was innocent. The whole order was innocent. His destruction had been the work of his rapacious enemies.

The Master of Normandy joined his voice with that of de Molai.

As this happened beside the scaffold which had been erected in the forecourt of Notre Dame, there was no way of hushing it up because many people had gathered to see the end of these men. Their voices rang out clearly and the crowd was hushed and it seemed, said some, that God himself was speaking through the Grand Master.

In view of the fact that they had rescinded their confession and to placate the growing apprehension and rising anger of the crowd, it was announced that their death sentence should be temporarily waived and the men taken back to their prison.

When the King heard what had happened he was furious. He could not rest while de Molai lived. He had waited a long time to finish him, as he said, and now to have the matter delayed again was more than he could endure.

Meanwhile the prisoners had been sent back to the Provost of Paris.

'More delay!' raged the King. 'There will be no real peace until those men are dead.' He made a sudden decision. He was not going to wait for more arguments. 'Today is the day when they shall meet their end,' he declared. 'They shall be burned at the stake in the Ile de la Cité at the hour of vespers.'

The King's word was law; and news of what was about to happen spread through the city. That was why shortly before the appointed time, the streets were crowded and it seemed that the whole of Paris was making its way to the spot where the burnings were to take place.

The people were overawed by the sight of Jacques de Molai and his companion for they seemed to glow with some special power.

The poor broken men they had been were no longer there. Jacques held his head high and the light in his eyes seemed to illumine his face. People noticed that his hands did not tremble as he bared his chest.

When his hands were about to be tied he said to the guards, 'Suffer me to fold my hands awhile and make my prayer to God for verily it is time. I am presently to die, but wrongfully, God knows. Death is near, and I am innocent of that of which I am accused. Because of this woe will come ere long to those who have condemned us without cause.' Then he cried out on a loud voice which could be heard throughout that crowded square: 'God will avenge our death.'

There was a deep silence. Some lowered their heads and prayed. The spectacle of men burning to death no longer excited them. There was a deep sense of foreboding in the crowd that day.

The crackle of the wood seemed ominous and as it burst

into flame and the smoke rose many people fell to their knees and prayed.

No good would come to France, they believed. The King of France was cursed. So was the Puppet Pope. For it was those two who had been at the very heart of the Templars' destruction.

The legend grew and when one month later the Pope died, people were certain that the curse existed. Philip himself lived only eight months after that day when Jacques de Molai and the Master of Normandy were burned to death in the Ile de la Cité.

BANNOCKBURN

EDWARD had something on which to congratulate himself. Since the death of Gaveston his people had warmed towards him. This was largely due to the Queen whose beauty appealed to them and whose outward resignation to her husband's conduct won their admiration. The fact that the King and Queen were seen more frequently together and that they had the lusty young Edward as a certain sign that they now and then lived together as husband and wife, had pleased the people. The King could never be like great Edward the First but perhaps with his evil genius Gaveston gone for ever, there was hope of a return to a normal way of life.

Moreover the feud between the barons was in his favour for they no longer stood together against him. Lancaster's party was strong but the powerful Earl of Pembroke had quarrelled with it over the death of Gaveston, and Pembroke had joined himself with the King.

Edward felt that he could enjoy a period of peace, as far as that were possible without Gaveston. Then there was trouble from the North.

The Scots had rejoiced in the death of Edward the First and the accession of his son which had resulted in their salvation. Scotland under Robert the Bruce had grown stronger as England under Edward the Second had become weaker. Bruce was just the man to take advantage of such a position. He had gradually but steadily begun to free his country from the English domination set up by Edward, the Hammer of the Scots.

It was clear that the second Edward had no heart for a fight.

He was not the strong warlike figure that his father had been. He had retired from the scene of action as soon as it was possible for him to do so and had left the Earl of Richmond in the north bestowing on him the title of Guardian of Scotland. His task was far from enviable and intermittent warfare had taken place between the Scots and English and recently Bruce had made raids over the Border into England on each occasion returning with valuable spoils.

The situation was becoming dangerous. One by one those fortresses held by the English were falling to the Scots. Edward groaned and cursed the Scots but he did little to prevent the disintegration of English power. Bruce, inwardly exultant, often wondered what Great Edward would think if he could see what was happening. Had he lived the conquest of Scotland would have been brought about. Indeed, it was a happy day for the Scots when he died and his son took the crown.

The Scots had no respect for Edward and an army without a leader, however well equipped, could not fail to arouse wild hopes in the hearts of its opponents.

One by one the fortresses fell. Perth, Dumfries and Roxburgh were taken. Linlithgow had been cleverly taken when a soldier from the Douglas clan, disguised as a carter, had asked leave to take a hay cart into the castle. As it drew up in the gateway beneath the great portcullis, from under the hay armed men sprang out, entered the castle and took the defenders by surprise. Such incidents put heart into Bruce's army. They were not so well equipped as the English and must rely on cunning. It seemed they had plenty of this and under Bruce's leadership their hopes ran high.

The Castle of Edinburgh seemed to present the greatest difficulty of all as it was surrounded by three sides which were declared to be impassable precipices. The Scots were in despair when one of the soldiers came to his commander Randolph and told him that as a youth he had had a mistress who was in the castle and he had cut out steps in the cliff face so that he might visit her. He realized that every time he had visited her he had risked his life but he had come through safely and now he could show them the way.

They decided to try it and with the aid of rope ladders actually made their way up the steep cliff-face to the walls of the castle. They ascended, invaded the castle, killed the unsuspecting sentinels and took it.

This was the greatest triumph and incidents like this were, said Bruce, worth a thousand men.

At this time only three important castles remained in English hands: Stirling, Dunbar and Berwick. Of these Stirling was the most important and Bruce decided that they must take it, but the castle was well defended and Bruce knew that to attempt to storm it would mean the loss of men and ammunition which he could ill afford to lose. As a great soldier he was less sanguinary than his men and he realized that while they would achieve successes in the existing circumstances it would be a very different matter if the English army marched up to Scotland. However, the more fortresses he could wrest from them before the main attack the better, and Stirling was of the utmost importance.

Therefore he sent his brother Edward Bruce to besiege the castle; Edward harried its occupants in every way and the Governor, Sir Philip Mowbray, was unable to procure the supplies he needed. Edward Bruce however lacked the astuteness of his brother and was beguiled by Sir Philip Mowbray into conferring with him. To take the castle would be expensive for the Scots in men and arms; moreover there was a possibility that the operation might not be successful.

'Edward's armies are on the way to defend Stirling,' was Sir Philip's argument. 'I can hold out until they arrive. This could spell a defeat for you which could be disastrous to the Scottish cause.'

Edward Bruce replied that all knew the nature of the King of England. He was not like his father. It seemed likely that he had no intention of bringing an army to Scotland. In which case in due time the Scots would have Stirling as they had Edinburgh, Linlithgow and the rest.

'That is true,' replied Mowbray. 'So I will make a truce with you. If the English army is not within three leagues of this castle by the Feast of St John the Baptist I will surrender to you without the loss of one life on either side.'

Edward Bruce agreed. When his brother Robert heard what he had done he was greatly displeased but, determined to make the best of the situation, he began to see that the arrangement would give him a chance to gather together an army to stand against the English should they come.

*   *   *

Pembroke came in haste to Edward.

'My lord,' he said, 'you will see the urgency of this matter. Mowbray must be relieved at Stirling and we have little time in which to do it.'

Edward sighed. 'These tiresome Scots.'

Pembroke went on a trifle impatiently: 'Mowbray is a gallant soldier and a faithful servant. He needs assistance and he must have it.'

'Then let us send it.'

'My lord, that is not enough. Since your father's death we have lost a great deal of that which he gained. One by one the garrison towns are slipping away from us. We must stop this and the only way to do it is to amass an army and march on Scotland.'

'The barons ...'

'It is an opportunity to unite them in a single cause. No matter what their quarrels with each other, their duty to the Crown remains. I am ready to forget my differences with Lancaster and Warwick until this matter is resolved and so must they.'

'I see this could be so,' said Edward.

'There must be a full-scale invasion from sea and land. The Scots have a great leader in the Bruce. Never have they been so united ... even under Wallace. Now is the time, my lord. If we allow Stirling to fall into the hands of the Scots it will be a disaster. We owe it to Mowbray to send relief as soon as is possible.'

'It shall be done,' cried Edward. He felt a sudden enthusiasm for the fight. It was true that it would bind the barons together and he was tired—and a little afraid—of their continual bickering. It would help him to forget Gaveston. People were always comparing him with his father, now they should see that he could be warlike too. He would teach the Scots a lesson.

'We should summon the earls and barons without fail,' said Pembroke.

'Let it be done,' answered Edward.

Within a few days the commands were issued to eight earls —among them Lancaster—and eighty-seven barons.

They were to meet at Berwick by the tenth day of June.

*   *   *

Preparations went on apace. Edward ordered that a fleet of twenty-three vessels be assembled at the Cinque Ports and their purpose was to invade Scotland.

In all this Pembroke was beside the King. He tried to instil into Edward a respect for his opponent. It would not be the first time Pembroke had faced Bruce. He had been victorious against him at Methven and beaten by him at Loudoun Hill and he knew him for a formidable foe. Edward laughed aside his warnings. Bruce was a man to be reckoned with, yes, he accepted that. But such an army would come against him that his would be completely outnumbered.

'Even my father could not have withstood such an army had he been on the opposing side,' said Edward.

''Tis so, my lord,' replied Pembroke. 'But we must not make the mistake of expecting easy victory.'

Pembroke was a master at the art of war. He made sure that the army should have the necessary provisions; he set up men whose efficiency he could rely on to take care of the stores. They must have in their train smiths, carpenters, masons and armourers, wagons to carry the tents and pavilions and all that was necessary to warfare. Many a battle he reminded the King had been lost through neglect of such details.

Nor must the King neglect to ask the help of God and it would be a good gesture for him to make a pilgrimage with the Queen and his young son to St Albans.

Isabella was nothing loath. She enjoyed displaying herself to the people, and that she should show off her son delighted her.

Along the roads people came out to give loyal greetings as they passed. It was like the old days when Great Edward went to war, they said. There was the King with his beautiful Queen and his son, the heir to the throne. The Gaveston period was over. That man had been evil. He was the son of a witch and temporarily had cast a spell on the King. All Edward needed now was victory in Scotland and the people would be certain that the old days were back again.

Alas, it was not going to be so easy, as he found when he arrived at Berwick.

It was Pembroke who brought the news to him. 'Lancaster, Arundel, Surrey and Warwick will not come in person,' he told the King.

Edward was filled with sudden rage. 'Why not? How dare

they? Have I not summoned them?'

'Aye, my lord, and they have sent token troops in accordance with their feudal vows to the Crown. They say that they should have been consulted before you took up arms.'

'Traitors!' cried the King.

'We cannot say that, my lord. They have fulfilled their commitments though in the minimum degree it is true and we shall not have the force we expected from them.'

'I thought at a time like this they would have considered their duty to their country.'

'They consider only gain to themselves, my lord. And they would say that they have performed what was required of them. We must forget them at this time. We have the service of good men. Many have seen service in Scotland before this and Wales too. Their services will be of the greatest value to us.'

The King agreed and he glowed with pride and optimism when he surveyed his army. There must be some forty thousand men, a band of which even his father would have been proud.

Edward was going to show the Scots that his father's spirit lived on. He was going to make them eat their words. This was going to be as great a victory as had ever glorified his father's name.

He with his men marched on to Edinburgh.

*　　*　　*

Robert the Bruce, aware of the advancing English, should have been filled with apprehension. He was, and yet there was in him a surging hope, for he believed that it was his destiny to drive the English out of Scotland and when Edward the First had died and he had begun to realize the nature of his successor he had been certain that he was going to succeed.

There had been so much failure; the Scots could not hope to raise an army which could compare with that of Edward's in training; in equipment they were vastly inferior; yet the spirit was there. Men who were defending their homeland always had the advantage over the invader. If they had an inspired leader they could work miracles. Bruce was inspired. He had suffered many defeats but he knew he was going to win in the end. He liked to tell the tale of the spider which had somehow caught his imagination and that of his followers.

He would sit by the light of the camp fire and talk to them of the time when he had been lonely, depressed and defeated, when he had been routed and had barely managed to save his life. He would tell how he had lain in his bed and watched a spider try six times to attach its thread to a balk and each time fail. The spider went on trying until on the seventh attempt he was successful. This seemed significant to Bruce because six times he had raised armies and attempted to defeat the English and each time he had been defeated.

'Now shall this spider teach me what I am to do,' he said. 'Even as the creature failed so did I; and even as he succeeded in the end I shall also. He has taught me a lesson which I shall never forget and that is never to accept defeat. If I fail yet will I try again and go on trying until defeat turns into victory.'

It was spoken of often in his camps. They knew that their King would never harm a spider, and nor would they for it had become a superstition that ill luck would follow any who did.

It had helped him, that spider, because the legend which had grown up round it was that one day Robert the Bruce would succeed even as the spider had. He was going to turn the English out of Scotland.

This might be the time. It *must* be the time for the King himself was in Scotland with a mighty army and the battle which would inevitably follow could be a decisive one. True Great Edward was no more, but the army was there and how could the Scottish army one third the size stand up to it?

Robert the Bruce had mustered his men at Torwood close by Stirling where he reviewed his chances. With a smaller army he must rely on his own generalship, his men's determination and his knowledge of the ground on which the battle would take place. He must manoeuvre so that he should choose the spot and as he had few cavalry men and the English were well equipped in this field, he decided that the battle must be fought on foot. He himself chose the battleground. It was to be New Park between the village of St Ninian and the little stream of the Bannock which was known in the district as Bannockburn. Here by the water the land was marshy and this would provide a danger for the English horses.

He called together the principal generals of the Scottish

army. There was his brother Sir Edward Bruce, Sir James Douglas, Randolph Earl of Moray and Walter, the High Steward of Scotland.

He was very sober as he addressed them. 'We are outnumbered three to one, but do not let the men know this. I have carefully examined the ground and I want the right wing of the army to rest on the banks of the burn. There we can be sure of not being outflanked. The front of the army shall extend to St Ninian village.'

'The left will be less protected than the rest of the army,' pointed out Moray.

'You speak truth. It will be exposed to the garrison of Stirling castle. That is why I have ordered that pits be dug in that area and in these shall be placed iron spikes.'

' 'Tis a grand idea,' cried Douglas.

'And the hollows will be filled with brushwood,' went on Bruce.

'No horse will be able to pass over that ground,' commented the Steward.

'That was the intention,' smiled Bruce. 'Now, let us go forward with a quiet confidence. The odds are against us but we can succeed.'

'We must succeed,' said Randolph.

'I thank God that it is not the English King's father who comes against us,' murmured Bruce.

'Doubtless they will carry his bones before the army,' said the Steward who was not a veteran of battle as the others were.

Bruce smiled at his smooth young face.

'We learn to believe only in those omens which bring good to us,' he said.

'But if they are good or evil ...' began the young man.

'Evil ... good ... either is born in the mind. And so are victory and defeat. My friends, let us say together, "This day we shall succeed." Come, I will speak to the men. I want every man who fights under my banner this day to be there because he wishes to see Scotland free. I want no reluctant men in my army.'

He rode forward on his small grey mare, an unimpressive animal but surefooted and chosen for this reason. He was clad in armour and on his helmet he wore a circlet of gold that all might recognize him as the King, and in spite of his somewhat unkingly mount there was that about him which inspired men and never had it been more apparent than at that moment.

He spoke in clear ringing tones. The enemy was close. Many of the men here this day would remember the bloody battles between Scotland and the late King. That King was dead now and he believed they had little to fear from his son.

'If there is a man among you who is not fully resolved to win this field or die with honour, let him throw down his arms and go. I want no such man in my army. I would rather have but half the men who stand before me now and they good brave men, loyal to Scotland, than double the present numbers with traitors or reluctant men among you. Now is your chance. Speak now if you will. I offer you liberty to go or stay.'

There was a deep silence. Bruce's heart was beating uncertainly. What if there were cowardly men among them? What if they, sensing death close by—for assuredly it would come to some this day—grew faint-hearted and thought with longing of their bairns and their firesides away in some remote corner of Scotland far from St Ninian's and Bannockburn?

Not a movement in the ranks. No sound to be heard but the ripple of the burn.

Then a great shout went up. 'Victory for the Bruce and Scotland for ever.'

I have good and faithful men to serve me thought Bruce. That augurs well for Scotland.

* * *

Edward's great desire was to get the battle over. He had no doubt of the outcome. He had a fine army. If his father were looking down on him now he would be pleased with him. The Scots could not stand out against him. He had been angry because of those barons who had refused to join him but now he laughed to think how sorry they would be when he returned victorious to England.

The first thing to do was to relieve Mowbray at Stirling Castle. That would be a fine gesture. He sent for Sir Robert Clifford and ordered that he take an advance party of eight hundred cavalry and capture the castle.

Sir Robert rode off. It was certain that the Scots would be expecting this move. Stirling Castle was a strategic point and it was to relieve the governor that the English army had come to Scotland. He must therefore be wary. He knew where the enemy army was situated and instead of taking a direct route which could have resulted in his being seen, he with his men rode quietly round the village of St Ninian's taking care to keep themselves out of sight as much as possible. Thus Randolph Earl of Moray whom Bruce had commanded to be watchful of just such a move did not see what was happening and it was Robert the Bruce himself who caught sight of Sir Robert and his band making their way cautiously to the castle.

The Bruce rode hastily to Randolph and demanded to know what this meant.

'You have thought too lightly of the charge I gave you. A rose has fallen from your chaplet this day, nephew.'

Overcome with horror Randolph rode off immediately in pursuit of Clifford who hearing the approach gave the order to his men to wheel round and attack.

Randolph had only five hundred men and he was outnumbered but he formed his troops into a square with spears held before them. The English rode forward but they could not break through the Scottish spears and Clifford gave the order to surround the Scots. The English cavalry was heavily armed and the Scottish weapons were only their long spears, short knives and battle-axes. The Scots put up a magnificent fight but they were against the heavy arms of the English cavalry and surrounded as they were it seemed inevitable that they must be defeated although they might inflict heavy casualties upon their opponents.

Bruce was watching the affray from some distance, Sir James Douglas beside him.

'By God, my lord,' said Douglas, 'this will be the end of Randolph. I must go to his aid.'

'Nay,' said Bruce. 'To do so would mean a change of our plans. Randolph should have stopped them before they got so far. Let him fight his way out of this.'

'It will be death for him. They will be wiped out ... the whole force.'

While the conflict between Randolph and Clifford was in progress the English army had been brought to a halt while it was considered whether to begin battle that day or wait until the next. Both men and horses were tired from the long march and it was finally decided that the following day would be more appropriate.

Robert the Bruce was of the same mind regarding the time to begin the fight. The possible loss of Randolph had meant that he must make certain adjustments to his plans, and he was riding along the line of his army, seated not on a warhorse but on his small grey mare, carrying as his only weapon his steel battle-axe when he was seen by one of the knights who was suddenly filled with a desire to win glory for himelf. The de Bohuns belonged to one of the leading families of the nobility and their prestige had been greatly enhanced when Humphrey the fourth Earl of Hereford and third Earl of Essex had married Elizabeth, the daughter of Edward I, after she had been widowed by the Earl of Holland. It was true that the King might not have chosen this match for his daughter but Elizabeth had taken a fancy to Humphrey de Bohun and declared that as she had married once for State reasons she should be allowed the second time to marry as she wished.

Such a connection was highly desirable and Henry, Humphrey's young nephew, had the sudden wild urge to bring greater glory not only to the family but on himself and so win the admiration of his influential uncle.

There was Robert the Bruce, the King of the Scots, already a legend, and de Bohun remembered the old and honoured custom that battles could often be settled by single combat and that if the leader of an army could be thus slain the battle all but won.

What honour would befall the de Bohun family and in particular Sir Henry if he called out the mighty Bruce and slew him? And there he was seated on a small grey mare—with nothing but a battle-axe in his hand and the only reason he could be seen to be the King was due to the golden circlet he wore over his helmet.

Young Sir Henry rode forward.

Robert the Bruce was taken momentarily by surprise. He glanced at the young rider magnificently equipped on a fine warhorse, armed for battle. It was madness to answer the challenge. He was seated on his steady grey mare. She was agile and surefooted in marshy land but how could she stand up to this mighty armoured figure?

To refuse the challenge was unthinkable yet to take it

was perhaps foolhardy. But he *must* take it. He could imagine the rejoicing there would be in the English ranks if it was said that he had been afraid to ride out against the young knight.

He had to go into the attack and he had to act promptly.

He heard the gasp of those around him as he spurred the grey mare and rode out to meet de Bohun.

'Madness, madness!' murmured Douglas and he thought: Where will this day end? Randolph on the point of being taken by the English, the King accepting this unequal challenge ...

The hoofs of the warhorse pounded the earth as de Bohun, lance ready, came thundering towards Robert the Bruce.

The Scots watched with fear, the English with exultation. There was scarcely an English soldier who did not wish he was in de Bohun's shoes. His name would be remembered for ever.

Then the surprise. The lance should have pierced the Bruce's heart but it did not for with incredible agility he swerved at precisely the important moment. The lance thrust missed him and raising himself in his stirrups Bruce lifted his battle-axe and brought it down on de Bohun's head which was all but cleft in two.

The Bruce rode back to his men. They surrounded him.

'My lord, my lord, you could have been killed. This could have been the end.'

He looked rueful. 'I have broken my battle-axe,' he said. 'It was a good one.'

Inwardly he was exultant. He could imagine what effect this would have on the enemy and his own soldiers for that matter.

They would regard it as a good augury and when a small army faces a large one auguries are very welcome.

Douglas had witnessed the King's adventure and, considering it extremely rash, decided that he would himself take action. He was not going to let Randolph be entirely annihilated by Clifford's men no matter what Bruce said. If the King could act rashly on an impulse so would Douglas. The King had risked his life for a gesture. Well Douglas was going to do all in his power to see that Randolph did not lose his.

He summoned his men and rode swiftly towards the castle where the fighting between Randolph and Clifford was still

going on, but as he approached he could scarcely believe his
eyes for the ground was littered with the English dead and
he could see that Randolph was not only holding his own but
winning the day.

'Hold!' cried Douglas. 'We will not help him. To do so
would be to take from him the honour which is his.'

He was right, even as he stood there watching, the English
cavalry—or at least that which could get away—was galloping
off with some Scots in pursuit.

It was like a miracle.

Randolph had driven off the proposed attack on Stirling.

'God is smiling on us this day,' said Douglas.

*   *   *

Night fell on the camps. The English had been sobered
by the death of de Bohun and the defeat of the cavalry on
the way to the castle, but not unduly so. They outnumbered
the Scots and the spirit of Great Edward marched with them.

On that Monday, the twenty-fourth of June of the year 1314,
as dawn broke the Scottish army heard Mass performed by
Maurice Abbot of Inchaffray.

Every man was on his knees. Edward, from afar, saw this
and remarked to Robert de Umfraville, 'Do you see? They
are kneeling.'

Robert, Earl of Angus since the death of his father in 1307
and who had fought against the Scots on many occasions and
as Earl of Angus was regularly summoned to the Scottish
parliaments, knew Scotsmen well and he answered, 'Yes, my
lord, they kneel. But to God, not to us. I tell you this, my lord,
that army will either win the day or die on this battlefield.'

'We must see that they die on the battlefield then, Angus.'

'My lord,' went on Angus, who had become anglicised and
believed that the alliance of Scotland with England would be
advantageous to both countries and had therefore sworn fealty
to the English crown, 'I know the Scots. They will be great
fighters but they lack the discipline of your armies. If you
feign to retreat beyond the encampment they will rush forward to attack and fall out of order.'

'Make semblance of retreat,' cried Edward. 'Never.'

In his shining armour he felt supreme. He thought momentarily, I wish Perrot could see me now.

He was going to win. He was going to confound them all, those who had been critical of him and had sworn that he could never compare with his father.

He glowed with excitement as he sounded the call to charge.

Gloucester and Hereford prepared to advance towards the right wing of the Scots which was under Edward Bruce.

Gloucester muttered: 'I shall go ahead of you, Hereford.'

Hereford retorted, 'My lord Gloucester, that will be my place.'

'You mistake me, my lord,' cried Gloucester, 'if you think I shall follow where you lead.'

While they argued the Scots advanced and Gloucester with a small company of men rode forward. It was folly for they found themselves surrounded by Scots and without sufficient support to withstand them. Thus the wrangle had put both Gloucester and Hereford at an initial disadvantage.

The battle had begun.

The English should have had the advantage. Their cavalry were magnificent, but the Scots employed the custom of the schiltrom which was a formation like a hedge with each man holding his twelve-foot spear before him, so that even the heaviest cavalry must hesitate before throwing itself against those formidable spears.

The archers provided the worst hazard for the Scots and even the schiltrom could not withstand those showers of deadly arrows which kept falling and decimating them. The Scots however carried battle-axes beside their arrows which meant that when they had exhausted their supply of arrows they could rush forth with their axes and wreak havoc.

The hours passed and the battle raged. Bruce's spirits were high. Luck was on his side. He had chosen the right place in which to fight and he was on his home land. The English were exhausted by their journey north; they were not in their native land. There was not a Scotsman who would not have died that day for Scotland for who knew what his fate would be if he fell into the hands of the English?

The sounds of battle were deafening. The knights shouted their war cries as they plunged into the fray and spear clanged against spear in the deadly conflict; arrows flying through the air pierced the horses' flesh, driving the creatures to madness before they died, and the air was filled with the groans of wounded and dying men; banners trailed on the ground among pennants and broken spears and the grass was spattered with the blood of Scots and English. And still the battle persisted.

The Scottish army had in its wake the campfollowers—men too old for battle, women who wanted to be with their men, young children not of an age to fight but who were eager to see how the battle progressed and to be on the spot when the victory was complete, perhaps to take a share in what booty was available. In any case they would not stay in their homes while Scotland's future was being decided.

Bruce had ordered them to remain hidden by the hill and with them was the army's baggage and extra supplies of which they were in charge.

There was no doubt that the battle was going in Scotland's favour. Gloucester had been killed so had Sir Robert Clifford and Hereford had been taken prisoner.

The King's bodyguards clustered round him and the Earl of Pembroke cried: 'My lord, it is unwise for us to stay longer. We must leave the field without delay.'

'I shall not desert my army,' cried Edward fiercely.

But Pembroke took the bridle of the King's horse and went on: 'I am responsible for your safety. My lord, consider what would happen to England if you were to fall into Bruce's hands.'

'Where my army has died so shall I if need be,' replied Edward.

'Nobly said, my lord. But we must think of England without a King. Nay, if you will not come willingly then must I take you by force.'

The knights closed round the King. They agreed with Pembroke The battle was lost, that was clear. The King was in danger. His only hope of survival was in flight.

Edward was desolate. Why should ill luck so dog him? Was there nothing he could do which would succeed? If his father had been here . . .

No, no. It was no fault of his. Bruce was a genius just as Edward the First had been. None could stand against men like that. There was something superhuman about them. They could not be judged by the standards of other men and it was no use deploring the fact that one could not stand up to them.

He felt sick with disappointment.

The day had begun so gloriously. He had had everything on his side. But Bruce was his enemy and men like Bruce, Wallace, his own father Edward, were feared and respected; they had half won their battles before they had started them.

Dejected and disconsolate the King allowed himself to be taken from the field. He almost wished that he might be slain and so he might have been if Bruce had been able to give chase.

They rode to Linlithgow and finally reached Dunbar. There they found refuge for a while before they were able to take ship for Berwick.

It was a miserable homecoming for Edward. He could not stop thinking of all that had been lost—the lives of so many men, thirty thousand some declared. So much lost apart from lives, arms, horses, apparel, vessels of gold and silver, treasures .. all gone. And perhaps chief of all—honour. None would respect the King of England now. And he must return to England where it would be said: 'Ah, if it had but been his father.'

The theme of his childhood and youth. It was hard on an unworthy son to follow such a father. He must live in the shadow of greatness which made his shortcomings the more conspicuous.

In Scotland there was great rejoicing.

'For years to come,' said Robert the Bruce, 'Scotsmen will glow with pride when they talk of Bannockburn.'

THE KING IS WARNED

THE King was in despair. Nothing had gone right for him since the murder of Gaveston, he mourned. Oh, for a return of those happy days when he and his dear Perrot had sung and danced and conversed so gaily! Why could people not have let him alone? Why did they have to take Perrot from him? He often dreamed of the last ordeal of Perrot. How had he felt when they had taken him out to Blacklow Hill? A common soldier had run him through his heart; another had cut off his head; Those brave bold knights had dared not do the deed themselves. No matter. They were the guilty men. He would never never forgive them, and at their head was Lancaster.

Lancaster was his enemy, and since Bannockburn Lancaster's power had risen. It was said by some that Lancaster ruled the country now.

Lancaster was too rich, too powerful and too royal. He had too grand an opinion of himself and since he had assumed the titles of Earl of Lincoln and Salisbury (in addition to those he already possessed) he saw himself as the most important man in the country. It was amusing that his wife—through whom he had come by the titles of Lincoln and Salisbury— did not think so much of him. There were rumours that that marriage was in such a parlous state that the lady was seeking a means of escape from it. Good luck to her, thought Edward viciously.

Lancaster had refused to come to Bannockburn although he had acted within his rights by sending a token force. Would it have made any difference if he had come? Would the battle have been won instead of lost? None could truthfully say and yet that was exactly what people were saying. Unpleasant rumours were in circulation. If Lancaster had been Edward's son instead of the son of his brother ...

God in heaven! thought Edward. Lancaster wants to rule this country.

And there were many who would support him.

Bannockburn. Disaster, defeat, disgrace to the Crown and to England! Edward knew that all through his life and perhaps after people would talk of Bannockburn. Ever since King John had been involved in conflict with the barons that company of ambitious men had had grand ideas of their own importance. They would not allow a man to be a king. They wanted him as their figurehead to move this way and that as pleased them.

It was a wretched life. And no Perrot to enlighten it!

Perrot had never really had a proper burial. He would give him a grand one. He would have a tomb made for him so beautiful that it was worthy of him—one of which Perrot himself would approve. He would give himself up to grief and be thoroughly wretched and he would forget those rebellious barons gathering about him crying Bannockburn. Bannockburn ... as though it were all his fault.

How humiliating it had been to fly from the field of battle as he had been obliged to do. He would never forget it: riding fast with Pembroke beside him, making for Dunbar and pausing for a brief respite there before taking ship to Berwick. The horror of it, with the entire army in flight. Many of them were drowned trying to cross the Forth; many of them fell into the pits which Bruce's men had dug; the amount of treasure that was lost horrified him. Rarely had there been such a disaster in English history. All his father's victories had been wiped away in one great blow.

At Pontefract Lancaster had been waiting with an army —men who should have been beside their King at Bannockburn and Lancaster could not hide his satisfaction at the sight of the fugitive King.

An army! Why had he assembled an army? It was because, he had implied, he believed that if Edward had been successful in Scotland he would have turned his victorious army against Lancaster and those earls who had not been with him at the battle.

Then Edward must ride, side by side, with Lancaster to York, where a parliament had been called. Was there no end to the humiliation an unkind fate was heaping upon him?

In York he was made aware of his subjects' contempt. He wanted to shriek at them when they continually invoked his father's name. *Great* Edward, they called him as though to differentiate between him and his ineffectual son.

I will be revenged on them all one day, Edward promised himself.

He was clearly told what he must do, and it was maddening to realize that he had no alternative but to obey. He must confirm the Ordinances; he must receive back into favour those earls with whom he had recently been at cross-purposes. That meant the murderers of Perrot and most humiliating of all he was informed that his allowance would be cut to ten pounds a day.

He listened quietly but inwardly seething with rage.

Lancaster was contemplating him blandly. Edward was the King in name but Lancaster was in command now.

* * *

Lancaster faced the King. Edward was thinking: Perrot always hated you. He knew you meant me no good, my cousin though you might be. But perhaps it was because you were my cousin and so close to the throne that you always believed you would make the better king.

Lancaster was indeed thinking how feeble Edward was and he was still exulting in the defeat at Bannockburn. Surely that showed the people the kind of man they had as King. How many English were saying this day: 'If only Lancaster had been the son of Edward the First.'

It mattered little now. He was in command. Edward was aware of that for it was obvious.

'My lord,' said Lancaster, 'there will have to be some change of office. I have long felt—and others share my view—that those who hold the highest posts in the country are not always worthy of them.'

Edward wanted to scream with rage. He controlled his anger and said coldly: 'It is not an unusual state of affairs for those who would rule to dislike a king's friends.'

'Ah, if they were but your friends, my lord, none would

rejoice in them more than I. It is as you know, dear lord and cousin, my earnest wish to serve you.'

'I am glad to hear that,' answered Edward grimly.

'So, my lord, it is agreed that Walter Reynolds having bestowed on him the high office of Canterbury should relinquish the Great Seal. One cannot expect him to serve two such great offices in the manner demanded of them.'

So Walter was going now Thank God he had given him Canterbury. They could not oust him from his archbishopric.

'And on whom would *you* bestow the Great Seal cousin?' The sarcasm was lost on Lancaster. He had never been a man to look for subtleties. He had the answer promptly.

'I—and others agree that John Sandale should have the Seal. John Sandale. A good churchman and one of Lancaster's men.

What could he say? It was true Walter held both offices and many would agree that he had not the qualifications to do so. In fact, a great many thought it was unfortunate that such a worldly man should hold the office of Archbishop of Canterbury. Edward knew he dared not protest.

Lancaster triumphantly went on to mention other members of the King's household whom he thought it would be better to replace.

Inwardly Edward writhed with shame. Yet what could he do? Who was there to stand with him now? Those who had supported him at Bannockburn were no longer esteemed by the people. They shared the shame of defeat. Pembroke and Hereford had emerged from the battle it was true, but shorn of the honours they had won in the past. Gloucester who might have stood beside him was dead. He would never forgive Warwick for the part he had played in Perrot's murder and in any case Warwick's health had deteriorated so much that he was a sick man. He could not be sure of Warenne, whose loyalty fluctuated. His political life reflected his domestic affairs which were invariably in a turmoil. His marriage with Joan of Bar, the only daughter of Edward the First's daughter Eleanor and the Count of Bar, was unhappy and he was at this time living with Matilda de Nerford, the daughter of a Norfolk nobleman—a fact deplored by her family and the Church itself; and the Bishop of Chichester had threatened to excommunicate Warenne if he did not mend his ways. He was attempting to get his marriage with Joan annulled on the time-worn pleas of nearness of kin. Meanwhile he continued to live with Matilda who had already borne him several sons.

No he could hardly look for help to a man in Warenne's position. There was nothing he could do but give way.

Very well, let them do as they would. He would forget them. He would give himself up to contemplating the burial he would give to Perrot.

Dear Perrot. He had always comforted him. He was comforting him now.

* * *

Lancaster left the King and rode back to Kenilworth well pleased with life. He could see that what he had always hoped for was falling into his hands. That Edward was not worthy to be King most men knew. Strange to think he was still drooling over Gaveston. He was thinking of giving him a grand burial. Let him. It would keep him quiet while weightier matters went ahead.

King in all but name. The position could not be better. For if Edward were deposed there would still be the young Edward King of England, and who better to guide him than his royal kinsman Lancaster. Yes, let Edward concern himself with showering honours on his dear dead friend. It would keep him occupied and remind the people—if they needed to be reminded—of that liaison which had played a strong part in bringing him to his present humiliating position.

He rode into the castle. Grooms hurried forward to take his horse.

He was momentarily depressed thinking how pleasant it would have been to have found a devoted wife waiting for him, eager to hear of his triumphs.

Alice was there, as good manners demanded, to greet her lord, but her gaze was as cold as ice. It always had been for him, he remembered. Alice was beautiful, dignified as would be expected of the daughter of Henry de Lacy, Earl of Lincoln and Salisbury. Impious Gaveston had called him Burst Belly because of his girth, but that could not detract from his standing in the country as one of the first earls of the realm—rich and powerful. And Alice was his heiress. Something she never forgot.

The marriage of Lincoln and Salisbury with Lancaster,

Leicester, Ferrers and Derby should have been an ideal one—
and it was in one sense. But Alice had quickly shown that she
had little regard for him and that she knew it was the titles
of Lincoln and Salisbury which had been her great attraction. Perhaps if they had had children ... But they never had
and never would now. Alice had made it perfectly clear that
even for the sake of handing down these high-sounding titles,
she would not resume a relationship from which children
might result.

It was very unsatisfactory.

Dutifully she poured the wine for him and offered him
the goblet. He took it warily thinking of the cold glitter in
her eyes. He wondered lightly whether she would be glad
to see him dead. He doubted it. She seemed entirely indifferent to his existence.

'I have come from the King,' he said.

'And suitably subdued him?' she asked.

He looked over his shoulder nervously. Alice should remember that they must speak with caution.

She saw his concern and seemed amused. He wondered
then if she would smile in that way to see him carried off as
a traitor.

'The King is eager to win back the approval of his subjects,' he said. 'He takes Bannockburn to heart.'

'Small wonder,' she replied. 'And I'll warrant he is none
too pleased with those who did not follow him there.'

'He is grateful to be spared. He had to fly with Pembroke
and might easily have been taken by the Scots.'

'We live in stirring times,' replied Alice. 'The country will
be thankful that there are men who, having preserved their
strength during the Scottish campaign, are at hand to guide
the reins of government.'

She was smiling superciliously, hating him. And he hated
her. He thought: Would I could be rid of her? Would I could
take to wife a pleasant woman, one who would welcome me,
applaud me, take an interest in my actions, be proud that her
husband was royal and now was the most important man in
the country.

She was despising him instead, and he believed secretly
criticizing him for not being beside the King at Bannockburn.

In truth the Countess was not thinking much of her husband, nor the defeat at Bannockburn and his rise to power.

Her thoughts were all for a squire she had met when out riding. Her horse had gone lame and he had come to her assistance and taken her to his house. It was a small house by the standards to which she was accustomed, but to her it had seemed warm and comforting. He was lame that squire and walked with a limp, which oddly enough she had found attractive.

They had talked while his blacksmith had shod her horse and during that time something had passed between them.

He was quite humble really, merely a squire, but proud of his land and eager to look after it and those who served him. She found that rather charming. He laughed a great deal, was well read and witty. She enjoyed their encounter so much that she had decided it should be repeated.

That had been some time ago.

Now often she rode over to his house—grey stone with turrets covered in clinging creeper. It had become like an enchanted castle to her when she and her squire had become lovers.

Now as her husband talked of how his power over the King was increasing she wondered what he would say if he knew that his wife had taken a lover and that he was Squire Ebulo Le Strange, a very humble gentleman when compared with the mighty Earl of Lancaster.

*   *   *

How delighted Perrot would have been if he could have seen the beautiful ceremony!

Edward had ordered that his dear friend's remains should be taken from the Black Friars of Oxford, who until now had had possession of them, and brought to Langley.

It was appropriate that it should be Langley, that place where they had perhaps been happiest. There they had arranged their plays. What a clever actor Perrot had been; and an expert in showing others the way. And what fun there had been when Walter Reynolds had surprised them with boxes of clothes and articles they needed for their plays. And now Perrot was dead and Reynolds was Archbishop of Canterbury. As for Edward he was still the King but scarcely that with Lancaster standing over him and making it clear to everyone that orders were issued from him.

A pox on Lancaster! This day he could think of nothing but his grief for Perrot.

The funeral had been costly. Never mind. He would pledge everything he had for Perrot.

Walter was with him—Thank God for Walter who had ordered that four of his bishops and fourteen abbots attend the ceremony. The barons stayed away, which was significant. They no longer thought it necessary to please the King, and Lancaster might consider it an act of defiance against himself if they attended the obsequies of a man in whose murder he had been the prime instigator.

However the ceremony was an impressive one, and Gaveston was laid to rest in the Church of the Dominicans at Langley.

The King wept openly, and it was said: 'None can ever take the place in his heart which Gaveston held.'

* * *

During the next few days it seemed as though God had turned His face against the English. The weather was so bad that the crops failed which meant famine throughout the land and starvation for many. The price of wheat, beans and peas had gone up to twenty shillings a quarter, a price beyond most purses, and due to the shortage even the royal table could not always find supplies.

The country could have recovered in time from that first disastrous harvest but the following one was equally bad. Corn was so scarce that the brewers were forbidden to convert it into malt, so there was not only a shortage of food but of drink also.

All through the summer the rain fell in torrents; fields were under water, many villages were completely flooded so besides being without food many people were without homes. The crops were rotting in the fields and people were forced to kill horses and dogs for food.

Disease was rife. Many who did not die of starvation did so of mysterious ailments and there was a growing discontent throughout the land.

Moreover it was hardly to be expected that after the great victory of Bannockburn the Scots would rest on their laurels. That energetic man, Robert the Bruce, consolidated his gains and made forays over the Border coming as far south as Lancashire. The Welsh, seeing their opportunity, had risen under Llewellyn Bren. Llewellyn had six stalwart sons and these seven men had soon taken the whole of Glamorganshire.

The Marcher Barons had gathered together and driven the Welsh back and as a result Llewellyn Bren was captured and brought to the Tower. This was the one success since Bannockburn and was no credit to the King for it had been brought about by the might of the Marcher Barons chief among them the powerful Mortimers.

Edward Bruce, brother of Robert, had landed in Ireland. Edward Bruce was an ambitious man; he was a great soldier but lacked the genius of his brother, though that did not prevent his desire to share the crown of Scotland. Wisely Robert had decided that to be King of Ireland might satisfy Edward; and now that the English had been so firmly routed was the time to make a bid for that crown.

It was disconcerting to know that Edward Bruce had landed in that troublesome island and with the Earl of Moray taken possession of Carrickfergus and been crowned King of Ireland.

It seemed there was no depth to which England could not fall.

The people, weary of famine and illogically blaming their rulers for that, were beginning to be disenchanted with Lancaster who seemed incapable of helping them any more than the King had.

It was frequently said that had Great Edward been alive he would have found some way of righting their wrongs. The fact that Edward the Second looked so much like his father made them more critical.

Beset by famine, disease and the knowledge that Robert the Bruce despised them so much that he had penetrated far into the country, that the Welsh had dared raise a rebellion and that Ireland was in the hands of the Scots, they began to look round for a scapegoat.

The Queen sitting quietly at her tapestry with her women about her was not inwardly as serene as she appeared to be.

Young Edward was four years old. A sturdy child whose health gave no cause for concern, he was long-legged, flaxen-haired, full of high spirits and devoted to his mother. Isabella had made sure of that. On this child rested her hopes. She was certain that the time would come when they would stand together—perhaps against his father. She had thought that day might be soon when Lancaster had taken the King's power from him; she had admired Lancaster, but now she was not so sure. He was not an energetic man; in fact he was inclined to be lazy. What was he doing about the famine and the disastrous incursions of the Scots in Northern England and Ireland?

Lancaster was not the man she needed and it would seem that the time was not yet ripe. But she must remain watchful.

While she sat stitching one of her women said to another: 'It is such a silly story. I am sure no one believed it.'

Isabella aroused herself and wanted to know what this story was.

The woman was confused. 'I scarcely like to say, my lady. It was clearly a madman ...'

'Nevertheless I wish to hear.'

'My lady, it is so very foolish ...'

'I have said I wish to hear,' retorted the Queen coldly.

Her women were afraid of Isabella. She had never been severe with them and yet they were aware of a certain ruthlessness in her. They had often admitted to each other that they would not care to displease the Queen. And they would shiver, and then wonder why they felt this fear of her so strongly.

Now the woman said quickly: 'Just a bit of gossip, my lady. They were talking to the King ... It was nonsense.'

A faint colour showed itself under the Queen's skin; her eyes glittered and the woman hurried on: 'They said ... oh forgive me, my lady ... it must have been the words of a madman ... they said that the king was a changeling ... not the true son of Great Edward. They said that one of his nurses dropped the Prince when he was a baby. He was killed and this maid being so terrified put another baby in his place.'

The Queen burst into loud laughter in which her women joined, relieved.

'A ridiculous tale indeed! You are right to think so.' She smiled at the woman who had told the story. 'Did you ever see one who more resembled his father than the King?'

'No, my lady, never.'

'I have heard it said that he is the image of what the old King was at his age.'

'It is certainly so, my lady.'

'That nurse was very clever, was she not ... to find a baby who looked so like the King?'

They laughed and, chattering, recalled other absurd bits of gossip they had heard from time to time.

But the Queen did not treat the matter as light-heartedly as she pretended to do. It was true it was a ridiculous story, but the fact that it had been invented in the first place and been passed round was an indication of how people's minds were working.

They were growing disillusioned with the King. There must be an idea—faint as yet—to dispossess him; which was why the notion that he was a changeling would be allowed to flourish.

The people no longer admired him. They wanted a King like the first Edward, a strong ruler, victorious in battle, one at the mention of whose name the enemy quailed. Robert the Bruce had never been greatly in awe of Edward the Second. What had he said? 'I am more afraid of the spirit of Edward the First than the armies of Edward the Second. It was more difficult to get a square inch of land from the First Edward than it would be a kingdom from the Second.'

Oh yes, they were beginning to despise the King. So the changeling story was welcomed.

That night she went to Edward's chamber and talked to him of the funeral of Piers Gaveston. She wanted to hear how impressive it was and how magnificently Walter Reynolds had presided.

How she despised him as she listened! What a fool he was! At this time when the people were suffering from the disasters of the harvest how could he spend so much money on the burial of the man whom the people had hated more than any other!

Did he not see how precarious his position was? Had he forgotten what had happened to his grandfather King Henry III and his great grandfather King John?

Edward was a fool ... a weak fool.

She stroked his hair. She must have children. What would her position be without children? She had her stalwart young Edward but he was not enough. Children were so delicate—particularly it seemed were boys. Her powerful father was dead—the victim, they said, of the curse of Jacques de Molai. She could look for little help from her family. Her brother

Louis, called le Hutin because he quarrelled with everyone, was ailing. It was being said throughout France that none of the sons of Philip the Fair could prosper because of what their father had done to the Templars. Isabella shivered to contemplate what that awful scene must have been like with the Grand Master calling his curse on the royal house of France as the flames consumed him. His Queen was with child and there were fears that the curse might prevent her producing a healthy male child which was so urgently needed.

No, there was no hope of help from Louis.

Isabella must stand on her own, and now she knew that Lancaster was a weak man, she would have to look for other support if ever she was going to save herself from the humiliation the King had made her suffer.

But she would never forget.

In the meantime the more children she had the higher her hopes. Desperately she needed a son.

That was why she made herself charming to Edward, and he, obtuse as he was, believed her attitude towards him meant that she cared for him.

*   *   *

The Queen was pregnant and, though the King was pleased with this, and when the Queen rode out through London the people cheered her, their resentment against him was growing.

It was the old trouble—King against barons, and there was always the danger that this would break out into civil war. Only a strong King could keep the barons at bay and Edward was scarcely that.

What had angered him most about Lancaster's high-handed manner was the fact that he had succeeded in robbing him of his friends. The departure he most regretted was that of Hugh le Despenser. Despenser, a man of more than fifty years, had served Edward the First well and he had been ready to do the same for his son. At Edward's coronation he had carried part of the royal insignia and from that time had shown himself to be the King's man.

When the barons had stood against dear Perrot, Hugh le Despenser had been the only one of them who had given him his support. That was something Edward would always remember.

Of course a great many cruel things had been said against
him at the time. They said he was avaricious and that he
thought by currying favour of the King and his favourites he
would be well rewarded. They were strong, those barons, and
they dismissed him from the council.

But there was something very resilient about Hugh. It was
not long before he was back. The King was delighted to see
him and presented him with the castles of Marlborough and
Devizes. When Gaveston was murdered it was Hugh who was
beside the King, trying to offer that comfort which no one
could really give. Hugh understood perfectly and the King
was fond of him.

They used to talk a great deal together. Hugh hated Lancaster.

'Forgive my anger, my lord,' said Hugh, 'for I speak of your
cousin, but I would I might challenge him to combat. With
what joy would I run my sword through that arrogant body.'

'Ah, Hugh,' replied the King, 'you are a true friend to me.
And God knows, I have little left to me. When Perrot was
alive ...'

Then he would tell Hugh about the wonderful life they
had had together and the King found he could laugh again
over the wit of Piers Gaveston with someone who could understand it.

Then Bannockburn where Hugh had been with the army
in the débâcle and afterwards, when Lancaster was saying who
and who should not serve him, Hugh was one of those who
were dismissed.

'To be a King and not a King,' mourned Edward. 'I would
be happier as one of my poorest subjects.'

Hugh le Despenser had a son named Hugh like himself.
Young Hugh was a most beautiful young man—one who came
as near to Perrot in that respect as anyone could come in
the King's eyes, and young Hugh had now become his chamberlain.

Strangely enough he had been sent by Lancaster, for this
beautiful youth had allied himself, against his father, to the
barons.

It was a pleasure to talk to him, for he was amusing and gay.
He was light-hearted, cheerful and whenever he was given a
present he would be so delighted that it gave Edward great
pleasure to bestow gifts on him.

Isabella had watched the King's growing absorption in young Hugh le Despenser with increasing irritation.

It is going to be Gaveston all over again, she thought. Why was I married to a creature like this?

There were times when she had difficulty in controlling her fury. She hated Edward; yet she was tied to him. She longed for a strong and passionate man, someone who would work with her, who was ambitious and above all aware of all she had to give. Yet here she was married to one whom she considered only half a man, but he happened to be a king and as she wanted power as much as adoration and affection she had to walk very carefully. If this child she carried was a son, she would have made another step forward. She must have sons.

She saw what was happening so clearly. She understood these people around her as Edward never could.

The elder Hugh le Despenser had sent his son to the barons. The artful old schemer! She understood it might well be because he thought one of them should be in either camp. 'You, my son,' she was sure he had said, 'will go to the barons and support them, while I stand beside the King. Then whichever way the tide turns one of us will be in the safe ship. Our estates will be saved and it should not be impossible for the winner to rescue the loser.'

Sound reasoning and worthy of the wily old Despenser.

Then bumbling Lancaster had stepped in. Young Hugh was a presentable fellow, one who could well find favour with the King. Let him go into the royal household, keep his eyes open and report anything worthy of note to his masters.

He should make a good spy for the Lancastrian party.

Clever! no doubt Lancaster thought.

Old fool, thought Isabella. It can't be long before even Lancaster sees what he has done.

And to think that she had once thought of throwing in her lot with him! Oh, how clever she was to wait, to play her game cautiously!

She would have a few more children by Edward—and there must be no doubt in anyone's mind that they were royal children—and then they would see.

In the early part of August she returned to Eltham Place there to await the birth of her child and to her great joy on the fifteenth of that month a boy was born.

There was great rejoicing and the child was christened John.

He was known as John of Eltham.

*   *   *

There was another year of famine. Rain had fallen continuously throughout the summer; the fields were marshlands and the crops once more were ruined.

The people declared that it was not the French who were cursed, but the English.

'This would never have happened in Great Edward's day,' was the constant comment. *He* would never have allowed his people to suffer. He would have done something. He would never have let the Scots beat him. He had been a great King. And what had they now?

There were jokes about the King's relationship with pretty Gaveston. Did they remember all that money which was spent on making a fine tomb for him at Langley? Such extravagance while the people went hungry.

There was something wrong with England as events were proving and they must look to their King for the reason.

Then John Drydas appeared.

He was the son of a tanner from Powderham and all his life people had commented on his long legs, his flaxen hair and his likeness to the King.

People used to nod and wink and say that if Edward the First had not been a moral man, never known to stray from his marriage bed, it would have been almost a certainty that John of Powderham was the result of some rural royal frolic.

The likeness was uncanny.

John of Powderham was a dreamer. He used to fancy that he was the son of the King. When famine struck Powderham he used to sit on the green with the villagers gathered round him and tell them what he would do if he were king. He would see that the people were fed; he would have prayers said in churches, he would have prayers and offerings made to the saints that they might intercede with God to shut off the rain and bring out the sun. There was so much he would do if he were king.

''Tis a pity you'm not the King, John Drydas,' said his friends. 'You'm wasted tanning skins.'

He began to think that he was. Ever since he was a boy he had been interested in the King for the likeness had been evident from early days. Some said that one of the King's ancestors might have fathered a son on some country wench years ago and the likeness had come through in her descendants. Faithful husbands Henry the Third and Edward the First could certainly not be blamed. But the royal streak was there.

When the story of the changeling had been spread about it had been of the utmost interest to John of Powderham. He had talked of nothing else for days.

Then the idea had come to him. 'It were like a dream,' he said, 'and yet t'were not a dream. It was some fancy I had of long ago ... I were lying in a room all silks and velvets ... I remember it hazy-like ... like there be a mist between me and that day.'

His friends urged him to try and remember. And it was amazing how the visions kept coming to him.

'Of course I were a very young baby,' he told them. 'But a baby has these flashes of memory like, I do believe.'

The village was excited. It was rarely there was so much to talk about and it was a relief from the continual discussions of poverty and hardship.

Then one day as his admirers sat in a circle about him he told them that he was in truth the son of King Edward the First and therefore their King.

He was beginning to remember. One night while he was sleeping in his magnificent cradle, men came and carried him away. He was too young to know what was happening to him and his first memories after that were of the tanner's cottage. It was perfectly clear. The man who called himself Edward the Second was a changeling. It was clear enough was it not? Look what had happened when he went to Scotland. Look at the life he had led with the wicked Gaveston. Was that what could be expected from the son of Edward the First? Everything he did pointed to the fact that he was not his father's son.

He looked very like him, pointed out some.

'He is tall and fair-haired. There are many men tall and fair-haired. What of me then? Do I not look the spitting image of him?'

They had to admit this was so.

'What will 'ee do about it, John?' asked the miller.

'I reckon I ought to do some'at,' said John.

'You should go around the country, telling people you be the true King.'

'Yes, maybe that's what I should do.'

John of Powderham was a little apprehensive. It was all very well to proclaim himself the true King in his own village. Going round the country telling others was a different matter.

But his friends were determined.

They had to put a stop to the present state of affairs as soon as possible. They wanted a real King to rule them and to see John Drydas, standing his full height with his yellow hair thrown back and his long shapely legs ... Well, if that wasn't the dead image of Great King Edward they didn't know what was.

* * *

The Queen said: 'This after the changeling story is too much. Every tall fair-haired man in the country will be setting himself up as the King. You have to make an example of this one, Edward.'

Edward agreed with her. He had talked over the matter with Hugh who had actually seen the man.

'He is handsome enough,' was Hugh's comment. 'Tall and fair. And he certainly has a look of the late King and yourself. But what a difference! The poor creature has no grace, no charm. He is an uncouth yokel.'

'What do you expect him to be?' demanded Isabella tartly, 'brought up by a tanner! I doubt you, my lord, would be as charming and graceful if you had been brought up in a hovel instead of the ancestral home of the Despensers.'

Hugh tittered sycophantically. They were beginning to hate each other. In due course, thought Hugh, he would not have to placate *her*. It would be the other way round.

The Queen said: 'I do believe this man should not be treated lightly.'

Edward looked at Hugh. Oh God, prayed Isabella, let me keep my temper. This is going to be darling Perrot all over again.

Hugh was not completely sure of his position, so he said quickly: 'There is much in what you say, my lady.'

'Poor fellow,' said Edward, 'I doubt he means any harm.'

'He is only helping to make you more unpopular than you already are.'

Edward said petulantly: 'The people are so tiresome. Am I to blame for the weather?'

'They won't blame you for the weather,' said the Queen, 'but for doing nothing to combat the effects of it. They don't realize that Lancaster rules them now ... not their King.'

She was not going to argue with them. If the King liked to be lenient with this man let him. His folly was leading him to disaster fast enough.

She left the two friends together. Now they would put their pretty heads together and talk of the past. Hugh must be sick to death of hearing of the talents and virtues of Darling Perrot.

But John of Powderham was not allowed to go free. He was arrested and imprisoned. He was given a chance to bring forward proof which might substantiate his claims to be the son of the King.

Of course, the poor fellow could do nothing of the sort. But he insisted on his claim. He *knew* it had happened the way he had said. What more proof did they want than the character of the present King.

He had given his accusers the opportunity they needed.

Poor John Powderham was sentenced to that horror which had become known as the traitor's death. He was hung drawn and quartered.

An example to any of those who might have notions that Edward the Second was not the true King of England.

* * *

There were further signs of unrest.

Soon after the affair of John Drydas, a certain Robert Messager was in a tavern having drunk a little more than his wont when he remarked that it was small wonder things went wrong with the country when the manner of the King's way of living was considered.

There was quiet in the tavern while he went on to speak very frankly of the King's relations with Gaveston and now it seemed there was a new pretty boy favourite. It was a wonder the Queen—God bless her—endured the situation. Many in the tavern agreed and the more Robert de Messager drank the more frankly he discussed the King's friends.

There was bound to be someone who reported this conversation and the next night when Messager was in the tavern
there was a man there also who plied him with wine and led
the conversation to the habits of the King.

Messager, seeing himself the centre of the company and that
he had the interest of all, used what were later called 'irrever-
ent and indecent words' about the King.

As he uttered them the stranger made a sign and guards
entered the tavern.

Shortly afterwards Messager found himself a prisoner in a
dark little dungeon in the Tower. Realizing what he had done
he became quickly sober when he was seized by despair and
a realization that his own folly had brought him there.

There was a great deal of talk throughout the capital about
Robert de Messager. He was a citizen of London and London
looked after its citizens. Messager had spoken of the King in a
London tavern. He had merely said what everyone knew to
be true. Perhaps he had been indiscreet. Perhaps he owed
the King a small fine. But if he were to be condemned to the
traitor's death there would be trouble.

The Queen as usual was aware of the people's feelings.
When she rode out they cheered her wildly. It seemed that
the more they despised Edward, the more they cherished her.
They saw her as the long-suffering Princess who had tried to
be a good wife and Queen to their dissolute monarch.

'Long live Queen Isabella!'

Then she heard a voice in the crowd: 'Save Messager,
lady.'

Save Messager! She would. She would show the people of
London that she loved them as they loved her.

She looked in the direction from which the voice had come.
There was a shout again: 'Save Messager.'

She replied in a clear voice, 'I will do all I can to save him.'

More cheers. Sweetest music in her ears. One day everything
would be different.

She had some influence with Edward. He did respect her.
The fact that she never upbraided him for his life with Perrot
and Hugh won his gratitude. She had given him the children
—two boys. What could be better? They must have more, she
had said. Two were not enough. He really owed her a good
deal for being so considerate. She was prepared to receive

him that they might have children, and she loved their two boys—even as he did. There was a bond between them and he was ready to listen to her.

'You must pardon Messager,' she said.

'Do you know what he said about me?' asked Edward.

She did know. She did not add that Messager had spoken the truth.

'Nevertheless,' she said, 'I want you to pardon him. The people have asked me to intercede for him and I think it well for them to believe you have some regard for me.'

'But they know I have. Have you not borne two of my children?'

'The Londoners wish him to be pardoned and they have asked me to do what I can. They want him pardoned, Edward.'

'But to speak of his King thus ...'

'Edward, it is better for you to waive that aside. The people will gossip less if you do. It is not often I ask you for anything. But now I ask you for this man's life.'

Edward rarely felt fully at ease with his wife, and the prospect of her begging for this favour and that it should be for the life of a man appealed to his sense of the romantic.

Let the man go. Show the people that he cared not for their calumnies and make a pretty gesture to his Queen.

When Robert de Messager was released the crowds gathered to cheer him. He had struck a blow for freedom. He had come near to horrible death and thank God—and the Queen—that he had escaped.

'God save the Queen,' shouted the people of London.

She rode out among them.

'How beautiful she is!' cried the people.

'Shame on the King,' said some. 'Such a good and lovely Queen and he turns to his boys!'

And she smiled and acknowledged their loyal greetings.

They loved her. They were on her side. One day she would have need of them.

* * *

Another unfortunate incident occurred soon after that.

It was Whitsuntide and the Court was at Westminster and the celebrations took place in public according to the custom. At such times the doors of the palace were wide open and it was the people's privilege to come in if they wanted to see the royal family at table.

At such a time as this, with famine throughout the country, it was asking for trouble to allow the poor to see how well stocked the royal table was. There had, it was true, been certain shortages in the kitchens, even of the most wealthy, but to the poor the joints of beef and the golden piecrust looked very inviting.

The King and Queen sat side by side at the great table and the King was beginning to realize that if the Queen was beside him—as a queen should be—the people were more inclined to look with favour on him.

However, while they sat at table there was a commotion from without and then suddenly there appeared at the door a tall woman on a magnificent horse. The woman's face was completely covered by a mask so that it was impossible to see who she was.

She rode into the hall and brought her horse right up to the table where the King was seated. Then she handed a letter to him.

Edward was smiling, so was the Queen.

'A charming gesture from one of my loyal subjects,' said Edward. 'I wonder what the letter contains?'

He gave it to one of his squires and commanded that it be read aloud so that the whole company could hear.

He was expecting some panegyric such as monarchs were accustomed to receiving on such occasions when, to his amazement, this squire began to read out a list of complaints against the King and the manner in which the country was ruled.

'Bring back that woman,' he said, for the masked rider was already at the door.

She was captured and immediately gave the name of the knight who had paid her to deliver the letter to the King.

The knight was brought before the King who demanded to know how he dared behave in such a manner.

The knight fell on his knees. 'I wish to warn you, my lord. I am as good and loyal a subject as you ever had. But the people are murmuring against you and I believe you should know it. I meant the letter to have been read by you in private. I was ready to risk my life to tell you.'

A deep silence fell on the hall. Edward was uncertain. The Queen spoke to him softly.

'You must let him go as you did Messager. To punish him would arouse the fury of the Londoners.'

Edward saw the point. He had no wish for trouble from his capital.

'You may go,' he said to the knight. 'I like not your conduct but I know it was done out of no ill wish to me. Another time speak to me yourself. You need have no fear of that. Let the woman go too. The matter is over.'

It was the only way to deal with such a situation. But it showed the mood of the people.

BANISHMENT

LIFE was not going smoothly for the Earl of Lancaster. He was President of the Council and the people were complaining about his bad rule; he was commander against the Scots and the state of affairs at the Border went from bad to worse. Edward Bruce was reigning as King of Ireland and people were saying that he, Lancaster, who had been full of criticism for the manner in which the country had been governed under Edward, had made as much a disaster of affairs as Edward himself had.

It was time Lancaster was put out of office. This was the opinion of John Warenne, Earl of Surrey and Sussex, and he was ready to join with the King to bring about that desirable state.

Warenne was not the most reliable of allies; his loyalties wavered, not so much because he sought his own gain as that his opinions changed from time to time. He had hated Gaveston from the time the latter had humiliated him at the Wallington joust but he had disapproved of Gaveston's murder and had been of the opinion that the favourite should have been brought to trial as had been promised him.

His domestic affairs gave him great cause for concern as he hated his wife Joan of Bar and had been trying for some time unsuccessfully to divorce her. He had several children by his mistress Matilda de Nerford and being devoted to her and to them, was anxious to see her securely provided for. The King had been sympathetic to him on these matters and at this time Warenne was veering towards Edward.

It was on Warenne's advice that the King called together a council at Clarendon. Here it was decided in secrecy that an attack should be made on Lancaster, and Warenne himself would be in charge of this.

In due course Warenne with a selected band of troops marched north to Pontefract but as he approached Lancaster's country and realized the wealth and power of his opponent he suddenly took fright and made up his mind that if he attacked at that point he would most certainly encounter defeat.

He called a halt and decided to return south and think up some other plan of action.

On the way he was joined by one of his squires who had been travelling in the south-west. This man had stayed at Canford in Dorset where Lancaster had estates, and while there had been the guest of Lancaster's Countess. He had quickly realized that she was an unhappy woman.

'She confided in you?' asked Warenne in surprise.

'In a manner,' was the answer. 'Of course, my lord, it is no secret that the Countess finds little satisfaction in her marriage.'

Warenne nodded in commiseration. He of all people knew what it meant to be unhappily tied to someone from whom it was difficult to escape.

'A most charming and beautiful lady, my lord. And in despair, I think.'

'I am not surprised. Lancaster must make a sad bed-fellow.'

'So it would seem.'

'I should like to meet the lady,' said Warenne.

'There is a whisper, my lord, that the lady has found a lover.'

It was then that the notion came to Warenne.

'We will ride to Canford,' he said. 'I should like to meet the lady. I would condole with her and perhaps help her in some way.'

'She was most hospitable, my lord.'

'Would she not be to her husband's enemies?'

'Doubtless especially so to them, for if they were his enemies they might be her friends.'

Warenne laughed aloud.

'You have a point there, my friend.'

*　　*　　*

Alice de Lacy welcomed the visitors.

The Earl she told them was in Pontefract. She had heard
there had been an assembly at Clarendon which he had not
attended.

She was indeed a beautiful woman, and sprightly. Lancaster
should have counted himself lucky, since as well as all that
charm and dignity she had brought him Lincoln and Salisbury.

That she hated her husband was obvious; his name only
had to be mentioned and there would be a flash of contempt
in her eyes.

Warenne's sympathies were touched. These arranged marriages could ruin one's life. How different it would be if he
had never been married to Joan and if he and Matilda had
met before he had been forced into marriage. Then he would
have stood against all coercion. It would have been so simple.
All this fuss with all the frustrations could have been avoided.
The children would have been secure ... Life would have
been so much more smooth and easy. Yes, he had great
sympathy with Lancaster's wife.

'The Earl is rarely under your roof, my lady, I believe,' he
said.

' 'Tis so and thankful I am for it,' she replied.

He did not press the matter then, but as the evening wore
on and the minstrels sang songs of hopeless love, he talked
of his own predicament.

'Married when one is too young to protest and then to find
oneself unable to escape. My dear lady, I have been unhappily
married for years. I get no help from Rome. I have had some
good fortune though. I have a lady who is devoted to me, who
has given me the only home I have ever really cared about.
There, does that shock you.'

'Indeed, it does not. I rejoice for you, my lord. You have
been bold and your boldness is rewarded. Have you any children?'

'Yes, Matilda and I have a fine family. Would my son could
inherit my title and lands. Our laws can be ridiculous at
times. Would you not think that if two people were un-
suited it should be the easiest thing in the world to untie the
knot?'

'Alas, my lord,' sighed the lady, 'you are not the only one
who is in this position. I can think of one who is far less hap-

pily placed than yourself. What think you it is like to be married to Lancaster?'

Warenne nodded gloomily as though there was no need for words.

'I had no wish for the match,' she went on. 'It was made for me. My father thought it good for me to be allied with Lancaster and Lancaster had his eyes on Salisbury and Lincoln.'

'They greatly enriched him.'

'They did not make him more acceptable to me. I would I could be free of him. You at least, my lord, are not forced to live with a partner whom you dislike.'

'No, I left my wife. I went to Matilda and we share a home. I found someone whom I could love and cherish.'

'And I ...' said the Countess and stopped short.

Warenne allowed a short time to pass in silence.

'I talk too freely,' said the Countess.

'My lady, you may talk to me as you will and I promise what you say will go no farther than these four walls.'

'It is a great relief to talk ... and to one who has suffered similarly.'

She told him how she had been riding one day and had met a man who had helped her with her horse which was in difficulties. They had met again.

'Charming,' murmured Warenne.

'We are in love,' she said, 'but what hope is there for us? What chance have we of happiness?'

'That is how Matilda and I used to talk and then we learned that opportunities have to be seized, that if one is bold enough, fearless enough, most things are possible.'

'You left your wife and set up house with your Matilda. It was easy for you.'

'My dear Countess,' replied Warenne, 'would you have the courage to do what I did?'

She was looking at him with shining eyes.

'I am a woman,' she answered. 'It is not so easy.'

'True, but still not impossible. Matilda did it.'

'You mean I could, if I were brave enough, leave this place ... leave Lancaster and set up house with Ebulo le Strange.'

'You could. Who is this man? I know him not.'

'You would not. He is merely a country squire.' Her voice softened when she spoke of him. 'Oh, how I long to share his house, to live quietly ... to live in harmony, to have child-ren ...'

'Then go to him.'

'My lord of Surrey, can you really *mean* that!'

'Yes,' cried Warenne, 'go to him.'

'How could I? Could I take my servants with me ... *his* servants? Would they come ... ? How could I trust them?'

'Go without servants.'

'What would Lancaster do to him? Lancaster is the most powerful man in the country.'

'His power is waning. He is a fool. He had everything—all the power a man could have but he has not been clever enough to use it. Now he is fast losing it. If you want to leave Lan-caster now is the time.'

'I would do it, but I fear for Ebulo. He would trump up some charge against him. Ebulo is nothing but a humble squire. Lancaster's power may be waning but he is the King's cousin still.'

'If you were given shelter in one of my castles, somewhere where Ebulo could visit you in secret, none need know that he was involved.'

'My lord, you think of the most outrageous acts.'

Warenne's eyes were sparkling. All the mischief of his nature was uppermost. He liked the Countess. He liked attrac-tive women. She was charming and when she talked of her lover she was quite beautiful. He liked to help lovers particu-larly those for whom life was not running smoothly. And what a truly marvellous way of attacking Lancaster. It was so much better than marching on Pontefract and engaging in battle.

'It is necessary to be outrageous to win happiness,' he said.

'Then ... what, my lord?'

'You and I will leave here tomorrow. We will go off as though to the hunt. Take with you what jewels you can carry. Have you a few trusted attendants, those who will serve you with their lives? Let them pack other valuables and be ready to follow you with a saddle horse.'

'Are you truly serious?'

'If you are, my lady. Let us plan this with care and who knows perhaps tomorrow you will have left Lancaster for ever.'

Alice de Lacy clasped her hands and said: 'I believe Pro-vidence sent you to Canford, my lord Surrey. For it is true that I could not have endured this state of affairs much longer.'

'Then ... tomorrow, dear Countess, we cut the knot. We shall escape together and ere long you will be making arrangement for your lover to be with you.'

'What can I say to you?' she asked. 'How thank you?' Then a shrewd look came into her eyes. 'You have your reasons. Perhaps you dislike Lancaster as much as I do.'

'I dislike him, my lady, as much as I love to help a lady in distress.'

It was a good enough answer.

It had to come, she told herself. And now is the time.

* * *

By this time the Queen was pregnant again. Her plan was working well. She had young Edward, now aged six years old and sturdy; there was John aged two and now another child coming. John was not quite as healthy as his elder brother but perhaps he only seemed a little delicate because Edward was so lusty; however, his health gave no real cause for concern. She was gathering together her little family.

It was irksome that there should be so much delay, but inevitable. Each day she despised Edward more but she could remind herself that in time she would be free of him. There would come a day when they would part, when she would make him pay for all the humiliations he had heaped on her; and that day would be worth waiting for.

She cherished news from France because her hopes were fixed on her native land. Louis le Hutin was dead. His Queen had borne a son shortly after his death, a boy, Jean, but he had died within seven days. Poor little King of France who never knew that he had inherited a crown! Her brother Philip was now King. He was called The Tall because of his unusual height. People said that the curse of the Templars was working in the royal family of France. It had killed first her father a few months after it had been uttered and now her brother Louis and his infant son. She knew that the people were asking themselves what other disasters were awaiting the family of the man who had destroyed the Knights Templars. Isabella had no great hopes of her brothers. They were weak. It would have been different if her father had lived.

Still, she would wait and when the opportunity came she would be ready to seize it.

A great deal was happening in the country. Everyone was talking now of the abduction of the Countess of Lancaster by John le Warenne Earl of Surrey and Sussex.

What an extraordinary affair that was. Of course she had long known that Alice de Lacy disliked her husband and had refused to live with him as his wife. Poor Lancaster! Why had she ever admired him? She might at one time have been tempted to take him as a lover; that would have been if she had not been determined that no one should cast suspicion at her until she was in a strong enough position to withstand such an attack; and she was determined that no one should dare whisper that her children might not have been sired by the King.

Warenne was the devoted husband in all but name to Matilda of Nerford, so it was strange that he should have eloped with Alice de Lacy. It was understandable that Lancaster should have been furious, and had given vent to his anger by attacking Warenne's lands in the north. A private war was going on between them and being conducted with all the methods of a civil war. She had told Edward that he should stop it. It was not good for battles to be fought in his country by his barons—one against the other.

It was better, said Edward, that they should fight each other than fight against him.

He was right in this but it was demeaning for him to have to stand aside and watch these two men fighting their own war. He might have called a halt as far as Warenne was concerned but Lancaster was too strong for him. And for Warenne too it seemed, for already Lancaster had captured the castles of Sandal and Conisborough and the only way in which Warenne could save Grantham and Stamford was by handing them over to the King.

In vain had Edward ordered hostilities to stop. Warenne had pleaded that it was impossible for him to desist while Lancaster attacked him and Lancaster, of course, was a law unto himself.

And the Countess? wondered Isabella. What of her? It was a mysterious affair, for she could not believe that Warenne and Alice de Lacey were lovers. There was more in this little adventure than there appeared to be.

Perhaps in due course she would discover, but her own affairs were of far greater consequence. And the biggest irrita-

tion of her life was the young Despenser. She could see what
was happening there. The handsome young man was creeping
into that place which had been occupied by the detestable
Gaveston; and, like Gaveston, young Hugh knew that she
hated him, as indeed it was natural that she should. Gradually
he would work against her. She must beware of that.

In the meantime there was the child.

She was at Woodstock in Oxfordshire for the birth. She had
always loved Woodstock, a place which took its name from the
magnificent forests which surrounded it. Vudestoc was the old
Saxon name meaning a wooden spot. Ethelred had held his
Wittenagemot there, but it was chiefly noted for being the
place where Henry the Second, Edward's great great grandfather, had kept his mistress, The Fair Rosamund, and where
this little intrigue had been discovered by Henry's vindictive
queen, Eleanor of Aquitaine.

There was a woman Isabella admired. She had taken strong
action against her erring husband. True it had resulted in her
imprisonment but she had had sons to stand by her.

Yes, she was glad that she had come to Woodstock to bear her
child.

It was an easy birth and this time a girl.

'I will call her Eleanor,' she said, 'after her great ancestress.'

*   *   *

It seemed as though that period of ill luck was passing. The
summers had returned to normal, the harvest had improved;
and there was good news from Ireland where Edward Bruce
had set himself up as King. Edward Bruce, great soldier that
he was, lacked the genius of his brother Robert; it was said
that his pride was immense and that he yearned to stand
above all others. The English colonists in Ireland had been
fighting against him ever since he landed but he had usually
come through victorious, for when he had been in difficulties
his brother Robert had joined him with reinforcements and
all went well while the two were together. But Robert could
not leave his newly acquired kingdom for long and there was
constant trouble on the Border, so Edward Bruce was left
to command alone.

There came the battle of Leinster. Edward Bruce's advisers
warned him that his enemies were a strong force and that he

should wait for reinforcements before going into attack, but he replied scornfully that one Scot was as good as five English and he cared not for the disparity in numbers. He was proved to be wrong, fatally for him. He was slain at Dundalk and his army routed. His head was sent to King Edward and his quarters set up in four towns so that all might know that the erstwhile King of Ireland was no more.

The Scots no longer held Ireland.

Edward was euphoric. 'All comes well in the end,' he said.

He had ceased to mourn so sadly for Gaveston now that there was Hugh le Despenser to comfort him.

Lancaster was once more in the ascendancy. He had been victorious over Warenne though he made no attempt to insist on his wife's return and she remained living in comparative obscurity although all knew that she was under Warenne's protection.

Warenne had been forced to surrender his estate in Norfolk and his possessions were considerably reduced by the action he had taken. Eyebrows were lifted when it was known that Alice de Lacey had granted Warenne tenancy of several of the manors she had inherited from her father.

It was a mysterious affair, and the fact was that although Lancaster had come out of it ostensibly the victor his enemies mocked him behind his back and the fact that he could not manage his domestic affairs better caused them to ask each other how he could hope to deal with the country's.

Outwardly though he was still the strong man, the King in all but name.

The Despensers—the two Hughs, father and son—were taking possession of the King. There seemed to be no limit to their avarice; the more that was bestowed on them, the more they wanted, and resentment was rising against them.

A dispute was now in progress, because since the death of the Earl of Gloucester at Bannockburn his estates passed to his family and they were to be divided between Gloucester's three sisters, one of whom had been married at an early age to young Hugh le Despenser. The other two husbands were Hugh d'Audley and Roger d'Amory, and these two complained that Hugh le Despenser had not only claimed almost the whole of Glamorgan as his share but, because he was married to the eldest sister, had taken on the title of Earl of Gloucester.

It was an uneasy situation. Isabella watched it with calculating eyes. She was aware that the Despensers were creeping farther and farther into the King's favour and the measure
of their success was reflected in their attitude towards her. She
was not entirely sure but she believed she detected a veiled
insolence.

Trouble in the north broke out and this meant that all
attention was focussed on the Border. Edward marched north
with Lancaster to besiege Berwick. Isabella and her ladies
were left behind in Brotherton, a village near York. She was
growing impatient. She was advancing well into her twenties;
she had three children, born as she often thought, in humiliation. She, reckoned to be the most beautiful princess in
Europe at one time, and none could deny she was still a handsome woman, was a notoriously neglected wife. She would
never never forgive Edward for the humiliation he had made
her suffer. The people of England loved her—but it was partly
because they were sorry for her. Well, one day she was going
to make use of that sympathy. She was going to show Edward
that she had always despised him, and that she had borne her
children out of expediency. Her nature had revolted. She
could not deeply love those children, because they were
Edward's too and conceived in necessity. But she was devoted
to her first-born, which might have been due to the fact that
all her hopes rested on him. She visualized the day when he
might stand with her against his father. During her stay in
Woodstock she had thought of herself as resembling Eleanor of
Aquitaine whose sons had stood with her against their father.

There was a commotion below. Men were riding into the
courtyard. Starting to her feet she went down to see what was
happening and was startled to find men she recognized as the
servants of the Archbishop of York.

'Something has happened,' she cried.

'My lady,' said the spokesman of the men who she saw were
troops, 'the Archbishop has sent us with all speed. He begs
you to prepare to leave without delay. The Black Douglas
is at hand with ten thousand of his men and it seems that his
plan is to take you hostage.'

Hostage to Black Douglas! A great soldier and patriot with
a complexion so dark that it had earned him his name. Her
eyes sparkled at the thought of adventure. At least she thought
Black Douglas was a man.

'Is this indeed so,' she said. 'And how has this come to your knowledge?'

'My lady, if you will prepare to leave at once you shall hear all when you are safe.'

She hesitated.

'There is a force of loyal troops surrounding the castle,' said the spokesman. 'You must leave at once or you will be in acute danger. The Scots are uncouth. They might not know how to treat a Queen.'

In less than an hour she was riding away from the castle in the company of the Archbishop's men.

It was then that she heard what had happened. One of the Scottish scouts had been discovered in the town and because of his strange accent suspected. He was taken to the Archbishop and asked to explain his business. This he could not do to the Archbishop's satisfaction and finally on being threatened with torture he had admitted that Black Douglas was marching on York, his plan being to abduct the Queen and hold her prisoner.

When she arrived in York she was greeted by the Archbishop who was delighted to have saved her but at the same time he believed that it would be dangerous for her to stay and that she should leave at once for Nottingham.

* * *

The King had expressed little concern for Isabella. She was aware of this and hated him for it. She remembered how distraught he had been when Gaveston had been threatened and how he had once left her behind at Scarborough in his need to escape with his beloved friend. If Hugh le Despenser had been threatened he would have been in a state of panic.

Oh yes, indeed, it was unforgivable.

Edward could not continue the Scottish war. The Scots could not be driven out of Yorkshire. They had a grand leader in Bruce and what the English lacked was just such leadership. Edward was weak; Lancaster was little better. It was a sorry time for England.

Edward had been forced to suggest a two-year truce with Scotland, and rather to his surprise Bruce had agreed. He did not know then that Bruce was becoming alarmed by the state of his health. Years before he had been in contact with lepers and the dreadful disease had begun to show itself. It was alarming and he needed rest from the rigours of a soldier's life and for this reason he was ready enough to agree.

Edward was jubilant. He was the sort of man who could live happily in the moment and shut his eyes to the disasters threatening the future which to the discerning eye would appear to be inevitable. He was behaving as foolishly over Hugh le Despenser as he had over Gaveston and the lesson of that earlier relationship appeared to have made no impression on him. The Despensers were as greedy as Gaveston had been, as power-hungry and because of this growing as unpopular with the people.

He will never learn, thought Isabella.

She was pleased that Edward was to go to France to pay homage to the King—Isabella's brother Philip V—for Ponthieu. It would give her an opportunity of sounding Philip and trying to discover how much help she could get from him if she should need it. She wondered whether it might be possible one day to place herself at the head of those barons who had had enough of the King and the Despensers. She had often thought of it when Gaveston had been alive, but it had not been possible then. At that time she had not been the mother of two fine boys. Young Edward was growing up long-legged and flaxen-haired like his father and his grandfather; he was also showing a certain seriousness which seemed to please everyone.

She had heard it said: 'That one is going to be Great Edward over again.'

That was what she liked to hear.

Now there was the journey to Amiens. She liked to travel and in her own country she was always greeted with loyal affection. She noticed that the people were less effusive towards Edward. It was natural. News of his neglect of her would have reached the country and the people were offended on her account.

It was pleasant to be at the French Court again. She found it more graceful than that of England. The clothes of the women were more elegant. She was ashamed of her own and determined to have some gowns made to wear in France and take back with her.

Edward did the necessary homage and she had an opportunity of talking alone to her brother.

Poor Philip! He looked far from well. His skin was yellowish and he had aged beyond his years. He had only been on the throne for four years and it seemed as though he were going the same way as Le Hutin.

'You are much thinner, Philip,' she told him anxiously. 'Have you consulted your doctors?'

Philip shrugged his shoulders. 'They are determined I am to die shortly. The curse, sister.'

'I should snap your fingers at them and tell them you refuse to die at the command of Jacques de Molai.'

'Do not mention that name,' said Philip quickly. 'No one does. It is unlucky.'

Isabella shook her head. If she had been in her brother's place she would have shouted that name from the turrets. She would have called defiance on the Grand Master. She would have let the people of France see that she could curse louder than the dead Templars.

But she was not subject to the curse.

'Charles is waiting to step into my shoes,' said Philip.

'That will be years hence and perhaps never.'

Philip shook his head. 'I think not. And then ... his turn will come. Tell me of England, sister.'

'Need you ask? You know the kind of man I married.'

'He still ignores you and prefers the couch of his chamberlain to yours?'

'I would my father had married me to a man.'

'He married you to England, sister. You are a Queen, remember.'

'A Queen ... who is of no importance! I hate these Despensers.'

'The two of them?'

'Father and son. He dotes on them both but it is of course the pretty young man who is his pet.'

'Well, sister, you have a fine boy.'

She nodded and whispered: 'Yes, brother. I rejoice. Two boys and young Edward growing more like his grandfather every day. People comment on this.'

'What England needs now is another First Edward.'

'What England does not need is the Second Edward.'

'But that is what it has, Isabella.'

'Perhaps not always. Perhaps not for much longer.'

He was startled. 'What mean you?'

'There is whispering against him. The barons hate the Despensers as much as I do. If it should come to ... conflict ...'

She saw her brother's face harden and she thought: How wrong I was to expect help from him. All he is concerned with is his miserable curse.

'It would be wise for you to continue to please him.'

'Continue! I never began to.'

'Oh come, sister, you have three children by him.'

'Begotten in shame.'

'You should not talk so. They are his and yours.'

'They are indeed. But what I have to endure ...'

'Princes and princesses must always accept their fates, sister.'

What was the use of trying to get help from Philip?

But there was one other who was brought to her notice during that visit to France. This was Adam of Orleton, Bishop of Hereford, who conveyed to her that he had great admiration for her fortitude regarding her relationship with the King.

It was not long before they were finding opportunities of talking together.

He deplored the state of the country and the troubles between the barons. He hinted that he thought the Despensers were responsible for a great deal of the people's growing dissatisfaction.

'My lady,' he said, 'it is the affair of Piers Gaveston over again.'

How she agreed with him! How she longed to talk of her ambitions, but she was too wily for that.

So she let him talk.

He told her that there were growing suspicions of Lancaster.

'I have heard it whispered, my lady, that he has been in communication with Robert the Bruce who has paid him bribes to work with him against the King.'

'I cannot believe it. Lancaster would never work against England, and Robert the Bruce is hard put to it to pay his soldiers. How could he afford bribes?'

'It is something which is being said,' the Bishop replied. 'It may be that Lancaster thinks he knows the way to bring about peace with Scotland better than the King. It is a fact that when the Scots make raids into England they never touch Lancaster's land.'

'I must look into this,' said the Queen. 'Have you told the King?'

'My lady, I thought it wiser to tell you.'

She was exultant. What did that mean? Could it really be that men were beginning to turn away from the King and look to her?

She felt the trip to Amiens had been successful even though she realized that she would get little help from the King of France.

*   *   *

The Despensers must have been aware of the resentment against them, but so blind were they to anything but their personal gain and their certainty that they had the King in leading strings that they ignored the warnings.

It was the trouble over the Gloucester inheritance which brought matters to a head. The three brothers-in-law were still squabbling over their shares when Young Hugh in a rage seized Newport which belonged to Hugh of Audley.

Audley complained to Lancaster who, believing that his prestige had been restored since the affair with Warenne whom he had beaten so unreservedly, called the barons together.

'We must rid ourselves of these Despensers,' he announced.

'The King will never hear of it,' was the answer.

'The King would not hear of Gaveston's banishment, yet he was banished,' retorted Lancaster. 'Aye, and lost his head too, and although many liked to pretend they had no hand in that affair, I was never afraid to admit that I was there and I believe—and so do other right thinking men—that one of the best deeds any Englishman ever did was to rid the country of that parasite.'

This was the old Lancaster. Many of the barons were now turning to him once more for leadership, and it was certainly not difficult to rouse them against the Despensers. Even Warenne was on Lancaster's side in this, so were Hereford and Arundel; and the fiery Marcher barons hated the Despensers too as they had taken land near the Marcher country.

The foremost of the Marcher barons were the Mortimers. They were kings in their territory and had been for centuries. The Conqueror had used them to keep peace on the Welsh border and their power had grown even greater since the subordination of the Welsh. The leaders of the Mortimer clan were the two Rogers—the elder, the Lord of Chirk, had taken an active part in the battles of Edward the First, but he had always been a man of strong will and had fallen out of favour with the King for leaving the army in Scotland without permission. At that time his lands and chattels had been confiscated but after the first Edward's death Edward the Second had restored his possessions and given him greater power. It suited Edward's indolent nature to set up a man like Mortimer and give him authority over many Welsh castles making him like a king in his county.

His nephew, that other Roger de Mortimer, Baron of Wigmore, joined him and they had been working closely together for some years. Roger de Mortimer the younger was a man of overpowering personality. He was tall and extremely handsome in a dark bold way. He had become Earl of Wigmore when his father had died. Roger was then in his very early teens and since he had been under age Edward the First had put him under the wardship of Gaveston for at this time Edward had not realized what an evil influence Gaveston was having on his son. Roger had been noticed for his outstanding good looks when he was created a knight at the same time as the Prince of Wales and at the coronation of young Edward he had been a bearer of the robes. Along with his earldom he had inherited important estates and a marriage was very soon arranged for him which would enhance his possessions still further. Joan de Genville was connected with the Lusignans and therefore had associations with the royal family and among other advantages she brought to Mortimer the town of Ludlow and estates in Ireland.

In that troubled country he had achieved great success, for his experiences with the Welsh had taught him how to deal with the Irish.

It had come to Roger de Mortimer's ears that the young Hugh le Despenser had been warning the King that it was time he curbed the power of the Mortimers, who, in the Despensers' opinion, were becoming too powerful in the Marcher country and regarded themselves as rulers there in subservience to none. Thus when it was known that Lancaster was rousing the barons against the Despensers the Mortimers were ready with their support.

Being somewhat wild and lawless men they could not wait for conferences. They went into the attack at once, and as the young Despenser had taken lands bordering on the Marcher country which he swore belonged to him because they were part of the Gloucester inheritance, they ravaged those lands, seized the castle, made off with valuables and cattle and declared open war.

The young chamberlain came to the King in despair.

'See what these Mortimers have done,' he cried. 'Oh, it was a mistake to allow them so much power.'

'My dear Hugh,' cried the King, 'we will punish them, I promise you. Everything shall be restored.'

'But how?' cried Hugh.

'My dear, I promise you something shall be done. I shall issue a writ forbidding anyone to attack you and your father. I shall threaten them with death. It is treason. Yes, Hugh, there shall be a writ and all that the Mortimers have taken shall be restored to you.'

But neither the King nor Hugh had realized how strong was the opposition. Under Lancaster the barons stood together insisting that Edward call a Parliament to discuss the matter of the Despensers and when it was assembled the barons were present in large numbers all wearing white badges on their arms to indicate to the King that they were unanimous in their decision to get rid of the Despensers.

It was Lancaster who led the attack. The Despensers had appropriated funds from the royal exchequer, he said. He had proof of this. They had become richer than their deserts warranted. They must be banished from the land and their ill-gotten gains taken from them.

The King's furious despair was of no avail.

Hugh the elder saw that the country was on the verge of civil war. The King would find that there was scarcely a nobleman ready to support him. He would be defeated and deposed. His son was nine years old; the Queen would not stand with the King and she had friends in France; they could set up a regency under Lancaster. Because of this state of affairs the elder Despenser decided that they should go quietly.

The Despensers left Court and the trouble subsided.

Edward wept. It was the Gaveston problem all over again.

The Queen was amused. Everything was working her way. She was pregnant once more and at the time of the banishment her time was very near. She had decided to go to the Tower this time for her confinement. There she would brood on the future. She had two boys and her daughter Eleanor. They were all in good health. If her fourth child was a girl perhaps her plans would be delayed. But she had two boys already. No, after this fourth child there should be no more. She had done with humiliation, with standing aside for Edward's favourites.

She had borne enough. It was her turn now.

*   *   *

As she lay awaiting the birth of her child she wondered why she had chosen such a gloomy place. Although it was the month of June there was a chill in the stone walls and she had noticed that much of the place was in need of repair.

The roof was not watertight and when it rained her bed-clothes were wet. The whole place had been neglected, and she knew who was to blame for that. The Despensers had used money for their own needs which should have been spent in repairs. It was a well known trick, and it was one of the reasons why people considered it a boon to get the custody of such places.

Oh the cursed Despensers! First Gaveston and now them. And if some evil fate overtook young Hugh le Despenser what then? Some new young man would appear in due course.

What a man to have married her to! And what a joke that she had managed to get four children by him. Something of an achievement.

But no more. This is the end, she promised herself. Now she would start to work towards that goal which had been in her mind for some time now.

The birth was not difficult. She bore children easily; and this was another girl.

She decided to call her Joanna and she became known as Joanna of the Tower.

Edward came to see the baby.

'Another girl,' said Isabella, watching him closely. He was good-looking still. She felt angry when she regarded him because in the beginning if he had been prepared to be a good husband to her she would have loved him and worked with him. Then there would not have been this perpetual trouble which time and time again grew out of his infatuations—first Piers Gaveston and now Hugh le Despenser. If only he would be more reasonable with them; if only he did not have to make the relationship so blatant, it would have been so much easier. As it was it gave rise to utterances such as those which had almost cost the man Messager his life, and incidents like that of poor Drydas which had brought him to hideous death. If only he could have been discreet; if only he did not have to have them with him all the time, to pamper them, to bestow costly gifts on them. Oh Edward, you fool. I wonder what will be the end of you. Our son Edward is growing up. Nine years old, a reasonable age and showing every sign of being like his grandfather. That is what the people say when he rides out. He is a growing danger to you, you foolish Edward.

Edward was laughing to himself as though enjoying some private joke. He had scarcely looked at the baby. She waited for him to tell her.

'It's Hugh,' he said.

Her expression was cold, but he did not notice.

'Did you know he is on an island in the Bristol Channel?'

'I did not, and should he be?' she answered. 'Wasn't he banished from the country?'

'He has turned pirate.' Edward was laughing so much he could scarcely go on. 'He has an armed vessel and has captured two merchant ships. They were coming up to Bristol full of rich cargo. He has taken their cargo and sent them on empty.'

'Does he know the penalty for piracy?' asked Isabella.

'Oh, Isabella, come now. It was only meant to be a joke.'

'Do the captain of the ship and the owner of the vessel think that?'

'They will be made to understand. But is it not just like Hugh?'

'Exactly,' she retorted with asperity. 'The role of pirate should suit him well.'

'It will not be long before he is back,' mused Edward. 'And I shall not rest happy until he is.'

The Queen regarded him cynically. You fool, she thought. You are signing your own death warrant.

MORTIMER

THE AFFAIR AT LEEDS CASTLE

IN gratitude for another birth and quick recovery, the Queen must go to the shrine of St Thomas in Canterbury to give thanks.

She set out from the Tower and what a joy it was to ride through London where the people cheered her so loyally! She was their beautiful Queen who had remained faithful to the King and bore him children even though he behaved so badly with those leech-like friends of his.

'God save the Queen!' they cried, and she was amused to think that if the King had been with her she would still have been the one they cheered.

It was a long way to Canterbury and her marshal suggested that it would be a good idea to break the journey at her Castle of Leeds and he would send a messenger on to warn the custodian, Lord Badlesmere, of their approach.

The messenger arrived at Leeds but unfortunately Lord Badlesmere was away and Lady Badlesmere was in charge.

The Badlesmeres were firm adherents of Lancaster's cause and stood firmly against the King. They had been incensed by Edward's attitude towards the Despensers, and Lady Badlesmere who was a very forthright woman had been heard to declare that royalty was only to be respected when it was worthy of respect.

Lord Badlesmere had given instructions that none—no matter who—should be allowed into the castle unless they carried an order from him or from the Earl of Lancaster. And when she heard from the Queen's messenger that the visitor was to be Queen Isabella, she decided that she was not going to swerve from the orders she had received even for her.

'Begone!' she cried to the messenger. 'I will admit none to the castle unless he bears an order from my lord or the Earl of Lancaster.'

'My lady,' replied the messenger, 'do you understand that this is the Queen of England?'

'How can I be sure of that? How do I know that you may not be an enemy in disguise?'

'You will see for yourself when the Queen arrives.'

'My good man, go back to your mistress. Tell her that I shall admit no one—*no one*, do you understand—unless they come from my husband or the Earl of Lancaster.'

The perplexed messenger was wondering how he could go back and tell the Queen that she was denied access to her own castle when he heard the sounds of approach. The Queen's party had arrived at the castle walls.

'The Queen is here,' said the messenger. 'My lady Badlesmere, have you considered that this castle belongs to the Queen and your husband is merely the custodian?'

'I repeat my orders and these I intend to carry out,' insisted Lady Badlesmere. 'If this is indeed the Queen, she must needs find lodging in some other place.'

The Queen hearing the dispute was astounded and commanded her guards to approach the drawbridge, but Lady Badlesmere gave an order to her archers and from the castle walls came a stream of arrows which struck six of the Queen's company, killing them.

Before the furious Isabella could advance one of her bodyguard seized the bridle of her horse and forced her to retreat.

'We must escape from this mad woman, my lady,' he said and galloped off with her.

The Queen was shaking with anger. How dared a subject behave thus to her! She knew Lady Badlesmere of old. A woman who thought she was always right and knew how to manage other people's affairs. 'By God,' she cried, 'she shall be taught a lesson for this.'

The Queen's party minus the six dead, rode away to spend the night with more hospitable hosts. Lady Badlesmere was, in truth, a little disturbed when she found the six dead at her gates. She had them removed and immediately sent a messenger to the Earl of Lancaster.

She knew that there would be trouble. The Queen had been grossly insulted and six of her servants had been killed. Perhaps, thought Lady Badlesmere, she had been a little rash. She believed though that Lancaster would be delighted with this insult to the royal family. After all, she had been acting on his orders and it was yet another proof that he was more important than the King.

She waited a long time for a reply from Lancaster and finally she sent another messenger. This time the answer came back. It had been folly to deny the Queen admittance to her own castle. The Queen was seething with rage and unlikely to allow the matter to pass. Lancaster dissociated himself from the affair. The Badlesmeres alone would have to face the storm they had stirred up. He, Lancaster, had had no hand in it and he did not intend to become involved now.

*   *   *

Even Edward was roused from the lethargy into which he had fallen on the banishment of the Despensers.

Isabella raged at him. 'It must not be allowed to pass. What would the people think of a King who did not avenge such an insult to his wife?'

Yes, he agreed, something must be done. Lancaster had declared he was not involved so it should not be a difficult matter to take Leeds and let Isabella have her revenge on the Badlesmeres.

When the people of London heard of the insult to the Queen they were enraged. They marched through the streets demanding she be avenged. Many of them were strong able-bodied men and had taken part in battles when the need had arisen. They were ready to do so again for their darling Isabella.

Edward caught their enthusiasm and within a short time he was marching at the head of a sizeable army to Leeds. It was exhilarating to find that his men were with him. They could not wait for the battle. They were determined to take Leeds and then let those who had dared behave so callously to their beloved Isabella begin to say their prayers.

Leeds Castle had been built on two islands in a lake of about fifteen acres in size. The islands were connected by a double drawbridge but the two separate buildings were capable of making a separate defence. The water passed between the buildings in three places, which was of great use to the defenders.

Nevertheless Edward had brought up a formidable army and they made a fierce attack. Within a few days Lady Badlesmere was forced to surrender. Her husband had given her his support in what she had done but he had not returned to the castle to help her withstand the siege.

The army stormed in, at its head Edward the King.

Lady Badlesmere was brought before him. She faced him boldly, and showed no sign of fear.

'What made you treat the Queen in this way?' he asked.

She answered: 'I was custodian of the castle in my husband's absence. It was my right to say who and who should not enter.'

'You are mistaken, woman. Leeds Castle belongs to the Queen. Yet you denied her admittance. That is treason.'

She did not flinch even then, knowing the penalties.

She said: 'Lord Badlesmere will support me.'

'We will leave it to him to cut down the rope on which you shall hang on your battlements.'

She shrugged her shoulders. 'So be it,' she said. 'I shall be another victim to the tyranny of kings.'

Edwards was astonished that she could talk thus in face of death and in his heart he knew it would be impossible to put such a woman to death.

In fact he could not bring himself to hang a woman. She should be imprisoned, he said. Let her be taken to London and lodged in the Tower.

His advisers shook their heads. She deserved hanging. Think what she had done to the Queen. But Edward would not listen. Instead they hanged the seneschal Walter Colepepper and eleven of his servants, which was grossly unfair for they had merely obeyed their mistress's orders.

However punishment had to be meted out to someone.

The bold Lady Badlesmere was taken to London and as she passed through the streets the people came out to jeer at her and throw rubbish at her and threatened her with what they would do to her.

The guards managed to protect her from the angry crowds and she was taken to a dungeon in the Tower.

*   *   *

Edward was triumphant. The capture of Leeds was his first success in battle. He felt like a conqueror.

Isabella was delighted. He had acted for her and for the first time had shown he had some regard for her. She received him warmly in London. It was good that the Badlesmere woman had not been hanged but had been brought to the Tower. Had she been hanged they could have made a martyr of her.

'You must take advantage of your success,' she told him. 'Look you, Edward, the whole of London is on your side. The barons will see this and perhaps not be quite so eager to stand against you.'

She was right. Several of the barons who had been dismayed that the Queen should have been denied access to her own castle now came to the King with their followers to show him that they had had enough of Lancaster's vacillating.

'Now is the time to break Lancaster's power,' said the Queen.

They were together, she and Edward, as they had never been before, but if he thought she would forget past insults at the turn of fortune he was mistaken. The victory at Leeds had been an easy one—an army against one woman defending a castle—and the Queen was working towards a goal which did not include the King. But she would make use of him now; and as Lancaster had proved to be no real friend to her— although in the beginning it had seemed that he might be— she was ready to eliminate him.

'You know Lancaster is a traitor,' she said to the King.

'I have had ample evidence of that,' replied Edward. 'He has been against me constantly.'

'And have you wondered why in their raids the Scots never touched his lands?'

'I know there are rumours that he has an understanding with Robert the Bruce.'

'An understanding with Robert the Bruce! When he is your subject!'

She said: 'We must if we can, lay hands on the letters which have passed between Bruce and Lancaster and if we do ... oh if we do ... then who can deny that we have a traitor in our midst?'

Edward's mood had changed. He was all set for success now.

He marched up to the Welsh border and the Mortimers' land.

The Mortimers immediately sent word to Lancaster that

the King's army was on the march. They should join together and then they could defeat him. Edward was not famous for his prowess in battle and with the might of their two armies they would be invincible.

Lancaster's reply was that this would be so but he failed to send his army, and without him the Mortimers were not strong enough to face those thousands of the King's supporters who now that they had a more resolute Edward at their head (since his victory at Leeds), were ready to throw their hearts into the fight.

The result of the encounter was the débâcle of the Marcher men and much to Edward's surprise he found that two of his most formidable enemies were his prisoners—Roger de Mortimer, Lord of Chirk, and his nephew, Roger de Mortimer, Lord of Wigmore.

They were immediately sent to the Tower.

It was success such as Edward had never dared dream of. He knew now how his father had felt throughout his long fighting life.

THE END OF LANCASTER

HE now turned his attention to Lancaster.

Letters had been found. It was true that Lancaster had been in communication with the King of Scotland and in the letters he had sent to Bruce he had signed himself King Arthur. That was ominous and Isabella was right. He must destroy Lancaster. There could be no peace for him until that was done. With this object in view he planned to march north.

It was now clear that Lancaster was taking a firm stand against the King. He did indeed parley with the Scots whose great desire was to see a civil war in England. Sir Andrew Harclay, who was the warden of Carlisle, was aware of this and came in great haste to Edward to inform him of what was happening. Edward sent him back to Carlisle with instructions to attack the English traitors and inform him at once if they were joined by the Scots.

Action took place at a long bridge which crossed the River Ure. This bridge was very long but narrow and at its approaches the Lancastrians came face to face with Sir Andrew Harclay and his force which was drawn from the counties of Cumberland and Westmorland. These man had very good reason to hate the Scots and their allies; and that the latter should be English incensed them.

Humphrey de Bohun, Lord Hereford, attempted to take the bridge on foot, while Lancaster tried to cross the river on horseback and attack Harclay's men from the flank. Lancaster however found Harclay too strong for him and he suffered great losses. Meanwhile de Bohun while on the bridge was killed by a spear being run through a gap in the planks of the bridge from below and entering his body.

The Battle of Boroughbridge had ended in the annihilation of Lancaster's forces and his own capture.

At Pontefract Edward was waiting to receive his cousin.

Lancaster faced him with a lack of animation. He knew that the long battle between them was over. He despised Edward and wondered what the future held for him. He shrugged his shoulders. Whatever it was it would have no consequence for him.

He did not attempt to remind the King of their relationship; he would not plead for his life.

It was over. He had enjoyed power but he had not possessed the talents to keep it.

'Your trial will take place at once,' said the King.

Lancaster bowed his head and was led from the King's presence.

The trial was quick and Lancaster was found guilty of conspiring with the Scots against the King. He had used the soubriquet of King Arthur in his dealing with Robert the Bruce. King Arthur! the court tittered. It was clear that Lancaster had had a high opinion of himself and where his ambitions lay.

Papers had been found addressed to Bruce containing a suggestion that he come into England with a good army and Lancaster would see that a good peace was made.

Edward sat watching his cousin, and he was thinking: You killed Perrot. You boasted of it. Yes, you were proud of it. And when he thought of that beautiful body being destroyed he almost wept. But this was revenge. This would be the end of Lancaster.

He could almost hear Perrot laughing beside him. Dear Perrot, he should be avenged.

Edward listened to the words of the prosecutor.

'Wherefore our Sovereign Lord the King having duly weighed the great enormities and offences of the said Thomas, Earl of Lancaster and his notorious ingratitude has no manner of reason to show mercy . . .'

He was to die the traitor's death, that horrible one, which had now become the custom—hanging, cutting down alive and burning the entrails after which the body was cut into quarters and distributed for display.

But in the case of noblemen the sentence was diverted to death by beheading, and as Lancaster was royal this should be done to him.

They put him on a grey pony, and thus he rode through the town where the people came out to jeer at him and throw at him anything they considered disgusting enough. Stones cut his face and he turned neither to right nor left and it was as though he was completely unaware of the blood which ran down his face.

'King Arthur,' cried the mob, 'where are your knights, eh? Why don't they come and rescue you? Let them take you back to your round table.'

He looked straight ahead. Gaveston had suffered a similar fate to this ten years before. Was this why they were taking him to the hill? Was this why they made him ride on the little pony, why they sought to rob him of his dignity?

All men must die at some time, but it was sad that a royal earl should come to it this way. Then suddenly the enormity of what was happening to him seemed too strong for him.

'King of Heaven,' he murmured, 'grant me mercy for the King of Earth has forsaken me.'

They reached St Thomas's Hill outside the city of Pontefract. He saw the block. He was aware of the watching faces—avid for blood, eager to see the ignoble end of one who had not long before been the most powerful man in the land.

He turned his face to the east.

Someone cried: 'Turn to the north, man. That's where your friends are.'

He was roughly pushed. Now he was looking ahead to where beyond the Border was the land of the Scots.

He knelt and placed his head on the rudely constructed block.

The axe descended and Lancaster was no more.

*　　*　　*

Warenne brought the news to Lancaster's wife.

Alice de Lacy looked at him with disbelief.

' 'Tis so,' said Warenne 'He was found guilty of plotting with the Scots and that has been his undoing. He was sentenced to the traitor's death but because of his noble birth he was not hanged drawn and quartered but taken to St Thomas's Hill near Pontefract where they cut off his head.'

'Pontefract,' she murmured. 'It was his favourite spot.'

'Well, it is over, Alice. What now?'

'I am free,' she said. 'It is what I and Ebulo have longed for. But I wish it could have come about in a different way. Poor Thomas, he was so proud ... and clever in a way, but he did not understand how to treat people. It has been his downfall.'

'There is no longer the need for you to remain in hiding.'

'I have so much to thank you for.'

'Lancaster was my enemy, you know. It was my pleasure to disconcert him.'

'I think you had a certain kindness in your heart for a woman placed as I was.'

'It could be so,' he answered. 'And now?'

She answered: 'I am going to Ebulo. We shall be married.'

'The daughter of the Earl of Lincoln, the wife of royal Lancaster to marry a humble squire!'

'Even the daughters and wives of earls have a right to marry for love,' she answered.

Very shortly afterwards the nobility was astonished to learn that the Countess of Lancaster had married Ebulo le Strange, a squire who was not only far below her social standing but who was also lame.

THE LOVERS IN THE TOWER

THE lust for power had now seized Edward. It was as though with Lancaster's death he himself had taken on new life. Moreover the truce with Scotland had come to an end and Robert the Bruce was celebrating this by attacking the English towns in earnest. When he came as far south as Preston it was decided that it was time to attempt the invasion of Scotland once more.

Everyone was astonished by the change in Edward. The Londoners were with him to a man. He had avenged the insult to Isabella and they liked him for that. The Despensers were banished. A plague on them. Now perhaps the King had outgrown his follies and was going to show them that he was a true son of Great Edward.

At one point the English crossed the Border into the Lothians. They reached Holyrood House and took it. They should have been astonished by the lack of resistance of a commander like Bruce. It was too late when they realized that he had crossed the Border and had come as far as Yorkshire, his object being to attack Edward's army from the rear.

Isabella was travelling with the army and was staying outside the town of York. She was in a pensive mood. Events were changing her outlook rapidly. Edward was winning the confidence of the people. For him the affair at Leeds Castle had been a blessing in disguise. By avenging her he had won general approval and particularly that of the Londoners and was enjoying a popularity which he had never known before.

Whatever happened now she did not want Edward. The plan which had been forming in her mind for some time was

not yet fully developed, but nothing Edward could do now
would make her want to change it. In brief it was that Edward
should be deposed and their son Edward take the crown, with
his mother beside him as Regent. But if Edward was going to
reform his ways? If he was going to be a victorious king and
a faithful husband, what then?

I shall never forgive him for the humiliation I have suffered
at his hands, she thought.

Even as she sat brooding she heard the sound of arrivals
and there was an urgency about those sounds. She rose and
went down to the great hall to see what was happening.

At the sight of her one of the men who had just come cried
out: 'My lady, make haste. We must go from here. The King's
army is routed and the Scots are on their way to take you
prisoner.'

It was the old pattern. Why had she thought for a moment
that Edward would become a successful general?

No, he had failed once more.

Never mind. That made it all the easier for her to continue
with her plan.

Hastily she prepared to leave. After the gallop to Tynemouth
she boarded a boat. It was a rough passage but she did not
care.

It could not be long before events began to go her way.

*   *   *

There was despair in the north among those who had been
loyal to Edward for it was clear that he was no match for Robert
the Bruce. Once again he had been put to flight and had nar-
rowly escaped. He was not meant for battle. England's tragedy
was that the old King had borne such a son and had himself
died before he had been able to complete his task.

Edward was impatient. He wanted no more war with Scotland. He disliked war. Only briefly had he had good fortune
and that was when he had attacked Leeds Castle which was
held by a woman.

There was disillusion and it was disconcerting that his supporters in the north were now beginning to realize the futility
of depending on him.

They were actually attempting to come to private terms with
the Scots because it seemed likely that the harrying of the

Border would continue for a very long time.

The Bishop of Durham and the monks of Bridlington sent their valuables south and were attempting to make a treaty with Bruce, a fact which showed clearly that they had no confidence in Edward and were looking out for themselves. Edward was deeply shocked when he heard that Andrew Harclay, the Earl of Carlisle, had actually travelled to Dumfries and held a conference with Bruce in which he offered to recognize him as King of Scotland in return for peace between them and security from attack for his own property.

Isabella heard the news and said to herself that this man of the north showed good sense. Anyone who relied on Edward was a fool. They had at last learned the lesson. Let the whole country learn such lessons. They would be all the happier to see him go.

She had many friends to support her. The chief of these and the one in whom she placed most reliance was Adam of Orlton. He hated the Despensers as much as she did and had rejoiced to see them banished. Since the arrest of the Mortimers he had been in some danger, for now that Lancaster was dead and the Mortimers imprisoned people were looking to him as the most important man in the party which had stood against the Despensers. Edward hated him and had wanted him out of the the way, and had even managed to bring him before a lay tribunal—the first time this had ever happened to a Bishop. He might have been condemned to death if he had not been under the protection of the Archbishops of Canterbury and York—who must naturally protect their Bishops—for they commanded that violent hands should not be laid on a man of the Church. The King, however, insisted on the trial's proceeding and Adam was found guilty and although he could not be condemned to death his possessions were confiscated. He was at this time protesting to the Pope and was living in the Tower, not exactly a prisoner but as one who would have been, but for the influence of the Church.

Isabella often visited the Tower and stayed in the apartments where her daughter Joanna had been born. She was in constant communication with Adam.

In spite of what was happening in the north Edward could have changed the whole course of his life at that time. His enemies were either dead or imprisoned. The chief of these were Thomas of Lancaster who was dead and the Mortimers who were in the Tower, though with his usual lack of vision he underestimated Roger de Mortimer the younger. Edward could have had him executed and given the traitor's death instead of which in his usual dilatory manner he allowed him to remain a prisoner in the Tower.

Poor Edward, thought Isabella. He would never learn from his mistakes. One would have thought that having seen the country brought almost to civil war through Gaveston and then through the Despensers, he would have recognized the signs of danger.

But it seemed he could not. The small success which had brightened his career of failure had blinded him to facts.

He recalled the Despensers.

Alas, there was no one now to stop him. He was no longer merely the King in name. Lancaster was dead and it was he, Edward, who now gave the orders.

The Despensers responded with alacrity, and it was not long before they were flaunting their authority as blatantly as they had ever done.

It was they who ordered a friend of Harclay's to call on him at his castle and when he arrived, to arrest him in the name of the King. Thus this brave soldier, who would have served the King if he had not seen the hopelessness of such service, after a brief trial suffered the agonies of the traitor's death.

It was with the Despensers' help that Edward obtained a thirteen-year truce with Bruce and congratulated themselves on having won the peace, forgetting that it was the state of Bruce's health—the dreaded disease of leprosy was now apparent to all—which had been the main reason for his agreement.

Then it was a return to the old ways. The Despensers must be placated at all costs. The King was beside himself with joy to have his dear Hugh back with him. He was never, never to go away again, declared Edward.

* * *

The Queen had taken up temporary residence in the Tower. She liked, she said, to be near her good friends the people of London. In truth, now that the Despensers had returned, she was getting impatient for action and she wished to have secret conferences with her good friend, Adam of Orlton.

A gloomy place, the Tower of London. Strange that it should contain a prison and a palace. Here many prisoners had lain in despair. At night the fanciful believed they could hear the moans of those long dead. It was said that on the winding staircases and in the cold dank rooms ghostly figures appeared, men and women who would never rest until they had restitution from those who had given them a life of hell-on-earth in these dark walls. There was no place in the country which was so haunted.

William the Conqueror had ordered it to be built and Gundulf, the Bishop of Rochester, had designed it. It had stood a symbol of the Conqueror's power to a conquered people. Of course it had been added to since then and was no longer the bleak fortress it had been in the days of William. It had been surrounded twenty years after the first fortress had been erected with an embattled stone wall and a deep ditch. Then that inveterate builder Henry the Third, the King's grandfather, had built the Lion Tower and added to the improvements to the White Tower. The moat had been enlarged by Edward's father. It seemed that every King must make his mark on the Tower of London. Not the present one though, thought the Queen grimly; Edward was too indolent. The Tower to him was just a strong fortress to which he could retire when his subjects were in revolt against him.

There was a melancholy about the place but there was something which excited her too. From the narrow windows she could look out on the river and see the good merchants going about their business and it comforted her to realize that they were her friends.

There was no reason why anyone should speculate because of her presence there. It was after all one of the most important of the royal residences. Young Edward was in the good hands of Richard de Bury who had been appointed his tutor and guardian; the other children were at Pleshy in Essex in the household of the Earl of Hereford who was their guardian. She was not exactly a doting mother and made no pretence of being. It was true that she kept a firm hand on young Edward and saw him frequently. She was eager that he should feel dependent on her and she was careful to do everything to win his devotion.

From her window she could see one of the small gardens of the Tower shut in by tall pales and one day there appeared

there a tall dark, somewhat emaciated, man in the company of
Gerard de Alspaye whom she knew as the Sub-lieutenant of the
Tower. There was something about the manner in which he
held himself which attracted her attention. She thought: He is
obviously a prisoner but he walks like a king.

She watched for him and saw him on another occasion and
on impulse she sent for Alspaye and asked him who the dis-
tinguished-looking prisoner was.

Alspaye looked confused and she guessed that it was against
orders that the prisoner had been given an airing.

'You need have no fear,' she said. 'I'll swear this man is one
of the King's prisoners, and I know that you made sure no harm
could come of his taking the air.'

'That is so, my lady. He has just become bereaved. His uncle
who shared his dungeon has died.'

'Of what did he die?'

'The rigours of prison, my lady. Lack of food. The dungeon
is airless, without one window; the walls run with damp; it is
stifling in summer and bitterly cold in winter.'

'What was the crime of these men?'

'They were captured in battle.'

'By the King?' She could not keep the note of contempt from
her voice but Alspaye did not seem to notice.

'In the Marcher country, my lady.'

'Then he is ...'

'Roger de Mortimer, my lady, Earl of Wigmore, and his
uncle recently dead was the Lord of Chirk.'

'I have heard much of these Mortimers,' she said. 'I can
remember the surprise when they were taken.' She smiled suddenly. 'I should like to speak with this man. Do you take him
into the garden again soon?'

'I would take him there when you wished, my lady.'

'Walk there with him tomorrow and I will join you. Do not
let him know that I have mentioned this. Let it be as if by
accident.'

'It shall be as you wish, my lady.'

She was filled with an unaccountable excitement. Ideas
flashed into her head and were discarded almost before they
came. Roger de Mortimer, one of the great Marcher barons!
She had heard Edward talk of the Mortimers with something
like fear in his voice. Yes, he had certainly regarded the Mortimers with awe. The uncle and the nephew. They lived as

kings in their territory. Edward had said it was a mistake to allow those not royal to hold such power.

And now, one of them was dead and the other, this emaciated prisoner, still held himself like a conqueror.

The next morning she took a ride through the streets of London—always a heartening experience. She had taken great pains with her appearance. It was gratifying to hear the shout for Isabella the Fair. Whatever happened, she thought, the people of London would be on my side.

In the afternoon she went to the garden. True to his word Alspaye was there with Roger de Mortimer.

The Queen stood looking at them, her eyebrows raised as though in surprise.

Roger de Mortimer stepped forward and bowed low.

'Pray tell me who you are,' she said regally.

'Mortimer at your service, my lady.'

Alspaye had taken a step backwards and she turned to him.

'One of your prisoners?' she asked.

'My lady, the Earl of Wigmore has recently suffered a great bereavement.'

'Ah, yes,' said the Queen, 'the Lord of Chirk. The rigours of prison were too much for him.'

'He was an old man, my lady,' said Mortimer.

She nodded. 'And you are being given a little exercise in case you too should succumb. Is that so, my lord Lieutenant?'

'It seemed a merciful thing to do,' was the answer.

'It was so. My lord Mortimer, take a turn with me.' She glanced at Alspaye who withdrew a few steps. Then to Mortimer: 'Come, my lord.'

'You have been here some time, I believe,' she said.

'Some two years, my lady.'

She looked at him closely. The pallor of his skin accentuated the fierce dark brows; and she thought how handsome he was in spite of the privations he had suffered.

'You have felt deeply the death of your uncle, I'll swear,' she went on.

'We had been together so long. My father died when I was seven years old and from that time my uncle was a father to me. Yes, my lady, indeed I feel his loss deeply ...' He clenched his fist. 'One day ...'

She felt an exultation gripping her. He was a man of violent passion, this Mortimer.

'Yes, my lord, one day?'

'My lady, you must pardon my emotion. This was a beloved uncle ... one who had been as a father to me. I have been long in prison ...'

'I know it,' she answered gently. 'But you could say you were fortunate. The King might so easily have condemned you to death.'

'He did, but—and it seems strange to me—he commuted the sentence to life imprisonment.'

'Life imprisonment! Perhaps death would have been preferable.'

'Nay, my lady, I think not. It is true I am the King's prisoner. I spend my days in a hideous dungeon ... except when my good friend Alspaye gives me a breath of fresh air. But I still would cling to life. I still hope, my lady, that one day I shall be free of this place.'

'You think the King would pardon you?'

'Not while the Despensers are with him. But it may be they will not always be there.'

'You think he will rid himself of them?'

'Nay, my lady, but it may be that others will. Did they not despatch Piers Gaveston somewhat hastily to his Maker? But I talk too much. Forgive me. I have been shut away so long. It is years since I have had the good fortune to speak with a lady and yet here I am ... in this prison garden talking and walking with the queen of them all.'

'You have not forgotten how to pay compliments, my lord.'

'In your presence, my lady, they would rise naturally to the lips of any man.'

'So you know who I am?' she asked.

'My lady, I have been long in this noisome prison. They say that many have suffered from visions. I cannot but help wonder whether that is what is happening to me now. It may be that this is a dream from which I shall shortly wake. In this dream I am speaking to the most beautiful woman in England and France and in the whole world, I dareswear. The Queen herself.'

'Yes, indeed you pay pretty compliments. I am no vision, Mortimer. I am your Queen. I will say adieu. The lieutenant is bewildered.'

'My lady, if I could ...'

'Yes, Mortimer, what would you have of me?'

'I am afraid to ask it.'

'You afraid? I doubt it. You have the look of a man who knows little of fear.'

'If I could see you again ...'

'Who knows. It may come to pass.'

She turned away and left the gardens.

* * *

In her apartment she went to a window and looked out. He was still in the garden and talking earnestly to Alspaye. As for herself a wild excitement had taken possession of her.

What fierce eyes he had—large dark passionate eyes. She had sensed the vitality of him—the essential masculinity. 'All that time incarcerated in the Tower,' she murmured. 'Recently bereaved of a beloved uncle and yet I never saw a man who had more fire in him. How his eyes flashed when he spoke of Gaveston and the Despensers! How such a man as he is would despise such as them. How he would despise Edward!

Mortimer—the King of the Marcher lands. Such a man she thought I have wanted to meet all my life.

She *must* see him again soon. She would make Alspaye understand that he was to be taken to the garden on the next day and she would be there.

Perhaps she should be a little more discreet. But she was tired of discretion. She had been humiliated too long and it might well be that this was the time for action.

She scarcely slept that night. She could only think that somewhere in this Tower he too was sleeping.

Alspaye was eager to please the Queen. He was also under the spell of Mortimer; she saw that and she was not surprised. Alspaye was delighted that the Queen was interested in his prisoner.

The Queen joined them in the gardens.

'You see your vision has returned, Mortimer.'

'To put such hope in my heart that I dare not believe in it,' he replied.

'*You* would dare anything,' she answered.

'I was once known for my daring,' he agreed.

'And will be again, I doubt not.'

'That is for the future.'

'And you believe in your future?'

'I am beginning to my lady.'

'Rest assured your faith will not be displaced.'

'You are good to me,' he said.

'I like your kind, Mortimer,' she answered.

He understood at once that this was a reference to the King and his kind.

He answered: 'When a man has lost his freedom he is reckless of what else he might lose. He speaks his mind. I will say this that I have always felt deeply for you. If you had raised an army to drive out of the country those who displeased you, I should have been at the head of that army.'

'Yes, Mortimer, you speak rashly indeed when you talk of raising armies.'

'How could I raise armies, madam, when I am a poor prisoner?'

'But a moment ago you admitted that was but a temporary state. One of these days ...'

He turned to her and they faced each other. Some understanding passed between them. In that moment they both realized the deep significance of this encounter.

'Mortimer,' she said, 'I believe there is much you and I should say to each other.'

'Standing here with you,' he answered, 'is for me complete delight. Here am I a prisoner, death could steal up on me at any moment, yet I can say that I never was as happy in the whole of my life as I am at this moment.'

'And why is this?'

'Because I have found you.'

She was shaken with emotion and she said: 'It was I who found you, was it not?'

'Let us say we found each other.'

'We have met but twice and that in this prison garden with Alspaye keeping guard on you.'

'Alspaye is a good friend to me. He hates the Despensers.'

'How many people in this country hate the Despensers?'

'Myriads. We have but to find them ... to rouse them. Then I swear to you in a very short time the pretty Despenser will go the way of Gaveston.'

'How you hate the Despenser.'

'I hate him more than ever now I have spoken with my incomparable lady Queen.'

'The King is as he is ...'

'It is no way for a King to be.'

'He has done his duty. You know I have a fine son ... two sons.'

'Young Edward is growing up. That is a matter for rejoicing.'

'You are speaking treason, Mortimer.'

'I know it. How could I help but be treasonable to the King when I am standing so close to the Queen.'

'You mean ...'

'I mean what is best not said. But being a woman as well as a queen you will know.'

She said: 'I must not stay here. What if we were seen?'

'It would be noted.'

'And then we should meet no more.'

'My lady, we *must* meet again.'

He had taken her hand and the pressure of his fingers thrilled her. She thought: I have waited too long. Mortimer is the man for me.

She said in a somewhat breathless voice: 'I will arrange it.'

*　　*　　*

She sent for Alspaye.

'Your prisoner Mortimer interests me,' she said.

'Yes, my lady.'

'When I talked with him in the gardens he spoke very freely.'

'Prisoners become reckless, my lady.'

'It occurs to me that I should have further talk with him. I should discover what is in his mind.'

Alspaye bowed his head. 'Do you wish to go to his cell?'

'That would create certain speculation, would it not?'

She thought of the cells, damp on the walls, airless and stuffy. No, that was not the place where she and Mortimer should be together.

'If I sent for him to my apartments ...'

'He would come with his guards, my lady. The King's orders were that he should be very specially guarded.'

'Yet he walks with you in the gardens.'

''Twas so, my lady, but the guards were behind the doors which led to the gardens. It was only because he was with me that they allowed him out of their sight.'

'And if I sent for him, to have talk with him ... here ... say in my apartments ...'

'Then I should bring him and stay within call, my lady.'

'And his guards?'

'They would expect to escort him and be at hand.'

She felt irritated. There was no way in which she and Mortimer could be alone without its being known.

She did not mind Alspaye's knowing. He was a man of discretion and had already witnessed their meeting in the garden. But she must be free to be alone with Mortimer. The desire for excitement and adventure, having been suppressed all these years, would remain so no longer. She was ready to take any risks.

'I doubt not the guards take a little wine now and then.'

'When they are on duty my lady they take very little. There is much carousing when they have their free time though. Life in the Tower seems to give them a fancy for wine.'

'Let them be given extra wine and make sure that it is potent.'

'Drugged, you mean, my lady?'

She did not answer but her smile was enough. 'When they are asleep let Mortimer be brought to me ... by you. I will be responsible for his safety.'

'If you will be responsible for him, my lady ...'

'I have told you I will.'

'Then I will see what can be done.'

'Not only see,' she retorted, 'but do it. I shall remember you ... with gratitude, Lieutenant.'

*   *   *

He came into her apartment. He looked different. He wore his confidence like a garment.

He came swiftly towards her and taking her hand kissed it fervently. His lips were warm. Then he raised his shining eyes to her face.

She stepped towards him and laid her hand on his shoulders. It was enough. The next moment he had picked her up in his arms and held her closely against him.

She felt his lips on hers, demanding, certain of himself ... Impertinence! she thought indulgently. Am I not the Queen? She was laughing to herself.

'Mortimer,' she murmured. 'This is part of the vision perhaps.'

'Nay, nay,' he said. 'Since I first saw you it has happened often in my dreams ... now comes the reality.'

'I ... the Queen,' she began.

'*My* Queen,' he said, 'my Queen for evermore.'

He was a practised lover. He had known many women, she guessed that. And what had she known? Reluctant Edward! How she hated Edward, more so now she knew what it was to lie with a real man.

'Mortimer, Mortimer,' she moaned, 'my dearest Mortimer ... from the first moment I knew it was you ...'

His answer was in his fervent love-making. They lay side by side, fingers entwined.

'There is so much we should talk of,' she said.

But there was no time for talk. They must make love again and again. Nothing else would satisfy him ... or her.

How she wished that she could hold back time! How was she going to live without Mortimer after this? She was a passionate woman who had been stifling her real emotions for too long. Now they were breaking forth. It was a flood which was bursting the banks; it was flowing over her resolutions, her ambitions, everything. There was nothing in her life just now but her need of Mortimer.

It was more than consummation of their love. It was the beginning of a new life for her. Mortimer was going to be more than her lover. That was something they both knew instinctively; and she would never forget that although he was aware of this yet he must cast it all aside that they might first slake this fierce desire which possessed them both.

'Have you any doubt,' murmured Mortimer, 'that you and I were made for each other?'

'None,' she answered. 'Oh my dear one, how thankful I am that I have found you.'

But they must part. How frustrating that was. If only they could have lain together through the night and talked in between bouts of love-making. What bliss that would have been.

'Yes, at least we have had this. Let us not forget that,' said Mortimer.

'And when shall we be together again?' cried Isabella. 'Alspaye will know what has happened.'

'I believe we can trust Alspaye.'

'And the guards? We cannot drug them every night.'

'Nay, but we must find a means.'

'How? Where? In the garden? In your cell? No, gentle Mortimer, my love, we must find a means for I cannot endure to be away from you. You have shown me what I have missed. Oh Mortimer, why were you not the son of the King of England?'

'My Queen, my Queen! I could never have believed there was such a woman. I would I could carry you off to my Marcher country. There I would hold you against all who came to take you from me.'

'One day, Mortimer ... One day. I swear to it. I swear. Oh there is so much to say. But you are here. We must free you ... That is the first thing. We must free you from the Tower.'

'When can I be with you again?'

'We must go carefully. There is so much at stake.'

'But I must see you soon. How can I stay away from you ... after this? Knowing that we are both in this Tower together ... and these thick walls divide us ...'

'I shall arrange something. Dear Mortimer, you must dress now. You must go back to your dungeon. Alspaye cannot wait much longer. The guards will be awakening from their sleep. Dear Mortimer, your life is the most precious thing on earth to me. It must be preserved ... for the future. One day, my love ... one day ...'

He saw that she was right. They dressed hastily. One last embrace and Alspaye came in to conduct him to his dungeon.

*   *   *

She was being driven mad. She had seen him in the garden but what could they do there but touch hands? She could stand close to him, feel the strength of his body. It maddened her, and he shared her feelings. They had wakened such massive floods of passion in each other that it was almost impossible to restrain them.

'What can we do?' cried Mortimer in despair.

It was not easy to arrange another night even with Alspaye's connivance. He had of course guessed the state of affairs and understood the Queen's emotion. Poor woman, had she not been married to Edward all these years?

There was one night when it was arranged that a few doors

should be unlocked and the guards drunk again and this time when the lovers had slaked their passion to a certain degree, Isabella insisted that the first thing that must be done was to arrange Mortimer's escape from the Tower.

'I will go to the Marcher country and you will join me there,' he said. 'We will raise an army against the King.'

'No,' she said, 'not the Marcher country. That could be unsafe. You must go to France.'

'And you?'

'I would find some means of joining you there. My brother would help us. And we would come against Edward and the Despensers. I will get my son with me and I shall be fighting to put him on the throne. You and I, gentle Mortimer, will rule for him until he is of age.'

'If this could but be achieved . . .'

'Why should it not? The people love me . . .' She paused. They had loved her because they said she was not only beautiful but virtuous; she had allowed herself to be humiliated by Edward and had still borne him children. When they knew that Mortimer was her paramour would they love her just the same? But of course they would. She would charm them with her beauty and she would only be giving them her son—so like his grandfather—in place of their dissolute King. 'Yes,' she went on, 'the people would be on my side. They hate the Despensers. They want them banished. We should have the people with us.'

'It shall be,' cried Mortimer. 'Oh, my Queen, you have brought love such as I never dreamed of into my life and with it hope.'

She had never been so excited. Everything she had always wanted was coming to her. She had always known that hers was a sensuous and passionate nature and she marvelled that she had been able to suppress her natural desires so long. But then she had needed a Mortimer to arouse them. And here he was and with him came the possibility that the dreams she had long cherished were about to come true.

What she had wanted was a strong man to stand beside her. Here he was without the slightest doubt. And this man, who was to have her complete trust and who was to stand beside her no matter what happened to them, must inevitably be her lover.

Life had never seemed so promising.

Now she must give herself to the task with her unbounded energy. It would help to take her mind from the yearnings of her body.

And that task was to free Mortimer from the Tower.

*   *   *

She rode out of the Tower. She was leaving the Palace for a few days. It was better so in case there should have been talk. Moreover she had work to do. She was going to see Adam of Orlton, the Bishop of Hereford.

It was never easy for the Queen to go anywhere without taking with her a large company so it was fortunate that Adam was at this time in London and she could ride out as though merely taking the air.

The Bishop received her warmly. He was in disgrace with the King but the Queen had never been unfriendly towards him. He was against the Despensers and none could be more so than she was. She believed that she could rely on Adam's help.

He himself would have been in the Tower if it had not been that he was a churchman and under the protection of Canterbury and York so she could be sure of his sympathy.

'My lord Bishop,' she said, 'I have matters of great moment to discuss with you. I need your help.'

'My lady,' replied the Bishop, 'if it is in my power to give it, that help is yours.'

'I can no longer endure the rule of the Despensers.'

'My lady, you are not alone in your feelings. If it could be put to the country I'll warrant there would be few who did not agree with you.'

'It is time they went. The King should never have recalled them.'

'Alas, he has done so.'

'My lord Bishop, it is clear to me that if we rid ourselves of the Despensers before long they would be replaced ... even as this young Hugh has replaced Gaveston.'

The Bishop nodded in agreement.

'It must not be allowed to happen, my lord Bishop,' insisted the Queen.

'My lady, can it be prevented?'

'In one way. The King's son and mine is growing fast.'

'But a boy yet, my lady.'

'Old enough to be crowned King. There have been others of his age.'

'A Regency?' asked the Bishop eagerly.

'Chosen with care. My lord Bishop, what we talk of is of the utmost secrecy. It is only because of the dire need that I would speak thus.'

'I know it well, my lady. But these matters are in men's minds and it is well that they be spoken of ... among those who could have it in their hands to avoid disasters.'

'Even so. I need your help, Bishop. There is a man in the Tower who has sworn to stand with me.'

The Bishop raised his eyebrows and waited.

'Roger de Mortimer.'

Adam nodded. 'A strong man, indeed. He ruled the Marcher lands with his uncle and he was as a king there they say.'

'His uncle has perished in his prison. His nephew still lives. He is young and vigorous. He would stand with us.'

'You have tested him?'

'The Queen smiled slowly: 'Aye, my lord Bishop, I have tested him.'

'Yes,' said the Bishop, 'a strong man. He could rouse the Marcher country.'

'He must first escape.'

'From the Tower! I'll swear he is most rigorously guarded.'

'He has friends.'

'Who, my lady?'

'The Sub-lieutenant, Gerard Alspaye.'

'That is good. He could do much.'

'My lord Bishop what could *you* do?'

'Nothing from inside the Tower. Outside. I could have horses waiting at an agreed spot. I could have a boat waiting to take him across the river to that spot and another at the coast.'

'And would you do this, my lord?'

'I would do my best for you, my lady.'

'I thank you with all my heart.'

'If we can rid this country of its evil influences the whole of England will thank *you* with all their hearts.'

'I can and will with the help of God and my very good friends.'

'Then the first thing is to get Mortimer from the Tower. What will he do in France?'

'Go to my brother. Let him know how I am held here. Get help from him. I shall try to join him ... if that is possible. But I must have my son Edward with me.'

'I see. It would mean civil war.'

'If the King can find any to stand with him.'

'There will be some I doubt not. The Despensers will be there and mistake not behind the pretty face is a wily mind.'

'I know it well. But first we must free Mortimer. I pin my hopes on him. My lord Bishop I rely on you to provide what we shall need once Mortimer is free of the Tower.'

'Let the rest be arranged from within and then we must be sure that we work together.'

'God's blessings on you, Bishop. You are a good friend to me and to your country.'

'With God's help, my lady, I will serve you both until He sees fit to take me.'

She was satisfied. Her excitement was intense. All was going as she could wish.

*   *   *

There were whispered conversations in the darkness of the night. They were getting reckless. The need to be together obsessed them; as did the knowledge that soon they must be parted. Alspaye was getting anxious. It was possible to arrange these meetings but they must necessarily become increasingly dangerous as suspicions must inevitably arise. It might be feasible one night, or even two, to leave a door unlocked, a corridor unguarded, to make guards sleepy with wine. But these occasions were becoming too frequent.

'We must not jeopardize the plan,' said Mortimer.

'Indeed we must not,' agreed Isabella, 'but when you are in France we shall no longer be together.'

'But you must follow me. You must use all your skill to do so.'

'I shall. I shall. You may rely on me.'

They embraced passionately; they talked earnestly; and they continued to meet.

Gerard de Alspaye was uneasy. What would happen to him, he wondered, when such an important prisoner as Roger de Mortimer escaped from the Tower? He would be blamed. His head would not be worth much he was sure.

There was only one course of action for him to pursue, said Isabella. When Mortimer went, he must go with him.

Alspaye's spirits were considerably lightened at the prospect. There were meetings with Adam outside. He had engaged the help of two rich Londoners, John de Gisors, and Richard de Bettoyne, who would provide the boat which would take Mortimer and Alspaye across the river and the horses which could carry them to the coast. They would see that these were waiting ready at the appointed places. Speed was essential and the fugitives must get to France immediately, for it would be dangerous for them to linger in England for even one day longer than they need. As soon as the disappearance was discovered the hue and cry would follow and even Edward would realize the danger of letting a man like Mortimer escape from his clutches.

'Well, let it be soon,' agreed the Queen, and she added that it was fortunate that summer had come.

Alspaye said: 'On the night of the first of August the Tower guards always celebrate the feast of St Peter ad Vincula.'

'On this occasion,' Mortimer interrupted, 'it should be a specially merry feast. We must make sure that the wine flows freely.'

'I shall put two notorious imbibers in charge of my lord,' went on Alspaye, 'and shall see that they are well supplied with liquor. I'll warrant it will not be long before we have them in a drunken stupor. That will give us an opportunity to make our preparations.'

Many plans had been discussed and discarded and they had come to the conclusion that the safest way was for Mortimer to escape by means of a rope ladder. He had, of course, to get out of his cell and although most of the guards would be drinking heavily there could be one or two abstainers and it was logical to suppose that on such an occasion they would be especially alert.

Mortimer's dungeon was next to the kitchens and from these it was possible to get out onto a roof of an inner ward. This was where the rope ladder would come in. For several weeks Mortimer with the help of Alspaye had managed to loosen a portion of the stones in the wall. It was not difficult for Alspaye to say he wished to speak with the prisoner and dismiss the guards while he did so. During the time they spent together the two men worked on the wall so that by the first of August it was a simple matter to lift out the stones which they had loosened and make a big enough hole for them to pass through.

They would then be in the kitchens where Alspaye must make sure that the servants were either carousing with their guards or too drunk to notice what was happening. From the kitchens they could reach one of the inner wards and there it was that they would need the rope ladder to take them into the outer ward and they could from there make their way to that spot on the river where the London merchants, John de Gisors and Richard de Bettoyne, would have a boat waiting.

They had gone over the plan in their minds, looking for possible defects. To be discovered would mean certain death for Mortimer and Alspaye. But they were determined they would succeed.

The Queen was perhaps the most anxious of the three. She had seen in Mortimer her great hope. Moreover she was passionately in love with him and to have found a man who was not only her lover but her saviour seemed miraculous to her.

She was terrified that something would happen to him.

The first of August dawned. She went along to the little church of St Peter ad Avincula on Tower Green and asked the saint's help in this project.

During the morning Mortimer was allowed to walk in the garden and Alspaye dismissed the guards with instructions to wait by the palings and while he and Mortimer walked they ran through the details once more.

The Queen joined them.

'I know I should not have come,' she said, 'but I had to. After tonight it will be long ere I see you both.'

'We must make sure that it is not too long,' said Mortimer.

'I shall be unable to endure it. I shall find some way to escape to France.'

'It would be better if it did not appear to be an escape,' said Mortimer. 'If you could come on some pretext and bring young Edward with you.'

'I will do it. I will do it.'

They clasped hands. It was the nearest to an embrace.

She was amazed and delighted by Mortimer's calm. He was a man of action and he could not help but be exhilarated at the prospect of escaping from imprisonment even though it would mean a temporary separation from the Queen. He had no doubts of the success of the venture.

Nor, when she was with him, had she.

They did not linger too long in the gardens. Alspaye escorted Mortimer back to his dungeon and in her apartments the Queen told her attendants that she wished to be alone. She was too tense for light conversation and she was afraid that her manner might betray something.

Throughout the Tower the festive spirit was apparent. St Peter ad Vincula was a very special saint and the warders and guards told each other it was only right that on this day he should be honoured.

Dusk fell. Now was the time. There were sound of revelry throughout the Tower. The Queen said she was pleased that the servants of the Tower should celebrate the occasion but she would retire early and rest.

She waited. Everything had been timed perfectly. She prayed that there might be no hitch. Alspaye had seen that those guards in the vicinity of Mortimer's dungeon had been given a wine which was particularly potent; it had also been laced with some special herbs reputed to add to the soporific effect.

It would be soon now.

She visualized the scene in the dungeon. The guard at the door slumped on the floor. Alspaye and Mortimer removing the stone, slipping quietly through to the kitchens. Would there be a hitch there? Suppose one of the cooks was not completely drunk? Oh, but they would be. They, like the guards, had had their wine specially treated.

How much they owed Alspaye! This could never have been arranged without him. They had been clever. Help from within, help from without. It was certain to succeed.

Wrapping a concealing cloak about her she came out of her palace quarters and made her way to the inner ward.

There was no sign of them. Her heart seemed as though it would fail her. If anything went wrong she felt she would die, for if Mortimer were caught trying to escape there would be no hope for him.

Oh what a fool Edward was to have imprisoned him in the first place! Oh, but thank God for Edward's folly! Anyone but Edward would have recognized Mortimer's superb qualities and never have let him live. Oh thank God again and again for Edward's folly.

A sound behind her. A movement. There they were. Relief flooded over her. Safe! The most difficult part accomplished.

They saw her and Mortimer ran towards her. He had her in his arms.

'Oh, gentle Mortimer,' she cried, 'if I could but come with you.'

Alspaye said: 'There is no time to lose. At any moment they could discover we have gone.'

'Where is the ladder?' said Mortimer.

It had been her task to bring that to them. She produced it and Alspaye threw it over the wall.

'Now, my lord Mortimer, you go first.'

'Let me hold it for you,' said the Queen. 'Good-bye, dear gentle Mortimer.'

One last embrace. 'To France and our meeting,' he said. 'Pray God it be soon.'

He was over. She looked down and saw him standing there ... safe on the other side of the wall.

It was Alspaye's turn. In a few seconds he was standing beside Mortimer. She threw down the rope and returned to her apartments to await the discovery of the missing captives.

* * *

It was not difficult to find their way to that spot where the boat was to be ready for them. The merchants had not failed them. It was there.

'We have done it!' cried Mortimer.

'Not yet, my lord,' replied Alspaye. 'We have escaped from the Tower ... no mean feat, I agree. But we cannot boast of our success until we are safe in France.'

Indeed they had good friends. The horses were waiting for them—fresh and ready for the journey, with seven men from Mortimer's household attending them.

This was indeed good fortune.

'My lord,' said Alspaye, 'you have friends who love you dearly.'

'Or mayhap hate the Despensers,' replied Mortimer.

They rode through the night until they reached the coast of Hampshire.

Out at sea lay a ship. It was the one which would take them to France.

It was not difficult to hire a small boat.

Mortimer bade his men be cautious for by this time it might

well be that his escape had been discovered and warning given to look out for anyone leaving for the Continent.

'Tell them,' he said, 'that we want a small boat to go to the Isle of Wight.'

This was done, the boat procured and very soon it was skimming across the water.

Mortimer boarded the big ship. The Captain who had been waiting for him gave orders to sail as soon as the tide and winds were favourable.

Later that day Roger de Mortimer and Gerard de Alspaye landed in France.

As they drank wine in a riverside tavern and congratulated themselves on their good fortune, Mortimer said: 'We have come so far. Now the real work begins.'

THE QUEEN PLOTS

EDWARD was in Lancashire when a messenger arrived from London with the news that Roger de Mortimer had escaped from the Tower.

A fury seized him. He realized at once that he should never have allowed this to happen. Oh what a stupid thing to have done! To have allowed Mortimer to keep his head.

It was because dear Hugh had not been with him at the time of Mortimer's capture, and Mortimer had been in the Tower by the time Hugh was back. Hugh was so clever. He foresaw disaster. And now Mortimer was free!

Hugh came in to see him and was clearly perturbed by the news when he heard it.

'Never mind, sweet lord, we need not fear him. We shall stand against him and all his Marcher barons.'

'I know, Hugh, I know. But to think he was allowed to get away from the Tower. What could have happened?'

'The feast of St Peter ad Vincula was it? You know what these people are. Give them a chance to carouse ... and they forget their duty.'

'Someone should answer for this.'

'They will, dear lord, they will.'

When they learned something of how the escape had taken place they were even more disturbed.

'He could only have done it with help from within,' declared Hugh.

'Help from within and without!' agreed the King. 'It would appear we have enemies.'

Hugh smiled sadly. Enemies! They surrounded him and they were the King's enemies because of him.

Never mind, the King was his very dear friend; he could not do enough for his beloved Hugh. They were together through the days and nights and Hugh and his father were becoming the richest men in England. It was so rewarding to have royal patronage and when that patronage grew out of a doting fondness then indeed a man was fortunate.

'He will have gone to the Marcher country, I'll swear,' said Edward.

'His home of course. That is where he will rally support.'

'Let us plan a campaign to the Welsh coast. We'll get him, Hugh, and this time it will not be a dungeon in the Tower for him.'

'He is a handsome man, that Mortimer,' mused Hugh, 'but I doubt he will be so handsome without his head.'

Meanwhile Mortimer, having landed safely in Normandy, was on his way to Paris.

* * *

By great good fortune Isabella's involvement in the escape of Mortimer did not occur to her husband. There had been some in the Tower who had seen the meeting between the pair and the Queen's connection with Alspaye who was now branded a traitor as it was soon discovered that he had escaped with Mortimer. Adam of Orlton, too, was suspected as the outside influence who had helped to make the escape possible. No doubt it seemed incredible that Isabella should have taken a hand in the affair, and it was presumed to be merely a coincidence that she had happened to be in the Palace of the Tower at the time.

However her attitude towards the King had changed. She made it clear that she wanted no more intimacy with him. Not that he pressed that. It had only occurred because of the need to give the country heirs. They had stalwart Edward who was nearly thirteen years old and growing conscious of coming responsibilities.

They will come sooner than you think, my son, thought Isabella grimly.

For the rest of the children she had little time to spare. That they were well and happy was all she wanted to know. Young

Edward was her concern and she did make a point of being often with him.

Her great desire was to get to France, to join Mortimer, and to begin the plan of action which was to depose her husband. She could tell herself that she had right on her side. The country was going from bad to worse. The Despensers were an evil influence. Edward and his hated favourites must go. Isabella visualized an ideal state of affairs with her and Mortimer ruling through young Edward.

She was beginning to build up a little coterie about her— all enemies of Despenser, all with the same grievances against the King, and since the Queen had suffered more humiliation than any through this unfortunate liaison, it was to her they were beginning to look. They all had one aim in common, to destroy the Despensers who, it was believed, were at the very heart of the King's unworthy kingship—just as in the earlier years of his reign Gaveston had been.

Thomas Earl of Lancaster was remembered and it was beginning to be said that he had been wrongfully treated. He had been humiliated and beheaded in a manner very unseemly for one in his position. Stories about his goodness—which had little foundation in truth—were circulated about him. Isabella could scarcely believe her ears when she heard that he had been called a saint. It was not long before miracles were being said to be performed at his grave.

His brother Henry, now Earl of Lancaster, came to see the Queen and to tell her how much he understood her dislike of the Despensers.

It was significant. Henry of Lancaster—certainly not the fighter and leader his brother had been—was offering her his support. Even the King's two half-brothers Thomas Earl of Norfolk and Edmund Earl of Kent came to see her and to pay her very special homage because they too were heartily tired of their brother's preoccupation with the Despensers.

'It will not be easy to bring about his banishment,' she told her brothers-in-law.

'It should be done,' replied Kent.

'The King would fight to the death to save them,' said Isabella.

'Still,' repeated Kent steadily, 'it should be done.'

It was an indication of the way people were thinking and of great gratification to Isabella.

She was desperately looking for an opportunity which would take her to France where she could rejoin Mortimer.

*   *   *

Although the Despensers seemed at times to rush madly down that path of folly which had led Gaveston to disaster, they were shrewd. They had noticed a change in the Queen's attitude towards the King. They had been well aware that she previously tolerated them and had received the King for the sole reason of getting children. They understood that now she had four she had decided that was the end.

This was reasonable enough but she was turning more and more against the King—a fact which would have been no cause for concern but for the popularity she enjoyed with certain people.

The chief of these were the Londoners who had always favoured her and had particularly disliked the King's handsome young men. The Londoners were at this time annoyed with the King because he had removed a plaque from St Paul's which had been set up to applaud the good deeds of Thomas Earl of Lancaster. Since he was dead—and had died so ignobly —they had decided to make a saint of him. They forgot his indolence and incompetence; they endowed him with virtues he had not possessed; they were constantly telling each other that if he were there life would be different. It was dangerous and particularly so when miracles were said to take place at that spot where the plaque had been as well as at Lancaster's tomb. It was a sign of the times.

Their chief cause for concern was Isabella.

'Everywhere the Queen goes the people cheer,' complained Hugh.

'They have always thought very highly of her,' replied Edward.

'Yes, at your expense! I like that not.'

'Dear Hugh, you are too mindful of me.'

'And should I not be of my liege lord?'

'There, I have made you scarlet with indignation.'

'Indeed I am indignant at anything which bodes ill for my lord.'

'What bodes ill now, dear nephew?'

Edward had taken to calling Hugh nephew. He said it was a pleasant relationship and some people would take it from the name that he regarded Hugh in that light.

'The Queen, I think, my lord.'

'The Queen! In what way?'

'She is restive. She is jealous of me. She sees too many people.'

'What should we do? You tell me, Hugh.'

'Let us consider her.'

'Do so, Hugh.'

'Her brother is the King of France and she writes frequently to him. There are complaints in her letters of your treatment of her.'

Edward shrugged his shoulders. 'I doubt her brother has time for her gossip.'

'The King of France would always have time to hear evil spoken of the King of England.'

'She speaks no evil. She merely complains that I spend more time with you than with her. Well, I do not intend to spend more time with her if it means missing your company.'

'I know it and rejoice in it. I wonder whether the Pope would grant an annulment.'

'An annulment! And she the sister of the King of France.'

'No, he would be afraid of France. He would never grant it. But we might try.'

'It would have to be in secret.'

'It would be. But I believe you should take over some of her lands. She is very well endowed.'

Edward nodded. 'Then let it be done.'

'It is unwise that she should keep her French servants. How can we know that these may not be spies for France?'

'What would you suggest?'

'That they be sent away. Her allowance should be cut to twenty shillings a day and that is enough for her. With more she might use it to make mischief. I believe she is in correspondence with someone in France.'

'She writes now and then to her brother I know.'

'Yes . . . and maybe others.'

'What mean you, Hugh?'

'I am not sure, but for your sake I should like to put a watch on her.'

'A watch, dear boy?'

'I thought my wife might be her . . . what shall we call it . . .

keeper of the household. She will be able to report to us what is going on there.'

'Would she undertake such a task?'

'She would if she were told to.' Hugh's wife was the daughter of the Earl of Gloucester and the Princess Joanna, daughter of Edward the First and therefore Edward's niece. Hugh had already come into his share of the Gloucester estate through her, so he was pleased with his marriage. Whether Eleanor le Despenser was as gratified with it was another matter.

However she could be made to act as keeper of the household for Isabella and report where her correspondence went.

So it was arranged.

The indignation of the Queen when she realized what was happening was great; but much to the surprise of those about her she made little complaint. She was biding her time. Soon she would be the one to call the tune.

*   *   *

How maddening it was that she should be submitted to such indignity. The King's niece to be her guardian—that foolish little creature who was afraid of her mincing husband! How dared she! And yet of course the poor little thing was afraid to do otherwise. She had an idea that the silly girl tried to take her letters and give them to her spying husband. Did she think Isabella would be such a fool as to allow her to do that? Did she think she had not friends who would take what she wrote in secret and deliver it unopened to its destination?

Charles, the last of her three brothers, was now the King of France. He was known as Charles the Fair having inherited the good looks of his father Philip IV. It was said that he was doomed as we're all the descendants of the direct line of the Capets and really it seemed that the curse was working. First her father, then Louis le Hutin, then Philip the Tall and the only one who was left was Charles.

He still lived but like the people of France she was ready to hear that some catastrophe had overtaken him.

She wrote fiercely to him, letters which were for his eyes alone. Could he stand by and see his sister—a Princess of France—treated thus? He already knew—the whole world knew that her husband preferred the couch of his chamberlain to hers. Her husband was a miser. He had robbed her of lands and possessions; he had ordered that she should receive a pittance. He was depriving her not only of her status as a Queen but of everything she possessed. The greatest indignity of all had been to set a keeper of the household over her. A woman who—poor creature—had been married as a child to Despenser on account of her fortune. This woman's task was to spy on her, to steal her letters, to treat her as a prisoner. Could he, her brother and King of France stand by and see this happen to a member of the great royal family of France?

Charles le Bel decided that he could pacify his sister by reminding Edward that he owed him personal homage for the provinces he held in France and he considered it the duty of the King of England to come to France and do his duty.

'Depend upon it,' said Hugh le Despenser, 'the Queen has stirred up trouble. Letters from her have got through to the King of France and this is the result. Let your young half-brother Edmund go to France. It will keep him out of mischief. He can explain to Charles le Bel that you are too engrossed in matters of state here to make the journey just yet.'

Edward always made a point of taking Hugh's advice and Edmund Earl of Kent was sent to France.

Charles received the Earl with a show of hospitality and gave some magnificent entertainments in his honour.

The young Earl was no match for the King of France. Moreover, while Kent was on a visit to Aquitaine, Charles de Valois, a younger brother of Philip the Fair and uncle of the King, invaded the Duchy and so successful was he that the earl was forced to agree to a peace which was greatly to his disadvantage and gave the French possession of almost the whole of Aquitaine.

Isabella watched these events very closely and believed that she saw through them the chance she had been waiting for.

Humbly, she sent word to Edward asking if she might see him. He could scarcely refuse such a request and he was surprised to see how meekly she came.

Hugh was wise as usual, he thought. They were treating her in the right manner.

She made no reference to his neglect of her. She came straight to the point and said how grieved she was to see the conflict between him and her brother. She could not understand what her uncle was thinking of to attack Aquitaine so villainously.

'The French have always been after it,' said Edward. 'I'm afraid my brother Kent was not experienced enough to handle the situation.'

'Poor Edmund, he did his best.'

'His best was poor statecraft,' said Edward.

She wanted to laugh. And you, my fine man, she thought, what of your statecraft? Edmund's ineptitude is nothing when compared with yours.

'My brothers were always fond of me,' she went on. 'Edward, I believe that if I went to Charles I could put your case to him. I believe I could make him see reason. Perhaps I could bring my uncle to reconsider the treaty. It would please me to try.'

'*You* go! That would be useless. They would never listen to you.'

'I was always treated with great respect in my father's court,' she said with pointed dignity. 'I doubt I should receive anything less in my brother's.'

Edward looked at her thoughtfully. She had managed to win the approval of the Londoners. Hugh had been talking about that the other day. He had said she had always been careful never to do anything which might lose that respect.

'It is a matter I should have to consider,' he said.

Oh yes, she thought, ask Master Hugh whether he will allow your Queen to visit her brother.

Her spirits dropped. She might have been able to delude Edward. Hugh le Despenser was another matter. In spite of the fact that he allowed his acquisitive nature to bring him more and more unpopularity every week, he was shrewd. He could surely not have connected her with Mortimer's escape. She had been very careful about Mortimer. She had not written to him at all. That would have been too dangerous even though she had her faithful friends whom she could trust to deliver important letters. She had been afraid of putting him in danger. No, Hugh le Despenser could not know of the relationship between her and Mortimer.

There was nothing to be done but let Edward consult with his dear Hugh. Meanwhile she must pray that she could get that permission to leave. It would be so much more satisfactory than attempting to escape, for they were not quite ready yet to come out into the open.

*   *   *

Hugh considered the matter.

'So she wishes to go to her brother?'

'That is what she said. She would mediate for better relations between us. This treaty my brother has made is disastrous for us.'

Hugh was silent and Edward went on, 'She has proved herself in the past to have a certain grasp of affairs. I believe too that her brother is fond of her. He might listen to her.'

'He is going to insist on your going out to do homage to him.'

'I shall not go.'

'It could mean trouble if you don't.'

'That's why I thought it would be a good idea to let Isabella go and see what she can make of things. I am sure she is eager to impress us.'

'Yes,' agreed Hugh. 'She has changed of late. She has become resigned. There was a time when I thought there was a smouldering lioness inside her, waiting to strike. Now, she has changed.'

'It was having the children. She dotes on young Edward you know.'

Hugh nodded. 'Let her go then. I see no harm in it.'

'She shall go,' replied Edward.

When Isabella heard the news she could scarcely believe her good fortune.

She lost no time in setting out for France.

*   *   *

She could scarcely restrain her exultation as she made her rapid preparations. The scheming of years was coming to its climax. How clever she had been! How wise to act so discreetly through the years! Now she had her son, her little Edward— not so little, old enough to be crowned King, with hands to guide him . . . hers and Mortimer's.

Oh gentle Mortimer, soon to be with him, to embrace him, to lie at his side, to make love, to make plans.

Nothing must go wrong now.

May was a beautiful month with the trees in bloom and the birds mad with joy—a manifestation of her own feelings. This was the springtime of her life—although she was twenty-nine years of age. It was a beginning, and twenty-nine was not old. A little mature perhaps but one needed maturity to plan carefully. She was inclined to think that everything was set fair.

Her company consisted only of Lord John Cromwell and four knights, apart from her personal attendants. The wind was with them and as she stepped onto French soil she could not restrain her expressions of joy. Lord John remarked that a love of one's native land was something which never left one. And she allowed him to think that this was the reason for her exultation. If he but knew, her thoughts were in England— but not England as it was today ruled by an effete King and his minion.

She was happy. Soon she would be with Mortimer.

It was sooner than she had dared hope, for he had heard of her arrival and came in haste to greet her.

He bowed low. He must not show undue familiarity before the company, but in his eyes she saw all she wished to know.

'My love,' he whispered as he bowed before her. 'So long it has seemed.'

'At last I am here.'

Then he was saying that he had heard of her arrival and had come to escort her to her brother's court in Paris.

Mortimer had arranged for them to stay the night at a *château* put at her disposal by her cousin Robert d'Artois who had heard a great deal of her humiliation at the hands of her husband and had been incensed that a daughter of the royal house of France should be so treated.

As they rode along Mortimer talked to her of his adventures since he had left England. He had found favour with her brother the King, which was perhaps not surprising for French Kings were always ready to favour the enemies of the Kings of England. He had told Charles a great deal about the influence Hugh le Despenser wielded over the King and naturally Charles, seeing clearly Edward's folly, was not displeased about that.

'I am happy to say,' said Mortimer, 'that the King your brother has shown nothing but friendship towards me.' He bent his head and whispered. 'Tonight ... It must be tonight.'

And she answered, 'Tonight.'

When they arrived at the *château* her cousin was eager to give her a royal welcome. He made it clear that he was very impressed by her beauty. She felt that she had come to life, recognized for what she had always known she was, a charming and desirable woman.

Lord John Cromwell was a little uneasy about what he called Mortimer's undue familiarity. 'He was, my lady, the King's prisoner,' he explained to Isabella. 'Now he is an exile. If he were to return to England he would lose his head.'

'True enough, my lord,' answered Isabella and appeared to reflect. 'But it seems to me that I am on a difficult mission. I have to get good terms for my husband from my brother and if Mortimer speaks truth he is on friendly terms with Charles. I shall need all the friends I can get. It would not be wise to alienate Mortimer.'

Lord John agreed with this. 'But I would not trust him too far if I were you, my lady, if you will forgive my mentioning the matter.'

'You are forgiven, Lord John. I know that you are faithful to me and to the King.'

'The Mortimers were always a wild family, my lady. They ruled the Marcher land and it is in them to rule.'

'I agree with you. Trust me, I shall be careful.'

How she laughed when that night she lay in Mortimer's arms.

The reunion had been one of complete satisfaction. The fact that it had been planned with care gave it an added delight. They talked in whispers through the night for before dawn he must be gone. It would never do for any to guess at this point that she had come to France to join her lover.

'I shall never go back without you,' she told him.

'When we go back it will be with an army. We shall succeed.'

'Of course we shall succeed.'

'Gentle Mortimer, it must be so. You and I together and Edward with us ... my young Edward. We must find a way of getting him here.'

'How does he feel about his father?'

'Bewildered. He is but a boy. But a clever one ... one who knows his destiny. He hears gossip of Hugh le Despenser. It disturbs him.'

'Oh, my love ... my love,' cried Mortimer. 'What a happy day when I was sent to the Tower!'

'In the gardens that day I knew I had been waiting for you all my life.'

'None ever loved as we do.'

'And none ever planned such a great project as they lay in their bed of love.'

'How long till dawn? I would I could hold back time.'

'The future is for us, my love.'

'Ah,' he answered, 'for us.'

'The day will come,' she said, 'when you will not have to creep away before the first streaks of light appear in the sky.'

He wondered then if she meant she would marry him. Could the Queen of England marry a Mortimer? He had a wife. She had a husband. But such obstacles could be removed.

Ambition. Love. How glorious when these two walked together. To make love! To make plans! Life was good. Never had either of them dreamed of such bliss as life now offered them.

'Would we could stay like this for ever,' said Mortimer.

'Nay, my dear love,' answered the Queen. 'This is but the springtime of our union. Glorious summer lies before us.'

'And autumn and winter?' he said.

'Autumn will come with the fruits of our endeavours,' she said. 'And if there is winter we shall know how to keep each other warm. What talk for lovers; Let us make talk when we cannot make love. Do you agree, dear Mortimer?'

Mortimer agreed.

ISABELLA

LETTERS FROM ENGLAND

THERE was a royal welcome for Isabella at her brother's court. Charles did not look in good health and as soon as she saw him she thought of the curse of the Templars. He possessed those outstanding good looks which came here and there in the family. Isabella herself had them, so had her father, and they had appeared again in Charles. Now there was an air of fragility about him.

He immediately gave her a private audience for he was very eager to hear whether rumours he had heard concerning the King of England were true.

Isabella began by telling him how delighted she was to be in her native land. She had had a most unhappy life in England and it was all due to the warped nature of the King.

'He is abnormal, brother,' she said. 'You will know that his great favourite was Piers Gaveston. He has been followed by Hugh le Despenser. They were always together. I scarcely saw him.'

'You have four children,' said Charles.

'I insisted that we try to get children and we succeeded.'

'So he was not with his favourite then.'

'Can you imagine my humiliation? Daughter and sister to Kings of France to be so treated.'

'It was well that you had your children ... and two sons among them.'

Charles spoke bitterly. The curse of the Templars implied that the line of Capet would end with them. It was all very well to snap one's fingers at the curse but it was working out. Louis and Philip had gone and left no heirs. If they had children they were sickly. They desperately needed a male heir for the salic law reigned in France and this decreed that the crown of France was of such noble estate that it could not come to a woman.

Charles could not help being envious of his sister's two sons. There had been great rejoicing when his wife the Queen had become pregnant. But what bitter disappointment when she had given birth to a girl. People talked of the curse again, and it did seem that the kings were doomed. What would happen when he died without heirs he did not know. He supposed his father's younger brother Charles of Valois or his cousin Philip would take the throne. It would then be the end of the direct line of the Capets when the House of Valois took over.

But he was not dead yet. There was still hope. But for the miserable curse ...

Isabella guessed what her brother was thinking but she was little concerned with the affairs of France. Those of England absorbed her.

'I seized this opportunity to get away,' she said, 'so great was my longing to see France and to leave the husband I have learned to despise.'

'He is a fool,' agreed Charles. 'Roger de Mortimer has told me much of English affairs. Now there is a man of vitality. Edward was a fool to let him escape. A fool to make a man like that a prisoner. He should have had his head while he had the chance.'

'Edward will always make the wrong decisions. He was foolish to send Kent here to deal with important affairs. Kent is too young.'

'I had thought he would have sent Pembroke.'

'Pembroke died before he could send him. Ah, yes, it would have been different if Pembroke had come. His old friends are either dying or deserting him. Edward loves the Despensers but no one else does.'

'He readily gave his consent to your coming here?'

'Oh, the Despensers were glad to be rid of me, so I was allowed to come. You see the people like me. They cheer me in the streets. It infuriates Edward because when he rides out they can be very sullen.'

'And the Despensers?'

'They would tear them limb from limb if they had a chance.'

'Not a very healthy state of affairs.'

'A diseased one I should say, brother. Oh how happy I am to be here. Everything is so much more elegant. I am going to summon some of the French dressmakers to court. No one makes clothes as they do. See how unbecomingly we dress in England. I look unworthy of you, brother.'

'I have heard several comment on your beauty. They say you are looking radiant. Not as though you have been ill-treated in England.'

'It is because I have come home. I wish to have French clothes. You will have no objection to my summoning the seamstresses?'

'Do so if you will, sister.'

'Then I shall give orders immediately. Then I must talk with you of State matters. You know I am here to plead for Edward.'

'I know it well. Can you plead for one whom you so assuredly dislike?'

'I have a son, Charles. I plead for him. He is young yet, but he is a clever boy. I want him to have a kingdom when the time comes for him to take it.'

Charles alternated between indignation at the manner in which his sister had been treated, amusement at her ability to think of her appearance at such a time, gratification that the King of England had had to send the sister of the King of France to plead for him, pleasure at having the sister for whom he had always had some affection restored to him, and certain doubts in his mind as to whether there was something behind all she said and did.

* * *

Now she was exquisitely gowned. She had summoned the finest Paris dressmakers; she had chosen the most magnificent materials and indeed she looked like a queen. Never, even in the days of her early youth had she been so beautiful. She glowed with that inner radiance which had come to her when she had found Mortimer. She was deeply in love; and she was full of plans for success. Never had she lived so fully, so danger-ously and so excitingly as she did at this time.

She became the centre of a little court. She discovered her

latent fascination. She lured people to her by her glowing
beauty, her wit, her vitality and her charm. It was said that
she was the most beautiful woman in Europe.

Mortimer adored her and she was entirely Mortimer's. But
others fell in love with her. There was her cousin Artois for
one. He grew more and more indignant at the manner in which
she had been treated in England; he told her that his great
desire was to serve her.

Those Englishmen whose duty had brought them to France
formed a coterie about her. Mortimer was of course at their
head, and joining him and Artois were the Bishops of Winchester and Norwich who were acting as Edward's ambassadors
in Paris. Others who were disgusted with Edward's way of life
and despaired of England's future under him paid homage
to his Queen. They guessed that there was something more to
her being here than to plead with her brother for her husband.
Young Edmund Duke of Kent who was feeling very depressed
because of his failures in France came to her and she comforted
him, assuring him that what had happened was no fault of his.
There was no respect for Edward abroad, she said, and any
mission of his must fail while this was the case. She spent
several hours with Kent placating him, winning him to her
side. He was one of those who was half in love with her.

'It is good,' said Mortimer, 'to have the King's brother with
us.'

Others like the Earl of Richmond and Henry de Beaumont
were in constant attendance. All useful adherents, all enemies
of the Despensers who had offended them too often.

So the plan progressed well.

But of course she must appear to be doing the task which
she had come out to do.

At length Charles agreed that he would send no more troops
into Gascony and would consider returning the conquered
provinces to England if Edward came and paid long overdue
homage to him for his French possessions.

She had many opportunities of talking to Mortimer because
he formed part of that little court which surrounded her and if
she could talk in private with her cousin Artois and the Bishops
of Norwich and Winchester so could she with Mortimer.

'What if he comes?' she asked.

'The Despensers will persuade him against it.'

'He and they are eager for peace.'

'Yes, but they are not going to let him come without them
and would they be welcome at your brother's court? There
is an alternative.'

'I know,' she said. They looked at each other and marvelled
at the manner in which they even thought alike.

'Do you think he would allow it?' asked Mortimer.

'He is fool enough to.'

'If we had the boy here, we should be half way to victory.'

'We can try it,' said the Queen.

'With the utmost care. Let him think you but do it to ease
him and because you think it is time the boy began to realize
his obligations.'

'I will do it,' said Isabella. 'But first I must get my brother
to agree.'

'First,' said Mortimer, 'let us wait and see what Edward's
answer is. We must by no means seem over eager for the boy to
come in his place. We have to tread very warily, my dear love.'

'How well I know it,' replied Isabella.

*   *   *

When the Despensers heard the terms the King of France
had set they were, as Isabella and Mortimer had guessed they
would be, very disturbed.

The matter had been before the Council and there it was
agreed that Edward should go to Paris. The Despensers were
worried. They discussed the matter earnestly together and
came to the conclusion that the King must on no account be
allowed to go.

'Without his protection,' said the elder to the younger, 'there
would be some excuse to seize us. Then I would not give a
penny for our chances.'

'Edward would never allow them to harm us.'

'My dear son, they would not wait for Edward. Look how
they treated Gaveston and even Lancaster was hurried to his
death. Once they had us, depend upon it we should be dead
men before Edward could do anything to save us.'

'To go is the only way he can save his French possessions.'

'To stay is the only way he can save us. No, Hugh my son, the
King must not go to France. You must persuade him against it.
He *must* remain here. Without him, with the country in the
mood it is in, we are lost.'

'Is it really as bad as you think, Father?'

'My dear son, you are constantly with the King. You divert him. You are his greatest friend. *I* have time to look around at what is happening. I happen to know that Henry of Lancaster has been writing to that Adam of Orlton who I am sure had a hand in Mortimer's escape from the Tower. He had put up a cross to his brother's memory at Leicester and is circulating more stories about more miracles at Lancaster's tomb. No, Edward must not go. You must seek means of detaining him. Do not let him give a direct answer.'

Edward was only too ready to be detained. He had no fancy for going to Charles of France and doing homage. It was an act never relished by any of his predecessors.

He was delighted when the communication came from Isabella.

She had spoken with the King of France and he had agreed that if Edward found it difficult to leave his realm at this time he would accept the homage from young Edward. She believed that it was an excellent notion and if the King agreed to send their son it would be a good exercise in diplomacy for the boy and she would take good care of him.

If he agreed young Edward could be created Duke of Aquitaine and Count of Ponthieu and could then pay homage to her brother Charles for these provinces.

Edward was delighted. The Despensers discussed the matter together. It would keep Edward in England and their lives could depend on that.

'Let the boy go,' said Hugh to the King. 'It will be a good experience for him. He is growing up. It is time he began to take part in affairs. He can lessen your burden, my lord. Yes, let the boy go.'

Edward's life had been one long series of mistakes, but in sending his son to France he made the greatest mistake of them all.

Isabella and Mortimer could scarcely believe their good fortune. Their plan was progressing beyond their wildest hope.

* * *

With what joy she rode to the coast to wait the coming of the Prince! Mortimer was beside her.

'Soon,' he whispered, 'we shall be going home. We shall go

at the head of an army. Nothing could have served us better than the coming of young Edward. The fact that the King sends him shows that he is unworthy to rule. It is now our task to see that the boy is on our side.'

'Fear not that I can win him to us,' replied the Queen.

'None could withstand your charm,' Mortimer assured her, 'least of all a young boy ... and he your son.'

It was a wonderful moment when young Edward stepped ashore. He was such a handsome boy, showing promise of Plantagenet good looks. He was going to be tall as his father and grandfather had been; he was flaxen-haired with keen blue eyes, alert, intelligent, eager for life, aware of his destiny and determined to fulfil it.

He was accompanied by the Bishops of Oxford and Exeter and a train of knights. All these, thought the Queen, must be won to our cause.

The boy was clearly overwhelmed by his mother. He would have bowed to her but she would have no ceremony.

'My son,' she cried. 'My dearest son, it makes me so happy to see you. So handsome, so healthy. Oh my dear boy, I am so proud of you!'

Young Edward coloured faintly. He had always admired his mother; she was so beautiful and she had always made it clear that he was the favourite of her children. He had heard it said how patient she was in enduring her humiliations. He was beginning to understand his father's way of life and deplored it. He knew that there was trouble in the country because of it and that one day he would be the King. When that time came it would be different. He would make sure of that. He had heard a great deal about his grandfather and he wanted to be like him.

Walter Stapledon, Bishop of Exeter, had talked to him of his duty and had impressed on him that his life must be dedicated to the service of his country. So he was delighted to be with his mother and to ride beside her to Paris. He was not sure how he should feel towards Mortimer. He knew that the Earl had been his father's prisoner and had escaped from the Tower. But his mother seemed very friendly with him and Mortimer certainly made a great effort to please the young Prince. And even his uncle, the King of France, showed affection for him and told him how glad he was that his father had agreed that he should come.

On a September day in the Castle of Bois de Vincennes near Paris young Edward paid homage to Charles IV of France in place of his father. It was an impressive ceremony and enacted with a show of amity, but the French King was too wily to stick entirely to his bargain. He might restore Gascony and Ponthieu but he had suffered considerable losses in the action, he complained, and for this reason, he thought it was only fair that he should keep the Agenais.

Isabella and Mortimer looked on with pleasure at the ceremony. The trouble was that now the homage had been paid and the King of France satisfied there was no longer any reason why the English party should remain in France.

To leave would mean saying good-bye to Mortimer. Moreover if she went back to England Isabella would be in the same position as she had been before. Of course she must not return and the task now was to gather as many people as possible to their banner, and when they had a considerable army, then would be the time to strike.

There already existed a nucleus of discontented people from England and this grew daily. But it was not an army. Isabella wondered whether her brother would help, but Charles was disenchanted with war and he had no intention of carrying on one in England.

He had offered hospitality to Mortimer because he thought he could supply useful information about England; moreover Mortimer was a declared enemy of Edward so therefore it was wise to have him at hand. Naturally he received his sister who was also Queen of England but he did not expect even her to outstay her welcome.

Mortimer and Isabella realized that although the first part of the mission was accomplished, they had had incredible luck. But now they had to conjure up an army from somewhere. How?

It was true the cause was growing. Many of the people who formed part of their circle could raise men back in England.

The situation grew more and more difficult every day. Even the King was beginning to wonder why the English party did not make preparations to leave. Isabella and Mortimer had anxious meetings together. They would not be separated. Moreover it would be very dangerous for her to leave now. There were surely spies at court and it might well be that someone had noticed the relationship between them and had reported it to Edward.

'It would give him an opportunity to be rid of you,' said Mortimer and added with a shiver: 'He could accuse you of treason. Time is what we need, my dearest. Time.'

'Then we must find it,' replied Isabella firmly. 'We shall not falter now.'

'Stapledon has a great influence over young Edward,' Mortimer pointed out.

Isabella agreed. 'I am a little concerned about Stapledon,' she added.

'He makes it clear that he regards me as a traitor,' added Mortimer.

'The old fool. I am going to sound him out. I am determined to discover what is in his mind.'

'Go carefully.'

'You may trust me,' replied Isabella.

'Edward must have had a high opinion of him to have trusted young Edward to him.'

'Edward would always put his trust in the wrong people. I will see what can be done with the old Bishop.'

Mortimer agreed. Isabella's power to fascinate had grown since she had come to France. She had changed from the humiliated Queen who at every turn was shown by her husband how much more attractive he had found his male friends.

*   *   *

Walter Stapledon, Bishop of Exeter, was reckoned to be a man of integrity. He was learned and a member of the University of Oxford. He was, in fact, the founder of Exeter College which at this time was known as Stapledon Hall. He had taken a great interest in the rebuilding of his cathedral and had spent a part of his income on making it beautiful.

He had gone into politics some years before when Edward the First had sent him on a mission to France. Later he had returned to France, this time with Edward the Second; he had deplored the differences between Lancaster and the King, and had tried to bring about a reconciliation between them; and Edward's trust in him was shown by his sending his son to France in his care.

The Queen approached him carefully.

'My lord Bishop,' she said, 'how think you my son responds to his responsibilities?'

'He has done well, my lady,' answered the Bishop.

'I am glad you agree with me. It is said that he will be another such as his grandfather. I pray this may be so.'

The Bishop did not meet her eye. He said: 'There is a resemblance between the Prince and his father and grandfather.'

'I trust he may be like his grandfather,' said the Queen firmly.

The Bishop was alert. He had heard rumours. Could it be true that the Queen was engaged in an adulterous liaison with Mortimer? There was that in their manner when they were together to suggest this might be true. Mortimer—a traitor to the King—a man who had escaped from prison where he had been condemned for treachery, and to be received as he was, to be honoured by the Queen and the Court of France! It was a state of affairs which made the Bishop very suspicious.

The Queen went on: 'My lord, like so many good men you must be saddened by what is happening in England.'

She waited for his response but it did not come and she went on somewhat impatiently: 'You cannot be happy about the King's obsession with Hugh le Despenser.'

'I respect the King's right to choose his ministers,' replied the Bishop rather coldly.

'Ministers, my lord,' said the Queen rather hotly. 'Would you call pretty Hugh a minister?'

'He holds the office of Chamberlain bestowed on him by the King, my lady.'

'My lord Bishop,' retorted the Queen, 'you must not think I should consider it treason if you were to speak your mind.'

'I can assure you, my lady, that my thoughts are not treasonable.'

The Bishop bowed with dignity and asked leave to retire.

She saw at once that she had made a mistake. He was not with them. He had the sort of blind loyalty which told him he must support the King at all cost.

She went at once to Mortimer and told him of the interview, repeating it word for word.

'He could be dangerous,' agreed Mortimer. 'And he will talk to Edward.'

'My dear love, what can we do about it?'

Mortimer stared into the distance. 'If he is a danger to our cause he must be removed.'

'How?' whispered the Queen.

'We must find the answer to that one, my love. It must not appear that we have a hand in it. This is too important a cause to be spoilt by a priest with a misplaced sense of duty.'

Walter Stapledon went to his chamber and shut himself in. It's true, he thought. The Queen with Mortimer is plotting to overthrow the King. It is for that reason they wanted the Prince here; this is why they will not go back to England but make excuse after excuse to stay.

What could they be planning to do? Raise an army? Invade England? How far was the King of France involved?

And the Queen knew that he was aware of what was happening. She and Mortimer ... her paramour ... Guilty of disloyalty and adultery ... They would stop at nothing. In the moment when he and the Queen had faced each other she knew that she had betrayed her evil schemes to him.

Walter Stapledon, he said, your life is not worth one little groat.

Perhaps even now the assassin was lurking in readiness for him.

He sent for his servant—a man whom he could trust.

'Have you some of your garments which would not look too ill on me?'

The man stared in astonishment.

'I will tell you something,' said the Bishop. 'I have to get away from the court with all speed. I need a good disguise. Can you procure something ... for yourself and for me. Then, my good friend, we will make for the coast with all speed and take ship to England.'

'If it is your wish, my lord.'

'It is not only my wish but my need.'

*   *   *

Luck was with the Bishop. He and his servant reached the coast without mishap and quickly found a ship to take them to England.

He went to his lodging and there discarded his disguise and garbed in his bishop's robes sought an audience with the King.

As might have been expected Hugh le Despenser was with him.

Edward expressed surprise and consternation at the sight of him.

'My lord Bishop, your mission was with the Prince. Is he with you?'

'I left the Court of France in a hurry, my lord,' said the Bishop, 'and disguised. Had I not done so I should never have been allowed to get away to tell you what is happening there.'

The King was puzzled but Hugh was alert.

'Pray go on, my lord Bishop,' he said.

'My lord, I hesitate to say this. Nor would I if I did not firmly believe it to be truth. The Queen and Mortimer are engaged in an adulterous intrigue.'

'Mortimer!' cried the King. 'Mortimer and Isabella!'

'It is clear that she had a hand in effecting his escape. They had planned this. They schemed to get the Prince with them and once they did were more careless than they had been before. They are gathering malcontents and their plots bode no good for you, my lord.'

'This is wild talk, Bishop,' said the King.

But Hugh had laid a hand on his arm. 'It smells of truth, dear lord,' he said. 'As you know I have long suspected the Queen.'

'What good can she do?' asked Edward.

'Is the King of France with her?' cried Hugh.

'I know not. As soon as I realized that my suspicions were correct I thought it my duty to make haste to you. I implied that I would not work with them and for that reason my life was in danger.'

'It is monstrous!' cried the King. 'What can we do?'

'We must recall the Queen and the Prince without delay,' said Hugh. 'Mortimer cannot stand without them.'

'I wonder how far it has gone,' mused Edward.

'My dear lord,' replied Hugh, 'it is nothing which we cannot handle. The King of France will not send men to England. He might help with arms and sympathy, but he will not be able to do anything against the army we shall raise. But first let us not make it known that we are aware of their villainy. Let us get the Queen and the Prince back. When they are here it will be necessary to restrict the Queen. I doubt the poison has seeped very far into the Prince's mind. We must be thankful to my lord Bishop for his loyalty.'

'My dear Bishop,' said the King, 'it shall not be forgotten.'

'I seek not rewards for my loyalty, my lord,' said the Bishop with dignity.

'I know it well,' replied Edward warmly. 'I thank God that I have many good friends in my realm on whom I can depend and who will serve me no matter who comes against me.'

On the advice of both Hugh and the Bishop the King that day wrote to the King of France telling him that now that the matter of homage was settled he would be glad of the return of his Queen and son.

* * *

The King of France sent for his sister and when she came he embraced her coolly and said: 'It is time you went back to England.'

Isabella looked as distressed as she felt.

'It grieves me to think of returning,' she said. 'It has been so wonderful for me to be here in my native country. Life is so different here. If you but knew, brother, what I have had to endure.'

Charles tapped the letter in his hand. 'Edward reminds me that it is time you returned. You should make your preparations.'

She hesitated. She wanted to tell him of their plans. How so much was going in their favour yet how they needed time.

'If you do not go,' went on the King, 'Edward will think I hold you against your will.'

'Does he say that?'

'No. He implies that the reluctance is on your part.'

'How right he is! Oh Charles, you do not know how I have suffered through those Despensers.'

'You have mentioned it now and then sister,' replied Charles with increasing coolness.

Oh God help me, thought Isabella. He is going to send me back.

'You want me to leave do you?' she asked bluntly.

'My dear sister, you have been long here. Your business is settled. It is natural that you should return to your husband.'

'You mock me. My husband! You know what he is.'

'You and your son should return to your home.'

'He asks that you send us, does he? In what terms?'

'He asks why there is the delay in your returning and

mentions that you have been away long enough.'

'Charles, I am afraid.'

'You Isabella ... afraid! I know you are many things but I am surprised to find *you* afraid.'

'They will kill me if I go back,' she said quietly.

'Kill you. *My* sister. They would have to answer to me if they did. I do not think they would wish that.'

'Charles it would not seem like murder. But it would be. The Despensers hate me. You know what it was like before I came. I was almost their prisoner. That is what they wish. Oh, they will not cut off my head. Nor will they give me a dose of poison which immediately removes me ... but they will kill me nevertheless. They will imprison me and slowly they will take my life away from me.'

'Isabella, you over-excite yourself.'

'Would you not be over-excited brother if you were faced with murderers? Let me stay here, only a little longer I promise you. I will make plans ... but I cannot go back to Edward and the Despensers yet.'

She had fallen to her knees and raised her eyes supplicatingly to his. She was very beautiful and she was his sister and they were the only two left of their father's children. Charles himself felt none too secure with the Templars curse hanging over him.

He raised her and kissed her lightly on the cheek.

'Do not be so dramatic, Isabella. Certainly you may stay a little longer. I will write something to Edward. But you must not get up to mischief. Do you understand?'

Mischief?'

'There are rumours. I have heard that you are over friendly with Roger de Mortimer.'

'What calumnies! Of course I am friendly with the English here in France.'

'You have gathered a good many about you.'

'Indeed why should they not speak with me? They are unhappy about the King even as I am.'

'I would not wish my court to be the plotting ground.'

'Dear Charles! You are going to be my good brother. I promise you that I shall make my plans for departure and as soon as I can bring myself to do so I shall leave.'

'And when you go take your malcontents with you.'

'And you will write to Edward.'

'And tell him that your departure has been temporarily postponed but that within a few weeks you will be making your plans to leave.'

*   *   *

The King of France was frowning over a letter he had received from the King of England. A few weeks had passed since he had told Isabella she might remain a little longer, but so far she had said nothing about her departure.

'Very dear and beloved brother,' wrote Edward,
    'We have received and well considered your letters ... It seems that you have been told, dearest brother, by persons whom you consider worthy of credit that our companion, the Queen of England, dare not return to us, being in peril of her life, as she apprehends from Hugh le Despenser. Certes, dearest brother, it cannot be that she can have fear of him, or any other man in our realm. If either Hugh or any other living being in our dominions would wish to do her ill, and it came to our knowledge, we would chastise him in a manner which would be an example to all others ...
    We also entreat you, dearly beloved brother, that you would be pleased to deliver up to us Edward our beloved eldest son, your nephew ... We pray you to suffer him to come to us with all speed for we have often sent for him and we greatly wish to see him and speak with him, and every day we long for his return ...'

Charles's brow was wrinkled. The letter was genuine enough and although he despised Edward as an incompetent ruler he could not believe he was capable of plotting the murder of his wife. Whereas he could believe of his sister that she was concerned in some mischief.

And whatever it was he wanted no part in it. He felt weak in health, lacking in vitality; he doubted he would ever get a son and heir. The curse of the Templars sat heavily upon him and he was not going to look for trouble outside his realm.

Isabella would have to take her problems elsewhere.

By the same messenger there were letters for Isabella and young Edward.

Isabella, with Mortimer beside her, read hers aloud.

'Lady, Oftentimes have we sent to you, both before and after the homage, of our great desire to have you with us, and of our grief at heart at your long absence; and as we understand that you do us great michief by this we will that you come to us with all speed and without further excuses.

Before the homage was performed you made the advancement of that business an excuse and now that we have sent by the honourable father, the Bishop of Winchester, our safe conduct to you "you will not come for fear and doubt of Hugh le Despenser" whereat we cannot marvel too much ...

'And, certes, lady, we know for truth, and so know you, that he has always procured from us all the he could for you, nor to you have either evil or villainy been done since you entered into our comradeship ... and we are much displeased, now the homage has been made to our dearest brother, the King of France, and we have much fair prospect of amity, that you, whom we have sent to make the peace, should be the cause (which God forfend) of increasing the breach between us by things which are feigned and contrary to the truth. Wherefore we charge you as urgently as we can, that ceasing from all pretences, delays and false excuses, you will come to us with all the haste you can. Our Bishop has reported to us that our brother, the King of France has told you in his presence "that, by the tenor of your safe conduct, you would not be delayed or molested in coming to us as a wife should to her lord" ... Also we require of you that our dear son Edward return to us with all possible speed for we much desire to see him and speak with him ...'

Isabella finished reading and looked in dismay at Mortimer, who said: 'It is clear that he is becoming anxious.'

'He will have written to my brother,' replied Isabella. 'My dear love, soon it will be impossible for us to remain in France.'

'And it is equally impossible for you to return to England. We *must* gather together an army. We must be certain of a good reception when we do return to England. If only we had a few more months.'

'My brother cannot force me to go.'

'I fear he can. And he doubtless will if Edward continues to demand your return.'

'There must be a way,' cried Isabella. 'We have come so far we cannot throw everything away now. Moreover in spite of Edward's protestations, I would not give much for my chances with the Despensers if I returned to England.'

'Let us not show panic. Let us see what is the effect of the letters Edward will have sent to your brother.'

'There is something else,' cried Isabella. 'He will have written to my son.'

There was silence. 'I must go to Edward and see what his father has written. The boy is asking direct questions.'

'He will not wish to leave you,' Mortimer assured her. 'You have cast a spell over him as you have over us all.'

'It is true that he loves me well, but he is clever. He thinks often of when he will be King.'

'There is no harm in that. The sooner he is, the better.'

'Still, Stapledon instilled some filial feeling in him. A curse on that man. These letters are the direct result of his escape and reporting to the King.'

'It is done. Let us go on from where we now stand.'

'You are right, my love. I will go at once to young Edward.'

The young Prince was at that moment reading the letter from his father.

'Very dear son,

As you are young and of tender age, we remind you of that which we charged and commanded you at your departure from Dover and you answered then, as we know with good will "that you will not trespass or disobey any of our injunctions in any point for any one". And since that your homage has been received by our dearest brother, the King of France, your uncle, be pleased to take your leave of him and return to us with all speed in company with your mother, if so be that she will come quickly and if she will not come, then come you without farther delay, for we have great desire to see you and to speak with you; therefore stay not for your mother, not for anyone else on our blessing . . .'

Of course they must return to England, thought Edward. He wondered why his mother waived the matter every time he suggested it. It had been pleasant at the Court of France but he was looking forward to returning home. He would speak to his mother at the earliest possible moment.

He did not have to wait long. As he was putting the letter into a drawer his mother came into the room.

'Oh Edward, dear son,' she cried embracing him, 'did you enjoy the hunt? I hear you brought in a fine buck.'

'I don't think I ever saw a finer,' replied Edward enthusiastically. 'My lady, I have heard from my father.'

'So have I.'

She waited and Edward said: 'He is impatient for my return. He wants us to leave as soon as we possibly can.'

She went to him and slipped her arm through his.

'Edward, my dearest,' she said, 'I have begun to rely on you. I look upon you as my protector. You wouldn't allow any harm to come to me, would you?'

Edward flushed. 'I would protect you with my life.'

'Oh my darling child, what should I have done without you? Mine has not been a happy life you know. Your father and I ...'

Edward frowned. He hated to be disloyal to his father. Walter Stapledon had impressed on him that the King was supreme and must always be obeyed. But at the same time he had been taught to protect the weak; and he had sensed that of late he had become very important to his mother and he knew that she spoke the truth when she said she relied on him to be beside her. When he came into a room her eyes sought his at once. An understanding always passed between them. She was saying to him, he fancied, that she felt safe now he was there. And he replied to her that he would always be at her side if she needed him.

'This is not easy for me to say, dear Edward. May I proceed?'

'You must do as you wish, my lady.'

'You will understand I hope and not think badly of me.'

'I could never think badly of my beloved mother,' answered the boy.

'Then I will speak ... but with reluctance. You know there is much discontent in our country.'

'Yes, I do.'

'Your grandfather, whom you so strongly resemble, knew how to keep the barons in order. England needs a strong King, Edward. You are going to be a strong King. I have heard it said that it is a pity you are not older and that the crown is on your head.'

'But my father has many years before him yet.'

'Dear love, it is your father of whom I must speak. That is why I hedge and prevaricate because I cannot bring myself to say it.'

The boy was suddenly firm, giving a hint of what he would be when he came to the throne. 'You must tell me. It is not fitting that I of all people should be kept in ignorance.'

'So thought I as I wrestled with my conscience. You shall know. Your father is not like your grandfather. Your grandfather was a good and faithful husband.'

'My father is unfaithful to you!'

She nodded. 'Not with women. Dear Edward, you must have heard of Gaveston. He was the love of your father's life while he lived. Those who cared for this country's well-being took him out to a hill and cut off his head. Then he was replaced by Hugh le Despenser. You are old enough to know what humiliation I suffered.'

'Oh, my dear mother!'

'I knew your sympathy would be for me. For years I endured this humiliation. I even forced myself to bear children because I thought it was my duty to provide heirs for the country. Now my life is in danger. If I go back to England the Despensers will kill me.'

'They would never dare.'

'They would do it subtly, as I have tried to explain to my brother. Edward, if we return to England now, in a few months time you will have lost your mother.'

He turned to her and put his arms about her. She embraced him fiercely.

'You will not let that happen to me, my son.'

'I would kill any who attempted to harm you.'

'So thought I. Cursed was I in my husband but blessed am I in my son. Edward, I have good friends here. You know how they rally round me. Good men all. They knew what was happening in the court. They understand the power of the evil Despensers. I must stay here for as long as I can. Will you bear with me? Will you turn from your father's pleas?'

'I swore to obey him.'

'Yes, dearest son, but it will not be your father whom you are obeying, it will be the evil Despensers. He is in their power. They have woven a spell over him. Trust me, dear son.

Trust me ... just for a little while and then I will prove to you the truth of all I have told you.'

She leaned against him and wiped her eyes. Edward was overcome with emotion. That his clever, beautiful mother should be so treated was unendurable!

'You will stand with me, dear Edward,' she pleaded.

'Dear Mother,' answered the boy, 'I will defend you against all who come against you.'

'All?' she asked.

'All,' he replied fervently.

'You have made me so happy,' she told him, and when she had taken her leave of him went straight to Mortimer.

'Edward will be with us,' she said. 'He will never stand against me.'

'That is good work,' said Mortimer. 'Now let us be patient while we look to the future. We must find some means of raising an army. My spies from England tell me that the country grows more and more angry against the Despensers. If we could land with a reasonable force we should be welcomed.'

'It will come,' said Isabella firmly. 'Meanwhile, as you say, patience.'

FOUR SISTERS OF HAINAULT

IT was an uneasy situation, thought the King of France. He was gratified in a way that his brother of England was in an uncomfortable position, but from the first days of the marriage it had been clear that Edward preferred handsome young men to his beautiful wife. Isabella's French relations had been quite angry about it at the time. They had known of the existence of Gaveston of course but had believed that once the King was married to a beautiful woman like Isabella, that side of his nature would be suppressed.

On the other hand Charles had no wish for his court to be used as the centre of rebellion. He wanted peace and such a situation could so easily erupt into war. Edward was writing more and more letters; they were coming every day. He was quite clearly growing restive.

In the last one he had referred to Mortimer and there was a hint that Isabella and Mortimer were lovers.

'We would wish you to remember, that we have at different times signified to you by letters, how improperly your sister, our wife, has conducted herself in withdrawing from us and refusing to return at our command, while she so notoriously has attached her company and consorts with our traitor and mortal enemy, the Mortimer ...'

That could mean one thing. Isabella and Mortimer were carrying on an adulterous intrigue in his court.

Edward was growing more and more determined and,

doubtless on the advice of the Despensers, had informed the Pope of the most unsatisfactory state of affairs. The result of this was that the Pope had written to Charles—he would never have dared to write to Charles's father so, but the monarchy had grown debilitated since Jacques de Molai had been burned to death and uttered the Curse—declaring that excommunication would be considered if he kept his sister at his court where it was rumoured she was living in adultery with Roger de Mortimer.

This frightened Charles. Excommunication allied to the Curse would be the end of him.

He would write to Isabella. He knew her wiles too well to try to convey what he must do verbally.

Accordingly Isabella received a note from her brother in which he commanded her to leave his kingdom without delay or he would be forced to make her go.

She was filled with rage when she read her brother's command. That he should behave so to her and not even see her, shocked her deeply.

'I do not believe he will force me out,' she said to Mortimer. 'He would never have the courage. He is getting weaker every day. I have a feeling my brother will not last very long.'

'The Pope is threatening him with excommunication.'

'Let him threaten. We will delay a while yet.'

During the following evening Isabella received a visitor. It was her cousin Robert d'Artois. He came in great haste and wished to speak to her urgently and privately.

No sooner were they alone than he said: 'I come to warn you, fair lady. There is a plot to take you and the young Prince prisoner and to send you back to England without delay.'

'You mean my brother ...'

Robert nodded. 'I could not resist my desire to come and tell you, though it would cost me my life doubtless if the King knew I had done this. He has said that the only way to avoid trouble is to force you to leave. You are therefore to be put in restraint and sent back to England.'

'When?' she asked.

'Tomorrow. You have little time.'

'Oh Robert, how can I thank you for this?'

'You know I would serve you with my life.'

She put her arms about him and for a moment he held her in a passionate embrace.

'Dearest cousin,' he said, 'you know full well what you mean to me, and have for some time.'

'You have always shown yourself a friend ...'

'A friend ... a mild way of describing my feelings! I know Mortimer has your heart and you his. But my feelings for you are so deep, and so tender that I will say to you, Fly ... Fly with him now. Tomorrow may be too late. Make for one of the independent states. There you may well find refuge until you can gather together the army you need.'

'Oh, my cousin, how can I thank you?'

'It is I who thank you for allowing me to serve you.' Such devotion was stimulating.

She went at once to Mortimer. They must not hesitate, she said.

They would go during the night, replied Mortimer. She, he and young Edward, with as many of their friends as they could muster. The rest could follow.

That night they crept quietly to the stables and fled from the Court of France, making their way towards the province of Hainault.

*   *   *

They had not ridden far from Paris when they were joined by the rest of their company who had been warned of her flight and had come to join her. All agreed that it would be safest for them to get as quickly out of France as possible and it was with great relief that they crossed the border into Hainault.

Weary with the day's riding and feeling now that they could afford to rest awhile, they came to the town of Ostrevant and stopped at a house which proved to belong to a knight named Sir Eustace d'Ambreticourt. When he realized that the lady was the Queen of England he was overcome with the honour of meeting her and he and his family insisted that she rest in their house with the few of her followers whom they could accommodate and lodging should be found for the rest within the town.

Isabella was delighted with such hospitality. How different, she said to Mortimer, from the way in which we were treated in France! 'Ah, my love,' laughed Mortimer, 'we were well received by your brother until we stayed too long. But I agree the welcome of this simple knight warms my heart.'

Sir Eustace said that he must inform the Count of Hainault that he had such august visitors for he was sure that the Count would wish to greet the guests.

The Count's response was to send his brother to meet the party and offer them the hospitality of his castle. It was thus that Isabella first met Sir John Hainault.

Sir John was young, romantic, idealistic and eager to prove himself a chivalrous knight, and here was a lady in distress. And what a beautiful one! Isabella quickly summed up his nature and decided to appear feminine and pathetic. She played her part well and he was overcome with the desire to serve her.

'It is so good of you to come to me thus and offer such kindness,' she told him. 'I have been treated harshly of late where I would expect to have received love and understanding.'

'My lady,' cried Sir John, 'rest assured that you will know nothing but warmth and affection in this land.'

Isabella allowed the tears to show becomingly in her beautiful eyes. Sir John saw them and was most distressed.

'Lady,' he declared, 'you see before you a knight who swears he will do everything in his power to aid you. He will not hesitate to die in your service. Though everyone else should forsake you I will be there.'

This was fulsome devotion on such a brief acquaintance but Isabella knew that Sir John in his youthful exuberance meant what he said. It was gratifying and she felt better than she had since she had discovered her brother really meant to turn her out of his court.

Sir John went on: 'Lady, you can rely on me. I will help you back to England with your son when you wish to go. When I have stated your case to my brother, he will give you men and arms, I am sure. He will want to help you ... even as I do. I will risk my life in adventure for your sake. I promise you you will have no need to fear either the King of France or the King of England.'

The Queen rose from her chair and so overcome with delight was she that she would have cast herself on her knees at the feet of Sir John, but with a horrified gesture he prevented her from doing so.

'God forbid that you should kneel to me, Madam. Be of good cheer. My promise to you stands firm. My brother will listen to you. He has expressed admiration for you many times. I will take you to him and present you to his Countess and their children.'

The Queen wiped her eyes. 'You are kinder to me than I dreamed any could be. You have shown me goodness of heart and courtesy. I promise you, this I shall never forget. My son and I will be eternally grateful to you and we shall ask you to help us govern England as it should be governed.'

They talked awhile and it was clear that the young man was completely overwhelmed by the charm and beauty of the Queen and meant what he said when he declared again and again that he would die in her cause.

He was eager to take her to his brother and she said a grateful farewell to Sir Eustace d'Ambreticourt, telling him that when she returned to England she wanted him to come there and bring his family and she would see that they were entertained right royally.

She then rode out with Sir John who took her to the court of his brother Count William of Holland and Hainault. There with his wife the Countess Jeanne who was the daughter of Charles of Valois, a son of Philip III of France and therefore related to Isabella, he received the company very warmly and took great pleasure in presenting Isabella to his four young daughters, Margaret, Philippa, Joanna and Isabel. They were rosy-cheeked, merry, typically Flemish girls, homely, skilled in domestic arts and charmingly innocent.

When Isabella proudly presented Edward the girls dropped curtsies to him and Isabella was immediately struck by the lack of formality in the family. Edward was approaching fifteen years old—an outstandingly handsome boy, already tall for his age, long-legged, fair-haired and blue-eyed.

The girls, the eldest of whom was about his own age and the youngest not so much younger for they had quickly followed each other in getting born, were clearly intrigued by such a handsome boy and Edward was amused by them and their efforts to please him.

The Countess was eager to show that they could entertain their guests at Hainault as lavishly as they could in France which she remembered as a girl and a great many feasts, banquets and general entertainments were given.

Meanwhile Edward was left a great deal with the four girls. They rode together, played games, introduced each other to the customs of their countries and it was an enjoyable time for them all. Edward felt he had been lifted out of the fearful doubts which beset him. He knew that his mother was working against his father. He loved her dearly but he was uneasy; and to rest awhile in the rather simple but honest court of Hainault, where the Count and Countess were devoted to each other and their four merry daughters had no conception of family conflict, was for him a wonderful respite.

*   *   *

Of the four girls Edward selected Philippa as his favourite but he was too polite to show his preference. However when they rode out into the forest together he did contrive to get Philippa to himself.

'Let us lose the others,' he said.

Philippa's habitually rosy cheeks were a shade deeper. 'Do you think we can?' she asked.

'If you would wish it,' answered Edward. 'Would you?'

'Oh yes,' she cried, too honest to say anything but the truth.

'Follow me,' he told her.

He heard her high-pitched laugh as he spurred his horse. She obeyed and very soon they had galloped away and had come to a clearing in the forest. He pulled up and they were silent for a moment, smiling at each other.

'Are you glad we came here?' asked Edward.

'Oh yes. It was so *dull* before you did. Do you find it dull here, Edward?'

'Not when I am with you.'

She blushed charmingly and smiled at him shyly. 'Do you really mean that? But you must, must you not, since you say it? You mean the others as well, I suppose. Margaret is much cleverer than I and Joanna and Isabel prettier.'

'That is quite untrue,' he answered.

She looked astonished and he realized that she had really meant it, and was finding it hard to accept the fact that he really preferred her to her sisters.

'What strikes me most about you,' he told her, 'is your honesty. Do you never say what you do not mean?'

'What would be the point of that?' she asked. 'Speech is to express what we feel.'

'I like you, Philippa,' he said. 'You are different from other people. I begin to fear that I live in a world of deceit.'

He was frowning. He could not tell innocent Philippa that he believed Mortimer was his mother's lover and that his father had treated her badly because he would surround himself with favourites whom he loved better than he loved her.

'What do you mean, Edward?' asked Philippa, but he shook his head.

'Never mind,' he said. 'It is too beautiful a morning to talk of such things. Tell me about your childhood here. It was a happy one I know. Your father and mother love you and each other dearly.'

'But of course. We are all one family.'

He felt an impulse to lean forward and kiss her which he did.

She drew back blushing a little.

'I like you so much,' he explained.

'I like you too, Edward.'

'As a girl,' he went on, 'you will have to leave your home and marry one day.'

Her brow clouded. 'I know my parents think of it sometimes. I heard my father say to my mother that she wanted to keep us all children for ever.'

'And do you want to stay a child for ever?'

She was thoughtful. 'No,' she said. 'Not now. Besides it would be no use, would it? I dare swear one day I shall have to go away. Margaret will go first because she is the eldest.'

'Boys are more fortunate, especially heirs to crowns. They do not have to leave their countries.'

'No. You will stay in England and your bride will come to you. But she will have to leave her home of course. She will not mind that, though.'

'How do you know?'

'I know she won't mind once she sees you.'

'Philippa, would *you* mind?'

She shook her head. 'No,' she said, 'I should be glad.'

Then she feared she had said too much for his eyes had taken on a deeper shade of blue and he was smiling.

It seemed as though there was a sudden silence in the forest. Then Philippa said: 'You will be a King and a King of England. They will have to find you a very grand princess to be your Queen.'

His mouth was firm and his shining eyes rested on her as he said: 'I shall choose my own.'

Philippa was a little afraid. Instinct warned her that she should not be alone here with the Prince. Her mother would say it was wrong for her to allow herself to be led away. She had always obeyed her mother.

Instinctively she turned away, urging her horse forward. Edward walked his horse beside her and soon they were out of the clearing.

Before they returned to the castle they had joined the rest of the party.

*　　*　　*

The Queen knew that she could not stay too long even when offered such hospitality. The Count and Countess treated her like an honoured guest and Sir John hovered adoringly, but, as she said to Mortimer, they must move on. However, she had a notion that coming to Hainault was going to prove one of the best courses they could have taken. She was going to speak to the Count of her predicament but first she would confer with Sir John. Sir John was only too delighted to enjoy a tête-à-tête with her, and posing as the pathetic lady in distress —which was the role in which he liked her best, she fancied— she gave him a long account of her sufferings during her life with Edward and how it had come to the point when she could endure it no longer. He turned pale with horror when she mentioned the fear she had of the wicked Despensers and how she believed that if she set foot in England that would be an end of her.

'You must not go back without adequate protection,' he declared.

'You are right of course, my dear good friend, but how can I find that protection?'

'I will go with you.'

'You are so good to me, but one man alone, however valiant, could not save me.'

'I shall not go alone. I shall take an army with me.'

Isabella's heart leaped in triumph.

'You would do that?'

'It would be my joy and my privilege.'

'An army . . .' she began.

'Yes, an army to join your own. We would march on Westminster and force the King to offer up those despicable men.

I shall not rest until we have their heads for I see that you will be unsafe while they live.'

'I cannot believe anyone could be so good to me as you are.'

'You will see,' he promised. 'You will see.'

'Do you realize, my dear Sir John, that this means going to a foreign country and fighting someone's else's cause?'

'It is fighting *your* cause, my dear lady, and I ask nothing better than that.'

'You would have to have your brother's consent.'

'Fear not, I shall speak to him.'

Her heart sank. This was a romantic young man. His brother, the more mature Count who controlled Sir John and his armies, might not consent.

'Do you think he will agree?'

'I shall beg and implore him and continue to do so until he becomes so weary of my importunings that he will be glad to be rid of me.'

'Oh how I thank God for throwing me into your path.'

He kissed her hand. He would go at once to his brother, he said, and tell him that he proposed to go to England with her in order to set her son on the throne and depose that Edward who had lost the confidence of his people ... and most heinous sin of all had ill-treated the most wonderful woman in the world.

*   *   *

While he was sympathetic, the Count was far from enthusiastic at the project.

'My dear brother,' he said, 'you are proposing to go into a foreign country and embark on a war which is really no concern of yours.'

'The fact that Edward of England has ill-treated a lady is surely of concern to any knight.'

'You are young and romantic,' replied the Count. 'That is not good politics.'

'What would you suggest I do?'

'Escort the lady to the coast. Wish her well. Offer her friendship but not an army.'

'I could not do that.'

'You cannot involve Hainault in English affairs.'

'It is not a matter of politics. It is one of chivalry.'

'Oh, brother, I fancy the Queen of England is a very astute lady. She will know how to look after herself. No, I cannot give you permission to take an army to England.'

'*I* should raise that army. It would be my responsibility.'

'You are my brother, remember. No, I could not give my consent.'

Sir John's lips were stubborn. For the first time there was a coolness between him and his brother. The Count thought: If I do not give my consent, he will act without it. That much is certain.

Isabella, knowing that the interview had taken place, was eager to know the result. She waylaid Sir John and was immediately struck by his dismal looks.

'You have spoken to your brother?' she asked anxiously.

Sir John nodded gloomily. 'He is against it. Oh, believe me, he has the utmost sympathy for your predicament. He would do a great deal to help you ...'

'But his generosity would stop at sending an army.'

'That is what he says. But I do not despair. I shall persuade him ...'

'And if he will not agree ...'

He kissed her hand. 'I should never desert you,' he answered.

Isabella sought an opportunity of talking to the Count alone, but she did not mention the fact that his brother had spoken to him.

She said: 'It has been a great pleasure to rest awhile under your roof, Count, and do you know what has pleased me as much as anything? It is to see the friendship which has sprung up between our children. Edward is quite enchanted by your delightful daughters and I fancy they are not displeased with him.'

The Count was alert. He had a great respect for Isabella's strategies. 'He is a charming boy. Handsome, tall, strong and of noble character. That much is clear.'

'It is gratifying,' she answered, 'to perceive these qualities in the heir to a great crown.'

'He is indeed kingly in his bearing.'

'I am eager that he should make a good marriage,' went on the Queen, 'and by that I mean a happy one. I shall never forget my own arrival in a strange country and what was revealed to me when I came.' She shuddered. 'I want Edward to have a little choice when it comes to his marrying. I would like him to have met his bride first and found that he was fond of her ... before the ceremony.'

The Count's heart had begun to beat fast. Was she suggesting one of his daughters might be Queen of England? It was a dazzling prospect. He and Jeanne wanted good marriages for their girls but happy ones at the same time and it was clear that all four girls were already a little enamoured of the handsome Edward.

He came straight to the point: 'My lady, do you mean that you would consider one of my daughters as a bride for your son?'

'That was what was in my mind,' answered Isabella. 'I believe you would consider it a worthy match.'

'I will not pretend, my lady, that I should not have thought of looking so high. I have heard however that the King of England is in progress of arranging a match for the Prince with Aragon.'

'What the King arranges will be of no moment when justice is done. It is I who will decide whom my son shall marry. When I take an army to England my aim will be to remove the villain-Despensers from the King and if he protests then it will be my duty to my son and to England to transfer the crown from the worthless father to the worthy son. Oh rest assured, my lord Count, it will not be Edward, at present King of England, who will decide whom my son shall marry. I shall do that. My son will listen to me, not his father; and if the the lady is one of his choice ... believe me, there will be no difficulty.'

'I confess,' said the Count, 'that your suggestion has taken me by surprise.'

The Queen bowed her head. Indeed it must have done. The future King of England to marry the daughter of a Count of Hainault! But anything ... anything for an army.

'I should like to discuss this with the Countess,' went on the Count. 'She has always been most concerned about our girls' future.'

'Do so,' said Isabella. 'But remember that this happy state of affairs could only come about if I were successful in ridding the country of the Despensers.'

She did not add: And by deposing the King and setting my son on the throne. But that was what she meant.

The Count hurried to his wife and they discussed the matter long into the night.

'There would never be such another opportunity,' said the Count.

The Countess agreed. 'Moreover,' she added, 'the girls are all of them already enamoured of Edward. He is a most attractive boy. I confess I should be very proud for him to become our son-in-law. And then ... the crown of England.'

'What if the Queen's attempts to depose the King should fail?'

'If she had enough men to go against him why should she fail? You know how matters stand in England. Our friends there tell us that people are turning against the King every day.'

'Yes, but they are really against the Despensers. If he sent them away ...'

'He never will. The weaker he grows the more he relies on them.'

'But to be involved in a war against England ... for that is what it amounts to!'

The Countess was astute. 'There is a way,' she said. 'You could provide the army without being personally involved.'

'How so?'

'The Queen of England wishes her son to marry one of our girls. We agree to this. You will provide the dowry which will be enough for the Queen to raise an army among our people. Then ... if aught should go wrong you have merely supplied a dowry not an army.'

The Count looked at his wife with admiration.

'It is the answer,' he said. They were silent for a while, both thinking how glorious it would be on the day when one of their girls became the Queen of England.

'It must be Margaret,' said the Countess firmly. 'She is the eldest and it is fitting that she should be the first to be married.'

'It shall be as you say,' replied the Count.

*   *   *

Isabella and Mortimer were overjoyed. The opportunity had come at last.

'Oh what a blessing,' cried Isabella, 'that the Count of Hainault has four marriageable daughters!'

Sir John was ecstatically happy because the matter had been so cleverly arranged, and immediately set about getting the army together.

The fact that the dowry provided by the Count enabled

this to be paid for was not mentioned and neither Edward nor the girls realized that marriage had been discussed.

They carried on meeting frequently and often Philippa and Edward managed to slip away undetected when they were riding with a party.

He told her a great deal about his youth and that there was trouble at home now because of a conflict between his father and mother. Philippa was most sympathetic. She could imagine how distressing that must be. He said he would like to show her England and that when he went home and all the trouble was over he would insist on her coming there. He would enjoy showing her his country.

'You will be King of it one day,' she said, her blue eyes wide with a kind of wondering admiration.

'I shall have to wait until my father dies. I mean to be a great King, Philippa. I am going to be like my grandfather ...'

He stopped, remembering that he was repeating what had been said to him so often and that it was disloyal towards his father. Philippa immediately understood. She and her sisters had become very interested in England since Edward and his mother had come to Hainault and they asked a great many questions about England. They had gleaned that there was something unusual about the King of England but they did not know what.

'He is not like your father,' the Countess had said firmly and left it at that; but she had implied that there must be something very wrong with someone who was so emphatically not like their father.

With Sir John's exuberance and the determination of the Queen and Roger de Mortimer the army was ready in a very short time.

The day came when they must leave.

The four girls, all saddened by the departure of the young Prince, stood beside their mother as the Queen took a fond farewell of them and said that she would never, never forget the kindness she had received from the Count and her dear cousin in her hour of need. She embraced the girls and at last it was Edward's turn.

He stood before them, startlingly handsome, looking as some noted, already a king.

He took leave of the Count and Countess and then turned to the rosy-cheeked girls.

He was telling them how much he had enjoyed his stay with them, how he would never forget their kindness, when he saw that the tears in Philippa's eyes had started to flow down her cheeks; and then suddenly before she could stop herself she was sobbing bitterly.

The Prince went to her and laid his hands on her shoulders. 'Do not weep, little Philippa,' he said, but she had covered her face with her hands. Then he said: 'Look at me.' She lowered her hands and he said: 'We shall meet again. I promise you.' The Countess had laid her arm about her daughter's shoulders while the Queen thought how informal they were in Hainault. She was glad that Philippa had been so overcome. It was most affecting.

But she was eager to be away.

She had her armies ... two of them ... the English contingent led by Mortimer and the men of Hainault by Sir John.

She was all set for conquest.

THE QUEEN'S TRIUMPH

THE Queen and her armies had arrived at Dort where they embarked on the ships which were waiting for them.

With Mortimer beside her the Queen watched the loading of the ships; the wind caught her hair and with the flush of triumph in her cheeks she had never seemed so beautiful.

'Gentle Mortimer,' she said, 'I have a feeling that God is with us this day. So much for which I have longed has come to pass. Thank God for Edward who shortly will be our King.'

'And whose betrothal to one of the giggling Flemish girls has given us our armies.'

'Forget not, dear Mortimer, that one day one of those girls will be the Queen of England.'

'You are the cleverest woman on earth as well as the most beautiful.'

'And you are the wisest man on earth, Mortimer, for joining with me.'

Mortimer left her to supervise his army. The Prince was with him and Sir John was similarly engaged.

Soon they were sailing away and the coast of Holland was lost from sight.

Alas, a storm arose and some of the ships were badly battered. Then the Queen was terrified that the elements were going to destroy all her well laid plans. She prayed to God not to desert her now. For hours the storm raged delaying their journey—there were moments when she believed this was the end. But her joy was overwhelming when she at last beheld the coast of England and she went on deck and looked

about her. She saw at once that many of the ships had suffered considerable damage, and some of them had actually
been smashed to pieces by the fearful tempest. It now
remained to get ashore and assess the damage in detail.

It was noon when she had glimpsed the coast but midnight
before everything was brought ashore. Although some men
and arms had been lost a considerable force remained. Her
knights and attendants made a tent for her from carpets and
they lighted a fire for her to warm herself. The wind was
strong and it was an uncomfortable night but she was relieved
to hear from Mortimer and Sir John that the damage and loss
had been less than they had at first feared.

As soon as day broke they were anxious to move from the
windy shore and in a short time they were in the town of
Harwich where Isabella's brother-in-law, Edward's half
brother Thomas of Brotherton, came to greet her.

She had always been on very friendly terms with Edward's
half-brothers, Edmund of Kent and Thomas of Brotherton;
their French mother, Edward the First's second wife Marguerite, was of course closely related to Isabella. Marguerite had
brought up her boys to observe certain French customs and
this meant that there had been an immediate rapport between
them and Isabella.

At times like this that was very apparent and it was fortunate for her that they were more ready to be on her side
than on Edward's. Moreover, like so many people in England,
they were with anyone who was against the Despensers.

The news of her arrival spread through the countryside.
She was the wronged wife of a pervert King, it was said; she
had flown from England out of fear of the wicked Despensers
who had bewitched the King even as Gaveston—of evil repute
—had done. They rallied to her banner; not only the common people but the barons who had for a long time been
determined to take the first opportunity of getting rid of the
King's favourite.

Adam of Orlton, Bishop of Hereford, who had done so
much to help Roger de Mortimer escape from the Tower,
was overjoyed when he heard of the arrival of the Queen and
her army. He had been living uneasily in England, protected
only by his calling; and he knew that if the King and his
friends ever had a chance of taking revenge on him they
would seize it.

Now that the Queen had arrived with her army that chance had receded even farther.

He set out to meet Isabella, to assure her of his devotion, which was unnecessary really; he had shown that when he had so ably assisted Mortimer's escape.

He was received with affection by the Queen and Mortimer and the very next day preached a sermon in their presence to which the people flocked so that the church was filled to overflowing and the people crowded into the porch and at the windows to hear him.

He took the opportunity of thundering against the King and took his subject from the fourth chapter of the second book of Kings when the man complained of the sickness in his head and shortly after died.

'When the head of a kingdom becometh sick and full of disease,' thundered Adam, 'it must be taken off and it is useless to resort to other remedies.'

The congregation listened in awed silence. The Queen glanced at Mortimer who was smiling quietly. The Prince was anxious but he now fully believed that what his father was doing was against the good of England and each day he was becoming more and more sure of his destiny.

He believed now that what was good for England must be done, and here was a Holy Bishop in his pulpit confirming all that he had learned from his mother.

It was sad. It was tragic. But it was right.

* * *

The King was in the palace of the Tower of London when news was brought to him of the Queen's arrival in England with one army led by Roger de Mortimer and another by John of Hainault.

And they came against him!

He sent at once for Hugh. He had never seen Hugh so disturbed before. Hugh had always comforted him, refusing to believe in harm, always seeing the bright side of life. It was one quality Edward especially loved about him.

'They will not succeed,' cried Hugh. 'We will raise an army.'

'How?' asked his father.

'We will do it,' insisted Hugh. 'First we must get away

from here. The Londoners have always disliked you and loved the Queen. Once the news reaches London it will be too late.'

Although it was a mild September day it was chilly as always in the Tower and yet the sweat was on Edward's brow and there was a terrible fear within him. They were going to take Hugh away from him. He would never allow that. He would accept anything rather than that.

He turned to Hugh with appealing eyes. 'We *must* stay together,' he said.

'So shall we, my lord. But we shall have to leave London without delay.'

'The children ...' began Edward.

His son John of Eltham and his two daughters Eleanor and Joanna were in their apartments in this very Tower. Could they take them with them?

Hugh shook his head. 'My wife will take charge of them,' he said. 'We should escape and as soon as possible.'

'And what of London? Who will defend it?'

'Good Bishop Stapledon has shown himself a friend to us. Let us leave him here to hold the city for you.'

'Excellent,' cried Edward. 'Let that be done.'

'I suggest,' said the elder Despenser, 'that we make for Bristol. Then, if the need should arise we can take ship to Ireland.'

'It must be so, I suppose,' sighed the King. 'Who would have believed it possible that my own Queen should so turn against me!'

'She was always jealous of me,' replied Hugh.

'But she did not appear to mind. She was always so ready to be with me ...'

'We did not realize, my lord, that we had a she-wolf in our midst.'

'And she has Edward with her! That I find hard to bear.'

'She has John of Hainault and Mortimer ...'

'That traitor! There shall be a price on his head. Oh God, why did I not have that head when I had a chance to take it?'

Edward sighed and looked back over a reign of lost opportunities but there was no time for regrets now. The Earls of Arundel and Hereford had arrived at the Tower. They had come to warn the King.

'I have some friends left then,' said Edward.

They agreed that the best plan was to leave London with all haste and make for Bristol.

* * *

It was impossible to keep the departure a secret and very soon it was being whispered throughout the streets of London that the King had fled and the Queen was on the way.

The streets were full of shouting people. 'Down with the King! Down with the Despensers! Long live the Queen and Prince Edward.'

There was no doubt that, to a man, London was for the Queen.

Walter Stapledon was deeply disturbed by the shouts he heard in the streets of London and was making his way towards the Tower, the custody of which the King had left to him. He was wondering whether the royal children there would be safe in charge of Hugh le Despenser's wife and thought that perhaps she had not been a good choice. Anyone connected with the Despensers would be unpopular with the mob.

He intended to fortify the Tower lest the Londoners should attempt to take it. He must act quickly.

As he was hurrying along he heard his name spoken.

He shivered. Someone had recognized him. He quickened his pace but he realized that he was being followed.

'Stapledon,' he heard. 'The King's Bishop! He spied on the Queen.'

He was in the midst of his enemies. He hurried through an alley and changed direction. He would make for St Paul's and sanctuary. If the mob were aroused against him it would be the end.

But he was too late. They were all around him.

'It is the traitor Bishop,' they jeered. 'Dear friend of Edward and the Despensers. We know what to do with such like, do we not, even if he be a Bishop?'

He heard the ribald laughter; he saw the leering faces ... he was conscious of the merciless mob.

Someone tore at his cloak. In a few seconds they had his shirt from his back. He was naked before their jeering eyes.

'There stands a spy and a traitor to our lady the Queen.'

He felt the stab of a knife piercing his flesh. The blood

was trickling down his face and he was swaying before them.

He fell and they kicked him; they trampled over him; vaguely he could hear their jeering voices. 'Spy! Enemy! Friend of the minions ... Bishop or not he must die ...'

He believed he was praying but he was not sure. But he did know that he was dying. They meant to kill him but not too quickly. They wanted first their sport. They were dragging him along the ground. His body was mangled and cut in places. Obscenity was in the air. Were they speaking of him? What did it matter what they did to him? He was slowly slipping away.

'He's finished,' said a voice in the crowd.

'What shall we do with him now ... our fine Bishop?'

'We'll carve him up and send his head to the Queen ... a gift from the loyal people of London. Would we had the Despenser here.'

So they marched to the Tower carrying the bleeding head of the Bishop and there they demanded that Prince John and the two Princesses be given into their care to be sent to join the Queen.

This was a token of London's love for that lady.

*　　*　　*

The messengers were brought to Isabella in the castle of Gloucester, one of them carried the head of Walter Stapledon.

Isabella stared at it and remembered how the owner of that head had refused to join her in Paris and had slipped away to report her deeds to the King. 'His just reward,' she said.

'With the compliments of the people of London, my lady,' said one of the messengers.

'Return to them and tell them that I love them even as they have shown they love me.'

The messenger bowed and left.

Another messenger was brought to her. He told her that the people of London had released her children from the Tower and because they believed she would wish to have them with her they had sent them to Gloucester.

'My blessings on them,' she cried. 'Let my children be brought to me.'

She embraced them fiercely. It seemed so long since she had seen them: ten-year-old John, eight-year-old Eleanor and five-

year-old Joanna. They clung to her for they had been frightened by everything that had been happening. Their father
had gone away suddenly and left them and there had been a
great deal of shouting outside the Tower before people had
burst in. Then they had been told that they were being taken
to their mother.

'It is my friends who have brought you here, my darlings,'
cried the Queen. 'There. All is well now. You shall see your
brother Edward, for he is here with me.'

'When shall we see our father?' asked John.

'Of that we cannot be sure,' answered their mother glibly.
'Never mind, you are safe with me now.'

Joanna was ready to be happy but the two elder ones were
uneasy, thinking of their father. He had been strange when
he and Hugh had gone away and he had told them to do
all that Lady le Despenser told them to; and Lady le Despenser had been crying a great deal so they knew that something was wrong.

John had comforted the little girls and told them that it
would be all right when they saw Edward, and they were
going to see Edward now.

At the moment they could not help being overawed by
their beautiful mother who had suddenly grown so fond of
them though she had never taken much notice of them before.
All her attention had been for Edward. But they forgot that
now. It was pleasant to be embraced by her and made much
of and told how glad she was to have them with her.

They were presented to Roger de Mortimer and Sir John
of Hainault, both of whom smiled affectionately at them and
made as though they were delighted to see them. So they had
suddenly become important which was very gratifying.

Delighted by the arrival of the children and the head of
the Bishop of Exeter, Isabella was anxious to show the Londoners her appreciation.

She told Mortimer that she intended to appoint a new
governor of the Tower and a Mayor of London and she
believed he would approve of the choice.

'You remember the two merchants who were so helpful
when you escaped from the Tower?'

'Indeed I do. I don't think we could have managed so
well without them.'

'Adam arranged it of course.'

'Ah yes, a good friend Adam, but we do owe a good deal to de Bettoyne and de Gisors.'

'So thought I. That is why I have decided to appoint de Gisors Constable of the Tower and de Bettoyne Mayor of London.'

'An excellent choice,' smiled Mortimer.

'It will show them that I remember those who serve me well,' murmured Isabella.

* * *

Edward, accompanied by young Hugh, retired to the Castle of Bristol leaving old Hugh and the Earl of Arundel to hold the city for him.

There was not a hope that Bristol would resist the invading forces of the Queen. The people had no wish to. Like the rest of the country they were against the King.

So the Queen's army was welcomed and the people came out to cheer the troops as they marched through the streets with Roger de Mortimer at their head.

When he discovered that old Hugh was in the town he was delighted. Now had the time come to settle old scores.

'There must be no delay,' he said. 'Despenser and Arundel with him must be tried and sentenced immediately.'

The Queen agreed with him and the two men were brought before her and the barons, at the head of whom were Mortimer and Sir John of Hainault, for she said that they must be judged according to their deeds.

Sir Hugh lifted his head high and met her gaze unflinchingly.

'Ah, my lady,' he said quietly, 'God grant us an upright judge and a just sentence. And if we cannot find it in this world, we may find it in another.'

Death was imminent, he knew, for he could not expect pity from either the Queen or her lover. The fact that he was a man of sixty-four did not move them in the least. He was one of the Despensers loathed by the Queen and the country. He had been avaricious, it was true, but he had tried to do what he thought was right for the country providing it did not interfere with his personal gain. He was not a good man, not a great man; he had committed sins; but there were many who prospered and were more deserving of death than he was.

This was what he wanted to tell his judges, but they were not interested in his defence. They had determined at the start of his brief trial to prove him guilty.

They did and he and Arundel were sentenced to the cruel death which it had become the custom to bestow on traitors. They believed right to the end that their nobility would save them from that barbarous end and beheading be substituted. But this was not to be.

There should be no mercy for a Despenser and those who upheld them, decreed the Queen and Mortimer.

So the two men were taken out and hanged, drawn and quartered.

The Queen was exultant.

'There is one Despenser the less,' she said.

'And still one to suffer a similar fate,' replied Mortimer grimly.

*   *   *

Edward in Bristol Castle was almost mad with grief and fear.

Hugh from a window in the castle had heard the shouts of the people. He had seen the body of his father dangling on a rope and he knew what tortures followed.

He felt sick with grief. He and his father had worked together all their lives; they had revelled in each other's triumphs and commiserated with each other's failures. And to think of that revered old man in the hands of his rough executioners was more than his son could bear.

Edward tried to comfort him, but there was no comfort for Hugh.

What there was was the awful realization that very soon they would come for him and he knew well that a similar fate awaited him.

Edward clung to him in terror. 'Hugh, they have done *that* to your father! Oh they are devils! They will burn in hell for this. Your dear dear father ...'

Hugh said quietly, 'They will come here seeking me and you will see that they will do the same to me.'

'No,' cried Edward shrilly. 'I would never allow it. I should forbid it. They would have to listen to me ... the King.'

Hugh looked at him sadly. He thought: They will never

listen to you again, poor Edward. This can be the end of you
... and if it is for you it is for me also.

But they were not taken yet, though it could only be a
matter of hours before their enemies came. They would
watch the hideous spectacle of his father's execution and then
they would come to take him and make him the next chief
actor in their grisly performance.

He stood up suddenly. 'There is time yet. Edward we must
not stay here. They will march on the castle. It may be they
are preparing to do so now. We must get away.'

'Where to?' asked Edward. 'You mean just the two of us?
Oh where are all my loyal friends? There must be some of
them left.'

'My father is dead. Arundel is dead. And they died cruelly.
No, Edward, we have no one but ourselves. We must get away.
There is a boat on the shore. Perhaps we could go to Lundy.'

'To Lundy, yes. To Lundy. We shall be safe there, Hugh.'

'Come then. There is not a moment to lose. Take a thick
cloak. You may need it. Stop for nothing more. It may be that
they are already at the castle gates.'

Swiftly and silently they made their way out of the castle
and came to the shore.

The boat was there. They got in and Hugh seized the oars.
The strong wind caught at their hair but they were free.

'To Lundy!' cried Edward. 'Once there we will make plans.
Perhaps we can escape to France. Oh, this will not last, dear
Hugh. The people will turn against that she-wolf whom I made
my wife. My son Edward would never work against me.'

Hugh did not remind the King that young Edward was
with his mother and had come with her to Bristol. It might
be that the boy would turn against such perfidy in time, but at
the moment he was under the spell of his beautiful mother
and while he was with her he must work against his father.

The wind grew fierce and the boat could make no progress.
Again and again it was blown back towards the shore. It was
no use trying to row against such a sea.

They would never reach Lundy at this rate.

Hugh shook his head sadly. They would have to abandon
all hope of leaving the country. With some difficulty Hugh
brought the boat back to land and they disembarked on the
coast of Wales.

*   *   *

Hugh and the King slept the night in the shelter of a wood and the next day they walked until they came to the town of Cardiff. Hugh sold a jewel to buy them food and they rested at an inn where they talked with men who had heard of the Queen's coming to England and setting herself up against the King.

''Tis no more than a whore she be,' said one man. 'The true King will rise up, depend on it, man. God will not be with those that live in adultery.'

Such talk tempted the King to reveal his identity and he was warmly welcomed and several men swore they would stand with him. His father had defeated the Welsh but he had brought good rule to the country and they wanted no adultress and her paramour ruling them.

The King was filled with hope. Hugh was more realistic. A few men at an inn would count for little against the armies the Queen had raised.

Still it was good to see Edward in better spirits and they talked through the night of how they would raise men and Edward should win back what he had lost.

In the morning they were less sanguinary. The terrible fate of the elder Hugh had sobered both of them. Edward was terrified more for his friend than for himself. He was certain that they would not dare harm him.

'What we must do,' said Hugh, 'is to disguise ourselves, sound the people and if many feel as this innkeeper and some of his friends do we may raise men to fight for us.'

'You are right, dear Hugh,' said Edward.

'I think we could take the innkeeper into our confidence,' replied Hugh.

They did and the man was clearly excited to be drawn into the conspiracy. Welshmen of strict morals, he reiterated, will never support a whore and her paramour.

For some days they lived in high hope. Edward pinned his faith on his son.

'He is but a boy yet,' he said. 'When he is a little older he will never stand against his father, that I know.'

'But he has to grow up and much can happen before that,' Hugh reminded him.

There were days when their cause seemed hopeful but although there were some who sympathised with him they had no desire to go to battle for his sake.

It was not long before the Queen and Mortimer heard of his adventures.

Mortimer said: 'It is a pitiful attempt, but it would be wiser to put an end to his wanderings. Moreover, we want the Despenser. We will send a force to take them and bring them to us. A certain amount of harm can be done by these wanderings.'

'Let us send Henry of Lancaster, Edward's cousin. That will show that people of authority are with us. Lancaster should not have much difficulty in finding him.'

The news that Henry of Lancaster had come into Wales in search of the King quickly spread and Hugh suggested that they go into hiding because he was not altogether sure who were their friends.

They disguised themselves as peasants and left the small band of supporters they had managed to muster to wander the country like two itinerant farm hands. They were discovered by a farmer sleeping in one of his fields. He wanted men to help dig a field and they would be given food and lodging in payment for their work, he told them.

Hugh said quickly that they would be glad to earn a lodging and a meal but they were so urgently in need of the latter that they must eat before they worked.

The farmer studied them suspiciously and at length agreed as he said to humour them, so they were given cold bacon and bread with ale which due to their hunger tasted good to them.

Then they were set to work. Strangely enough it was Hugh rather than the King who betrayed them. Edward was quite handy with a spade. As a youth he had gloried in physical labour as a release from lessons. He had enjoyed working with the blacksmith and had often helped with thatching and digging trenches. In those days too he had sought the society of grooms and workmen, so he slipped naturally into the role of farm worker.

Not so Hugh, and it was very clear to the farmer that he had an unusual pair in his house.

There had been rumours about the King and the Despenser and he had heard that they were in the neighbourhood. He wanted no involvement in these matters. God alone knew where they could lead a man. Someone would be calling him traitor next.

He sent one of his workers into a nearby town with a message for the mayor. He had a strange pair working for him and he thought it was his duty to tell someone who was wiser than he was and would know what a man should do in such circumstances.

The messenger was asked questions. Indeed the itinerants were interesting. They sounded uncommonly like that much sought after pair, the King and his favourite. Bearing in mind what had happened to the latter's father—and the whole country was aware of that—no one wanted very much to do with these matters. Careless dabbling could bring a man to the terrible fate of that new law against traitors which made honest men shudder in their beds to contemplate.

It was not long before Lancaster's men arrived at the farm.

'We are betrayed,' said Hugh. 'My lord, this will be the end.'

The King was treated with respect. Not so Hugh. He was roughly seized by men who delighted in heaping indignity upon him.

'Come, pretty boy,' they said. 'It will be rather different for you now.'

They dragged him away from the protesting King.

'Where are they taking him?' demanded Edward.

'To his Maker I'd take wager, my lord,' was the answer.

Edward covered his face with his hands. He wanted to shut out the sight of Hugh's appealing eyes as he was dragged out of his sight.

He was courteously treated. He was to go to the castle of Llantrissaint,' he was told.

'On whose orders?' he asked.

They did not answer.

'You forget that I am your King,' he said.

And they were ominously silent.

But he was not really interested in his own fate. He could only think of what they had done to Hugh's father. Oh, if they should do that to Hugh he would die of despair.

So they were parted at last. Their attempts to escape had come to nothing, as they might have known they would.

And he was to go to bleak Llantrissaint Castle, the prisoner of someone—his wife he supposed. Mortimer?

Meanwhile Hugh le Despenser was on his way to Bristol to be delivered to the Queen.

*　　*　　*

Hugh stood before them. They were seated on chairs like thrones—the powerful beautiful Queen who had once made a show of humility and had been so careful to hide her hatred from him, and Mortimer, strong, bold, virile, as different from Edward as a man could be. It was said that the Queen was besottedly enamoured of him and their association was now of some duration. Looking back Hugh could see that it had been inevitable from the moment they had met. They were a match for each other—passionate ambitious people. The Queen was as ruthless as her father who had destroyed the Templars. What did she plan for Edward? He trembled to think. That it would be diabolical, he did not doubt. Her father had brought on himself the curse of the Templars. Perhaps she would bring retribution on herself too. And young Edward? Where was he? If I could but see young Edward, he thought, there might be a chance. I could move him to pity for his father's plight.

'So here is Hugh le Despenser,' said the Queen. 'You look less happy, my lord, than when I saw you last.'

'That was a long time ago, my lady.'

'Indeed it was. Why then you were like a petted dog. You sat on your master's satin cushion and were well fed with sweetmeats.'

'There will be no more sweetmeats for Hugh le Despenser,' put in Mortimer grimly.

'I do not expect them,' replied Hugh with dignity.

'Well, you gorged yourself while they were fed to you,' laughed the Queen. 'Oh, it is going to be very different for you now, you know.'

'So I had thought.'

'We are going to London,' said the Queen. 'We are going to receive the homage of my good and faithful people. Alas for you, I fancy they do not like you very much.'

For a moment he thought of good honest Walter Stapledon and wondered what his last hour had been like in the hands of the London mob.

'I must accept my fate for all come to that.'

'He relinquishes his life of luxury much more easily than I had thought he would,' commented the Queen.

'Oh he has much to learn yet,' responded Mortimer grimly.

Hugh was praying silently: 'Oh God give me strength to meet what is coming to me.'

'Take him away,' said the Queen.

*   *   *

They left Bristol for London. Isabella rode at the head of her army with Mortimer on one side and Sir John of Hainault on the other. Adam of Orlton was with them. He was determined to have a say in affairs.

Among the Queen's baggage was the head of Walter Stapledon. Mortimer had suggested it be placed on London Bridge but the Queen was too wily for that.

'No,' she had said, 'he was a churchman and many would say he had been a good man. He was our enemy and he never pretended to be otherwise. Such men have a habit of becoming martyrs and I fear martyrs more than soldiers. Nay. I shall show my virtue by sending it to Exeter and having it buried in his own cathedral. It will be remembered in my favour.'

'You are right, my love,' replied Mortimer. 'But are you not always right?'

She smiled at him lovingly. She wished as she had so many times that Mortimer had been the son of the King and she had come here to marry him instead of the unworthy Edward.

Hugh le Despenser rode with them. It had been their delight to find an old nag for him to ride on. He and the King had always cared so passionately for horses and they had once possessed some of the finest in the kingdom. This poor mangy animal called further attention to his degradation and in case any should fail to be aware of it as they entered the town through which the processions passed Isabella and Mortimer had commanded that there should be trumpets to announce the arrival of Hugh le Despenser and attention be called to him as he ambled along on his wretched nag.

Hugh felt sick with despair. He knew that a fate similar to that given his father was awaiting him and he knew there was no way of avoiding it. He fervently hoped that he would be able to meet his death with courage.

He had eaten nothing since he had been taken. He was growing thin and ill with anxiety more than from lack of nourishment.

Isabella watched him with apprehension.

'He looks near death,' she said. 'Are we going to be cheated of our revenge?'

'He could die,' agreed Mortimer. 'Indeed he looks near to it. I'd say there was a man who was courting death.'

'He need not go to such lengths. He does not need to *court* death.'

'We should not wait to reach London. I doubt he will outlast the journey. We should stop at Hereford, and try him there. It would be safer.'

'Alas, I wanted to give my faithful Londoners a treat. How they would have enjoyed the spectacle of pretty Hugh on the scaffold.'

'I'd say it was Hereford or just quiet death.'

'Then it must be Hereford,' said the Queen.

* * *

They had reached Hereford and there they halted for the trial of Hugh le Despenser.

His guards told him that the day of his judgment was at hand.

'Little did you think when you sported with the King that it would bring you to this,' taunted one of them.

He was silent. He felt too tired to talk. Besides there was nothing to say.

He was taken to the hall where his judges were waiting for him. They were headed by Sir William Trussell, a man who could be relied on to show him no favour. Trussell had fought against the King at Boroughbridge and when Lancaster had been overthrown he had fled to the Continent. He had returned to England with Isabella and had become one of her firm adherents.

He now harangued Hugh, listing the crimes of which he was accused. He had mismanaged the affairs of the kingdom in order to gain money and possessions; he had been responsible for the execution of that saint Thomas of Lancaster and had attempted to hide the fact that miracles were performed at his tomb. His inefficiency had been the cause of the deafeat of Bannockburn. In fact any ill which had befallen England since the death of Gaveston and the rule of the Despensers had been because of Hugh's wickedness.

Of course there was no hope for him.

'Hugh, all good people of this realm by common consent agree that you are a thief and shall be hanged and that you are a traitor and shall therefore be drawn and quartered. You have been outlawed by the King and by common consent and you returned to the court without warrant and for this you shall be beheaded; and for that you made discord between the King and Queen and others in this realm you shall be disembowelled and your bowels burned; so go to your judgment, attained wicked traitor.'

Hugh listened to this terrible sentence almost listlessly. It was no surprise. It had happened to his father.

It was their revenge and he had known from the moment they had taken him that it was coming.

All he could do was pray for courage, that he might endure what was coming to him with fortitude.

There was to be no delay, ordered the Queen. Delay was dangerous. He might die and defeat them of their satisfaction.

Almost immediately after the sentence had been passed, he was dressed in a long black robe with his escutcheon upside down. They had said he should be crowned because he had ruled the King so they placed a crown of nettles on his brow to add a little more discomfort and he was dragged out of the castle.

As they prepared to hang him on the gallows which was fifty feet high in order that as many as possible might witness the spectacle, the Queen took a seat with Mortimer and Adam of Orlton on either side of her that they might gloat over the pain inflicted on the King's favourite.

The handsome body now emaciated beyond recognition dangled on the rope and Isabella feared that he might die before they could cut him down and administer the rest of the dreadful sentence.

To her delight she saw that Hugh's lips were moving slightly as they laid him out and bared his body for the fearsome ordeal.

This is the man he preferred, thought Isabella. I was humiliated for his sake. He took away my friends; he deprived me of my rights. And now he is in my hands these are his just deserts.

There was little satisfaction though, for Hugh was so quiet. Once she heard a faint moaning, but there were no cries for mercy.

She reached for Mortimer's hand. He seized it and pressed it.

This was the end of Hugh, they were both thinking.

There remained the King.

EDWARD

KING NO MORE

EDWARD was numb with grief. Why was life so cruel to him? First they had taken Gaveston and now Hugh. Why was it that his love always brought disaster?

And what now? He was too numb to care.

They were taking him to Kenilworth. His cousin Henry of Lancaster had come to him and told him that he was to be his guest.

Henry had looked at him with compassion. Strangely enough he seemed to understand.

So they rode side by side to Lancaster's castle of Kenilworth which lay between Warwick and Coventry. Lancaster was proud of the place. Edward's grandfather, Henry III, had given it to his youngest son and so Lancaster had inherited it.

'Have no fear, I shall not harm you, my lord,' he said, and Edward thought how strange it was that a subject should speak to his King in such a manner. He might have been incensed, he might have been apprehensive but he could think of nothing but, Hugh is dead.

He lay in the room which had been prepared for him. There were guards at the door to remind him that he was a prisoner. An ironic situation indeed. A King the prisoner of his Queen!

Oh Isabella, Isabella, he thought. I never really knew you. All those years you were so meek; you bore my children. You waited patiently until I had time to spare for you. Gaveston never knew what your real thoughts were. Too late Hugh

discovered; and even then I would not believe it. And now
Mortimer is your lover. You ... Isabella.

She was like her father—Philip the Handsome, ruthless,
implacable, feared by all until that final day of reckoning
when he lay on his death-bed and knew that the curse put on
him and his heirs by the Templars was being fulfilled.

Isabella was cruel. Isabella was ruthless. She hated him.
He wondered what she and Mortimer would do now.

The days passed. Lancaster came to him—gentle and apologetic. It is not my fault that you are here, my lord, he seemed
to say, I but obey orders.

It was never wise to offend a King. However low he had
fallen, who could know when he would come back into power
again?

That was a heartening thought. Was that why Lancaster
was always respectful? Oh no, it was more than that. Henry
was his cousin; they were both royal; men who were close to
the throne had the greatest respect for it.

Henry and he played chess together. It whiled away the
hours.

'Henry,' he asked, 'how long will you keep me here?'

Henry lifted his shoulders. Doubtless it would be for Mortimer to say. Mortimer. That upstart from the Marcher country, a man who had been the King's prisoner and escaped!
Oh, what a fool not to have had his head long ago. But when
he looked back it was over a lifetime of follies. A headless
Mortimer would never have escaped from the Tower, would
never have become the Queen's lover, would never have captured the King.

But perhaps Mortimer was merely the tool. She would
have found another lover, another man to lead her armies.
She was his real enemy, the She-Wolf of France.

He tried to give himself to the game. Even in that he was
beaten. He had never been able to plan an artful strategy.
Lancaster could beat him on the board as his brother had done
in life. But Lancaster had come to a tragic end. He had not
won in the end.

'Checkmate,' said Henry triumphant.

The King shrugged his shoulders. He said: 'You are a
kinder jailer than I might have hoped for, cousin.'

Lancaster rearranged the pieces on the board.

'I do not forget your royalty, my lord,' he replied.

'You have never forgiven me for the fate of your brother,' said Edward. 'But I was not to blame. If he had not parleyed with the Scots ... he would be alive today.'

'He was a great man, my lord. His trial was hasty and he had no chance to defend himself.'

'Let us not go over the past,' said Edward. 'It is over and done with. There have been many mistakes. Let us not brood on them cousin. You have been my enemy and it is for this reason that the Queen and her paramour have given me into your keeping. You have done everything you could to preserve your brother's honour and that I understand. You built a cross for his soul outside Leicester. You proclaimed that miracles had been performed at his tomb and you tried to make a saint of him, knowing full well that the more men revered him the more they would revile their King.'

'It was your friendships, my lord, which made the people revile you.'

'I have been maligned and condemned,' cried the King. 'I have lost those whom I loved best. But what I can say is that I have received kindness at your hands and I did not expect it. You and I have not been friends, Henry, cousins though we be. And it is because of the enmity between us that I am put in your care. Yet you show me kindness. It is something which moves me.'

His cousin lowered his eyes to the board.

'Another game, my lord?' he asked. 'Would you wish to have your revenge?'

The King wanted to laugh aloud. His revenge. Yes, he would like to have his revenge ... his revenge on the murderers of Hugh and his father. Oh the tortures they had inflicted on that loved body. His revenge on Isabella, the traitoress.

Ah, if only he could move the men and women of his kingdom to the places where he wanted them to be as easily as he could move the pieces on the chessboard!

*   *   *

The Queen rode out in her silken dress adorned with shining gold buttons; her skirt flowed over her palfrey, and about her shoulders was an ermine coat. She looked beautiful and royal. The people of London cheered her. She was their ruler now. It was time the King was set aside. From the day

he had worn the crown he had shown himself unworthy. They
had always loved the Queen. She had responded to their admiration; she had shown them clearly that of all the people
of England the Londoners held first place in her heart.

Beside her rode her son Edward—his young face stern.
He had grown up quickly in the last weeks and was beginning
to understand what would be required of him.

She was going to the Tower to receive the members of
Parliament who would come to tell her what the decision had
been.

Already she guessed it. They would depose the King and
young Edward should be proclaimed Edward III. It was what
she had worked for! Her son King and she and Mortimer
the Regents who should control him and rule the land.

It was like the fulfilment of a dream.

She and Mortimer as they lay in bed the previous night
had talked of their coming power. Edward would turn to
them for advice and they would govern the land in his name.
She often thought how wise she had been to remain meek and
compliant until she had her children.

She said: 'Edward is behaving strangely. He is quiet ... too
thoughtful.'

'Oh come, love,' cried Mortimer, 'he is such a boy. He
regards you as a goddess. You will have no difficulty in making
him obey you.'

She allowed Mortimer to believe that she accepted this but
she continued uneasy.

Yet how sweet were the cheers of the Londoners in her
ears! She was foolish to have these doubts.

The prize was just about to be handed to her. A King who
was but a boy and would need a Regent and who should that
be but his mother who had raised an army and brought it
from across the Channel to depose his father of whom they all
wished to be rid?

She entered the Tower. In the royal apartments she and
Mortimer awaited the coming of the ministers.

She received them eagerly and their first words sent her
spirits soaring.

The Parliament had decided that Edward the Second must
be deposed and his first-born son Edward crowned Edward the
Third. This had the unanimous agreement of all the barons
and the clergy.

Isabella clasped her hands together and tried not to show her jubilation.

'My son is young yet,' she said slowly.

'There will be a Regency, my lady.'

A Regency indeed! The Queen. Who else? And she would choose her dear and gentle Mortimer to stand beside her.

'The matter has been given much consideration, my lady. The Parliament will select four bishops, four earls and six barons to form a Regency. It is the opinion that one bishop, one earl and two barons should be in constant attendance upon the young King.'

She could not believe she had heard aright. A Regency which did not include her! What were they thinking of? To whose efforts did they owe the King's defeat? Who but Isabella had rid them of the worthless Edward?

With admirable restraint she hid her fury.

She dismissed them saying she would impart their decision to the young King.

She went immediately to Mortimer and her rage burst forth.

'How dare they! I would hang them all. After all I have done. It does not occur to them to name me. Why? Because I am a woman? Is that it? Who raised the army? Who planned for years? Surely there is no one ...' she looked at Mortimer and added, 'nay two who would be the natural Regents?'

'My love,' said Mortimer, 'this is a cruel blow, but let us plan carefully. It is your son who will decide to whom he will listen. Let them give him his barons and bishops. You are still his mother.'

She held out her hand and he kissed it. 'How you always comfort me, Mortimer,' she said.

'It is my purpose in life, my dearest.'

'Yes, we shall defeat them,' she said. 'You and I will not be set aside for these men.'

'Assuredly we shall not.'

They sat down on one of the window-seats and he put an arm about her.

'How beautiful you looked this day in your regal ermine,' he said soothingly. 'A Queen in very truth.'

'But not good enough to be their Regent,' she said bitterly.

'Isabella, my love. We shall outwit them all. Do not forget. We have young Edward.'

She nodded but she was not completely at ease.
She had begun to have doubts about Edward.

*   *   *

She was right in thinking that the young Edward was
becoming apprehensive. He was beginning to understand
more of what was going on around him. He could not be
proud of his parents and he now knew why people had constantly compared him with his grandfather.

His father had been weak and dissolute, favouring handsome young men and frittering away the kingdom's wealth in
extravagant gifts for them. His mother was living in open
adultery with Roger de Mortimer, and they made no attempt
to hide it.

He often thought of that brief period when they had stayed
at Hainault and he and Philippa had talked together. He had
told her a great deal about his perplexities and, although
she had been very sheltered from the world and did not
understand half those problems which beset him, she had
shown him a wonderful sympathy, an adulation almost which
had been very sweet to him.

He had told her that he was going to marry her. It was
fortunate that there had been some arrangement between his
mother and her parents that he should marry her or one of
her sisters.

'Rest assured, Philippa,' he had vowed, 'it shall be you.'

She had believed him. Although he was but a few months
older than she was and they were only in their fifteenth year
there was a resolution about him which she trusted would
bring him what he wanted. To her Edward was like a god,
strong, handsome, determined to do what was right. She had
never met anyone like him, she had said; and he had replied
that she felt thus because they were intended for each other.

Strange events were happening all around him. His father
was a prisoner. It was wrong surely that a King should be made
the prisoner of his subjects. But it was not exactly his subjects
who had made him a prisoner. It was his wife, the Queen.

He had been fond of his father as he had been of his mother,
for he had always been kind to him, had shown him affection
and been proud of him. His mother, though, had charmed
him. When she had taken him to France he had begun to

feel uneasy because of the trouble about his father. Hainault had been a brief respite because Philippa was there. But since their return to England events had moved fast. There had actually been war between his father and mother and his mother was notorious. The Despensers had been brutally done to death and his father was a prisoner. What would they do to him?

A cold feeling of horror came over him.

'I like it not,' he said aloud, 'and by nature of who I am, I am in the centre of this.'

When his mother came to him with the Archbishop of Canterbury and his uncles the Earls of Kent and Norfolk he was ready for them.

They knelt before him; there was a new respect in their manner; he believed that something had happened to his father.

The Archbishop spoke first. 'My lord,' he said, 'the King your father, showing himself unworthy to wear the crown ...'

Edward caught his breath. 'My father is ... dead?'

'Nay, my lord. He lives, a prisoner in Kenilworth. There he is well cared for by the Earl of Lancaster. But because he has shown himself unworthy to govern he is to be deposed. You are the new King of England.'

'But how is that possible when my father lives? He has been crowned the King of this country.'

'The crown is too burdensome for his frail head,' went on the Archbishop. 'You are to be the King. You must have no fear. You are young and will have a Regency to show you how to govern.'

'I have no fear for myself,' said the young Edward. 'But I have for my father. I would see him.'

'That, my lord, cannot be,' the Archbishop told him.

The Queen said: 'It would only distress him, Edward. It is kinder to let him be where he is. I hear that he is contented enough. More, he is happy to be relieved of the duties of kingship which have been too much for him.'

'Yet he ruled for many years,' said Edward.

'And see to what state the country has come!' replied the Queen. 'Edward, you must remember you are young. For a little while you must listen to advice.'

'It is well that you should be crowned with as little delay as possible,' added the Archbishop.

Edward looked into their faces. He felt the blood rising to his.

'I would agree on one condition,' he said.

'Condition, Edward!' cried the Queen. 'Do you realize what honour is being done to you?'

'I realize fully what this means, my lady,' replied Edward firmly, 'but I will not be crowned King of this realm until I have my father's word that he gives me the crown.'

There was consternation. The boy had shown firmness of purpose which they had not expected. He stood straight, drawing himself to his full height which was considerable even though he had not yet finished growing; his blue eyes were alight with purpose, the wintry light shone on his flaxen hair. It might have been his grandfather who stood there.

Every one of them knew that it would be useless to attempt to coerce him. He was going to do what he believed to be right.

They saw that they would have to get the old King's permission to crown the new one before they could do so.

* * *

The January winds were buffeting the walls of Kenilworth Castle. Outside the frost glittered on the bare branches of the trees. It was a break prospect but not so bleak as the feelings of the King as he sat huddled in his chamber in Caesar's Tower in a vain endeavour to keep warm.

He had heard the clatter of arrivals in the courtyard below. He wondered what this meant. Every time someone called at the castle he feared the arrival might concern him and even these miserable conditions be changed for worse.

This was an important visit.

Lancaster stood in the doorway. 'Your presence is required below, my lord.'

'Who is it, cousin?'

'A deputation. They are in serious mood. The Bishop of Hereford leads them.'

'Adam of Orlton,' cried the King. 'This bodes me no good then. He was always my enemy. Who comes with him?'

'Among others Sir William Trussell.'

'Ay, an assembly of my enemies, I see. Tell me, do the greatest of them all come to Kenilworth to see me?'

Lancaster was silent and the King went on. 'You wonder who I mean? Come, cousin. You know full well. I mean the Queen and Mortimer.'

'They are not here, my lord.'

'Why do these men come, cousin? You know.'

'They have not told me their business, my lord. Come, dress now. They are waiting.'

'And the King must not keep his enemies waiting,' retorted Edward bitterly. 'Give me my robe, cousin.'

He threw off the fur in which he had wrapped himself and put on a gown of cheap black serge—the sort poor men wore in mourning, for he was mourning he knew for a lost crown.

He faced the party—the traitors who no longer showed him the homage due to a King. Leading them were two of his most bitter enemies Adam of Orlton and William Trussell. How he hated Trussell, who had sentenced Hugh to the terrible death which had been so barbarously carried out!

Trussell's eyes—like those of Adam of Orlton—were gleaming with triumph. This was a moment for which they had been working in their devious ways for many years.

They did not bow to him. They regarded him as they might a low-born criminal.

Then Adam began speaking; he listed the crimes of the King. Events long forgotten were recalled and the blame for them laid at his door. Bannockburn ... Would they never forget Bannockburn? How many had been blamed for that!

He lowered his eyes. He did not want to look into those vicious faces. He wondered what they planned to do with him. Not what they had done to Hugh ... beloved Hugh. They could not. They dared not. He was still their King.

Their faces seemed to recede and he thought Gaveston was beside him ... Gaveston ... perhaps the best loved of them all. Gaveston ...

Lancaster had caught him in his arms. He heard his voice from a long way off. 'The King has fainted.'

He was coming back to reality. The same chamber ... the same faces about him. So it could only have been for a moment.

They brought a chair for him. He was so tired. He did not want to listen to them.

Vaguely he gathered that they were telling him that he

was to be set aside, his crown taken from him, and that they wanted his consent to do so.

How kind of them, he thought. They wanted his consent! Why? Could they not do with him what they liked? Cut off his head ... Take him out and do to him what they did to Hugh ... No, he could not bear to think of what they did to Hugh. It haunted his nightmares. Hugh ... beautiful Hugh.

'It would be well for you to give your consent,' Adam of Orlton was saying. 'If you do not, who knows what might happen? It could mean that the crown would be lost not only to you but to your family.'

'My son,' he whispered. 'My son Edward...'

'Would be crowned King at once, if you consented to abdicate.'

'He is but a boy...'

'There must be no delay.'

'My son ... he *must* be your King.'

'So thought we,' went on Adam. 'Renounce your crown and he shall receive it forthwith. Refuse this and who knows what will happen.'

He gripped the sides of his chair. He thought of fair-haired Edward, the boy of whom he had been so proud.

He cried out: 'I am in your hands. You must do what seems right to you.'

The relief was intense. Sir William Trussell lost no time. He stood before the King to declare as he said on behalf of the whole realm that all the homage and allegiance owed to him as sovereign was now renounced.

Trussell then took the staff of office and broke it in two as a symbol of the dissolution of the royal household.

Edward Plantagenet was now a private person; his rights as King of England had been stripped from him. He felt humiliated and yet he knew that his own actions had brought him to this pass. He was glad his father was not there to see this day.

His voice shook with emotion as he said: 'I know that it is due to my sins that I am brought to this pass and it is a great grief to me that I have incurred the displeasure of the people.' His eyes were bright in his ashen face and his voice sounded firmer as he added: 'But I rejoice that my son Edward is to be their King.'

Neither Adam of Orlton nor Sir William Trussell made

any attempt to bow. He no longer represented the crown; he was an ordinary knight. They owed him no especial respect.

They left him and he sat on a stool and covered his face with his hands.

Lancaster found him thus, and he was moved to pity at the sight of him.

'Let me help you to your chamber, cousin,' he said gently. 'This has been a sad ordeal for you.'

'Henry,' Edward replied, 'I am no longer your King.'

'I know it,' answered Lancaster.

'He broke the staff before my eyes and in such a way, cousin, that I knew to him it was a pleasure.'

'Rest a while. I will have food and wine sent to you.'

Edward said: 'My son is King now. Young Edward ... He is young yet ... only a boy.'

'Yet old enough to force his will, cousin. He would not take the crown until he had your consent to do so.'

A smile touched Edward's ravaged face. 'Is that so then?' he asked.

''Tis true. He said he must first have your consent and would have none of it without.'

'Then someone still cares a little for me.'

Edward once more covered his face with his hands. He could see the young boy—tall, so fair, his blue eyes flashing, his mouth stubborn as he knew it could be. He would have faced his father's enemies as they tempted him with the crown.

His hands were wet with his tears.

'May God bless you, son,' he murmured. 'May you be happier than your father.'

Lancaster led him gently to his chamber where he lay on his bed and, though his black thoughts crowded on him like lowering clouds, there was among them a bright streak of hopefulness. 'My son, my son,' he murmured. 'You care a little for me.'

ESCAPE

THE winter was passing. Young Edward had been crowned at the end of January by the Archbishop of Canterbury, that Walter Reynolds who had once been a crony of the new King's father and who had now joined those who were against him. Walter Reynolds had always been a man who was ready to join the side where he could find the better advantage.

The Queen was in good spirits. She might not be Regent but she saw to it that she and Mortimer had great influence with the young King.

Sir John of Hainault had returned with his troops to his native land, for they had become restive after being away from home for so long. As for Sir John who had been of inestimable help to her she gave him a pension of four hundred marks a year which he was loth to accept declaring that all he had done had been for love of her.

She was at the height of her power and her beauty, for this had flourished since she had thrown aside the cloak of docility. She often laughed to herself to contemplate how everyone knew of her liaison with Mortimer and yet none raised a voice against it.

Often they talked of this but as the winter passed uneasy thoughts came to her. She discussed these often with Mortimer who attempted to soothe her. Mortimer was taking every advantage of his position. His success had been even beyond his dreams. All his estates had been returned to him together with those of his uncle who had died in the Tower. Honours had been secured for his family and he himself had been given the title of Earl of March. He was virtually king of the realm; all he had to do was please his mistress and that was easy, for she was a passionate woman long starved of that satisfaction which they had found so spontaneously together. The young King had to be handled with care and there were signs lately that he was beginning to fidget in his harness. The Queen noticed it but Mortimer refused to believe there was anything to be alarmed about.

'He questions everything,' the Queen insisted.

'Of course he does. He is very conscious of being King. But he is too young, too unversed in statecraft and the ways of the world. He will be a boy for a year or so yet.'

'He is not like his father, you know. He is clever. He learns quickly.'

'My dearest, do not fret about him. We shall know how to handle him when the time comes.'

'And his father? I worry about him.'

'Worry about the prisoner of Kenilworth! He will never rise to power again.'

'But he lives. What if he should rally men to his side?'

'Edward? My love, you cannot mean that. He is despised by all men. The people are delighted with their young King and their new rulers. They are devoted to you. Have you forgotten how they cheer you when you go into the streets?'

'The Londoners have always been faithful to me, I know. But can you trust the people? They are for you one day and against you the next.'

'They have long been faithful to you.'

'Because they hated Edward's friends, and he never made any effort to please them.'

'Come, my dearest, let us think of other more pressing matters.'

Mortimer laughed aloud as he held her close to him. He knew how to divert her thoughts. She was a woman whose sexual appetites were insatiable and for so long they had been suppressed; now that she had found the mate who was completely in tune with her he could divert her thoughts with amazing ease. Her ambition was great but slightly less so than her desire for Roger Mortimer. He exulted in it, exploiting to the full the power this gave him.

But although for the time her thoughts could be turned

in one direction there were occasions when she thought with increasing apprehension of her prisoner husband.

She began to notice as she rode through the streets that the people were less enthusiastic. She even heard murmurings against the newly created Earl of March. Roger was too rapacious. She realized there could be danger when she heard the whisper that it was Gaveston and the Despensers all over again, for the King and his lover had been replaced by the Queen and hers. She fancied too that young Edward's manner was changing towards her. She believed he was asking those around him questions concerning his father. He was growing up. Since the coronation he had grown very serious, leaving all his boyish pastimes, studying state papers and acting like a king.

It was all very well for Roger to say that they were in complete control. They might hold the reins at the moment but their young stead was getting frisky and at times she felt him trying to jerk himself out of his leading strings.

Then her thoughts would go to the prisoner in Kenilworth.

She determined to talk seriously to Roger. She would not allow him to lure her into a sensuous mood. This matter was vital and she was determined to make him see it as she did herself. She was a woman, she said, with a woman's intuition and she smelt danger in the air.

'Listen to me, my gentle Mortimer. I have heard that Lancaster and the King grow close together. They are cousins, remember, and Lancaster will not forget that Edward was once a king. It is said that they spend long hours talking together. Of what do you think they talk?'

'Of what did Edward talk to his dear friends?'

'You cannot compare Lancaster with Gaveston and Despenser. Lancaster is a man of power. He could become like his brother who, you could say, ruled this land at one time. Roger, I want Edward removed from Kenilworth.'

Roger was thoughtful.

'Yes,' insisted the Queen. 'They are together too much. He is not treated as a prisoner. They may well be plotting together. My son will be going to Scotland soon. It is expected of him. They are going to force him to act as his grandfather did and you know how he hammered the Scots. Lancaster must be recalled to join Edward's army and that means that he can no longer be the custodian of the prisoner king. Come, my dear, tell me whose charge my tiresome husband should be put into.'

Mortimer was thoughtful. Then he put his arm about the Queen and kissed her lips.

'As usual you are right,' he said. 'We must be watchful. Lancaster is too close to him. First we will remove him from Kenilworth. Let the King call Lancaster to confer on the Scottish expedition. I have it. My daughter's husband Thomas Berkeley shall be the jailer. My daughter's husband will wish to please me. Edward shall be taken to Berkeley Castle. I can promise you that he will not be treated there as an honoured guest.'

'As usual, gentle Mortimer, you succeed in calming my fears.'

'Then,' said Mortimer, 'this coming day I shall set this thing in motion. Our prisoner shall be sent to a more rigorous prison where he will find jailers not in the least inclined to be his friends.'

The Queen said: 'He deserves no kindness. He humiliated me bitterly for many years. If you but knew ...'

'My love, my love, I know full well. He turned from the most beautiful woman in the world to his despicable boys. But it is all over now, Isabella. Sometimes I wonder whether we could have known the fullness of our joy in each other if we had not had to wait for it.'

She was ready to be soothed, to be made love to.

She exulted in Mortimer.

*　　　*　　　*

Edward was glad that the winter was over. His cousin had seen that he did not suffer too much from the cold as he might well have done. In the chamber where they met and played chess there was always a great fire and there were furs for Edward's bed and others in which to wrap himself when the wind whistled about the castle walls.

Lancaster was changing, growing fond of his captive. He was beginning to ask himself whether it had been such a good exchange of rulers after all. Even in Kenilworth there came rumours of Mortimer's arrogance, of the blatant manner in which he and the Queen openly lived in adultery. Mortimer was not only the most powerful man in the land, he was fast

becoming the richest. Avarice had been the downfall of both
Gaveston and the Despensers. But here was as greedy and
grasping a man as had ever gone before.

The more dissatisfied Lancaster grew with the Queen and
her paramour the more sympathetic he became towards his
pathetic prisoner.

One May day when he had risen from his bed he found
that visitors had arrived at the castle. He received them immediately for they came from the court. He was quickly
informed that the King wished him to prepare to leave Kenilworth and join him in London. His counsel was needed with
regard to the Scottish campaign.

Lancaster was surprised. 'What of my prisoner?' he asked.
'Am I to bring him with me?'

Nay, was the answer. Within the next few days Sir Thomas
Berkeley and Sir John Maltravers would be arriving at the
castle. They would take over the Earl of Lancaster's duties.

Lancaster nodded slowly.

He had known that at some time Edward would be taken
out of his charge.

He did not greatly care for the task which lay before him
of informing Edward that they were to part.

He looked with compassion on the tall thin figure—now
almost gaunt, with the dark shadows under the faded blue
eyes.

'Thomas, cousin,' murmured Edward, 'they are going to
take me away from you.'

'It was to be expected,' said Lancaster. 'I have my duties. I
am to join the King.'

Edward closed his eyes and the lines of despair were obvious
about his mouth. Then he opened them and the stark fear
in them deeply disturbed Lancaster.

'It is because you have been too kind to me,' he said fiercely.

'I am told the King commands me to join him.'

'And we know who commands the King.'

'It may be that you will enjoy a change of castles.'

'Who, cousin?'

'Berkeley. Thomas Berkeley.'

'Did he not marry Mortimer's daughter?'

'I think that was so.'

'You see, cousin. I am to be put with my enemies. Berkeley!
He was no friend of mine.'

'His lands were confiscated,' said Lancaster. 'I believe they were bestowed on Hugh le Despenser.'

Edward shuddered. 'No friend of mine,' he murmured. 'And they will take me from here.'

'To Berkeley Castle, I doubt not.'

'Oh cousin, do not go. Do not leave me. Let us stay here together. You have made life bearable for me here.'

'My dear lord, I must obey the King.'

'*I* am your King, Thomas.'

But Lancaster shook his head sadly, and silence fell between them. It was Edward who broke it. 'Maltravers did you say?' he asked.

'Sir John Maltravers. A natural choice because he married Berkeley's sister.'

Edward shook his head. 'Another traitor ... to me. He fled from England and joined the Queen in France.'

'It is hardly likely, my lord, that they would choose your friends.'

'Oh, cousin, a great foreboding has descended on me.'

'It is the thought of change.'

'Nay, cousin. Here I have accepted my fate. I have grown accustomed to your company which has become very agreeable to me. And now ... and now ... I feel closing in on me, cousin ... a darkness, a horror ...'

'My lord, it is this sudden shock. All will be well. When you first came here we were not such friends ... In time you and Berkeley and Maltravers ...'

Edward shook his head.

'Oh, cousin,' he said, 'pray God to help me.'

Lancaster took Edward's hand and knelt and kissed it and it was as though Edward had become his king again.

'I shall pray for you, my lord. Be of good cheer. It may well be that life will be good to you yet.'

But Edward continued to shake his head. The deepest melancholy had settled upon him.

* * *

Lancaster had gone and his new custodians had arrived. Maltravers was outwardly insolent, Berkley almost shame-facedly so, as though he could not stop himself remembering that this poor emaciated man had once been his King.

'Rouse yourself,' said John Maltravers. 'There is a journey to be made forthwith. Should he be bound with ropes, think you, Thomas?'

'Let be,' replied Berkeley. 'He is hardly in fit state to run away from us.'

He who had once been a king before whom men bowed was now talked of in his presence as though he were a piece of merchandise to be moved whichever way suited his possessors. Humiliation indeed! But he was beyond humiliation. The terrible fear which had come to him when Lancaster had told him he was going would not leave him. He feared these men.

To Berkeley Castle they rode. How different it looked from when he had last seen it. Then he had ridden in as the King and there pageants and festivities greeted him. How different now! Gloomy! Foreboding! An impulse came to him to shout that he would not enter. Let them kill him here ... on the spot. He would not go inside that stone-walled fortress. His whole being cried out against it. He wanted to turn back to Kenilworth, to beg them to send his cousin Lancaster back to him.

Maltravers jerked his head as he might to a groom.

'Why the hesitation?' he cried. 'You waste our time, Edward Plantagenet.'

How they loved to show him that he who had once been their King was no longer of account!

He entered the outer court and went under the machiolated gatehouse. He wondered if he would ever come out a free man.

His horse was taken from him—a poor miserable creature to denote his state and the contrast between it and the steeds ridden by his captors was pathetic. Maltravers laid ungentle hands on him and hustled him forward. 'This way,' he muttered.

High-born Lancaster had never shown him such disrespect. He must now think of his days at Kenilworth as happy ones.

He was in the baronial hall—a fine place at the end of which was the chapel.

'I would like to say a prayer,' he said. 'Allow me to go to the chapel and kneel before the altar.'

'You can pray in your room,' said Thomas Berkeley.

Maltravers sneered: 'You should have thought more of praying when you had the time. You could have knelt before your altars then instead of before little Hugh.'

They were determined to torment him. He knew they would be cruel jailers.

He was mounting the great staircase leading to the keep and passing along a gallery when they came to a room which was heavily locked and barred.

'Your new palace, my lord,' said Maltravers with a mock bow.

Berkeley unlocked it and the door swung open with a creak suggesting it was long since it had been used. It was dark. The only light which came into the room was from a slit high in the wall. It was narrow with enough room for a man to get his arm through, nothing more. On the floor lay a straw pallet; there was a stool and a small wooden chest which would serve as a table.

'You cannot mean to lodge me here!' cried Edward.

'The man is ungrateful,' cried Maltravers turning his eyes to the ceiling.

Berkeley looked uneasy.

'My lord,' he said, 'it has been chosen as the room you shall occupy while you are here.'

Edward shivered and said no more.

They left him and he heard the key turn in the lock.

This was abject misery.

He knelt down and prayed. 'Oh God,' he said, 'let me die . . . now. Let this wretchedness end. God help me.'

He rose from his knees and lay on his straw pallet. And then it seemed that God answered his call for help for he began to think of his son. That dear boy had loved him. It was true he himself had neglected the child. There had never seemed to be time to concern himself overmuch with children in the schoolroom. Hugh had demanded so much of his attention. But he had always shown his son love and affection. Edward could not know that his father was being treated thus. He would never allow it.

Hope had entered the dismal room.

Edward, the King, would save him. If he could but know what was happening to his father he would come and rescue him.

If he could only get word to Edward. Meanwhile he was here in Berkeley Castle in the hands of men who hated him.

*   *   *

And how they hated him! It was their pleasure to heap indignity upon him. Maltravers was the worst. Sometimes he thought he detected a gleam of pity in Berkeley's eyes and when he visited him without Maltravers he behaved almost humanely. The discomfort of his room was intense. Fortunately it was summer. He did not think he could live through a winter in such quarters. But perhaps by then Edward would have come to save him. If he could only get a message to his son!

The food they brought him was almost inedible—the leftover slops from the platters of the serving men, he believed. They brought him cold muddy water from the moat in which to shave himself and Maltravers had brought with him a wreath of ivy to place on his head to resemble a crown.

He had steeled his mind against their mockery.

He had always enjoyed physical health. Like his father he had in his youth been full of vigour. He had preferred the outdoor life to study. So had his father but he had never let that preference prevent the attention to state matters and the study of documents which were part of a King's duties.

Lying on his bed, drifting back into the past, he knew he had failed miserably. He knew he deserved to lose his crown, but not this degradation. No, no man whatever his sins should suffer thus.

He could not eat the foul food they sent him. Sometimes he thought of Kenilworth as a kind of paradise. So it had been in comparison.

If only Lancaster were here that he might talk to him ... He would not have cared what they talked of as long as they talked.

The odour of the food on the platter sickened him. He longed for someone to take it away.

He lay on his straw and closed his eyes.

*　　*　　*

There were voices in his room.

'Perhaps we should send for a priest.' That was Berkeley.

'A priest! What matters it? Let him go unshriven to hell!' Maltravers indeed.

'Nevertheless I will send a friar to him. No man should be denied such a privilege on his death-bed.'

'Who would have thought he could have lived so long? He has the strength of an ox.'

'He is like his father. They are giants, these Plantagenets.'

'If his father could see him now . . .'

'Perhaps he does, Maltravers.'

'You are nervous, Thomas. You always have been. You can never forget, can you, that he was once a king?'

'I am going to send a friar to him.'

'If you wish it. I would save myself the trouble of sending for him.'

There was quiet in the room.

So they had gone and he was near to death—so near it seemed that Berkeley was going to send a friar to him.

I welcome death, he thought. If I went to hell it could be no worse than this. I have seen Satan himself in Maltravers. I have touched the bottom. I can go no deeper.

Edward, my son, you will come for me one day. If you knew what they were doing to your father you would not allow this to happen to me.

Edward, come to me, before it is too late.

*   *   *

Someone was kneeling by his bed. A cool hand was on his brow.

'Are you strong enough to pray with me, my lord?'

'Who are you?' asked Edward.

'I am Thomas Dunhead of the Dominican Order.'

'So you have come to pray for me?'

'And to pray with you.'

'I thank you. I have need of prayers.'

'So think I, my lord. Let us pray for your return to health.'

'Stay,' murmured Edward. 'If I return to health what is there for me? It is better for me to die. I am half way to death it seems and cannot have much farther to go.'

'Life is God's gift. We must wait until we are called to abandon it. Until that time comes it is our duty to cling to it, to preserve it, and to live it in that manner whch best pleases God.'

'You are a free man, Friar Thomas.'

'Let us pray together,' said the friar.

'Shall you come to me again?'

'Tomorrow.'

'If I am still here.'

'You must be. Your sins are many and you will need time to earn remission.'

When the friar had gone Edward felt better. It was comforting to have contact with human beings.

The next day the Dominican came again. When they were alone together from his robes he brought forth meat and bread.

'I have brought food for your body as well as for your mind,' he said. 'You are in need of nourishment if you are going to live long enough for repentance.'

Edward took the food and ate it ravenously.

'That is well,' said the friar. 'I will bring more tomorrow. And we will work together to save your soul.'

And the next day he came again.

They prayed at first and then the Dominican said: 'I have talked with my brother Stephen of your state. He is a bold fellow. He has many friends. When they heard of what was happening to you here they were enraged, for they know that your Queen lives in adultery with Roger de Mortimer.'

'It is all so remote to me,' said Edward. 'I scarcely ever think of it now.'

'The people are growing restive. My brother Stephen loves a cause, providing he thinks it a good one. My lord, when your strength is built up ...'

'Yes?' said Edward slowly.

'My brother is thinking of a plan of rescue.'

'God is answering my prayers,' said Edward. 'And my son ... could you speak to my son?'

'It would not be easy to approach the King. He is surrounded by men who are your enemies. His mother and Mortimer will let none approach him. My brother, who is a born conspirator, says that it would be better for you to escape from the castle first. Then you could rally supporters and let the King know where you were.'

'Am I dreaming?' asked Edward. 'I do sometimes, you know. Then I find it difficult to know whether I am in the past or the present.'

'This is no dream. We have friends outside. Now you must feign to be very sick. It must not be known that I bring you nourishment. When the time is ripe I shall come wearing two hooded robes. In the cell I shall take one off which you shall put on. We shall leave the castle together. Before this though I shall bring one of my brothers so that the guards are accustomed to seeing two of us. Do you understand?'

'Yes,' said Edward. 'Yes, indeed I do.'

'You must feign sickness. If they think you are too ill to rise from your straw they become careless. The doors are left unlocked until after I have left. It is possible that we can bring about your escape.'

'If you were discovered ...'

'It would cost me my life, I know. I should lose it most barbarously through the traitor's death. But then the sooner I should come to heaven. It may be that God has chosen me as his instrument. He cannot wish that adulterous pair to rule our country.'

'If I escape from here I shall never forget you.'

'My brother and I do not work for rewards but for the glory of God and the suppression of evil.'

'I can do it,' said Edward. 'I can see it is the answer to my prayers. I shall go from here and I shall see my son again. When I look on his dear face and see the compassion there for his father I shall know that God has taken me into His care once more.'

*   *   *

He was growing stronger. Such was his constitution that it responded quickly to the nourishment Friar Thomas Dunhead brought to him. He drew new strength from the knowledge that he was not deserted. He had some friends in the world.

Conspiracy was like new life to him. He would do it. It was not the end. He and Thomas Dunhead would walk out of this castle together. He exulted to think of what he would do when he was free.

Edward, my son, my son! You will come to your father's aid.

And then, all he wanted now was to live in quiet, peace and dignity.

It was not difficult to deceive Berkeley and Maltravers. They did not want him to die, it seemed. If he did they would be deprived of their post and their fun. Perhaps he should not think that of Berkeley for Berkeley was showing himself possessed of a conscience. Now that Edward's sense of perception was increasing he could see that Berkeley had no love for his task and that his repulsion for it was growing. He was not such a man as Maltravers.

So he lay on his straw during the day and waited for the moment when he should walk out of the castle.

Stephen came with his brother. Dressed as a Dominican he was allowed into the prison chamber. They must have thought he was very close to death, thought Edward.

Stephen had an exuberance his brother lacked. His eyes glowed with the love of adventure.

He thought it would be dangerous for one friar to enter and two to go out. Some of the guards might be observant. Then the whole plan would be wrecked.

He would come with his brother in the robes of a Dominican. Underneath these he would be dressed as a scullion. In the room he would give Edward his robe and Edward should go out of the castle with Thomas. He would slip out of the room in his scullion's clothes so that he might not be noticed. They would arrange the bed so that it appeared that Edward was in it. Then the escape might not be noticed until the next day.

It seemed a good plan if it worked.

Finally the day came. The two men entered the room. They knelt and prayed for a while. Then Edward put on the robe and he and Thomas walked out of the castle without protest. Stephen as the scullion left soon after.

Less than a mile beyond the castle horses were waiting.

To feel the fresh air intoxicated Edward. He felt suddenly young and strong again, full of hope.

'It is over,' he cried. 'I have come through hell. God is with me.'

* * *

He rode between the brothers Thomas and Stephen.

'To Corfe Castle,' said Stephen. 'There you will be received, my lord, by your friends. Once it is known that you have escaped from your captors there will be many to rally round you. The people are weary of rapacious Mortimer and the sinful Queen.'

'And the King...'

'The King is but a boy but there are signs that he is wise beyond his years and he likes not his mother's conduct. He is displeased with Mortimer ... Everything will be different soon, my lord.'

'I would not wish to be put back on the throne,' said Edward. 'I accept my unworthiness. But if I could but see my son ... if I could do homage to him as England's King ... I should be content.'

Corfe Castle rose before them. One of the strongest castles in the kingdom set there on the peninsular of Purbeck, impregnable, menacing to enemies, guarding the land.

'Henceforth I shall always love Corfe Castle,' said Edward.

The gates were opened. The party rode in. What a different reception this was.

'How can I ever thank you?' cried Edward.

'We but did our duty,' answered Thomas Dunhead.

'My first desire is to send a message to my son,' said Edward.

'It shall be done. First we will rest awhile and then we shall take your message. Stephen and I will take it together.'

'I thank God for his mercy,' said Edward.

They partook of food and wine and Edward was taken to the chamber which had been prepared for him.

He could not help but compare it to the misery of Berkeley.

'We shall leave at dawn,' said Thomas.

'I know my son will soon be with me,' replied Edward.

He fell into a deep sleep. It was light when he awoke. Something had awakened him. He had been prodded. He could feel the sharp pain in his back.

He opened his eyes.

It was a nightmare. It could not be true. Fate could not be so cruel.

Standing by his bed were Berkeley and Maltravers.

'My lord's attempt has come to naught,' said Maltravers in a tone of mock concern.

'What happened?' cried Edward starting up.

'It was not without its shrewdness, that plot,' went on Maltravers, talking over him, 'but we were not so easily deceived. The empty bed was discovered almost as soon as Edward Plantagenet had left. He must think we are fools at Berkeley. We discovered the direction in which he had fled and here we are at Corfe to continue taking good care of him.'

Berkeley said almost gently: 'We have our duty to perform, you will understand, my lord.'

'We have got the Dominican. In the short time left to him doubtless he will regret his recklessness.'

'His brother has escaped,' added Berkeley.

'But not for long,' said Maltravers. 'It will be the gallows and the traitor's sentence for them. Mayhap they will regret their folly when the rope is cut and the fire applied to their entrails.'

Edward shivered and Berkeley said: 'We shall await orders, my lord. In the meantime we shall stay here.'

So he lay on his bed and despair enveloped him.

It seemed to him that God had deserted him.

MURDER AT BERKELEY CASTLE

THE Queen was frantic.

'Think what might have happened. He might even have raised men to support him!'

'He could never have done it,' declared Mortimer.

'He might have sent word to the King.'

'But he did not, my love. And he must never have a chance to come so near to it again.'

Isabella looked at him, her beautiful eyes brilliant with the excitement which burned within her. There was something in the way Mortimer spoke which told her that his thoughts were the same as hers.

In such a case as this there was one way and one way only.

While Edward lived there would be danger and the older the King grew and the less popular the Queen and her lover became, the greater the danger.

Mortimer wondered what Edward's revenge on him would be if the tables were turned and he held the power.

Mortimer knew it would be the traitor's death.

They must not be squeamish. It had been obvious to him for a long time—and it must have been to Isabella too—that there was one course of action open to them.

The King must die.

They did not need to say the words. They understood each other's minds too well.

'Your son-in-law is too gentle,' she said.

'I know it well.'

'Then he should be removed.'

Mortimer nodded. 'Berkeley is hampered by his conscience. He cannot forget that Edward was once his King.'

'Then he is no man to have charge of him.'

'I want them to go back to Berkeley. Berkeley is the place. My son-in-law shall take him back.'

'And then...'

'I shall find some pretext to remove Berkeley and send another man to help Maltravers.'

'Who?'

'I am turning it over in my mind. Gurney perhaps, Thomas Gurney. There is a man who will work well for money and the prospect of advancement.'

'My dear,' said the Queen quickly, 'it must not look like murder. There must be no wounds.'

Mortimer nodded. 'You are right as ever. A slow death ... lack of food, lack of fresh air ... despair ... these should be our weapons.'

'But we cannot wait too long. Edward is restive. But for the Scottish matter he would want to see his father. Gentle Mortimer, we cannot afford to wait.'

'Nor shall we. Ere long I promise you this burden shall be lifted from us.'

'Never forget, it must seem as though it were an act of God.'

'So shall it,' Mortimer promised her.

*   *   *

So he was back in Berkeley ... not the same room this time. They had chosen one over the charnel house. The stench was nauseating. The food they brought him was inedible. Although he grew weaker his strength held out and he astonished his jailers by his grip on life.

Maltravers told him how his friend the Dominican had died.

'Quite a spectacle! They strung him up and cut him down alive...'

'I do not wish to hear,' replied Edward.

'But, my lord, you are no longer in a position to decide what you will and will not hear. It is my wish to tell you how your dear friend died.'

'Have done,' muttered Thomas Berkeley. 'It is a pointless

matter. The Dominican died bravely ... leave it at that.'

Yes, thought Maltravers, it was time Berkeley went.

That night Berkeley came into the room.

'I have come to say good-bye,' he told Edward.

Edward seized his hand. 'No, no. You must stay with me.'

'I have orders from the court to leave you. Another will be taking my place.'

'Oh no ... they are taking you away from me because you are the only friend left to me.'

'Oh, my lord,' cried Berkeley, 'I will pray for you.'

'It is strange,' said Edward, 'that it was only when you became my jailer that you were my friend.'

Berkeley did not speak. His emotion was too strong for him. He had deplored the conduct of the deposed King. He had been one of those who had worked to bring him down. But he must have pity for the man and he was convinced that none should be treated as he had been, no matter what his crimes. His instincts cried out against it; and he was filled with misgivings because he knew that this was why he was being withdrawn from his post. The Queen and her lover would have no mercy.

He knelt before Edward and kissed his hand as though he were taking leave of his King.

When he had gone blank despair came to Edward.

He thought of the brave Dominican being tortured; the only relief he felt was that Stephen had escaped. Lancaster had been taken from him and now Berkeley. And it was because these were humane men.

*　　*　　*

Isabella had sent for Sir Thomas Gurney. Mortimer was with her when the man arrived.

'Go at once to Berkeley Castle,' said the Queen. 'You are to take Sir Thomas Berkeley's place. He will have left by the time you arrive.'

Thomas Gurney bowed.

'You understand the position well,' went on Mortimer. 'The late King is an encumbrance to the good of the country. He is in a weak state. There can be no doubt that his days are numbered. It would be a blessing to bring him to his end.'

Gurney bowed. He understood that his task was to expedite Edward's departure.

'There must be no sign that the King has been helped to his death,' said the Queen. 'No outward violence. Such could rouse the people to revere him. You know how they are all seeking martyrs.'

'I understand, my lord, my lady,' said Gurney.

'We shall not forget those who are of service to us,' replied Mortimer.

So Sir Thomas Gurney took his leave and with all haste left for Berkeley.

* * *

Edward hated the man as soon as he saw him. He was another such as Maltravers. He knew they meant him ill.

He would lie in his bed at night and listen to footsteps waiting for them to come in and kill him.

For that was what they were going to do. He was taking too long to die and they were impatient. He saw that in their faces. In the morning they came in to look at him and he would pretend to be asleep.

'It would seem he has made a pact with the devil,' grumbled Maltravers. 'He has the constitution of an ox.' Maltravers had picked up the stool and seemed about to crash it down on Edward's head.

'Have a care.' That was Gurney. 'You know the orders. No sign of physical ill treatment. A blow from you could cost you your head.'

'True enough,' agreed Maltravers and Edward heard him put the stool down.

'They are strong, these Plantagenets,' murmured the new jailer Gurney.

So they insulted him and brought him muddy water to drink and food which cattle would have refused. But weak as he was he still lived on. There was a mischievous tenacity in him. He was not going to die to please them.

* * *

The messenger had risen with all speed from the Marcher land which had been restored to Mortimer since his return to

England. He had urgent news for his lord.

As soon as he was admitted to Mortimer's presence he threw himself on his knees for one always feared powerful men when bad news was brought to them. Perhaps in this case the great Mortimer, now virtually ruler of England, would reward his good servant.

'My lord, lord, I have lost no time. You will want to know that your enemy Sir Rhys ap Griffith is calling men to his banner. He is urging them to fight for the true King who now lies languishing in a prison.'

'By God,' cried Mortimer, 'I should have guessed Rhys ap Griffith would make trouble if he could. What response does he get?'

The messenger looked as though he would rather not tell and Mortimer shouted: 'Have no fear. I would know all.'

'Many Welshmen are gathering to his banner. They are saying evil things of you, my lord. They are saying they will free the King. I had thought you should know.'

'You did well to come to me,' said Mortimer. 'I tell you this; the upstart Rhys will find ere long that he has led himself and his followers into trouble.'

'Would my lord give me orders?'

Mortimer was thoughtful. 'Go back,' he said. 'Watch and send news to me of how he fares.'

When the messenger had gone he was thoughtful. No army Rhys ap Griffith could raise could have a chance against his and Isabella's. It was not the thought of that petty force which disturbed him.

It was the growing support for the King throughout the country.

When he and Isabella had come to England it had seemed the entire country was behind them. Now there was murmuring. First the Dunhead affair. That had been a warning. If that had succeeded and Edward had established his headquarters somewhere he might have rallied men to his cause. Thank God it had been frustrated before its fruition. And now this enemy was attempting to raise the one-time King's standard in Wales. What if men started doing that all over the country?

It would not be wise to take an army to Wales and crush Rhys ap Griffith. That would set others following his example.

There was one thing which must be done and that quickly.

The reason for rebellion must be removed. Why would he not die? He had been subjected to the utmost discomfort; he had been almost starved, set above the charnel house at Berkeley, the stench of which should have carried off a sick man by now.

But Edward lived on.

They had been gentle with him. Of course they had. It would be unwise for him to be seen to be murdered. Heaven knew what retribution would follow those who murdered a king.

They would be haunted by fear for the rest of their lives.

Edward must die ... but by natural causes.

He must be removed in a manner so skilful that all would believe he had passed naturally away.

But there must be no delay. They had prevaricated too long. They must act promptly now.

He would send for a man he knew—a man who had made a profession of murder, a man who was so skilled at the job that he could produce death by violence and none be able to detect a sign of it.

No, on second thoughts he would not send for the man. This was too private a matter. He would go and see him and tell him what must be done.

* * *

Days merged into night and night into day. It was dark in his room and he was scarcely aware of the coming of the dawn. He had recovered a little. He had a purpose in life. They wanted him to die and he was determined not to.

They had done all they could to impair his health. The smell from below was so obnoxious that at first it had made him retch, but a man can grow accustomed to most things. He noticed it less now. He dreamed of banquets when he had sat side by side with Gaveston or Hugh and imagined that the foul food they sent him was some special dish which one of his dear boys had concocted for him. He was not going to die to please them.

They watched him daily. He missed Berkeley, Berkeley would have changed towards him as Lancaster had. He and Berkeley would have become friends if left alone. He would have been given fur covers for his bed, a fur wrap, a glowing fire, a game of chess. They had known this so they had sent Berkeley away.

Maltravers and Gurney remained. There would never be any friendship between them and himself.

A dark shadow had entered the castle.

There was a third man. They called him William Ogle. What was there about that man? He walked softly with a cat-like tread. He laughed a great deal. It was loud, mirthless laughter. It began to worry Edward.

When darkness fell he was aware of the shadows. He had nightmares in which William Ogle suddenly appeared in the darkness of the room.

Whenever Ogle was in the room a strangeness came over Edward. His whole body felt as though it was covered in crawling ants. He shivered though his body felt on fire.

That was the effect William Ogle had on him.

Yet the man was respectful—more so than Maltravers and Gurney, calling him my lord and bowing now and then.

There is an evil about that man, thought Edward. I hope he will not stay here long.

*   *   *

Night. Footsteps in the corridor. Edward lay on his face breathing deeply.

The three men came into the room. One carried a lantern. They stood for a few seconds looking down on the sleeping man.

In the open doorway a brazier threw out a faint light and there was a smell of heating iron.

William Ogle was clearly in command.

He beckoned them close to him.

'Is all ready?' asked Maltravers.

Ogle nodded.

'Remember. Your hands must not touch him. There must be no bruises. Bring the table here and place it over him and hold it so that he cannot move. Quickly now ... while he sleeps. He must not be touched. Those are orders. No outward sign.'

Silently the two men lifted the table and placed it over Edward so that its sides pinned him to his bed.

He awoke and thought this was one of his nightmares.

He was naked. They had taken his robe. He caught a glimpse of Ogle approaching the bed and in his hand was a long spit glowing red hot.

And then such agony as no man had ever dreamed of. The red hot spit was inserted into his body.

He screamed violently as the fearful instrument of torture and death penetrated into his organs.

'Think of Gaveston,' cried Ogle. 'Think of little Hugh. Think of them, my lord ... Think of them ...'

Edward tried to struggle but the table was pinning him down. His screams were so loud that they penetrated the thick walls of the castle. Everyone within those walls that night must have heard him.

'He can't last long,' said Ogle, and even Maltravers and Gurney were shaken.

Edward was no longer screaming; his breath was coming in long tortured gasps.

'His inside will be a charred mass by now,' said Ogle. 'And there will be no mark on his body for any to see. The spit is protected by horn so there will not be a hint of a burn even.'

He seemed proud of his handiwork.

Edward lay still now. Ogle withdrew the spit. There was no movement from the body as he did so.

'Take off the table now,' said Ogle. 'There will be not a mark on his body. No sign of violence, no bruise, no burns. None will know that his intestines have been burned away.'

The table was set down. Neither Maltravers nor Gurney wished to touch the man. It was the experienced murderer who did that. He turned him over and gave a gasp as he did so.

'Bring the lantern nearer,' he commanded.

The three men stood at the bedside, looking down on the still dead face on which was an expression of terror and agony such as they had never before witnessed.

The features were set in that horrible grimace of pain. Nothing could have more clearly proclaimed that Edward the Second had died the most terrible, violent and cruel death which man could devise.

*   *   *

'He died in his sleep,' they said. 'It was a peaceful ending.'

There was no mark of violence anywhere on his body. But that expression on his face was clear for all who beheld it.

The three murderers conferred together.

'You said there would be no sign,' complained Maltravers.

'How was I to know it would show on his face?' grumbled Ogle.

He had only obeyed orders, he said. So had they all but they thought it wise to slip quietly out of the country and wait for the outcome.

The Abbot of Gloucester came to the castle and took the body away. It would remain in his care until a stately burial could be arranged. Throughout the country the people were talking of their late King. What had happened to him? There was some mystery about his death.

Was his wife not living in adultery with her powerful and avaricious paramour?

The young King was fast assuming his responsibility. He had been guided too long by his mother and her lover.

There were questions he wanted to ask. Where were those who had held his father prisoner? Why had they fled the country? There was so much he wanted to know. On all sides there were scandals concerning his mother. He was breaking free of his bonds. There was so much he had to discover and he was determined to learn.

The storm was rising and the storm would grow big.

JEAN PLAIDY HAS ALSO WRITTEN

The Norman Trilogy
THE BASTARD KING
THE LION OF JUSTICE
THE PASSIONATE ENEMIES

The Plantagenet Saga
PLANTAGENET PRELUDE
THE REVOLT OF THE EAGLETS
THE HEART OF THE LION
THE PRINCE OF DARKNESS
THE BATTLE OF THE QUEENS
THE QUEEN FROM PROVENCE
EDWARD LONGSHANKS
THE FOLLIES OF THE KING
THE VOW ON THE HERON
PASSAGE TO PONTEFRACT *In preparation*

The Tudor Novels
KATHARINE, THE VIRGIN WIDOW ⎫ Also available
THE SHADOW OF THE POMEGRANATE ⎬ in one volume:
THE KING'S SECRET MATTER ⎭ KATHARINE OF ARAGON

MURDER MOST ROYAL
(Anne Boleyn and Catherine Howard)
ST THOMAS'S EVE (Sir Thomas More)
THE SIXTH WIFE (Katharine Parr)
THE THISTLE AND THE ROSE
(Margaret Tudor and James IV)
MARY, QUEEN OF FRANCE (Queen of Louis XII)
THE SPANISH BRIDEGROOM
(Philip II and his first three wives)
GAY LORD ROBERT (Elizabeth and Leicester)

The Mary Queen of Scots Series
ROYAL ROAD TO FOTHERINGAY
THE CAPTIVE QUEEN OF SCOTS

The Stuart Saga
THE MURDER IN THE TOWER
(Robert Carr and the Countess of Essex)

THE WANDERING PRINCE ⎫ Also available in
A HEALTH UNTO HIS MAJESTY ⎬ one volume:
HERE LIES OUR SOVEREIGN LORD ⎭ CHARLES II

THE THREE CROWNS
(William of Orange)
THE HAUNTED SISTERS   Also available in
(Mary and Anne)   one volume:
THE QUEEN'S FAVOURITES THE LAST OF THE STUARTS
(Sarah Churchill and
Abigail Hill)